HOWLS FROM THE WRECKAGE
Edited by Christopher O'Halloran

Editing by Christopher O'Halloran
Formatting by Molly Halstead
Cover art by Maia Weir

Howls From the Wreckage published by HOWL Society Press
ISBN: 978-1-7367800-7-7

Visit our website at howlsociety.com

CONTENTS

FOREWORD
by Nick Cutter

I come, friends, to speak of disaster.

You'll find much of it between the covers of the book you're now holding…or e-reader, if you're one of that technically enlightened breed. Big, city-destroying ones and smaller, more intimate personal collapses. It's a great thematic tie-together for an anthology, and I'm shocked it hasn't been done before.

Horror so often dwells upon collapse, doesn't it? Of the body, or borders between sanity and madness or our world and other more hostile planes of existence. The collapse of the moral threshold separating right from wrong (a line many authors and their characters hurdle gleefully), and the collapse of bonds of family or friendship or parenthood that bind people.

Horror tends to traffic in disaster, doesn't it?

And this book is full of such wonderful accidents.

But sometimes—in the real world as well as fiction—events that seem unlucky on their surface are actually opportunities for growth that arrive cowled in disaster…in some cases, they can dictate the direction of your life.

As a boy, my family moved around a lot. My father was a banker, my mother a palliative care nurse, and in those days—the sad ole, bad ole eighties—it was often the father's career that dictated a family's trajectory.

Every time Dad earned a promotion, the movers would pack us up and we'd toddle on to our next home like a pack of modestly heeled hermit crabs.

My younger brother had a particularly hard time with it. These moves were, to him, an abject disaster, representing the unseating of his entire world. To me—more bookish than my brother and more malleable, my persona a bit like Silly Putty, able to compress and squeeze through a keyhole to take on the imprint of new surroundings…I consented willingly enough to these moves, but in retrospect perhaps it was just that I couldn't acknowledge our ill fate so readily as my brother did.

Thank god for libraries. They were my bomb shelter against disaster.

Every move resulted in the inevitable ordeal of being the new kid in school. Friendship networks had already been established, and there were times that I struggled to make a place for myself.

Which was where the library came in. Be it the public library or the one at school, they represented a sanctuary. I'm not alone in this: millions of bookish, mildly socially awkward kids flocked to those quiet nooks in the stacks, a safe place free from schoolyard pressures and the occasional predation.

On Sundays as a young boy, Mom would take me to the public library. I'd spend hours there, sitting amidst the old men who'd come in and read newspapers threaded onto long wooden dowels. We sat on big padded chairs that smelled vaguely of sweat or smoke or sweet saliva—it was hard to say, exactly, except it's a particular aroma that haunts the furniture of every library I've ever been in, a strange admixture of each and every body to have ever occupied them.

As a kid, I had no conception that libraries were organized along lines of division: fiction and nonfiction, genre, etc. To me, it was just a huge space full of books. If there was any separation at all, it was of my own conjuring and dead simple:

A: Books I'd like to read.

B: Books I'd prefer not to read.

Over time, though, I did see that libraries did divide the stock into categories. And you can likely guess which one I gravitated to.

If the library didn't have a "horror" section (and many didn't, a sad omission that seems to have migrated to a lot of contemporary bookstores), my kind of books weren't hard to find. Of course, back in the 80s—and since—that search started in the "K"s, with King and a dash of Koontz. There were further treasures in the "L"s (Lovecraft, Lieber), the "R"s (Rice, Ray Russell), "S"s (Shirley, Straub, Stine), and the "B"s were a particular goldmine: Barker, Beaumont, Blatty, Bloch, Bright, Bradbury, Bellairs, Blackwood, Bierce.

Even if the names were unfamiliar to me, the covers were often dead giveaways: red-eyed children with their hair blowing in a phantom wind; wrought-iron gates hemming shadowy manses; knives dripping blood and skeleton cheerleaders shaking pompoms.

These books, this genre—a genre often fueled by disaster, decay and calamity—nourished me in times of great loneliness and uncertainty.

What I didn't quite realize I was doing at that trembling age was calibrating my own writerly instincts and predilections. I've often thought of it as imprinting, that psychological process most frequently associated with baby goslings that intuit the first thing they see (ideally their mothers) as their caregiver, and follow her.

My own horror writing—*all* of my writing, but most powerfully the horror stuff—can be viewed as the out-welling of the books and authors I fixated on at an early age. All those hours in the library, squirreled away in a nook with a horror book…not only did it inform my desire to write horror, it absolutely set the rough boundaries for my own aesthetic, the things I wanted to write about, and the manner I've set about writing my books.

But let's set that aside so I can properly introduce you to the newest HOWL Society anthology: *Howls From the Wreckage*. As I read these stories—and there are many corkers in here—I saw the fascinating ways that influence works: that trickledown of an idea or concept that takes a new and (in these stories) radical form. I caught the vaguest whispers of Barker, Lovecraft, King, and others in some of these stories, but each is modern, fresh, and has something new and invigorating and often quite distressing to say.

It was my great pleasure to read these disasters, both great and small, and I know you'll love them too.

Happy reading,
Nick Cutter/Craig Davidson

Dear Recruit:

Congratulations. It is with great honour that we welcome you to one of the world's most eminent institutions: the cumulative global effort of 191 nations and the foremost organization for making sense of the unknown.

The HOWLS Bureau of Investigation exists on society's periphery, deliberately obfuscated. Utilizing unorthodox investigation methods, the HBI studies and attempts to explain cases of extreme disasters and accidents with unexplainable evidence.

Included in this dossier is a sample of cases similar to those you may be tasked to handle. They are not for the faint of heart, but if you've made it this far, that won't be an issue for you. You are encouraged to study this material until your formal orientation at the academy.

If you are receiving this letter, you have already accepted the position and thus been made aware that its receipt bars your option for withdrawal from the program. Should you wish to reach out with any questions regarding these documents, we regret to inform you they do not exist.

Regards,

Christopher O'Halloran
Director, HOWLS Bureau of Investigation
[REDACTED], Canada

DON'T PLAY IN THE CLOSET
by David Worn

"I don't like that song!"

Brian had been about to close the bedroom door when something in his son's voice stopped him. He turned the lights back on.

"What song, buddy?"

Sam pointed toward his closet. "*That* song."

Brian shook his head and smiled. Sam had always been good at finding clever ways to delay bedtime. Investigating noises in the closet, though, that was a new one.

The closet itself was empty save for a few bags of old toddler clothes and several shirts hanging from child-sized hangers.

"See? There's nothing there." Brian closed the door.

"Daddy, make the song stop."

"Head *down*." He used his *dad voice*, and Sam lay down on his pillow, hands over his ears.

"Thanks, buddy. Love you."

Brian turned off the lights, closed the bedroom door, and left Sam to stare at his closet in the dark.

"MOMMY. MOMMY."

It was just before dawn when Brian awoke with a start. He scrambled out of bed, his heart racing. His wife, Laura, pulled off her sleeping mask.

"What's going on?"

There was a gut-wrenching scream, and Brian bolted down the hallway. Bursting into his son's room, he slammed the light switch on.

Sam's bed was empty.

Brian yanked the rocking chair out of the corner. There weren't many places to hide in the small bedroom.

Where the fuck is Sam?

Another scream. Brian whirled around, trying to locate the source.

The closet.

He threw open the closet door.

Sam was inside, facing the back wall. His body trembled, and he screamed again at the darkness.

Laura came up behind him and gasped.

"Sam, I got you. You're okay." Brian got down and reached into the closet for his son.

Sam's clothes were wet with sweat, and his skin was cold to the touch. He instinctively put his arms around his father's neck, his body reacting to the comfort of a parent before his mind fully understood what was happening.

"I followed the song, Daddy," Sam croaked.

His voice, normally tripping over itself with excitement, sounded diminished. Sam buried his face in his father's chest and whispered something. Brian thought it sounded like, "Don't let them take me away." Then Sam cried in deep sobs that racked his little body.

On the floor of the yellow-colored room, as the first rays of dawn filtered through the window, Brian rocked his son, repeating "we're okay," over and over.

Laura sat with them, her hand on Sam's back. They exchanged looks, both thinking the same thing.

We've been here before.

Back before Sam, when the nursery lay empty. When they had doubted whether they'd ever be able to have children. When the endless tests and consultations had led them to that final appointment with their reproductive endocrinologist.

"Your chances of successfully carrying a pregnancy to term are remote."

Later that day, Brian found Laura sitting where they were now, her arms wrapped around her knees, staring at an empty crib. His heart broke when she said to him, "We'll have to return all of this stuff." He held her then, just as he now held Sam, telling her they would be okay.

Then baby Sam came crashing into their lives, and Brian would be damned if he'd ever let anything happen to him.

Sam went missing a few hours later.

Brian was in the video-editing suite at the production company where he worked, when his phone shrieked with an AMBER alert.

He picked it up and was stunned to see dozens of alert notifications stacked up on his lock screen.

What the hell?

The phone buzzed in his hand. A text from Laura: *Did you see the news? We have to get Sam now!*

Brian grabbed his bag and ran from the room. Rushing past the elevator, he burst into the stairwell, descending the stairs two at a time until he was in the parking garage. Another AMBER alert went off.

His tires screeched as he tore out of the garage. With one eye on the road, Brian fumbled with his phone and sent a text to Laura: *Driving now. Call me.*

Laura immediately replied: *Calls won't go out. WTF is happening?*

He scanned through the FM channels.

"—hundreds of children missing. No comment yet from the authorities—"

Brian ran a red light. *Fuck. Fuck. Fuck.*

The announcer returned, "I'm sorry listeners, I have to go, I have a kid." In the background, he heard muffled shouting. "You can't leave! We're on the fucking air!"

Traffic increased all around him. Like a pressure valve had exploded, flooding the streets with cars. He imagined other parents, hearing the AMBER alerts, hearing the news—what had the radio said?

"...hundreds of children missing."

His phone vibrated with a text. It was Laura's sister, Sonia. She texted: *At school to get Nick. Will get Sam too. Meet me out front.*

A police car sped by, sirens blazing, driving in the oncoming lane of traffic. At the next intersection, a sedan ran a red light and side-swiped the police car. The metallic boom of steel against steel reverberated off the buildings.

Brian drove past the wreck without stopping.

At Sam's school, the parking lot was jammed with cars, blocking each other in. They sat empty with their engines still running. Brian couldn't see a way around them until an SUV went by and hopped the sidewalk, driving on the grass to the school's entrance. Brian followed, his bumper catching the curb with a plastic crunch.

Outside his car, he became aware of the cacophony of distant sirens, as though the whole city was on fire. Running inside the school, he collided with a mother and her child on the way out.

"Get the fuck out of my way," she screamed.

Inside, the lobby overflowed with parents. They pushed and swore and shouted over each other as haggard teachers guided them toward groups of children seated on the floor, in the stairwells, and in the adjoining rooms.

Something scratched at the edge of his mind, but there was too much noise, too many people. As he looked around at the clusters of school-aged kids being reunited with their parents, it hit him.

Where are the little ones, Brian? Where are all the preschoolers?

Through the crowd, he saw Laura's sister carrying her son, Nick. Sam wasn't with them.

"Sonia!"

She looked his way and her face fell. Tightening her grip on her son, Sonia turned away and kept walking. She was seven months pregnant, and even in the chaos, people made room for her.

Brian pushed through the crowd and broke into the hallway that led to Sam's classroom. A cop walked in his direction, yelling into his phone.

"What do you mean you can't find her? I'm coming home right now. Keep looking!"

Sam's class was empty. The back door to the playground was open. Beyond, he could see a group of adults standing by the old wooden playhouse in the corner of the yard.

Sam had called it the "spooky house." And with good reason: its walls were soft with rot, and the windows were caked in grime and decades of greasy fingerprints. The inside was always dark. Like a closet at night.

As he approached, he recognized some of the parents. These were people he knew. People he had socialized with at school events and birthday parties. Now, they looked like ghosts.

"I'm looking for Sam," Brian said.

Panic welled up inside him. He thought that if he could just keep his voice steady, ask simple questions, then everything would be okay. That he could keep at bay the dark thoughts that stalked at the periphery of his mind.

Sam is missing. They're all missing.

One of the parents pointed at the playhouse.

He wanted to scream, to shake the shocked expressions from their face and get someone to fucking tell him what was going on. Instead, the flatness of his voice caught him off guard.

"I don't understand."

A little girl of about five or six stood with her mother just beyond the group.

"Tell Sam's daddy what you told me."

Brian recognized the girl. She was in one of the neighboring classes. A first or second grader.

"I...I saw the preschool kids go into the playhouse and close the door. They said there was music. I spied on them through the window and saw..."

Brian's heart raced.

"I saw them fall into the shadows."

The world slowed like a record player losing power. There was a ringing in his ears that increased as he turned toward the playhouse. In his head he imagined Sam, sitting on his legs, still wearing his PJs from that morning. His son looked back over his shoulder at Brian.

"I followed the song, Daddy."

Then he fell forward and disappeared into the dark.

Back in the schoolyard, Brian pulled his phone out of his pocket with shaking hands. His fingers felt numb, and he struggled to unlock the device.

There were several missed texts from Laura. The last one read: *I'm in the lobby. Where are you? Please tell me you got Sam.*

On the monitor, a young girl around Sam's age sat up in her cot and cocked her ear to one side.

Brian scrubbed the clip forward and noted the time. It was three minutes before she moved again.

Next to her, a boy turned over, and the girl said something inaudible.

Brian clicked on the audio track and amplified it. Over the noise, he made out only one word:

"Listen."

Brian didn't have to hear the rest to guess what they were saying. He had seen more than enough clips by now to know that the children were listening to something that no one else could hear.

"Daddy, make the song stop."

Brian shook his head and took a sip of coffee. The tools of his trade—laptop, external monitor, drawing tablet—were arranged into

17

a makeshift workstation on Sonia's dining room table. It was nothing like his home office, but here they were.

Somehow, in the chaos of that first day, after they'd lost Sam, they found themselves at Sonia's. Still in shock, they had watched from the kitchen table as Sonia moved about her house in a panic, turning on all the lights.

It was then that Laura made the decision. They would stay and help her sister keep vigil over Nick, at least until her husband could come home from deployment.

There was more to it, of course. Staying with Sonia had become a way for them to put off returning to their empty house. To put off facing the silence left by Sam's absence.

A flicker of movement brought his attention back to his computer. The boy stood up and joined the girl. Together, they slipped under a cot and fell into the shadows on the floor.

Brian scrubbed the clip back several frames and zoomed in on the space beneath the cot. The girl had already disappeared, but part of the boy's body was still in view.

There was no point. He knew he wouldn't find anything, but he opened the image-editing tools anyway. Playing with levels, exposure, noise reduction—it wouldn't matter. Between the cheap CCTV cams that schools used for security and YouTube's video compression crushing the blacks, he doubted whether he'd ever be able to squeeze anything but noise from those grainy shadows.

Swearing under his breath, he switched to his browser. In the window was an online spreadsheet, the cursor waiting on the row that read: *1:14 pm, Westbrook Elementary, Glenview, Illinois*. He wrote "N/A" in the cell next to it and watched as dozens of colored cursors moved around the spreadsheet. Other editors, photographers—experts in image manipulation—who, like him, were working late into the night. Trying to find some clue as to what happened to their children.

He took off his headphones. The sound of the TV drifted over from the next room.

"It's obvious that the planet has taken revenge on us. We've been pillaging her for centuries. Clear-cutting the forests, poisoning the oceans, driving wildlife to extinction. Gaia theory states that—"

"With respect," said an older male voice, "that is complete bullshit! Whatever is happening in Illinois is a scientific phenomenon. Not some half-baked hippie—"

Laura changed the channel.

"—schools continue to see record drops in attendance as parents move their children out of state over fears that the disturbance is spreading—"

Another channel.

"CDC guidelines remain in effect for all children under six—"

Brian stopped trying to listen. Nobody had any fucking idea what had happened. What was *still* happening. In the five days since Sam disappeared, Brian worked, trying to find some clue in the hundreds of videos posted on YouTube and social media. Hoping to squeeze out some new detail from the darkness—to understand what had happened to Sam. He needed to do *something*, anything to keep himself from accepting that Sam was—

Brian opened his next video.

So far it had been a waste of time. The only constant he'd seen was that the children heard something—a song only those around the ages of two to five could hear.

Some had been spared. Laura's nephew Nick survived by dumb luck. Other children had been asleep, on the potty, or in car seats when it happened. Unable to escape their caregivers and follow the song into the dark.

But they were still in danger.

Nick continued to hear the song. But in the frantic hours after the event, Sonia had put sufficient stock in online rumors to zip-tie her son's closet door shut and keep him under watch. And so he had survived when Sam had not.

Brian closed the video editor. On the monitor, an image of Sam smiled back at him. It was taken just a few days before the event.

"Daddy, look at the red leaf!"

Brian and Laura had taken Sam for a hike to see the changing leaves. They had walked hand in hand along the trail, and when Sam's little legs had tired, he had thrown him up on his shoulders. Tears gathered in Brian's eyes as he remembered how happy Sam had been.

It wasn't fair. Brian reached out and touched the monitor. Sam was their only child, the only one they would ever have. For years, everyone around them appeared to have no trouble conceiving; Sonia got pregnant with Nick on the first try. She had no idea how difficult it had been for them. How they'd struggled. Tests, injections, hormone assays. Always a negative pregnancy test.

It should have been Nick.

Brian hated himself for thinking it. But the thought was like a canker. Sonia had another child on the way, she could afford to lose Nick. But Sam...Sam had been a miracle.

Lost in thought, Brian didn't hear his wife come in. She put her hand on the back of his neck and touched Sam's image on the computer monitor just as he had done.

"That was a good day," Laura said.

Her eyes were red from crying. Brian squeezed her hand. After a moment, he nodded toward the notebook tucked under her arm.

"Anything?"

"No. Same as yesterday. All the crazies are blaming vaccines, Democrats, and aliens. The CDC did release a statement today."

"And?"

"They don't think it's a disease."

Brian snorted.

"I'm heading up to sleep. Do you have the pills?"

He handed her the prescription bottle of sleeping pills they'd been passing back and forth since that first long night without Sam.

After Laura left, Brian loaded up another video, this one captured from a cell phone. A mother was filming her child walking trance-like into a closet, thinking it was just a game. Brian muted the audio, not wanting to hear her reaction when it happened.

It was almost midnight. It would soon be his shift to watch Nick. He was just about to go upstairs when his phone buzzed with a text from a photographer friend.

It read: *I found something.* Followed by a link.

Brian clicked it and his screen filled with an image of a child's closet.

Holy shit!

Nick's door creaked as Brian opened it. All around the room, he saw the signs of Sonia's evening vigil: a book, a plate of crumbs, an empty glass of water. In his bed, Nick slept. His little head tucked under a stuffed animal. A barrage of LED lamps, battery backups, and photography lights were arrayed around the room, carefully positioned to kill any shadow that might have tried to gather there. Wires and extension cables ran everywhere.

Sitting in the glider, the same one that had once been in Sam's room before they'd given it to Laura's sister, Brian recalled the thousand nights he put his son to bed. His room was always so tranquil. The orange glow of his night light, the rumble of his noise machine. Sometimes, Brian stayed and watched his son sleep, wondering who this boy would one day become. Back when Sam still had a lifetime ahead of him.

Unlocking his phone, he examined the picture again. It was a photo of a child sitting in her closet. Unlike the low-quality videos Brian had pored over, this one had been taken with a professional

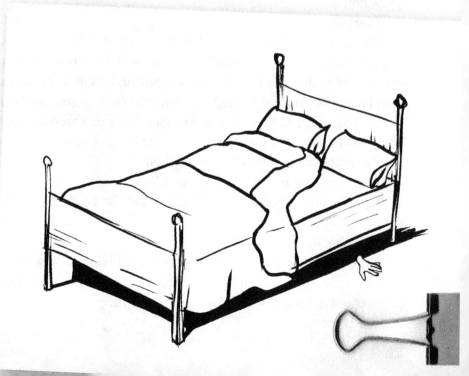

camera. The flash is what did it. It caught the darkness at the back of the closet moments before the child disappeared.

There was structure to that darkness. It looked vaguely like a wall; its edges were soft, and its inky black surfaces gave a faint impression of color. Like a slick of engine oil on wet pavement. It almost looked organic.

He adjusted the levels and rotated it this way and that. Trying to make sense of what he was looking at.

A tunnel?

As soon as he'd thought it, the possibilities exploded into his consciousness. The children weren't disappearing into nothingness. They were going somewhere. That meant…

Sam!

He could still be alive. Wasting away in the darkness.

The memory of that morning—of Sam crying into his chest after they'd found him in his closet—crept up on him. His nostrils filled with Sam's scent. The unmistakable perfect smell of his child.

"Don't let them take me away."

Brian was still for a long time.

When he finally looked up, it was 3:48 am. It would be sunrise in a few hours.

Don't do this.

His legs carried him toward the closet. A part of him wanted to be stopped, for someone, Sonia or his wife, to walk in on him. He pictured the look on their faces if they were to enter and see him sawing away with his pocket knife at the zip ties that held Nick's closet door shut.

He turned off the lights, one by one. Pools of shadows gathered under the bed, behind the chair, and inside the newly opened closet.

He hesitated over Nick's sleeping body.

Why are you still here and not Sam?

Brian gently shook Nick's shoulder and the boy's eyes fluttered open.

"Hey buddy, your closet is open."

Nick stared a long time at the doorway, his head cocked to one side. Just like the children in the videos. Listening to something that Brian could not perceive. The song from nowhere.

He got out of bed and shuffled over to the closet.

I only opened the door. That's all. It's not like I'm dragging him kicking and screaming.

Nick stood at the threshold, dropped his stuffed animal, and pointed toward the darkest part of his closet.

Brian listened close. There was nothing. Whatever the children seemed to hear, he was deaf to it. But still, he strained. And in that dark room, in the middle of the night, his body tingling with adrenaline, Brian could almost hear…*what? A song?* No. It was just phantoms in Nick's white noise machine.

He followed his nephew into the closet and closed the door behind them.

In the blackness, his heart raced. He waited with his hands raised, ready to grab Nick the instant something changed. What if it only works when they're alone? What if I'm too old for it to happen?

What if I can't follow?

He could still stop this, turn the lights on, and put Nick back in his bed. No one would know. His stomach twisted with revulsion at what he was doing. Brian conjured up that image of Sam alone in the dark, but it was no longer enough. He couldn't sacrifice someone else's child for his.

I'm so sorry, Sam.

He was about to open the closet door when it began.

A whisper of hot air rose from the floor by Nick's feet. As it passed over him, the skin on Brian's arms broke out in goosebumps.

Nick's body tipped forward, and Brian lunged, wrapping his arms tight around him, the momentum carrying them both into the dark.

Brian lay on his side, cradling Nick in his arms. Moments before, they had been falling. Then, the plane shifted suddenly, and they were lying on the ground. The break in the natural order of things had scrambled his senses, made him want to throw up. He took several deep breaths until the feeling passed.

The air was hot and humid and his eyes watered from an overpowering acetone-like stench, as though a thousand magic markers had just opened in front of him.

Nick squirmed in his arms. All around, walls like skin pressed down on them. There was a sound like cellophane crinkling and, all over his body, he felt tiny fingers press on him. They were moving. The fingers dragged them forward, like cilia pushing food along a digestive tract. The sensation grew stronger as the walls compressed around him. Brian groaned.

This was meant for children.

The fingers beneath him were pushing Brian back, trying to separate him from his nephew. He strengthened his grip, causing Nick to cry out.

"Uncle Brian?"

Nick's voice was pitifully small, but it sounded like *him*. Whatever trance he'd been in when he'd gone into the closet was over. He was just a little boy afraid of the dark.

An impression of light. Somewhere ahead, there was an end to the tunnel.

Distracted, Brian lost his grip on Nick and the fingers carried him away. Except they weren't fingers at all, in the faint light he saw the thousands of tiny oily black proboscises pulling Nick forward like a…

like a fucking conveyor belt.

Nick fell out of the opening and disappeared from view.

Brian pushed forward. The light was growing stronger. Near the opening, the tunnel appeared to widen; he could almost crawl on all fours if he could just make it a few more feet.

Through the opening, he caught a glimpse of a dusty red wall made of stone. He army-crawled toward it, dragging himself along the tunnel. The feeling of warm flesh and the hundreds of little finger-like cilia squirming as they were crushed under the weight of his body should have repulsed him, but he thought only of Sam. His son could be there, just a few feet away.

The light dimmed as a face occluded the opening. It was Nick. Another face appeared, that of an older girl. She looked curiously at Brian as he struggled to reach them. Then another child.

A shot of adrenaline surged through him and his entire body reached forward. Every muscle straining to get closer to—

"SAM."

Tears fell from his son's eyes, drawing rivers through the sweat and the dirt caked over his face.

"Daddy?"

"I'm coming, Sam," Brian yelled.

He fought for every inch of those last few feet. Ripping at the wall-flesh, tearing the soft wet cilia from their roots as he clawed his way forward.

The tunnel reacted to his progress, shuddering as if in pain. The flesh around him contracting and expanding in rhythmic pulses. His nasal passages burned as the smell of acetone grew stronger.

He pulled and kicked and willed himself forward, but he was getting crushed by the undulating walls of the tunnel. He felt a blinding pain in his chest as something cracked under the strain.

"Sam," Brian grunted.

He was so close. Ahead, Sam crawled partway into the tunnel and reached for his father. Brian's heart nearly tore out of his chest as he pushed every muscle in his body to their limit. Their fingers touched, and his son's desperate grip brought back the memory of Sam's first day of preschool, when he'd been so shy and afraid that he'd held onto his father's hand with an iron grip. As Brian left that morning, Sam had watched him go with pleading tears in his eyes. They'd both cried that day.

Through his hand, Brian felt Sam shudder. Something was wrong. Sam's fingers slipped from his.

No! Why did he let go?

Then he saw it.

The hand wrapped around Sam's shoulder.

It was not a child's hand. The arm was unnaturally long. Covered in red cloth, it extended upwards beyond the lip of the opening. The skin was like plastic stretched over bone.

The children were not alone.

Brian clawed at the walls of the tunnel, willing himself forward, trying to pull his entire weight with only his fingers as the walls constricted around him. *Just a little more, please God.*

Sam stood rigid, his eyes wide with terror. Tears streamed down his face as the hand guided him away.

Panic filled Brian with new strength, and he tore at the flesh, inching closer to the opening, pushing back against the walls with all his might, his broken ribs sending back shards of pain in protest. Darkness fell upon him as a sickening iris of flesh shut out the light and closed him off from Sam.

The wall-flesh shuddered and contracted as the fingers pulled at him, expelling him backward. He felt a tremendous surge of speed, and then his legs skidded on solid ground. He was back in Nick's closet.

He tried to return to the tunnel, but the darkness pushed back until the hot air dissipated and the floor was once again just a floor.

Brian lay wet and shaking. His body was bruised. Something in his chest was broken, and he breathed in wheezy, labored breaths.

Sam was gone. Nick was lost, and something unnatural was with them.

Lying against the floor, he was too shocked to cry. When it did finally come, it was slow and ugly. A howl filled with loss and shame.

The door to the room burst open and Sonia ran inside.

"Brian, the lights! Oh God, where's Nick?"

She stared at Brian's prone body in the closet, next to his feet were the remnants of the cut zip-ties. It didn't take her long.

"What did you do?"

She got down on her hands and knees and put her face close to his. One hand instinctively went to her stomach as if to protect the baby inside from him.

"WHERE IS MY SON?"

Brian didn't hear her; his mind was locked in those last moments. Touching Sam's fingers. The plastic hand pulling his son from the opening. Sam looking back at him.

And underneath it all had been the song. He hadn't registered it in the moment, but his mind had recorded it all the same. A song in no language. A clarion call. In his memory, he heard it as they did. Felt the power of that summons from the dark.

Sonia screamed his name, trying to get him to acknowledge her. She crawled past him and pounded on the floor of the closet. Tears fell from her cheeks onto the place where her son had gone.

At the doorway stood Laura. He knew she would come to hate him, be disgusted with what he'd done to her nephew, but right now the question hung in the air. She didn't need to say it.

"I found Sam," he said.

He had to bring him back, bring them both back. Get them away from that thing with the plastic hands.

He'd be better prepared next time. He'd have climbing gear, a rope, something to claw his way through. And a gun. Sonia would forgive him. Sam was family. They would come to understand…and then they would help.

And Brian needed help. For if this new plan was going to work, he would need someone else's child.

HOWLS BUREAU OF INVESTIGATION

HBI

SPECIAL AGENT *David Worn*

David Worn is a neuroscientist and Canadian expat. His short fiction has recently appeared in *Howls from the Dark Ages: An Anthology of Medieval Horror* and *Dark Matter Magazine*. When not writing, he enjoys patching Modular Synths and playing lightsabers with his kids.

worncassettes.com   @WornCassettes

MEMO: Evidentiary imagery and agent headshot provided by Maia Weir.

[>EXECUTERELEASE_]
By P.L. McMillan

I stare at my code, my shoulders aching, my hands limp in my lap. My desk is a graveyard of coffee-stained mugs and cardboard trays of frozen dinners. A scream rips through the eerie city quiet, and my guilt pulls me to my feet. I skirt around Arachne, avoiding her eight massive metal legs that curl slightly inwards, towards her open belly panel. At the window, I look out.

Four stories down, prone on the pavement, is a woman. She's dressed in sweatpants, a hoodie, and is surrounded by a halo of groceries, baby formula. My gut wrenches.

"Please, someone help me!" The woman rolls onto her hands and knees, scrambling along the street.

A four-foot-long, AI-operated spider skitters towards her, the digital interface screen on its back displaying a pixel-cute smiling face complete with eight cartoon eyes—one of Arachne's many sisters.

"Sign up for Express and get same-day delivery!" blares from the spider's speaker, and its digital smile widens as it winks one of its eight eyes.

"Someone! Anyone!" The woman manages to get to her feet but the spider is faster yet.

It leaps forward and pins the woman against a nearby car.

This is my fault.

So it is my obligation to watch as the spider uses its prehensile hands to crush the woman's arms into her torso. She falls. The spider works on her legs next. The echoes of her cracking bones reach all the way to my window, through the glass. Blood spreads on the pavement, glinting with snatches of sunlight.

The woman is a conveniently shaped package now, and the spider turns, using its legs to spin her as it spits plastic wrap out, silencing her screams with lime-green cellophane. The spider picks her up, holding her against its cheerful digital face with two legs.

"Thank you for being our customer!" the spider says. "And as always, smile with Naemcom!"

It carries the woman away, down the street, towards the Naemcom warehouse.

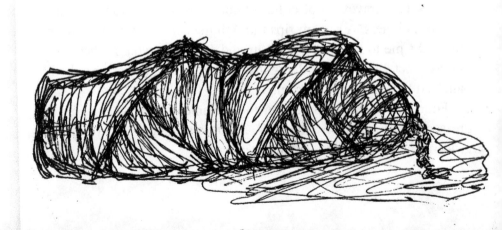

My stomach boils with acidic bile that threatens to rise into my throat, to fill my mouth. I turn away from the window and go to my fridge, pulling it open, revealing that my supplies have dwindled down to a few bottles of juice and some crumbs of cheese.

I drown my nausea in pineapple juice.

I ran out of food two days ago. And six days before that was when the spiders received the update. The accidental doomsday update.

My update.

The moment I hit ENTER rolls around and around my mind. An endless whipping. A flogging guilt stain.

I knew that more testing was needed when my manager told me to push the update, but Naemcom management wanted the spiders primed for when our competing company, Lornehead, released their new fleet of delivery drones.

I return to my laptop and look at the thumb drive plugged into its side. Transfer complete. Fear is a block of cold iron in my guts, weighing me down, trying to pull me away from the computer.

From the next step I must take.

As the lead software engineer, I was tasked with updating the spiders—*my* spiders—with new behaviours to target the drones, take them down, wrap them up, and bring them back to the Naemcom warehouse as returns. No evidence, no competition.

Illegal, of course. But, if my software update worked, then it would be untraceable unless the government raided the company warehouse, and there were too many politicians whose pockets were heavy with Naemcom bribes for that to ever happen.

I pull the drive out, thread a chain through its eyelet, and hang it around my neck. Three heavy thuds vibrate through the floor.

"Angelina Coors, your Naemcom Organic Farm Fresh delivery is here!" chirps a spider from out in the hall. "Yum, yum!"

I can hear my neighbour crying through the wall.

"Please! Please leave it on the floor!" she says.

"Angelina Coors, please sign for your delivery!" the spider replies, knocking, knocking, knocking.

"Go away! Leave me alone!"

I tested the update prior to releasing it, of course I had, but only in a controlled sandbox scenario. In that way, the spiders performed perfectly. I wish I could say I had known something was wrong, but I hadn't. The higher-ups told me to push the release so I did. It's what they pay me for, after all.

I hadn't imagined it could ever go this way.

"Angelina Coors!" the spider sings, slamming its legs over and over into the door, splintering the wood. My neighbour screams, begs, pleads.

I hadn't thought my logic through when I built the update. I'd designed it so the spiders would recognize a drone's four motors and use that to identify it as a "return" that needed to be retrieved. To be sure the spiders would do the job right, I'd also added simple AI to the update so the spiders could dynamically learn as they worked.

Looking back now, the flaw in that update was clear.

Returning to stand by Arachne, I touch one of her clawed hands tenderly. She is my prototype model. She is my favourite and, currently, the only Naemcom logistical spider that has not received the latest update. Because she's been here, with me, offline. As soon as I boot her up again, she will connect to my wifi and receive the update.

I open the Naemcom app on my phone and punch in an order for a return, specify the size of the box, and scan the barcode. The specifications match the large wooden crate that sits next to Arachne. Tenderly, I press Arachne's power button, watching as it glows blue. I yank open my front door, then return to my home office and climb into the crate, pulling the lid on after.

By programming the spiders to recognize an object with four protuberances—four limbs in essence—I'd placed a target on every cat, dog, person, and child in the city. When the spiders had powered on the following morning, ready to start delivering and meeting Naemcom quotas, they'd instead received an update that sent them out into the streets, to hunt down everything with four limbs they found.

The AI I'd added, thinking myself so clever, also allowed the spiders to change. To adapt their own base programming. It allowed them to evolve. They learned to knock down doors, open windows, mimic cries for help in order to get to their targets, and this change prevents a simple rollback command. This means new programming is needed to stop their massacre.

Angelina is silent, her screams likely muffled by plastic wrap. "Thank you for your order!" the spider says. "Please visit the Naemcom website and fill out a survey about your experience. If you do, you'll have a chance to win a $50 credit to use towards your next purchase at Naemcom!"

Arachne wakes, her motors gearing up, her circuits humming. Of her kind, she has a custom avatar and voice—mine.

Egotistical, I know.

"Wakey, wakey!" she trills, righting herself. "What a Naemcom kind of day!"

She pauses. I can picture her digital UI blank as she receives her new update. She beeps as the download and reboot completes.

"Jolene Hanover! I will collect your return now!" Arachne says.

My crate lifts, spins as she wraps it in plastic, cutting off my air supply. I reach for the box cutter I'd slipped into my pocket, pulling it free and slashing through the gaps in the wooden planks of the crate, creating air holes.

Arachne places me on her back and heads off, scuttling out into the hall, down the stairs. It's the first time I've been outside since after the software release and the city was overrun. Naemcom has hundreds of spiders and they are tireless, capturing solar power during the day, and charging as needed back at the warehouse.

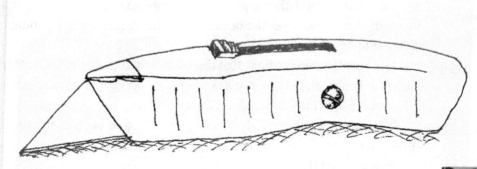

Bracing my hands on opposite sides of the crate, I try to steady myself as Arachne barrels through the streets. In the distance, guns rattle, the air throbs with helicopters. The government trying to bring the city back under control.

Over half its citizens dead—according to the latest news report I'd seen on my phone. Oh, but my spiders were as efficient at killing as they were at delivery.

I slam against the back of the crate as Arachne hurdles over a smoking car, the acrid stench of burnt rubber choking me. She takes me on the quickest route to the warehouse, through downtown, past abandoned boutiques, cutesy cafes, and overpriced restaurants that insist on serving everything on slabs of slate. The symphony here has changed. Gone is the cacophony of shoppers, of diners, the clashing music of competing bars and venues. Instead there are screams, the chatter of gunfire, the thunder of hovering helicopters.

I peek through a gap in the wooden slats at the passing chaos, the ruins of the city I call home, the destruction I caused. A man is dragged out of a store, kicking at the spider that pins him down and begins to break him into a better shape.

A copter swerves around a corporate office building, hovering above the street, facing us. Its gun smokes in the wind, a wreath of ethereal ghosts that are snatched in the copter's blades and dispersed.

My heart leaps into my throat, my palms slick with sweat, as I face down death. The copter's gun barrel begins to spin and this is it. I should have stayed in my condo—or maybe a quicker death by gunfire is preferable to starvation.

Then four spiders launch from nearby roofs, plastic wrap webbing spinning out behind them, giant metal legs spread like deadly starbursts as they shoot over the copter in lightning fast arcs, dropping on either side of it.

The plastic wrap is thick. Just thick enough to tangle in the copter's blades. Its engine stutters, smokes, then the copter body spins, jerking left, and crashes into the bank on the corner.

It's over in a second. My spiders should have been mercenaries. A dark part of my mind is proud. Look at my babies. Look at what I made. Unstoppable, beautiful, brutal.

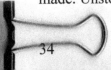

(*<executeRelease_*) *by P.L. McMillan*

The following explosion reverberates through the road, I feel it in my bones. Arachne carries me onward. We pass through downtown, entering the denser commercial district. The closer we get to Naemcom HQ, the more spiders I see. Carrying packages. Carrying bodies.

Arachne takes me in, scaling the wall to the intake bay only my babies can reach. The other entrances will have been sealed, locked, but my Trojan Horse takes me through. Through the logistical tunnels built for the spiders, deep inside the building, to the large echoing warehouse where returns are taken and processed.

"Logging return from Jolene Ora!" Arachne sings and I feel my crate tipping, me with it, as she sets me on top of another crate.

I keep still as she scans the barcode I stuck to the outside of the crate, silently processing it. A single beep, then Arachne steps back.

She's off and I'm alone in the darkened warehouse. I grip the thumb drive around my neck, closing my eyes, and picturing—as best I can—the inside of HQ. Returns, through to Processing, down the maintenance corridor to the Tech Center where calls were fielded, where ill-fated updates were made, and a possible redemption update could be initiated.

But the Returns Hub is a busy place. Spiders scuttle in and out, carrying boxes, carrying envelopes…carrying bodies.

I suck in a deep breath, perfumed with the smell of plastic, wood, chemicals, and rot. Decay. The thick, wet reek of hundreds of bodies melting away in their plastic cocoons, their juices soaking into the treated concrete floor.

As quietly as possible, I use the knife to slit through the plastic wrap around the lid. I have no idea if sounds will alert the spiders. They were never programmed to guard, just to deliver and retrieve, but I don't want to risk anything. Technically I hadn't meant to program them to kill people, dogs, cats, yet here we are.

Plastic cut, I close the knife, slip it into my pocket, and slide the lid off my crate. I pause, listen to the sharp tips and taps of spider claws along the floor, along the metal catwalks. One upside to this is I'm now too scared to feel how hungry I am anymore.

Palms pressing against the sides of the crate, I run the route again in my mind. Returns, Processing, corridor, Tech Center. On a normal day, it's a five-minute walk. Today? Well, that's anyone's guess.

Slowly, painfully slow, I peek my head above the edge of my crate. The dock is dim, lit only by rows of motion-activated lighting that follow the spiders as they roam in and out. Arachne set me on top of a five-foot-high pyramid of the larger, heavier returns, which also happens to be closer to the door to Processing than other areas of the Returns Hub.

With careful movements, I slip a leg over the side of the crate, ease myself out onto the pile. The smallest noise shouldn't matter, right? They were programmed for voice recognition, approaching cars, trams…still. My back to the wall, I keep my eyes on the floor, on my babies, the plague of the city. Kneeling, I fumble backwards, one foot, one hand at a time, making my way down the boxes.

My heartbeat is the rapid bassline, accentuated by the spiders' movement, echoing in the vast warehouse. My mouth is drier than it's ever been. Each movement is precise. Slide a toe along the edge and down the box's side, second foot to follow, then hand, and hand. A painful dance of fear and nerves. I make it to the base of the pyramid and freeze as a spider runs towards me. The lights overhead flash along with it, heralding its arrival.

My heart buries itself in my throat, choking me. I drop into a ball, wrapping my arms tight around my legs, tucking my face to my knees. Will it work?

Will it work?

I feel its heavy steps approach, stop.

My pulse pounds in my ears and insanely I need to sneeze, the floor—undusted for years—triggers my allergies and this will be it, the robot will know, it will grab me and wrap me and—

"False. No return identified. Returning to the field!" the spider chirps and tip-taps away.

Pressing my tongue to the roof of my mouth, fighting the sneeze, I look up. Coast clear, and I pinch my nose, sneezing so hard my ears pop, pain shoots through my skull, but it's silent.

And after the sneeze comes the feeling of nausea—fear and hunger, terror and despair. But I roll to my hands and knees. There are spiders everywhere. One drops off a cigar-shaped package that is still wiggling, still fighting to escape, blood stains the plastic and leaks onto the floor to join the ocean of other fluids, molding, reeking.

The door is closed. It will only take a dozen or so steps to reach it.

So I take a step.

And the light above me flashes on, triggered by my movement.

A drumroll of spider claws across concrete. "Return identified!"

I don't wait. I run.

Beneath my shoes, the rapid fire of mechanical hands pounding the floor, matching the thunder of my heart, and I feel my own reckoning approach, a death I programmed, my own design.

Like a knife maker murdered by a knife they forged. Poetic. Ironic, maybe.

Every second is an eternity. My one step for four of the spider's. My one breath for a million nanoseconds of processing and computing. I created the perfect monster—cold, unfeeling, efficient.

The door is an arm's reach away and I do reach, my hand sweaty, my vision focused down to a brutal pinpoint of hopeless precision.

My hand on the doorknob.

A flare of bright pain, the wet crunch of breaking bone, a reverberation of impact followed by a cold wave of numbness.

I twist the doorknob and fall forward, my legs buckling with the shock. The fact that the door opens inwards is my saving grace. I collapse into the Processing room and kick the door shut.

And what is pain but wave after wave of cacophonous decay that flows through every vein and nerve, killing time, killing awareness, until I am nothing more than a being of sensation and tears, bile on back of tongue, wails, and begging for mercy.

But the present seeps back in, as it always does, as with the guilt, the obligation.

I lie on the cold floor, clutching the stump where my left arm used to be.

One of my babies, my progeny, has managed to sever it from me, and I squirm in a hot pool of my own liquid, the crimson jam of my heart's creation.

I wonder at my own poetic waxings on the edge of death, the abyss makes artists of us all in the face of our own mortality.

The door in front of me is splintering. The spider is dedicated. Of course. That is my design.

Numbness is now my strength.

I slide up the wall, I the slug, my blood the slime.

So much blood.

The spider will take its return. But I hope to get the update done first.

Through the room, past empty desks with piles of paperwork and supplies, I grab an ethernet cable, tie it around my stump with help from my teeth, staunch the flow of death—for now. Trip over a trash can, scatter scraps of paper like leaves.

"Please." I don't know with whom I plead, through the door to the maintenance corridor.

Behind me the door to the Returns Hub breaks, falls. I feel it in my bones. The spider has reinforcements, crying for the statistics, fighting to fill their quotas. "Return identified. Collecting!"

A wave of dizziness, a fuzziness as thick as a blizzard. I fall against a wall, tilt, the impact to my knees awakens me and I bolt up again. I let go of my stump, grasping the thumb drive around my neck with a blood-stained hand.

Down the hall, no longer a steady tempo but erratic. Step, step, slide. Step, step, falter.

Behind me, desks are shattered, are thrown, chairs fall, monitors break. The spiders—my children—they come for me.

My doom. My design.

There it is. The door.

Behind me, a crash. They've breached the hall. But I'm through. Into the Tech Center, glowing with the blue luminosity of dozens of servers, thrumming with life. My computer is at the very back, in a small office. As team lead, I was given the honour. Now it feels like condemnation. My hip slams into the corner of a desk. I yelp but the pain brings clarity.

My shoulder, the gap where my left arm should be, it's still gushing blood. How much blood can one person lose?

Onwards, onwards. Footsteps. My own. The echoes of spiders. Also my own, in a way.

Past the desks of the people I once employed—dead now, most likely.

My door is open. I always left it open. A way to show I was one of them. A good manager. Death bringer. My own design.

At my desk, I let my knees buckle. It's final. The laying of a tombstone. My chair—ergonomic, within my yearly office budget, stupid thoughts, it's hard to control—catches me. It won't be long. My spiders are smart. They'll be here soon.

My computer fires all cylinders, I log in. Fail. Log in. My fingers are shaking, I keep hitting the wrong keys.

The door to the Tech Center shivers at impact.

I press my remaining hand to my face, suck in a breath. Grit my teeth so hard they creak.

I type. Slowly. One key at a time.

```
MotherArachne00
```

```
ENTER.
```

I'm in. Things are slower with one hand. A coldness spreads through my body like disease. Shock. Worse, maybe death.

I jam the thumb drive into a side port, open command prompt. Light blasts across the center, leaves spots in my eyes. The door is open. They have come.

Their animatronic hands beat a death march across the threshold. Their cheerful cries of war, of homicide, of genocide, are a falsetto of triumphant resolution.

```
(!committed_ || impl_->executeRelease_)
```

A running river of code. A new update. A chance. A hope.

Six spiders flow over desks, crush empty soda cans, puncture chair cushions.

Me. To be returned. To be crushed and wrapped and placed among the others.

I lean in my chair, kick my office door shut, first time in the seven years I've worked for Naemcom.

My fingertips are icicles and my heart is an iceberg, I type in the execute command.

My babies are at my door.

There's a chance this won't work.

The code runs, the prompt zigzags all over, I can't see though, my vision fuzzes, to match the static in my head.

The door shakes and shimmies in its frame. I press my hand against the place where my left arm used to be. The warmth of my blood gives my fingers a moment of life, despite the buzzing in my veins, bees of death, reapers of momentary despair.

I slip from my chair, my body limp, helpless.

Prostrate on the floor, the CPU fan whirs my dirge, my door breaks. I meant to define myself at Naemcom, to find meaning, to be a name to remember.

Arachne is the first one in. As it should be.

The daughter to take the mother in this necropolis.

I raise my arm to her. She seems to pause, legs raised above, guillotines of efficient logistics. This is my design.

I press my bloody fingers to the UI interface. To the pixel face I know so well. Leave her the baptism I should have given her when I first booted her up. Her birth, long forgotten in lieu of better versions.

She presses me, breaks me. The reversal of birth. Molding me into the shape needed to push me back. Rollback.

Past my thirty years, past adulthood, teenage-hood, childhood, into utero. My blood is my amniotic fluid, wrapped around me with the plastic Arachne spins out, weaving me into death.

Warm, hot, suffocating. I drink in my own copper. I hear the beep of a command executed.

Next cycle. Next reboot. Will my redemption be birthed?

Arachne takes me. Twists me. Roles reversed. Mother and child, creation and creator. Taking me to darkness. Taking me away.

It will only be a few hours if I did it right. Daily sync always at the same time. And I drift. Finally free. This, not mine, but Arachne's design.

HOWLS BUREAU OF INVESTIGATION

HBI

H.B.I.

SPECIAL AGENT — *P.L. McMillan*

With a passion for cosmic horror and sci-fi horror, P.L. McMillan sees every shadow as an entryway to a deeper look into the black heart of the world, meant to be discovered and explored. Infatuated with the works of Shirley Jackson, H.P. Lovecraft, and Ridley Scott, her dream is to create stories of adventure, of chills, of heartbreak, and thrills. Check out her short story collection, *What Remains When The Stars Burn Out* and her debut folk horror novella, *Sisters of the Crimson Vine* available now.

plmcmillan.com   @AuthorPLM

MEMO: Evidentiary imagery provided by Michelle Tang.
Agent headshot provided by Maia Weir.

SON OF YOKOZURO
by Caleb Stephens

I settle in next to Maru as he folds his hands behind his head and leans back against a mountain of discarded tires, staring up at the black velvet expanse that is the night sky. He has the cheeks of a Pokémon—Makuhita, to be exact. Two loveable brown mounds that make him look ten instead of fifteen.

My skin looks like a crocodile's; my features are as wrinkled as leather, my chin jammed with a riot of teeth.

We're chilling outside in the courtyard of the abandoned metal factory in Keiyō, a few miles from Tokyo, taking a break from playing *Monster Stalker* on Maru's Nintendo Switch. Well, mostly he plays, and I watch. My hands are much too big for the console. I'd crush it in a hot second.

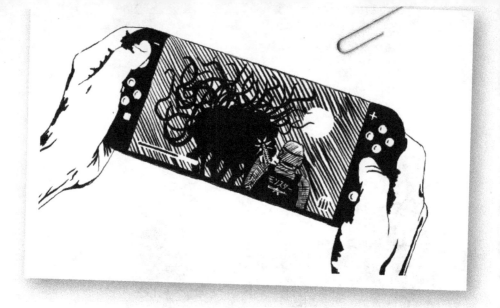

"Look, do you see those stars, Chibi? There, there, and there?" Maru stamps his finger with each *there* like he's punching little holes in the atmosphere. "That's *Tsuzumi Boshi*." He traces two circles, one above and one below a trio of glittering stars, connecting both ends of the drum that give the constellation its name. "Cool, right?"

It's kind of cool, I guess, but staring at the sky isn't really my thing; it's Maru's. He and his dad used to go stargazing every weekend. They spent an entire summer camping in Toyama just to escape the blinding city light. When his parents died in a train derailment near Ikebukuro Station two years ago, I wondered if Maru would ever look at the stars again. And it took a while, but when he did, I was right there, ready to look with him.

We sit there for a moment, both of us silent, until I say, "What do you think? Ready to kick some Domogato ass?" Domogato is the final boss in *Monster Stalker*. A black-scaled viper the size of Tokyo Tower. We've been trying to beat him for weeks without much luck, but I'm thinking tonight might be just the night.

"Hell yes, I am," Maru replies, firing up the Switch. "Let's harvest his guts!" He's just about to press the *Start* button when Dad roars for me from across the city. Maru groans. I can practically hear the eye roll in his voice. "Not *again*. You said he was taking the night off."

"I thought he was. I guess he changed his mind." I lay my hand on the ground so Maru can climb aboard. "Sorry, man. I gotta go. If he catches me hanging out with a human, he'll kill us both. How about a rain check? He's planning on burning down Hokkaido this weekend. He'll be gone until Sunday. We can play until our eyes bleed."

Maru brightens, his patented half-grin restored. I stand and set him on my shoulder, where he sinks into the fabric of my favorite Hawaiian shirt—the one I sewed myself using the flags I gathered from the courtyard of the Hamamatsuchō World Trade Center while Dad wrecked downtown (again).

"Promise?" Maru asks. "All night? Until sunrise? With pizza?"

I nod. "Yep. On my life."

After dropping Maru off at his apartment, I make for Dad's atomic beam. All that sparkling blue heat almost looks beautiful at times, but then you realize it's just his indigestion manifesting as radioactive fallout and it loses its appeal. Usually, it's spiking for the sky from the middle of the city, but tonight, it's closer than I'd like, radiating upward like some kind of malignant Bat-Signal.

If only he *was* Batman. That'd be sick. Him patrolling around Tokyo, keeping the criminals in check, making sure everyone is safe. Me, his Robin, right there with him. Father and son, the heroes of the city. How great would that be?

But he's not Batman.

He's Yokozuro, Lizard King of Tokyo and the scourge of Japan.

I find him in Makuhari, standing over a smoldering heap of rubble that was, until five minutes ago, a shopping complex replete with a tempura restaurant and a convenience store. Dad's hulking in the middle of the wreckage, looking extra terrifying as he devours what's left of the patrons, shoving them into his mouth like handfuls of M&Ms. His dorsal plates reflect the orange light of the fire consuming the condominium tower at the edge of the parking lot, his eyes a pair of glowing crimson slits. He's two hundred feet tall, and all braided muscle and glossy black scales.

I'm not even one hundred feet tall with a weight problem.

"Where have you been?" He plucks a body from the rubble and removes a leg, then works it between his teeth like a toothpick.

45

"You're late. You know to keep an eye on the clock tower."

"You *destroyed* it last week, Dad. Remember? And I thought you were taking the night off."

"No. Not until tomorrow."

"Why aren't you in the city?" Makuhari is mostly full of the elderly and the poor. They already have it tough enough as it is. Why Dad would want to add to their misery is beyond me. It's cruel, even for him.

"I grow weary of ravaging the city. The people there know to fear us. To give us respect. But out here—" he waves a black talon claw at the dense maze of apartment blocks cutting away in every direction "—they laugh at us. They treat us with disdain. It's time we remind them who we are."

I'm pretty sure I've never seen anyone laugh at Dad, *ever,* but I know better than to contradict him. The last time I did, I wound up in the middle of Tokyo Bay.

I cross my arms and sigh. They barely wrap over my chest. I'm basically the Stay Puft Marshmallow Man of the kaiju line. "So, what do you want me to do?"

Tendrils of blue flame leak from the corners of his mouth. "What do you *think* I want you to do?"

I scratch my head like I have no clue, like the answer isn't the same every time. "Wreck some shit?"

"Yes, Chibiuzza. Correct. 'Wreck some shit.'"

I do it, whipping my tail sideways into a four-story building across the street. There are no lights on, which means there's a pretty good chance it's abandoned. It cleaves in half, the top disintegrating in a shower of concrete and insulation. Dad tips his head in approval. I crouch and snag a dump truck parked in the handicapped spot.

My heart ignites. There's a woman cowering behind it, holding the hand of a toddler whose lower lip is wobbling like a slice of Jell-O.

A dark stain spreads across his crotch, and he flings himself, wailing, into the woman's arms. She barely reacts. Her mouth is stretched wide, ready to unleash the scream I know so well—the one that will earn her a first-class ticket to Dad's stomach.

I raise a finger and press it to my lips. *"Shh. Go."* My eyes flick to the alley behind them as I stand and launch the truck into the already-cratered shopping center, careful to avoid hitting the retirement home next door. *Rawr.*

When I look back, the woman and child are gone.

Dad glowers at me with his nostril slits flaring, the top right corner of his lip riding high in disgust. "Really? That's the best you can do? Use your breath."

"But it hurts." And it does. My atomic ray always comes out wrong. Sometimes as globs of burning tar mixed with jaundice-colored stomach acid. Sometimes as a gout of flame that fills my lungs with smoke and leaves me coughing for a week. Most of the time, as nothing at all. It isn't unless I'm really, *really,* pissed that I can fire my nuclear beam. It's the same orange hue as a pack of Kawaguchi Mikan Chan. I have to admit it's kind of cool when that happens. Starts a few fires. Enough to impress Maru, anyway. We use it to make s'mores.

"Go on. Do it," Dad orders with a menacing snarl which tells me if I don't, he will.

I turn and take a few breaths. Maybe, if I nail this, we can call it a night and head home. I pull in a deep lungful of air and hold it there, soaking it with my internal radiation, really letting it simmer, before I force it back up my throat and out of my mouth as hard and fast as I can. My spit rains down over the gas lines burning around my feet, hissing like a handful of water flicked upon a hot griddle. Nothing but halitosis rain.

The air tastes like rubber and scorched meat.

Dad shoulders me out of the way. *"Kuso!* How many times do I have to show you how to do it? Watch." And then his dorsal spines are lighting up, turning navy, turquoise, electric blue before he unleashes a bright stream of superheated vapor that carves a flaming canyon through the city, melting steel and iron and copper like giant pads of butter. Air raid sirens rise in response, the steady *thwack, thwack, thwack* of military helicopters echoing toward us not long after. Soon, they'll call in the jets and tanks just like every other night we do this, and we'll lay waste to them, too.

His lips stitch into a razorblade grin. He sets his hands on his hips and rocks back on his heels: the look of someone after a job well done. I briefly wonder if I should go fetch him a beer and his favorite recliner.

"See," he says, thumping his fist to his chest. "It's all internal. You must center yourself first, Chibiuzza. Focus your ki and unleash it."

"Uh-huh," I reply. I'm on autopilot mode, my mind already drifting to this weekend with Maru. If we can just find the Sword of Ishiri before facing Domogato, we might stand a chance of defeating—

Dad reaches out and gives me a shake. "Are you even paying attention, Chibi-kun? You aren't, are you? *Dammit*, boy, what am I going to do with you?"

I shrug. "Take me home?"

"Not a chance!" he snarls. "We aren't even close to done. I'll make a proper kaiju out of you yet. Come on."

I follow behind him, surfing the waves of his destruction as he levels government-subsidized housing and local businesses. I kick a few cars over when he looks back at me, and then put my fist through a petrochemical plant, making sure to limit the damage to the exterior itself—a hole that shouldn't be too hard to patch up in the morning.

Three helicopters bank over the plant's domed, aluminum roof and unleash a bevy of anti-tank hellfire missiles that pepper my body like rain on a warm summer evening. Dad obliterates two of them with a flick of his claws while I snatch the third by the rotor and set it gingerly on the street. The pilot raises his visor, blinking in awe as I wave at him and then turn toward Dad...

...who's shaking his head at me like we're not even related.

I know what he's thinking: *How is this my son?* I can see the loathing etched into the downward slant of his forehead, the anger baked into the squint of his glowing eyes.

And that's the thing—as much as he can't stand being my father, I can't stand being his son even more. After all these years, he still doesn't get me: I have no interest in destroying humanity. In fact, I like humans. Their television shows and their movies. Their video games and food. I mean, if pizza isn't a gift from the gods, I don't know what is. And it's not my fault I wasn't born angry like him, slithering over the bottom of the Pacific covered in nuclear waste. I don't have the same chip on my shoulder that he does.

I want to add to this world, not destroy it.

It's what's on my mind—how to tell him I'm done wrecking the city—when I spot the thatched roof of the Jikou-in teahouse on the corner ahead. My knees hinge and buckle. Across from it is Maru's apartment complex, with Maru standing on his balcony staring up from the ninth floor at Dad, who's staring directly back at him, lighting up his dorsal plates—indigo, arctic, cerulean blue—as he readies his nuclear ray.

"Dad, stop!" I shout, pushing past him and knocking over a bus in the process. It goes skittering down the street in a cloud of screams. *Shit, my bad.*

"Move, Chibi," Dad orders.

"No."

His eyes blaze red, and for a brief second, I think he's about to light me up with a heavy dose of radiation, but then they simmer and fade to their normal dull black. He analyzes me for a second before his lips curve into a smile. "You want to destroy it yourself, don't you?" He glances at Maru's building, practically beaming now. "Well, go on then, son. This one's all yours."

I grind my palms into my eyes and shake my head. "No, *Dad*, I don't want to *destroy* it. I want you to leave it alone."

The smile fades, replaced by disgust as the ridges and valleys of his reptilian face contort once more. Beyond him, rolling up the street from the industrial district, is a convoy of tanks and military jeeps bristling with soldiers carrying submachine guns and grenade launchers.

"Move," Dad orders.

"No," I repeat.

A pair of RPGs rip through the air and paint Dad's spine with shrapnel and fire. Guns chatter, sending volleys of bullets along his thighs and up to his waist, strafing his chest.

He doesn't even blink.

"I won't ask again." His voice is low. Pure smoke.

"I can't. My friend lives here."

Dad's eyes flicker and spark, two red torches burning in the place of his irises as he glances past me toward Maru. "A *human*. You're friends with a *human*? After everything they've done to us? After everything I've taught you about them, you would betray me?"

His skin peels back over his teeth in a way that tells me the question isn't one he's waiting for me to answer—Maru is already dead.

Unless I do something.

The war drums start in my chest; a steady beat that rises through my ribs and floods my heart. There, it swells, filling my blood with a simmering, liquid heat. A rage that spills through my veins like molten iron. I've *never* been good enough for him, *never* once made him proud. To him, I'm shame embodied: the disgrace of the entire kaiju line.

A column of blue radiance pulses up his throat. His jaw unhinges to unleash a wave of nuclear destruction, but not before I force all of the anger from mine.

"I HATE you! I *fucking* hate you!"

And then I'm roaring, sending a mandarin spear of neon light into the center of his chest. One that sends him hurtling back, back, back through a block of warehouses and into the exoskeleton of an abandoned construction project. Steel groans and bends. Iron cries out in bright, piercing snaps. The structure sways, pure tensile strength holding it in place for the length of a single breath before it falls. Several hundred thousand tons of metal shower over Dad and come to rest in a great billow of dust and cement.

I don't wait for him to rise. I'm already stomping in his direction, setting off little earthquakes with my feet.

Above, a squadron of fighter jets screams past and riddles the heap with tomahawk missiles, windows bursting all around me with the concussive thermal shock. The tanks on the street boom and thunder, shredding my Hawaiian shirt with hot belts of lead, pounding my legs with heat rounds, even though I'm trying to help them. Even though I'm the one attacking their enemy.

"Dad?" I whisper when I reach the debris pile. My tendons are rippling like the cables of a suspension bridge caught in a full-force gale. My joints feel hinged with liquid instead of bone.

The wreckage shifts.

Chunks of cement skitter down the pile. The air reeks of cinder and ash. Steel beams shift as a claw appears, followed by another, then Dad's leathered torso and neck. His chest is in tatters, venting black flags of smoke.

Around us, fringing the construction site, soldiers gather in rows to assemble howitzers and load mortars. Helicopters churn overhead like gnats. Clouds of asbestos light the air, interspersed with great tendrils of ash.

Dad's eyes glimmer up at me, pulsing red. His teeth burn white with moonlight as his jaw falls open. But no atomic breath ushers forth, no hideous blue luminescence ready to consume everything in its path. Only a single word…

"Chibi."

"Dad, I just…" I can't finish the sentence, don't even know what to say. Slick warmth oozes between my fingers, and I realize I've pierced my palms with my claws—that's how hard I'm balling my fists. Static swarms my vision. I can barely see straight as his hand rises from the rubble and comes to rest on my shin. He traces his thumb over my calf tenderly, the anger in his eyes gone, replaced by something I've never seen there.

Hurt.

"You can't trust them," he says. His voice is soft—a warm rush of wind scraping smooth canyon walls. Clear liquid runs down the gorges and cracks of his face. It takes me a moment to realize what's happening. *He's crying.*

The soldiers watch us with their artillery trained in our direction but don't fire. Beyond them lies a tableau of destruction. A cityscape etched in orange veins of fire, bright candles of flame licking higher toward the night sky.

"We've never given them a chance," I reply.

Wisps of smoke curl from between his teeth. His eyes narrow, his forehead creased. "Why do you protect them? Why can't you understand, Chibi? They hate us. They'll *always* hate us."

I picture Maru with his bright eyes and wind-chime laugh, and the way he's never once looked at me as anything but a friend. I picture his obaasan and the way she combs her fingers through his hair when he returns home at night. How she treasures him. He's her entire world.

How many worlds has Dad taken away? How many families has he obliterated? To him, people are ants to be crushed, maimed, destroyed, and devoured. To allow him to continue to unleash that destruction is a burden I can no longer bear.

"No, Dad. They hate *you*." My eyes grow hot, my teardrops falling like atom bombs that stream down the valleys of his ribs in a wet slurry of concrete dust and grease.

"Chibi-kun, you must listen to me. They are not your kind." His words rise and mix with the smoke staining the air. "They'll never change."

"And neither will you." The world blurs as I plunge my fist into the scorched carnage of his chest and wrap my hands around his still warm and beating heart. "I'm sorry, Father."

I tear it free and stand, the world unraveling around me into a series of still-frame images: Dad staring up at me with a dimming intelligence, fighting for focus, his eyes blinking against death's cavernous depths. His heart, a small, dark moon made of tissue and muscle sliding from my hand to the earth. The soldiers reforming their lines and aiming their weapons at me as I drift toward them in a daze.

It *has* to stop. I *have* to make it stop.

"Please, don't fire. I don't want to fight anymore." The words come unbidden as though spoken by someone else. I'm a bystander watching myself talk, trapped somewhere behind my eyes. I spread my clawed fingers and raise them. Dad's blood darkens the contours and lines of my palms. "Haven't we hurt each other enough?"

Nods filter through their lines. Guns falter. *It's working.*

"I swear on my life, I will never attack another human. I just want to live in peace."

There's a rustle in their ranks, movement, as a man wearing an officer's uniform threads his way through the soldiers. He gestures for them to lower their weapons, then brings a megaphone to his lips.

"How do we know we can trust—"

His voice is devoured by the thunder of jet engines. I snap toward a slice of white fire shrieking straight for me.

I jerk left, and the missile screams past, missing my head by a foot as it barrels straight for the buildings behind me.

There's nothing I can do but watch as a star is born in the middle of Maru's apartment complex—one that explodes outward like a dying sun. A dull, concussive shock reverberates through the earth as the structure implodes. The vibration rattles my teeth.

Oh, God. Maru.

By the time I reach the building, there's nothing left of it but a smoking crater of brick and cinderblock and body parts.

My heart disintegrates. My head throbs like a bruise.

They killed him.

My *only* friend. Dead.

They'll never change. Dad's words fill my head and run down my spine, dark and formless. His hate, now mine, saturates my brain and soaks into my soul until I know what he said was true. Every word.

They'll never change.

With a roar, I turn and light my internal fire.

And unleash hell.

HOWLS BUREAU OF INVESTIGATION

HBI

SPECIAL AGENT *Caleb Stephens*

Caleb Stephens is a dark fiction author writing from somewhere deep in the Colorado mountains. His short stories have appeared in multiple publications and podcasts, including *The NoSleep Podcast, Tales to Terrify, MetaStellar, The Dread Machine*, and more. His dark fiction collection *If Only a Heart and Other Tales of Terror* is available through Salt Heart Press and includes the short story "The Wallpaper Man" which was adapted to film by Falconer Film & Media in 2022. He has two novels releasing in 2023, *Feeders* from Timber Ghost Press and a yet-to-be-named psychological thriller from Joffe Books.

www.calebstephensauthor.com   @cstephensauthor

MEMO: Evidentiary imagery provided by Solomon Forse.
Agent headshot provided by Christi Nogle.

CRICKETS
By Solomon Forse

CONFESSIONS FROM THE CLASSROOM AND OTHER BLOGGABLE BUMMERS

user: @MissMiffed

Thursday, September 7

In my first year it was Flappy Bird. Then it was fidget spinners. A few years later it was Tech Decks. Then fluffy slime.

Now it's these god-awful Crickets.

If you haven't heard of them, then I'm assuming you teach older students—and that you probably don't have a 12-year-old at home. Otherwise, they would have already begged you for one by now, like my Caitlyn did. And of course I caved and bought her one for her birthday. But I'm starting to regret it.

I'll explain—but first let me help out those of you whose classrooms *aren't* chirp dungeons.

Crickets function sort of like Tamagotchis (remember those?), except they're shaped like little bugs. My students freak out over all the different customizable accessories, appendages, colors, and— the worst part for teachers—voices. Those reedy, squeaky, nails-on-a-chalkboard voices. The kids order them from that stupid Want app that sells everything from knockoff Apple gadgets to fake IDs to "personal massagers." We've all seen those Karens "parenting" their kids with iPads—they probably have no idea their little Braydens and Harpers are sending their debit card information over unsecure connections to China. Or wherever the heck all that junk comes from.

The factories must be churning out a million units a day. It seems like the more of them we teachers confiscate, the more we see in our classrooms. Or at least that's how it was until my school gave in and decided to meet the kids halfway.

Now we have Cricket-charging stations—or Hive Homes—in every classroom. The Want app sells the racks for next to nothing, and one of the younger teachers didn't mind collecting our cash and ordering

Crickets by Solomon Forse

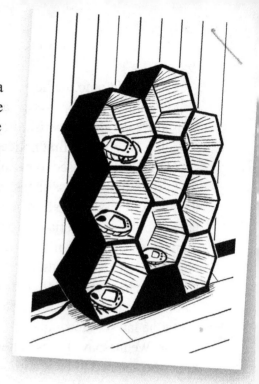

from her phone. So now, there's a black, hexagonal monstrosity—like a powered bookshelf with beehive cubbies—hanging from my wall, plugged into the nearest outlet. (Still looking for cute decoration ideas on Pinterest.) The kids get their toys charged, and I don't have to see them on their desks—or hear those annoying chirps. It's a win-win.

Well, until I get home.

Caitlyn's obsessed. She doesn't talk to me anymore. I can't even get her to eat dinner unless she's allowed to bring Jiminy Frickit (yes, I named it).

I tried grounding her, but that's exactly what she wanted, and I couldn't bear seeing the uneaten leftovers every time I opened the fridge. So I caved—again—and now we eat spaghetti on Tuesday nights while her Cricket sings to us like R2D2 auditioning for *American Idol*.

Would I be a bad mom if I ate dinner with earbuds in?

Friday, September 15

All right, I didn't really mean that—the earbuds thing. Props to @CanadianSaltQueen for the essay on parenting strategies though. Maybe I should have mentioned the other factor…Caitlyn has a crush. And she didn't tell me. Didn't plan to tell me. But guess who did anyway? Yep, my students. And Caitlyn's devastated about it. I'll have to see if I can find out who this "Sam" is, but I'm sure I'll like him.

More on that later, but for now here's the latest development with Crickets…

I once held onto the hope I could go the rest of my career without ever hearing "yolo" or "swag" again. But I'd take another year of that nonsense over the gibberish they're spouting now. I'm not even sure I'd call it language. I first noticed it during lunch duty this week.

While I'm supposed to patrol the entire cafeteria in endless circles for thirty minutes, dress shoes are no match for tile floors (God forbid the district dress code allow me to wear sneakers), so now, for every lap around the cafeteria, I stop and sit at a student table for a few minutes (never Caitlyn's though, that would be "Not cool, Mom"). And I haven't quite mastered the art of eating while walking, so it allows me to sneak a few uninterrupted bites.

Usually, they don't even notice me. They're too absorbed in talking about the latest video game or swapping cheese sticks for yogurt.

On Wednesday, I was relieved to sit with a particular group of kids who seemed to be ignoring their Crickets. A few still hung from lanyards on necks, but the toys mostly sat, unused, amongst wrappers and crumbs. They were still blinking and beeping, as usual, but at least the kids weren't interacting with them.

Maybe the trend is finally wearing off, I thought, but then I looked up and saw what the kids were *actually* doing.

At first, I thought they were busy play-acting a scene from that new Pixar movie about beetles going to the moon. Then I realized they weren't talking at all. I mean, they were communicating, but it was all in onomatopoeia—buzzing their tongues against their teeth, popping air from their lips, or droning in muffled notes from their throats.

And if that wasn't enough to get my WTF-radar bleeping, their limbs started jerking back and forth, like they were a little circle of houseflies rubbing their legs together.

Close to losing my appetite, I told them to stop. Well, in a nice way. It went something like this:

"What in the world are you kids doing?" I asked with a playful laugh, but none of them responded.

It was as if I wasn't even there.

And that's when I noticed it: all of the Crickets flashing perfectly in time with the children's movements and sounds.

Blink, buzz, jerk. Blink, buzz, jerk.

I pulled my cardigan tight against the goosebumps that crept across my skin.

"Real funny, kiddos." I slapped my hands on the table and stood up. "But let's get this mess cleaned up before the bell rings."

I'm not making this up—one of the boys (please don't let him be Sam) had a rivulet of frothy drool dribbling down his chin. Even worse, it was accompanied by a particular funk, a vinegary odor.

"Uh, is this one of those new TikTok trends or—"

I nearly jumped from my seat at the lunch bell (my principal keeps it at a deafening level because, well, she's about seventy years old, so it always takes me by surprise). But before I could even finish, the kids all stood up at once. They snatched their Crickets and scrambled from the cafeteria, darting down the hallways like roaches under a flashlight.

I tried not to get too weirded out by it—kids can be strange, and they can *smell* strange too—but when I noticed it again the following week, I just had to say something. I'm going to bring it up at the next staff meeting. And you can bet your money I'll be taking a closer look at Jiminy Frickit tonight.

Tuesday, September 19

Thanks to everyone who shared their own Cricket frustrations! I agree with @rabbi_shrimp that the trend will fade sometime soon— they always do. I talked to the math teacher next door to me after school yesterday, and he's certain the kids will forget all about Crickets when the new PlayStation release comes around this Christmas. I'm sure Caitlyn will ask her grandma for one, so maybe that will put an end to it. She's visiting next week. Maybe I'll bring it up then. But I don't know if I can handle three more months of Crickets—especially those creepy dances.

Years ago my students begged me to do the "whip" for Vine or the "Hey Julie" on TikTok. Of course, I went along with it every time. Building relationships is the key to classroom management. The embarrassment is always temporary, no matter how humiliating the dance. But the latest one with Crickets? Now I'm not so sure.

I've always been too clumsy for something *this* synchronized (I figured that out when my ex-husband once signed us up for salsa classes). The other teachers are referring to the new trend as "swarming," but I'm not sure what the students themselves call it. It requires a lot of room, so the kids mostly do it on the soccer field during recess. I've seen it while on duty. Maybe "synchronized" isn't the right word, though, because it isn't fluid and coordinated like an elaborate Super Bowl halftime show (well, except the Black Eyed Peas one). It's more...automated? Or networked?

Every time I see the kids doing it, I'm reminded of this time I went rock climbing with my dad as a little girl. My dad and I didn't use equipment or anything—he called it "scrambling." Anyway, when the both of us got about halfway up a mountain one summer afternoon, we reached a large vertical slab of rock about six feet high, which at that time was almost double my height. Just before I went searching for the first handhold, I noticed that the rock was moving. Not sliding or rolling or anything like that. It was the surface of the rock face itself. It was shivering. Or boiling. When I squinted real close, I saw that the rock was covered in a film of brown, gossamer-thin vines, and the whole mass was blowing in the wind. But there wasn't any wind. And that was when I realized they weren't vines.

They were spiders. Daddy long legs. Hundreds of them. Maybe thousands. Spindly legs all interlaced and crammed together and quivering in a massive meshwork, like they'd all gathered there for Spider Mecca.

And that's exactly what the students look like when they're doing that swarming dance out on the field: shivering and shimmying in unison as if they've all plugged into the same brain.

Caitlyn is saying goodbye to Jiminy.

Crickets by Solomon Forse

Wednesday, September 20

Thank goodness most of you agree with me. I won't go so far as taking a hammer to Jiminy like @EmpressThea did with her son's Cricket, but I won't deny the alluring power of the soda can crusher in our garage. But @ChelseaGourdGoblin is right—last year I *did* say I'd never turn into the "mean mom." Still, I have to put my foot down at some point, don't I?

I was almost late for school today—not because I couldn't get there in time, but because Caitlyn (more like Not-Caitlyn) refused to get out of the car after we parked in the teacher lot. She wouldn't even look at me. Just yelled and screamed about how everyone would make fun of her for not having a Cricket.

"Dad would've let me keep it," she said.

Ouch.

But I made it even worse.

"Do you think Sam won't like you if you don't have a Cricket? Boys don't care about stuff like that. He probably—"

"Sam is a *girl*. You would know if you actually cared about *me* and not my Cricket!"

I know I should have reacted differently, but I was too distracted by the flying elbows—she got so out of control that she unbuckled her seatbelt and started squirming and thrashing around the car as she cried.

I can't imagine what she might have done if I'd told her I'd already thrown her Cricket away. Even then, the whole problem wasn't about "having the thing" but instead feeling like she belonged. I remember what it felt like not to fit in at school. My parents never bought me the Trapper Keepers or Mr. Sketch markers. Or the Abercrombie & Fitch shirts or Tommy Girl jeans. I'd never want Caitlyn to feel how I did, but those creepy little toys aren't the solution. And like @rabbi_shrimp said, the fad's going to die eventually, just as surely as Pogs and Silly Bandz. So I begrudgingly dragged my daughter out of the car and all the way to her homeroom class.

Teachers can't be late.

Speaking of that, I have to rush off to a staff meeting—the IT team is presenting something about the Hive Homes breaching network security and infiltrating software on the student computers. That doesn't sound good.

Wednesday, September 27

I'm sorry you all had to wait so long for an update. I did check in to read the comments a few days ago, and @MollyMachine0101 couldn't be more on-point—I should have slowed down and supported Caitlyn in her most vulnerable moment.

But what I found in the garbage bin this morning changes everything.

Not only did I happen upon an empty shipping box with an address label to *my home* but also the torn-open packaging to a brand-new Cricket.

I don't know what to do. And no, I'm *not* secretly naming this one too.

A few weeks ago, I almost admired my daughter's attempts at rebellion. She'd dyed her hair and tried to conceal it under a beanie when she was around the house. I thought it was her passive aggressive way of saying, "Turn the freaking heater on, Mom," but a couple days after adjusting the thermostat, I noticed she was also wearing her beanie in the hallways at school.

And then I found an apple-green stain on her bedroom pillow.

I let it slide, other than making her buy a new pillow case with her allowance, but now that I've looked through my banking app this morning, I just can't anymore.

After scrolling past some bill payments and shopping trips, I found it: a hefty charge from "WantLogic, Inc." It took everything within me not to snatch the packaging from the trash, charge through the house, burst through Caitlyn's bedroom door, and shove it in her face. But I slowed and took a deep breath. I reminded myself that yes, she's questioning my authority as her parent, but she also needs to know that I support and accept her as she is. Ultimately, I decided to wait until Friday night to bring it up. We're holding another staff meeting after school, and I'm pretty sure I know what it's about.

Oh, and I was wrong about Crickets being manufactured in China. I saved the packaging. While the language printed on the box is pretty close to Chinese characters, the symbols look less like delicate brush strokes and more like…jointed limbs with sprouting hairs? I know it sounds gross, but I can't think of any other way to describe it. Any language teachers out there wanna help me out?

Saturday, September 30

The Hive Home is coming down! Just when I found a cool idea on Pinterest too. As per last night's staff meeting, Crickets are hereby banned district-wide. And all the other districts seem to be following suit too. No more chirping, no more swarming, and no more of whatever the heck I saw in the cafeteria. Effective Monday, any student who is

caught with a Cricket shall be sent to the office immediately with the toy confiscated until their parents come to pick it up.

One. More. Day. Do I want to be there on Monday when the kids absolutely lose their minds over the new policy? No. Do I have personal days saved up? Yes.

I'm getting a sub.

And no, I haven't confronted my daughter about the package yet. I will soon enough. I'm planning on spending my day off relaxing rather than arguing with Caitlyn again. I know that sounds mean, but I really, *really* need a break. As soon as I drop her off for school, I'm headed straight to the spa—I already booked the appointment for 9:00 a.m.

I'll talk with her later. She probably needs time to cool down.

Tuesday, October 3

She's gone. My little Caitlyn is gone.

If I could track down the headquarters for this "WantLogic, Inc.," who are so elusive they might as well be stationed on Mars, I'd be smashing down their door with an ax before making every last one of their employees pay for what they've done to my daughter and her classmates. But the reality is I don't know where to go or where to find them, so here I am. The best thing I can do is document what happened before I turn my memory inside out with grief.

Yesterday morning, there I was in a hoodie and sweatpants walking halfway from my car to the front door of the spa when my phone buzzed.

It was an email from my principal, not directly to me, but one of those staff-wide emails marked with "urgent" status. Since I still have access to my account—and who knows how long that will last—I will copy-paste the email here:

Staff—In five minutes, we will be announcing an evacuation alert over the intercom. DO NOT follow standard policy. Instead, as soon as you have ensured all students have exited into the hallways, you are to (1) turn back and remain in your classroom, (2) lock your doors, and (3) wait until an administrator contacts you. DO NOT share this information with students. DO NOT attempt any outside communication. Your life is in danger, and you will only remain safe by following these instructions.

Like any of you, at first I thought it was a terrible joke, or maybe a phishing email—but in today's climate, I can't imagine anyone trying a gag like that. And the email didn't ask for any personal data, so it couldn't have been phishing. It was the real deal, I quickly decided. But why did it seem like they were trying to hide everything from the students? Caitlyn would have no idea. I imagined her abandoned in the hallway, nervously clutching her backpack, not knowing where to go, running over to my classroom—only to remember I wasn't there. On the one day she needed me.

I immediately sprinted back to my car.

Just as I climbed in, my phone buzzed in my hand. It was my mother.

"Sweetie? Are you at school?"

I couldn't see her, but I knew her eyes were bugging out of her head, darting back and forth, the way they always did when she thought I was in danger.

"Mom, I can't talk right now, I have to—"

"Are you at school? Please tell me you aren't at school."

"No, I have a substitute today, but I—"

"Oh thank heavens," she said, exhaling as if she'd been holding her breath underwater and just burst through the surface. "Is Caitlyn sick? Did you stay home with her?"

"No. She's at school. I took a personal day. I'm at the spa. What's going on?"

"Oh, God." The silence that followed her trembling voice rushed over me in a chilling wave of dread.

"Mom, what's happening?"

"Haven't you seen the television? The reports? There's ambulances everywhere. Children pouring out the doors. You have to—"

"I'm going after Caitlyn."

And then I hung up.

I turned the key, threw the car into drive, tires squealing as I zoomed out of the parking lot and toward the highway on-ramp.

I don't recall much of what went through my mind in those fifteen minutes of speeding down the highway—foot flooring the gas, hands gripping the steering wheel, adrenaline coursing through my veins—but I was about a mile from my exit when I spied them off to my right.

The movement in the wide open field drew my attention, and at first I thought it strange to see such a large herd of animals—cattle maybe—stampeding like that. But as my car sped closer, I realized they weren't animals. There were too many colors: a conglomeration of neon shoes and blue jeans and striped shirts.

Children.

And they were carrying large objects—dark idols riding atop their shoulders, each one like a golden calf, frayed extension cord swaying behind it like a tail. Hive Homes. *Our* Hive Homes. *Our* students, all formed in a giant mass, hundreds of them, scrambling across a field like a horde of insects spilling from a nest.

My heart, already threatening to burst from my chest, could barely withstand the flood of icy panic.

Caitlyn was somewhere among them.

The car nearly spun out of control when I swerved to the right lane, veered onto the shoulder, and slammed on the brakes. The tires slipped as they hopped from asphalt to dirt and grass. I came to a bouncing stop. Throwing open the door, I leapt out of the car and rushed to the barbed-wire fence.

"Caitlyn!" I screamed.

The stampede continued.

Instinctively, I reached for my phone to call 911, but my hands shook so violently I could only fumble at my pockets.

So I flung myself over the fence.

After ripping my sweatpants on the wire, I clumsily rushed across the field in the slippers I'd worn for the spa. They plodded over clumps of roots and tufts of weeds as tall grass slapped against my knees.

The crowd of running children was within a hundred yards, but none of them acknowledged me. They all seemed to be looking forward, hurrying toward something—yet I saw nothing before them except more open fields.

It wasn't until I got closer that I could *hear* them. All making those popping and buzzing sounds with their mouths. If not for the rush of adrenaline I might have gotten sick from that awful noise. I can only compare it to something like the deafening spitter and sputter of water poured over a thousand campfires.

An even louder sound nearly ruptured my ear drums. A violent drone like an amplified rip from a brass section—it had come from the Hive Homes.

And then the children at the front of the mob, the ones carrying their idols, came to a grinding halt. I could see their flashing Crickets dangling from belt loops and hanging from lanyards. As one they pushed the Hive Homes together, unhinging some sections and inter-locking others until they combined to form a skeletal-like frame. And then the other children surged forward, piling on top of the Hive Homes and the children beneath them, still clicking their mouths as one layer after another assembled a growing, mountainous network.

I hoped to God that Caitlyn wasn't inside of it.

Still I ran.

When I was within fifty feet, the mass started to take shape, rising high above me. Children clambered over one another, intertwining arms with legs, entangling bodies to form separate structures. What first began as a tremendous puzzle transformed into an intricate design on an enormous scale. The main host elongated into what resembled a thorax. All about its mass sprouted squirming children who locked limbs and wriggled outward, bending into various angles to create a head, body segments, jointed legs, and curved antennae—all building higher and higher toward the open sky.

And it was only for a moment, a fragment of time, but I knew that momentary blip of color that flashed before me—that apple-green flicker passing across the monstrous amalgamation of children—was my daughter's hair.

I cried out to her.

And I jumped onto the pile. I scrambled up the mountain, clawing across arms and legs, my slippers gone within seconds. I jammed my bare feet into nooks and crannies among knees and elbows, crawling past glazed-over eyes. The children's mouths buzzed and popped in my ears, their breath vinegary and pungent.

Then I saw her. Wedged into the apex of a jointed segment, her legs twisted at obscene angles through a tangle of countless limbs.

Hands trembling, I climbed off the main body and crawled out over a bridge of children, straddling it as if I were traversing a log, inching across, wind ripping through my hair, the grass below me a thirty-foot fall.

Finally, I reached the apex. A torrent of relief washed over me as I clutched my daughter's arm.

I pulled myself closer, dug my face into the labyrinth of hair, skin, and digits illuminated only by the twinkling glow of Crickets.

I found her eyes. I pleaded with her, anything to get her to look at me. "Baby, it's me. It's Mom."

Her eyes stared right through me. I would have grabbed her, kissed her, held her to my chest, whispered her name softly into her ear, yet one wrong move and I would have plummeted to the hard ground below.

"I love you," I tried again, searching in her vacant eyes for even the tiniest twinkle of life. I begged her to answer me. Called her every sweet name. Reminded her of childhood memories—and then her mouth slowly opened.

I thought she would speak, but instead, from her lips spilled a frothy white substance followed by the sharp reek of vinegar. Her eyes rolled back in her head, mouth opened wide, jaw threatening to snap.

The fluid came rushing out like water from a hose, dousing me in the foamy spume.

I gagged at the wretched odor, throwing my face to the side, wiping my eyes against my shoulder. But the liquid kept coming and coming, soaking my hair, my clothing. And that's when I realized they were all doing it—hundreds of mouths vomiting all around me, spewing forth the yeasty solution, immersing the entire structure in a stinking bath.

Within seconds I found my movement restricted. At first I thought I'd been pulled into the network of intertwining children, but it was the foam itself—thickening, hardening. Like grease left in a frying pan overnight, it congealed into a waxy solid, gluing my skin against the bodies beneath me, jelling against my face. The more I blinked, the further it sealed my eyelids together, and when I quickly let go of Caitlyn to wipe at them—I lost my balance.

The weight of my body tore me from the structure like an old band-aid peeled away from skin. I fell, kicking and grasping at the air.

With a jarring *crack*, I slammed into the ground.

Somehow I didn't lose my breath. Somehow I maintained my consciousness. But I couldn't move. I could only stare at the gigantic mass rising up in front of me, now hardening into a pale-white carapace, the individual arms and legs of children lost behind translucent chitin.

When the sky grew suddenly dark, I thought that I was fading to black. But no, something had blotted out the sun. A cloud? Something else. Something terrible. Not the cemented children before me but a colossal shadow gliding thousands of feet over the field, two hulking wings stretched across the sky, long as skyscrapers.

For a moment the air was still.

Then from the darkened horizon came a peculiar whispering sound that grew to a deafening roar. The grass before me flattened, dust pluming upward into tidal waves.

A hurricane wind pressed me into the earth, soil clinging to my sticky skin. I was stunned by the terrible, sickly sweet stench carried with the storm.

When the wind subsided, I mustered the strength to break through the substance hardening around my joints, rising to my hands and knees. I looked to the imposing structure still beside me, Caitlyn somewhere within. It was flattening to the ground like a collapsing mountain, its bulbous head pressed down, thorax pressing against the earth, legs folding, crouching.

And with a single, coordinated movement, the structure of children uncoiled, springing into the air and hurtling into the sky.

"Caitlyn!" I shrieked, limp hand outstretched, yet she—or it— disappeared against the gloom of the gargantuan *thing* that now passed directly over the field.

But as the winged leviathan made for the horizon, the light once again returning to the sky, clutched against its underbelly was not just that single monstrosity that had leapt from the field, but dozens and dozens of them, like larvae nestled against their mother.

And with that I knew my little Caitlyn was gone.

As I sit here, her hoodie bundled tight against my body as I write these words, I can only hope that somewhere, wherever she is, wherever that thing went, I can find my Caitlyn and bring her home safe.

But I think I know the truth.

She's not coming back.

None of them are.

For this story Solomon Forse drew upon his eight years as a public school teacher. Although he is the founder of HOWL Society, he entered "Crickets" as a blind submission with the rest of the workshop writers in the community. When not managing the Discord server or handling publisher duties, Solomon spends his time role-playing horror with tabletop RPGs like Call of Cthulhu or shredding horror on the guitar in his Lovecraftian metal band Crafteon. Otherwise, he's busy attaining pilot ratings or pursuing his new career as an aviation accident investigator.

s.forse.writer@gmail.com   @SolomonForse

MEMO: Evidentiary imagery and agent headshot provided by Leah Gharbaharan.

YOU SHALL RETURN
by L.P. Hernandez

Life was never good or easy on these goddamned plains. Each day was a dance with death, and even death wasn't easy. Folk around here didn't die in their sleep, bellies round like a hillock of mashed potatoes. They died with claws for hands, skin drum tight with ribs you could count from across the room. They died with their eyes wide open, 'cause the hell they were glimpsin' wasn't so desolate as the hell around 'em.

Then the dust came, and from *bad* it got much worse. Pullin' life out of the soil was like squeezin' water from a brick.

The dust, oh the dust. Came like a brown mountain, down from Colorado like a bit o' Rockies broke loose and went walkin'. It took what we grew, what we pulled from the soil and broke it, and broke it again into smaller and smaller parts 'til it became the dust that coated our throats, filled the holes in our teeth. It was every word we didn't speak and half the words we did.

"If a handful of dust was worth a penny, we'd be clear of our debt with a million to spare," Daddy said once. Maybe it was a joke, but he didn't smile when he said it. I didn't understand the meanin' of that word, *debt*, only knew it was the reason someone might take everythin' away from us some day.

Hundred years ago, folk said *You can go to hell, and I will go to Texas.* Wonder what they'd think to see it now. It wasn't a place to go to. It was a place to forget.

During the storms it was just like night. The sun would go out and there was this sound like far-off cattle. But I ain't seen a cow in a year. Ain't nothin' worth slaughterin' now. It shook the walls of our home, roared dirt under the door like snow drifts made of ash. It brought misery. It brought death. It made me wonder what was goin' through Daddy's mind when he'd sit in his chair with his rifle waitin' for the storm to pass. It was hell. But it was a hell we understood until the day the storm brought somethin' else. Maybe Daddy had a suspicion about it, heard a rumor 'bout the storms from folk that left for California. Maybe that's what the rifle was for.

There's five of us in the house. Or, there was then.

My brother, Abe, was two years older but you wouldn't know it to see him. We was both a poor sight to look at, but it looked worse on him, like he already spent a day underground with a bouquet of dandelions in his hands and decided dyin' could wait 'til next week.

Daddy was like a scarecrow, skinny like us, sure, also 'cause he stood there in the field not movin', thinkin' about everything he lost and how he might get it back. Dreamin' of a life where a handful of dust was worth a penny.

Grampa was a ghost in the back of the house. Not a real one but brushin' up against it. It was him that built the house, raised a family there and squeezed water from those bricks until life was just short of miserable. There wasn't much left of that man, just his skin like the parts of the pig they dry out and feed to the dogs, and bones barely strong enough to stand on.

Mama was the roots to our tree, keepin' us in one place no matter what the wind wanted.

They called me Ellie, 'cause Eleanor felt too big for a small thing like me. Mama said I'd grow into it, but then she'd look to one of the clouded-over windows like that might be a lie and someone outside would be upset to hear it.

You could tell when the dust storm, the mountain-sized ones, was comin'. There wasn't much wind beforehand, like it was all bein' saved. We learned not to trust days like that, when the sun seemed so bright you forgot the decay it was shinin' over. By lunch we saw it, moved inside and pushed old rags under the doors. The wind would blow 'em back but tryin' was better than givin' up. Used to round up the chickens, but there's nothin' left of them 'cept some feathers stuck in a bush in Arkansas maybe.

Daddy didn't let Mama light the lamps or the fire. He just sat in his chair and stared at that picture over the mantle, the one he cut out of a magazine. Said it was called Mt. Rain-year or somethin', in a place called Washington. Daddy would sit there not movin' like he deserved the darkness, like it was his fault. Abe and me rode the storm out in the room we shared. He was growin' into a man and I probably shouldn't have known what that looked like, but it's tough to be modest when it's so hot, when your sweat-stiff clothes are scratchin' at your skin if you move an inch. Sometimes, I think Abe was hopin' Grampa would give up the ghost so he could take his room.

The mountain fell on us, and the room went dark. Them cattle was right outside, bumpin' into our house, snortin' under the door. Abe's bronze face went out like a snuffed candle. We just sat on our beds wonderin' if this might be the last one. Maybe the next storm would bring rain instead of sufferin'. Abe put a blanket over his head and stretched out like to take a nap. The storm can do that to you, lull you into a sleep you didn't know you needed. I played with my fingers, tried to breathe light so the dust wouldn't get in.

This part I turned over in my mind so many times I lost the shape of it. I don't know what's real and what I added to make sense of things. Abe or me or both of us at the same time realized the room was fuller than it had been a minute before.

People shapes, darker than the wood behind 'em. We screamed, all four of us, pushed our backs against the wall, me and Abe on one side and them on the other.

"Who are you?" Abe yelled.

"Who are *you?*" the boy yelled back.

I knew the voice right off. It was Abe. It didn't make sense then, and I won't pretend I understand it any better now. Abe's voice comin' from another body. How could I make sense of that?

There was commotion elsewhere in the house, but none of us moved. Abe patted the nightstand between our beds, lookin' for a weapon I imagine. All he found was a bible, which wasn't any help for this.

"Where you come from?" Abe said, lips barely movin'.

"*You* the one in my room. Where *you* come from?" came the reply.

Yellin' beyond our bedroom door, the sound of a chair tipped over. Mama's screams rose like a wave over Daddy's growl. Grampa, who hadn't spoke a clear word in months, joined in, his voice thick as the pulp that went in the sausage casings before all the hogs died.

"Grampa?" I said, turnin' to Abe.

The figures across from us was closer to the door and they headed that direction, still facin' us as if we might bolt across the room and bash em' over the head with Abe's bible. The smaller of the two opened the door and a bit of light come in. We was on the back side of the storm then, some of that sick yellow sun breakin' through.

I shoulda been scared at what I saw. It shoulda shaken me right down to the marrow. Instead I was dumbstruck. Dumbstruck by the way I looked, my shoulders sharp as a coat hanger, hair brown like a field mouse, matted in some places and wild with tangles in others.

I was lookin' at myself, and another Abe right beside her.

We followed behind, Abe brandishin' the bible as if it was a hammer instead. There wasn't much time for discussion right off. There was two mamas in the kitchen and two daddies in the living room, both with rifles aimed. But none of us paid attention to that. Right through the middle of the house there was a little river of blood leadin' to the open front door. Dust blew inside, turnin' the river into sludge.

Grampa's eyes was like a jackrabbit caught in a snare. There was blood on his naked chest, soaked into his beard so it looked like fox fur. He held a screwdriver in one hand, knuckles hard as walnuts from grippin' so tight. Though the metal was too dark to show any color, it did gleam wetly as the sunlight returned.

Grampa stumbled a bit and I wondered if some of that blood on him might be his. I reached for his arm but he shrugged me off and shuffled to the front door smearin' sludge as he did. I followed behind and the other me did likewise. We tracked the bloody lumps over the porch and into the yard, the dust mountain spreadin' our misery east.

He was belly-down in the dirt, arms trapped beneath him. A little rise and fall of his back showed he was still breathin', but as me and other me came close to him that stopped. His last breath was a blood-filled gurgle, a little stream of almost-black spillin' out of his mouth. I knelt beside him, and other me did too.

"Grampa?" I said givin' him a little shake.

He was so small, shriveled, a tomato forgotten on the vine. Rollin' him over was easy to do, but I regretted doin' it at once. His belly was a beehive, full of leakin' holes like he was hit by buckshot. His eyes was already losin' focus, murky like a mud puddle.

Two daddies, two mamas, and two Abes gathered around us. From my grampa's dead eyes I looked directly into his livin' ones.

"He tried to kill me," Grampa said, the screwdriver slippin' from his fingers.

There was a lot of yellin' between the daddies. Both said it was *their* house and the other was a trespasser. I wasn't payin' attention to 'em. Holdin' a thought in my head was like pickin' up a wet bar of soap. Other me felt the same, I imagine. Kept makin' eye contact and then breakin' from it. The yellin' calmed and the rifles pointed at the floorboards. I didn't catch the words leadin' to it, but an agreement was made.

The rifles was different kinds, needed different bullets. Both daddies said they kept an extra box o' bullets in the nightstand. So, whichever bullets was in the nightstand belonged to the gun and the rightful owner of the house. That daddy decided which of us was kin and the others would move to the barn while things was sorted.

A lot happened after that, but to put it simply, I didn't get sent to the barn. Daddy sat me and the other down and asked us questions. He sweat a lot while he did, picked at his face and passed his rifle from one hand to the other like he just pulled it out of a fire. Weren't no differences in our answers, but there was with Abe and other Abe. The Abe I was with when it happened, whatever *it* was, belonged to the house. Daddy figured that 'cause of a dog's name, one that died before I could make memories of it. The dog named Bandit belonged to the house and the dog named Rascal didn't. They was the same dog, I think, just named different. Because I was with the Abe that went with Bandit I belonged to the house.

Mama was sorted in a similar way, but there was only one Grampa left. What if Daddy decided Grampa was from the other family? He was a murderer and would have to account for it. I spoke about it with Abe, and I guess he was thinkin' the same.

"Grampa sure gotta spring in his step," Abe said, playin' with the coupla long hairs sproutin' from his chin.

"Oh?"

"Could barely keep soup on his spoon yesterday."

I swallowed hard, like tryin' to down a potato in one gulp. "Guess he gotta reason now."

Daddy spent a long time with him, voices so low and steady it was like they was hummin' to each other. But, with one man dead and the other stickin' to his story, wasn't much to decide. Finally, Daddy came out the room and shut the door behind. He nodded at us, and Mama bit her knuckles to keep from cryin'.

We talked more on that day than any I can remember. There wasn't much to say before the others came. Mama said some family from town packed up and moved to California. Abe thought he saw a whitetail but turned out to be a tumbleweed. Stuff like that. We talked about fetchin' someone who might make sense of things. Mama said the pastor at the church we stopped goin' to a year ago was an educated man. Daddy rolled his eyes at that and mussed my hair.

"What you think, Peanut, should we get the church man down to sort this out?"

I smiled so wide I thought my skin might split from it. I liked that nickname, *Peanut*. Daddy was in good spirits, which I wasn't used to. Grampa sat in the corner, lips movin' but not sayin' a word. Not that he could've helped. All we had was questions and more questions.

Where'd they come from?

How'd they get here and why?

I woulda thought it was a dream if not for the stains on the floor. Mama scrubbed 'em 'til the veins in her arms was like jumpin' ropes. It didn't help much and we couldn't spare the water.

No one mentioned the impossibility of it, that the storm brought another version of our family. Was a month or so ago, couple days after a bad one Daddy went to town lookin' for a deal. Usually, that's when folks decided they had enough, after the dust tore up what they coaxed from the earth. They was desperate to unburden themselves of anythin' might delay puttin' miles between them and some other place. He come back with the same handful of dimes he left with. Mama asked how it went and he just shook his head, kept shakin' it like he heard somethin' in town he couldn't let settle in his mind. I think Daddy knew. Even if he didn't believe it would happen to us. He knew it when it did.

"What do we do about him?" Abe asked, standing in the window.

Daddy stood next to him, rifle like a part of his arm he forgot about.

"Guess we should bury him. Got that hole we dug for the coyotes."

"But he's your—"

"He ain't my anythin'," Daddy said, cuttin' him off and noddin' at the barn. "He's with them."

Over my shoulder, I saw Grampa in the hall. Still had blood on him almost like he meant to do it. He stood tall, outside of the room. Felt like two prairie dogs was tusslin' in my belly watchin' his hands clench into fists.

Daddy and Abe went out to the barn to talk about the dead Grampa on the lawn, leavin' me and Mama alone with the livin' one. He took Daddy's place in the window, one thumb hooked inside the beltloop of his jeans.

What are you thinkin' about, Grampa?

He turned to me as if he heard the question and winked.

What do you see when you look at me? Your granddaughter or somethin' other?

The body was wrapped in burlap and lowered into the coyote hole, which welcomed no coyotes that year. Mama made an extra helpin' of supper, cooked ham hocks that been boiled a coupla times before, and a handful of beans you had to go fishin' for. Daddy, Abe, and me brought it to the barn. Found it hard to look at 'em, especially *my* other. She looked scared.

Inside the house, Grampa sat at the head o' the table 'til he caught the look Daddy was givin' him. For all the talk earlier in the day, our words ran out. Probably each of us was lost in our own heads.

Soon, it was night and I felt more tired than I had in ages. But when my head hit the pillow, I couldn't turn my thoughts off. I kept thinkin' about the storm, noticin' the others in the room with us, Abe's hand reachin' for the bible.

I picked up the bible then, paper so thin I thought it might melt between my fingers. I didn't find comfort in holding it again, just sparked a whole new flurry of thoughts I couldn't control.

Abe fell asleep quick. He snored the dust out of his lungs while I considered every ache in my body and wondered if my other was miserable on her bed of hay. I wanted to talk to her, find out about her life, mostly how it was different than mine. Maybe there'd be time in the mornin'.

The creaks of the house assembled into somethin' more purposeful after midnight. Wasn't just the wind against the walls but movement, slow, like someone tryin' to be quiet. I sat up in bed and turned my ear to the door.

Ksss Ksss

I pictured two snakes side-by-side tryin' to slither outta their skins. From the direction the sound started I knew it was Grampa.

Ksss Ksss

Down the hallway and into the kitchen. When there was a sound in the house, a groan or pop he'd stop and wait a bit.

Ksss Ksss

A creak of front door hinges and then a light rumble on the porch.

"Abe!" I hissed.

He snored louder.

I had an idea where Grampa was goin', and I decided it was better to follow alone than to try to keep the two of us hid. I slipped out of bed, quieter than a spider 'cause I'm smaller, and danced feather-light, like a Daddy Long-Leg over soap bubbles. I cracked the front door just enough to put my eye to it and saw Grampa's shape as it was swallowed by the dark of the barn. He was meetin' with the others. He was doin' it in secret. Couldn't think of a good reason he would wait 'til the house was asleep to palaver with 'em, but what could I do about it?

When the wind picked up, everythin' that hadn't been uprooted whispered, a thousand ghosts askin' us not to forget about 'em. It was loud enough to cover the sound of my steps as I scurried to the barn. I heard 'em talkin' in there, the other Daddy and Grampa, but couldn't make out the words. There was a loose board around the side, thought maybe I'd hear better at it. I groped around in the dark but only managed to add a few new splinters to my fingertips. Where was that board?

The voices was gettin' agitated, Grampa's mostly. I didn't need to hear the beginnin' or the end of the conversation.

"...fuckin' kill 'em tomorrow night and take their place!" Grampa yelled.

Other Daddy's words came back softer than I could understand. I sat on the ground and held my belly. If there was more than a spoonful of broth in it, I might have thrown up right then.

I crept back to the house, my spine stiff as a rake thinkin' Grampa would open the barn door and see me. I slipped inside and checked the window. No Grampa.

The house felt different, all the madness from the day wrung out of it like dirty water from a rag. In the dark, the snow of Mt. Rain-year glowed above the mantle. Daddy once said it was someone else's dream and tossed the picture in the fire. That was the first time the bank said they would take the property. Mama rescued it, and Daddy was glad of it later that week. We sold a few things and made it another month.

I dashed to my parents' room, mindful of the time passin' and the likelihood Grampa was on his way back.

"Daddy," I whispered, jostlin' his shoulders.

His eyes popped open like he knew I was comin'.

"Ellie? What is it?"

I nodded for him to follow, and he did after glancin' at Mama real quick.

"What is it?" he whispered again.

I opened the door to Grampa's room and pointed at his empty bed.

"Daddy, Grampa's with the others. I-I don't think he belongs with us. I know he don't. I heard him, Daddy."

He scratched his face, pulled a hair from his chin not thinkin' about it.

"Daddy, I followed him out to the barn. They gonna kill us."

His eyes fell to the dark spots on the floor, the blood Mama couldn't clean.

I grabbed his hands, "It's okay, Daddy. I gotta plan."

He sniffled.

"You trust me, Daddy?"

Knowin' somethin' happened and bein' able to explain why is two different things. They came with the storms that always felt like a mistake, like chaos, like they didn't belong in our world. Maybe there's somethin' to that. Our lives was chaos, but in chaos there's opportunity. After I asked Daddy if he trusted me, we both heard the creakin' of the porch floorboards. We skipped outta Grampa's room and huddled in mine.

Ksss Ksss

Those sneaky snakes slitherin' down the hall. Daddy was breathin' heavy, realizin' he was wrong about Grampa and we was in danger 'cause of what he didn't wanna admit. Grampa stopped outside my door like he could hear our hearts poundin' in our chests. Maybe... maybe he changed his mind about *tomorrow*. Maybe this would all happen right now.

Ksss Ksss

Daddy and I huddled together in the dark, sayin' nothin'. His breath hitched some, and his heartbeat never slowed even as I rubbed his back. I knew then I couldn't tell him the whole idea. I knew he wouldn't be able to see it through.

Half an hour passed before we heard Grampa's snore and Daddy sneaked back to his room. I crawled into bed, so tired it felt like my muscles would slough off my bones. But I couldn't sleep. I picked the bible up off the nightstand, let the weight of it settle on my chest.

I knew those people in the barn, knew who was snorin' in the room next to me. I remembered lookin' in the bible for some solace and findin' nothin' of value, nothin' that could improve my life. I remembered tossin' it in the fireplace when no one was lookin', the pages cracklin' like pork fat on a skillet. It burned bright, and I thought God might be mad at me. But I didn't save it. Now, here it sat on my chest. A second chance at life. That's just what it was. If I learned anythin' growin' up on those goddamned plains it didn't come from a book. It came from life, from knowin' in order for somethin' to live somethin' else has to die.

It began like I pictured it in my mind, waitin' for sleep to come. Daddy agreed to take us to Aunt Lynn's house, to give the others a proper roof over their heads while the matter was sorted.

"Why not send them?" Daddy asked.

I made sure Grampa wasn't around to hear.

"If they get there first they gonna get the first crack at tellin' the story. They gonna get Aunt Lynn on their side. Then we lose everythin'."

I worked on the other part of the plan, the part I couldn't tell Daddy about, in secret. A hammer, a coupla nails. No one paid me much mind, but I caught other me starin'. She looked like she wanted to talk, probably wanted to tell me our families was mixed up, that she belonged to the house, but I already knew that. Knew it when I saw the bible come back from the ashes.

Daddy called me *Peanut*. I liked that. He never done it before. But, that's because it wasn't my daddy. Just like I knew my Grampa wasn't knockin' on death's door like the one in the coyote hole had been. I learned that from Abe. I learned a lot by listenin'. I liked bein' called *Peanut*. I liked Daddy messin' my hair. I wanted him to do it more. This plan, it would solve everythin'.

Aunt Lynn was a two-mile trip from our house, near the edge of Pampa. We packed up the Ford and headed that way before supper. Grampa stayed back *"to keep an eye on things"* like I knew he would. Didn't have a phone so we just showed up. Aunt Lynn was Mama's sister, so they run off to talk. Daddy talked with Daryl, her husband. I don't know how it went over. I was outside with my cousins.

At supper I was deep in my own thoughts, so I didn't notice much of what went on around me. Not sure how much Mama and Daddy shared about what happened, but the cousins made up for it with their chatter. We had potato soup with bits o' bacon in it, and that was the best meal I'd eaten since Christmas. I fought to sleep on the porch.

It was necessary for my plan, and Daddy allowed it since I done it before, pretendin' to camp with my cousins.

I waited for an hour after the lights went out, then walked the two miles back to the house in the dark. I had a kerosene lamp with me but didn't light it. The dirt road held onto the heat of the day so that it was like walkin' over dyin' coals. By the time I saw the gray shape of the house against the backdrop of night I was soaked through with sweat.

There ain't any heroes in this story, myself included. In fact, you might think I am the villain after I tell you what I did next. Bad crops ain't grown from good soil. Think about that. You don't have to know more about my grampa than I already shared to understand he deserved what happened to him. The others, well, look away enough times and you might miss what's comin' at you. I did feel bad about other me, but like I said, I ain't a hero in this story.

I worried Grampa might have caught on to what I was doin' earlier that day. He didn't. He was too busy thinkin' of how to take control over the change to his plan to kill all of us and take our place. None of the windows of the house opened, but you could still throw a chair through the glass and get out that way. Grampa didn't notice I nailed boards to the window frame, on the side, hangin' like a sock on a clothesline.

The house was dark, and I put my lantern down to get to work. Hummed a church hymn 'cause I didn't know any other songs, and I didn't wanna think too much about what I was about to do. I nailed the boards across the windows, just a light *tap tap tap* when the wind blew. That's when I saw him through the window, almost dropped my hammer from fright.

Grampa was in Daddy's chair. Well, in *this* house it was Daddy's chair. In *our* house it was his. There was a rifle across his lap, and his head faced me right on. My heart was like a hundred crickets trapped in a glass jar. I froze, hammer up by my face, wonderin' if he was gonna aim the rifle at me. I think Grampa knew I didn't belong with the house. No one else was afraid of him like me. No one else knew him like I did.

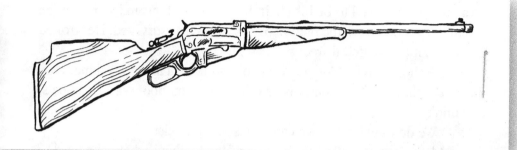

His mouth opened like he was about to scream, to wake the others I imagined, but instead his head lolled to the side and I realized he was asleep.

Tap tap tap

The wind covered the sound of my hammerin'. Kept one eye on the nail and the other on Grampa. Last thing to do was to slide Daddy's axe through the doorhandle. Weren't no other exits.

I hoped it would be quick for the ones sleepin' in their beds, 'specially other me. She didn't deserve it, but neither did any of the hogs we slaughtered before the dust came. Neither did the coyote Abe shot the leg off of. Neither did I. Grampa deserved it, though.

The air was so dry, the wood so old it went up like a matchbook. I stepped back to about the place where the other Grampa died, my kerosene lantern havin' served its purpose. After half a minute the shoutin' began. Poundin' on the front door, but that's where the flames was highest. A hand punched through the window, fingers turned to claws pullin' at the board blockin' the way. The arm flopped like a catfish on land, and then it disappeared and another window broke.

Not many folks can say they heard themselves die, but I did. I heard my own voice cry for help. A cry I didn't answer. But the fire, the fire felt good. Hot. It felt like redemption.

After all, in order for somethin' to live, somethin' else has to die.

All that was left of the house was the chimney. The evidence of my crime was gone, the nails I used lost within piles of ash among other nails. I let Daddy come to the decision on his own. He stood in a pile of what used to be his chair, hands on his hips and starin' at the chimney. Somehow, the picture of Mt. Rain-year survived. He strolled over to it and pulled it free.

He showed it to Mama. "We could go here. The debt's done."

He glanced at the femur near where the front door was. Grampa's, I think.

"We don't exist. Or, we can choose to not exist."

Mama's eyes drifted to the area of the kitchen, where she used to spend so much time. She nodded but it was like she was lost in a dream.

"What you think about that, Peanut? How 'bout we start over somewhere green?"

He draped an arm over my shoulder.

"I think that sounds wonderful, Daddy."

HOWLS BUREAU OF INVESTIGATION

HBI

SPECIAL AGENT   *L.P. Hernandez*

L.P. Hernandez is an author of horror and speculative fiction. His stories have been featured in anthologies from *Dark Matter Magazine*, Dark Matter Ink, and Cemetery Gates Media among others. He is a regular contributor to *The NoSleep Podcast* and has released two short story collections, *The Rat King*, and *Dreadful: Tales of the Dead and Dying*. His novella, *Stargazers*, was published under the My Dark Library banner with Cemetery Gates Media. When not writing, L.P. serves as a medical administrator in the U.S. Air Force. He is a husband, father, and a dedicated metalhead.

🌐 www.lphernandez.com   🐦 @thelphernandez

MEMO: *Evidentiary imagery provided by Leah Gharbaharan.*
Agent headshot provided by Cassie Daley.

THE RICHARDSON FAMILY REUNION
By Ryan Marie Ketterer

It wasn't easy to gather all the Richardsons in Mayport. Raised poor in the coastal Alabama town, most had scattered to other states in search of more money, a better education, or something new. Some had simply run away. Nora Richardson was impressed her grandmother had pulled off the feat of convincing her long-lost relatives to come visit her one more time—especially Nora herself, who had every reason to avoid the place she once called home.

Mawmaw was the only Richardson who still lived in Mayport. Nora was concerned, but not surprised, when her conversations with Mawmaw about coming back to visit were nearly incoherent. Mawmaw had spouted nonsense ever since Nora was a child, and that was no different now. But from what Nora could discern, a date was set and, thanks to Mawmaw's years of dedicated service at the country club, they had a venue. So Nora traveled south, back to the place she tried so hard to forget.

Mayport was a different place than it had been nearly two decades ago when her parents shoved her into their old, rusty van and drove north. Main Street was a ghost of its former self, just empty storefronts with cracked windows and ripped awnings. Nora stopped in front of a rusted newspaper machine when the yellowing paper inside caught her eye.

"NEVER FORGET THE MAYPORT FOUR!"

The article was dated two years ago—a grim reminder of the loss Mayport suffered. A reminder Nora didn't need. The faces of those little kids—so innocent and young—stared back at her. Polly's face stared back at her. A tear rolled down Nora's cheek.

Nora chased Polly across the back yard, the humid air not a hindrance.

"Slow down!" Nora tried to keep up with Polly, following the bright blue of her little sister's NASA jumpsuit as she ran towards the wetlands behind Mawmaw's house. "Mawmaw said we can't go in there."

"Oh Nor-Bear, why you always gotta follow them rules?" Polly spun around, grinning at her sister. The blue of Polly's outfit was stark against the bright green surrounding them. "You know Mawmaw won't know one way or 'nother if we go in there!"

Nora had a hard time taking her sister seriously when she used that silly nickname, but Polly was right. The moist forest, with its towering swamp pines and chestnut oaks, always scared Nora. That and she hated getting bit by the swarming mosquitoes, which were always worse inside the treeline.

"I'm not going in today!" Nora stopped and lowered herself to the damp grass.

Polly stuck her tongue out. "Ok-ay, lame-oh! I'll be right back."

Nora lay amongst the overgrown blades and smiled. Ma and Pa had dropped them at Mawmaw's earlier that morning, and days at Mawmaw's were always the best—no one to yell at them and unlimited sweet tea. Plus, Mawmaw's collection of mystery novels never disappointed.

As Nora speculated on her next Agatha Christie, Polly dropped to the grass beside her.

"Be careful or you're gonna get grass stains all over that jumpsuit," Nora said. The NASA outfit was her sister's favorite, and she saw herself as something of an astronaut ever since they visited the Space Center in Huntsville months ago. Nora noticed Polly's sleeve was pushed up her arm, which revealed a dark-gray mark leading up towards her elbow.

"Polly, what—"

Polly grabbed her sleeve and pulled it over the bruise. "It's nothing, Sis." Polly's smile never wavered.

A silence thicker than the Alabama air expanded between them.
A lump rose in Nora's throat when Polly's quiet words shattered the
saturnity. "It was an accident, he didn't mean it."

Nora was the big sister. Big sisters were supposed to protect. She
tried to shove her emotions back down, deeper inside her body where
no one would ever see them. Where Polly would never see them. Nora
needed to be the brave one. She needed to be the big sister..

"I won't let it happen again, Polly."

A sudden meowing from behind them dispelled the heavy moment,
and Nora collected the neighborhood cat into her arms.

"Shadow!" Nora said, as she snuggled her face into his wiry fur.

"Shadow gets to run off whenever he wants. Why can't we?"

Nora continued to nuzzle the wandering feline as she tried to
process what Polly said. Leaving wasn't an option, so she didn't see
any use talking about it. Pa knew the police; they'd never make it far.
Where would they even go?

"What if we could leave this place forever?"

Nora let Shadow glide from her grip and looked over at Polly,
shaking her head. "Pa would find us."

"But there might be a way. In the wetlands—"

"Stop Pol, just stop." Nora was angry now, upset that her sister
would consider something so stupid. "I let you sneak off all the time,
but not like that. Never like that."

Nora jumped up from the grass. As the sisters walked back towards
Mawmaw's house, Polly said, "I wish you'd listen to me. Just once."

When Nora arrived at the country club, dozens of family members
were already there, Mawmaw included. The old woman had only a
short walk on a path through the wetlands in her back yard to reach the
golf course. It was the same walk she had done every day of her life.

The manicured grass was profoundly green and looked surreal
around the white tents set up for the reunion. Under each one was a
collection of round, white tables, all decorated with pictures of the
Richardsons over the years.

Nora caught a whiff of barbecue pork from the cavalry of crock pots as she wove through the crowd, admiring the photos. In every one, there were smiles. Laughs. Nora lingered on a picture of her and Polly with their parents in Mawmaw's back yard, their faces glistening in the southern heat. Even in the photos that were supposed to be happy, she saw the anger. The hate.

Mawmaw approached from behind. "You be missin' her, but she okay. Polly's okay. Don't you worry." She spread her flabby arms and Nora collapsed into them, allowing herself a careful sob while she inhaled Mawmaw's stale butterscotch scent.

"I just wish she—" Nora broke off, grabbing a napkin from a nearby table. "I just wish I'd had a chance to say goodbye."

Since Polly disappeared, Nora's life had never been the same. She coasted through jobs, doing enough to get by, but not enough to move up. Her personal relationships fared even worse—the only men who wanted to spend time with her were carbon copies of her abusive father.

Nora watched as more Richardsons arrived at the country club and made their way to coolers filled with beer and crocks simmering with home-cooked meals. Mawmaw embraced each and every one, forcing them into a conversation with a proud smile on her face.

When Nora saw Ma and Pa approaching Mawmaw in the food tent, she cringed. Deep down, she'd hoped they would've stayed away, lost in their drunken haze.

As Nora pinballed between tables, she heard the bickering sneers from her Ma, directed at Mawmaw: "...just leave us alone, will ya?"

Pa shot Nora a glare as she approached, and they all turned to face her.

"Ma, Pa, how nice of—"

"What, you didn't think your ol' man wanted to waste his time comin' all the way back down here for a day?"

"I...it's nice to see you, too. There's barbecue right here—"

"Ya, ya, why don't you go get me a beer or somethin', huh?" Pa hadn't aged well. He grinned at her, his yellowing teeth poking out from behind his cracked lips like errant, drunken soldiers.

Ma was already halfway done with a sandwich, her sunken, pock-marked face stuffed with pulled pork and coleslaw, grease dripping down the front of her torn shirt. "Look at her jus' standin' there. She always was the useless one."

A razorblade twisted in Nora's chest, slicing into pieces what remained of her heart.

Pa grunted in agreement and sat at one of the tables, the edge digging into his distended stomach, and took a swig of booze from his flask.

Nora burned crimson, holding the sharp pain in her gut; if she managed to keep it in all those years, she could do it now. She turned to Mawmaw, vowing not to continue the conversation with her parents, and led the woman away.

"Make it an Ultra, hun!" Pa said, his voice chasing Nora from the tent.

As Mawmaw watched this confrontation, the wrinkles on her face deepened, carved like memories in an aging oak tree: enduring and permanent.

Despite this, the day carried on. Clouds danced in front of a slow-moving sun and the autumn air was crisp, a rarity in Alabama. Nora did manage to catch up with distant relatives she hadn't seen since childhood, politely laughing at the memories they shared of her and Polly, while trying to avoid the reek of stale beer that reminded her of those dark nights when Ma and Pa came home late.

When Mawmaw's screen door banged open well after dark, Nora's father stumbled in, the pungent scent of alcohol overwhelming the house. Ma followed, and Nora wondered how they made it home. A sick, dark part of her wished they hadn't. Mawmaw cowered in the corner.

Nora escaped out the back door, knowing a shouting match was coming. She paced in the grass as she overheard the confrontation, the clammy air sticking to her skin like plastic wrap.

"The damn girl knew she wasn't s'posed to go out there," Pa said, his tone grating.

"It's your damn mother's fault, we should never be leavin' our kids with her." Ma's speech was so slurred that Nora could barely understand it.

Nora wanted to walk across the crunchy, dead grass toward the wetlands, to try to find Polly and make them stop yelling, but she was scared.

"She went through, ya hear? She was done fed up and I told her to go." Mawmaw's incoherent ramblings were getting worse. Less and less of what she said now made any sense.

Several low growls echoed across the back yard and Nora spun. The noises came from the direction of the wetlands, and she took two steps toward the forest. She prayed her sister wasn't out there, having to defend herself against some vicious animal. The sounds stopped, and all she could hear was the cacophonous buzz of the cicadas.

Nora was so entranced by the heavy darkness in front of her that she jumped when the metal screen door slammed behind her. Mawmaw slouched into a cracked plastic lawn chair and let out a single sharp sob. *"Polly gonna be ok, ya hear? She gonna be ok."*

As midafternoon approached and the sun made its slow descent to the horizon, the food in the crock pots was depleted and the ice inside the coolers began to melt. Nora sat on the wraparound porch at the country club building, which was on a hill overlooking the reunion. She sipped a spiked seltzer and recalled memories of that night Polly never came home as she watched her family bounce between the massive tents from afar.

The blue lights. The search parties. Pa becoming more violent. Ma becoming more distant. The fear truly set in when they learned that three other kids also went missing that night. Lucas, Connie, and Shirley. Nora didn't think Polly was ever friends with them, but they did live in the same rundown neighborhood as the Richardsons. There were rumors of a serial killer.

After a while, Ma and Pa couldn't take it anymore—everyone looking at them, asking about them—so they drove north. Away from the dread. Away from the unknown.

Nora didn't think it was possible, but she realized now how much she missed Mayport. She wished Polly could be here today. She wished they could say goodbye to Mawmaw together.

Without warning, a great white light shot from the wetlands in the distance. The chatter from the reunion ceased. The solid beam rose straight into the air, its glow steadily fading into the clear blue sky. Nora rubbed her eyes and wondered if the blazing emanation was a trick of her imagination.

The Richardsons began to point, to call attention to the unnatural glare. At first, the radiant shaft was no different than a spotlight one might see at a concert, but with each passing second it became brighter, eventually brighter than the sun.

Nora rose from her seat and let her sunglasses fall to her nose, but she was still unable to look directly at the beam. The pressure in her ears began to change rapidly like that time her parents drove her and Polly through the Talladega Mountains. Out of the corner of her eye, the light grew not only in brilliance, but also in size.

As it continued to expand to the size of a skyscraper, the ground shook. The pressure in Nora's ears continued to increase, eventually popping and causing Nora to nearly stumble from the porch. She grabbed the sides of her face, her hands coming away red as blood dripped from her ears.

The apparent earthquake worsened, and Nora eventually faltered, plunging down the wooden stairs, but her eyes never left the wetlands treeline.

One by one and then all at once, the trees split apart, cracking and splintering and eventually flattening to the ground. Echoes from bursting hundred-year-old trees reached Nora across the golf course grounds, and before she could wonder what could cause such carnage, she saw it.

From the destruction rose a magnificent metal beast, like a long-forgotten and destroyed ocean liner breaching a white-capped ocean.

The sun reflected off the steel hull of the machine as it launched skyward. It vaguely resembled a modern spacecraft, with large round thrusters on the bottom expelling fire that burned the vegetation below. But its cobbled-together round shape was wrong. Different. It was like nothing Nora had ever seen before.

The spaceship traveled in a beautiful arc, peaking hundreds of feet in the air when its propulsion system died and gravity took hold, bringing the unfamiliar hunk of metal barreling towards the astonished family.

The pile of library books Nora had accumulated over several months crashed onto the desk in front of Mrs. Foley. It was her last day at Mayport Middle.

"You've worked up quite a collection here. Did you manage to read all of these?"

Nora nodded and forced a smile. Mrs. Foley was always nice to her, giving her all sorts of mystery recommendations.

"You'll be missed here, Miss Richardson. Polly, too."

The name of her sister cut like a hot iron through her gut. Nora forced a laugh and tried to make a joke. "As if Polly ever liked the library."

Mrs. Foley's smile was earnest. "You'd be surprised. She was here all the time, looking for proof of aliens or something. Some new planet."

Nora remembered that NASA outfit Polly always wore and sighed. It was hard not to always think, "what if?"

Nora woke with a pounding headache and struggled to remind herself what had happened. The spaceship, the crash. It must have knocked her unconscious. She pulled herself from the ground and wiped blood from her brow, from her face. Everything was silent. She stumbled down the hill to where the family reunion had been set up, hoping, praying, that people were okay.

The perfectly manicured golf course grass was now blackened and riddled with embers of fire. The tents that once provided shade were no more, the tables and chairs and crock pots scattered into pieces.

Nora stepped closer to the carnage. There were large pieces of the ship strewn everywhere, crackling from the extreme heat. One of these sheets of metal moved slightly then shifted to the side, and Nora watched as a distant cousin—Laura, she thought—rose from below the simmering steel.

The woman reached for Nora, tried to call for help. Her mouth moved frantically, but only blood poured out.

Nora was frozen in place, wanting to help but afraid any action she took would further injure the woman.

In a feat of inhuman strength, Laura pulled herself from under the rubble. A sharp edge of metal from the spaceship's hull caught the front of her leg and peeled an entire layer of skin from her shin, but she barely seemed to notice.

With blood dripping from her wounds and a scrap of flesh flapping below her knee, Laura lurched toward Nora. Her jaw continued to flop open and closed, but the only sounds she managed were grunts.

Nora opened her arms to catch the woman, but before she could, Laura collapsed. Her dying cousin's lungs rattled one more time as her own blood suffocated her, and then her eyes settled, losing their frantic plea for help, still focused on Nora.

Nora sobbed, falling to the ground as she stepped away from the dead woman's pleading stare. She was desperate. She needed to find someone to help. Anyone.

She pulled herself up and continued on, looking

for survivors. Fiery annihilation surrounded her as she searched for what felt like hours, kicking hunks of metal aside and extinguishing small embers with her shoes.

Eventually, Nora found her Ma and Pa. Her father's body lay twitching across the same chair he sat in while eating his lunch. There was a burning hole in his chest where his flask had popped open; the alcohol ended up killing him after all.

Ma didn't need to witness her husband's last raspy breaths as his guts burned from the inside out because her body was severed at the waist, her death likely instantaneous. A thin but very sharp piece of metal lay on the ground near Ma's body, coated with blood and entrails.

Tears fell down Nora's face. Seeing her parents dead like this, their bodies completely ravaged by some unexplained disaster, she felt hollow. After the years of abuse she endured, after driving away her little sister, they deserved this. And yet, she continued to sob.

The worst of all was when Nora found Mawmaw. She dropped to the ground next to her grandmother. Nora didn't care that the thin skin on the front of her knees was burning as she knelt on the simmering grass. Mawmaw was riddled with fragments of glass and metal, the materials incandescent and eating away at the woman's frail wrinkles. Somehow, though, Nora saw her eyes blink in recognition.

"I knew…" Mawmaw's voice was raspy, barely audible. Nora felt like she had cotton balls stuffed in her ears and lowered herself closer to her grandmother.

"It's okay Mawmaw, I'm going to find help." Nora didn't know how or where she might do that, but she needed to try. She looked around for anyone, anything, that might help her grandmother.

"I knew she'd come back," Mawmaw said, blood bubbling from her mouth and dripping down her withered face. "She promised…"

Her words, as had been so common over the past several years, made no sense to Nora. All she could do at this point was try to ease her grandmother's suffering.

"Help is coming." Nora's empty words had no audience, though, as the little life left behind Mawmaw's eyes finally extinguished.

Nora continued to shuffle through the cinders and still crackling chunks of Richardson meat as she made her way closer to the impact site. She saw someone there, moving. A child?

"Hey! You! I need help!" The small figure spun and stopped Nora cold. The faded blue jumpsuit the child wore was familiar.

Nora assumed she was hallucinating or perhaps suffering the side effects of some sort of head injury, and she dropped to the burnt grass. Her head felt like it weighed a million pounds, and black dots scurried like frantic ants across her vision. Nora assumed death was claiming her as the approaching image of her little sister became more and more real.

Nora looked away from the delusion her mind was forcing upon her, and instead stared straight up at the blue sky and puffy white clouds, while tears rolled down the sides of her face. She hoped the end would come soon.

Phone calls to Mawmaw back in Mayport became less and less frequent as Nora maneuvered her way through high school. When they did happen, Nora was always frustrated.

"The girl's alive. All them kids are. But no one wants to listen to Mawmaw."

Nora stopped arguing eventually. If her grandma thought Polly was alive, then maybe that was okay. Maybe she could be happy.

"Wake up, Nora! C'mon, Nor-Bear, wake up!"

Nora's eyes shot open.

She was propped against a tree. It felt like there was a man with a chisel trying to carve his way out from inside her skull. When her eyesight cleared, she noticed she was in the woods. Why was she in the woods?

Small fingers snapped in front of her eyes. "Earth to Nora!"

"Stop, my head," she said, trying to quiet the thundering voice that had brought her back from the brink of death. She brought her hand to her temple, as if her fingers could mask the pain. When her gaze lifted, the child with the blue jumpsuit stood in front of her.

NASA, she thought. *That's the NASA logo.*

Nora screamed. "Go away! Get away from me! You're not my sister!"

Yet it was. Or at least, it was close enough. Polly's young face stared down at her, just as Nora remembered it, same as all those photos she looked at earlier. Despite this, there was an unfamiliar wisdom behind those eyes, a wisdom that no child could bear.

The kid put her small hands on either side of Nora's face and smiled. "Shhh, quiet now, you're awake. Everything's going to be okay."

Nora's breathing was fast and raspy, and she couldn't seem to slow herself down.

"It's me, Nor-Bear. It's Polly. I promise it's me and I promise you're okay. Your vitals are normal."

"My vitals…?"

"I've been trying to come home all this time, and we finally figured it out."

"We…"

"We, yes. Lucas and Connie and Shirley. You remember them, right?"

Nora closed her eyes and tried to die. Or maybe she was trying to wake up. What she was seeing, what she was hearing, none of it made sense. She wanted—no *needed*—to escape.

"Nor-Bear, open your eyes. I know this doesn't seem real, I know it doesn't make sense, but I'm trying to show you. If you just look here, please, I can show you."

Nora sensed the child moving off to the side. Unwillingly, Nora opened her eyes. The girl was leaning over the edge of a massive hole in the ground.

It wasn't a normal hole, like one that was dug—it was something alien. Something awful.

Nora gazed at the unnatural occurrence, trying to process what she saw.

The hole was probably twenty feet across. It was pure darkness, a darker black than she thought possible.

Nora's instinctual urge to protect her sister kicked in and she lunged forward, trying to pull the little girl from the precipice.

Polly let Nora help her, but when they fell back to the muddy forest floor together, the kid laughed. The laugh was almost right; it was almost Polly. But Nora knew it wasn't really her, knew it couldn't be her.

"It's okay, sis," this Polly—Fake Polly?—said. "It's not dangerous."

Nora, finally feeling awake, looked around her. The wetlands. She was in the Mayport wetlands. Flattened and splintered trees surrounded her. This hole, or whatever it was, appeared to be ground zero.

"I see you're processing it now. Nor-Bear, it's really me. I came on the ship, I came home!"

Nora stayed silent, her eyes bouncing between the hole and Fake Polly.

"Look in, you'll see," Polly said.

Nora inched her way closer to the hole. When she looked down, she saw a planet. It was lush red and green, with oceans and atmosphere and clouds swirling above. It was beautiful.

"When we were kids, you know how much I loved the wetlands. This is why. I saw that planet." Polly's eyes glittered as she spoke. "I wanted to know everything about it, so I read all the books I could about space, but I never found anything about that place down there."

Nora was unable to process the words Fake Polly was saying. Everyone was dead, and this child was talking about what she used to read at the library?

"Reading books wasn't enough—"

"Stop. Stop stop stop." Nora held her head in her hands. "Everyone is dead. Mawmaw is dead, and Ma and Pa."

Understanding leaked into Fake Polly's face. "I'm sorry about that, about Mawmaw especially. The ship was meant to land…"

Nora laid back and curled her legs to her chest. This must all be from her head injury. None of this was possible.

"Nor-Bear, I know it's sad. I get that. But this discovery…it could change everything."

Nora remained in the fetal position, refusing to address the abomination that was talking to her.

Fake Polly continued with her absurd explanation. "When the books weren't enough, I went back to the hole. I needed to see what happened if I put something in it. First it was rocks and dead animals. But the most exciting was when I used the neighbor's cat. Remember that skinny little cat? The one always eating Mawmaw's garden?"

Nora was flooded with memories of Shadow. She cried for two days when he had gone missing. That same summer Polly, her Polly, had disappeared. "Bobcat got 'em, most like," the neighbor had said.

"When I threw him into the hole…" Polly stopped and shook her head. "Nora, you should have seen it."

"It doesn't make any sense," Nora said.

"There's so much to explain, I know, and it'll take time," Fake Polly said. "But we'll have plenty of time."

Nora spun. "What do you mean?"

"We live down on that planet now. Me and the others. Even Shadow."

Nora stared at Fake Polly, in disbelief at what she was saying.

"Not only that, Nor-Bear; the planet is magical. None of us have aged. I can't wait to show you what we've built."

"What do you mean..." Nora shook her head and backed away from the hole.

Fake Polly smiled. The same smile, but different, the one that didn't look right. "I want you to join me, Nora."

Nora couldn't just leave, abandon everything she knew. But then again, what was left?

"I won't force you Nor-Bear. I will only ask you." Fake Polly's face was almost sincere, but there was something in those eyes. Something else. "Follow me, please. You won't regret it."

And with that, the apparition that was her little sister was gone. Nora looked into the hole and saw Polly floating away, floating back towards that planet. She was holding out her hand, waiting for Nora to join her.

Nora, kneeling on the edge of a phenomenon she would never understand, closed her eyes and recalled the carnage and death she had witnessed. In her head, she could hear Polly all those years ago. *"I wish you'd listen to me. Just once."*

Nora finally did.

HOWLS BUREAU OF INVESTIGATION

HBI

SPECIAL AGENT *Ryan Marie Ketterer*

Ryan Marie Ketterer is from Malden, Massachusetts. Her work can be found forthcoming in *Clarkesworld*, and currently in *Dark Matter Magazine*, *Cosmic Horror Monthly*, and several anthologies. She's a fan of the weird and uncanny, and her writing draws most of its influence from the works of Shirley Jackson and Thomas Ligotti. When she isn't writing stories, Ryan is writing code for a software startup in Boston, MA or training for another road race.

https://linktr.ee/ryanmarie47   @RyanMarie47

MEMO: Evidentiary imagery provided by P.L. McMillan.
Agent headshot provided by Cassie Daley.

CASUALTIES OF A PREDICTABLE APOCALYPSE
By Joseph Andre Thomas

First—the sound of rattling glass.

"Buttermilk!" Early called out from the kitchen.

I'd been reading on the couch while Early, my boyfriend, cooked dinner. In my peripherals, his six-foot frame pirouetted around our tiny kitchen, a too-small BBQ apron strained around his not-precisely-svelt waist. Smells of vinegar, cayenne, and Worcestershire wafted through the apartment.

My cat, Sufjan, asleep on the other side of the couch, perked his head up, the gray fur of his face flat on one side. I looked up from my book—don't recall the title, it's long gone—to see the dozen or so half-empty liquor bottles on our small bar cart jiggling, jingling. Writer's Tears shoved against Pernod like moshers at a punk show.

"Hun?" I asked, lowering the book. "Are you using the food processor?"

"I'm telling you, Emily," he said, "people in this chicken-illiterate city default on water and eggs as a binding agent. Sure. Fine. For plebians. But if you *really*—"

A *clang* from the neighboring apartment interrupted him.

"What was that?" he asked, walking into the living room.

The floor started to move. My feet, flat on the carpet, trembled. The glass in the balcony door wobbled. Another noise from the apartment above—duller, louder.

Someone falling, I thought.

"Oh god," said Early.

Tiny pressure cracks appeared in the corners of the white ceiling, creeping inwards—then, with a *RACKK*—a massive bolt ripped through the plaster, easily as a child ripping paper. Plaster and paint chips coated the floor.

I stood, shoving Sufjan under my arm. The ground *lurched*, tossing me into the wall.

"Here!" said Early, running to the dining room and throwing chairs aside. "Under here!"

"Are you—?"

"Just do it!"

He dropped to his knees and crawled under the table. I held Sufjan, his claws digging into my skin, and followed.

"Don't worry, don't worry," said Early, forcing calm. "They taught us in school. Chill, don't move. It'll pass quickly."

Books tumbled from the shelf. The flatscreen fell with a dull crack. The bar cart toppled, tossing broken glass and liquor all over the ugly beige carpeting. Glass shattered in the kitchen, screams poured in from the hallway. The ground beneath us shuddered, as though the building's frame liquified.

I looked to Early—red-faced, sweating bullets. Sufjan had paradoxically calmed, as though he sensed the severity of the situation. After what felt like an hour—actually, I would learn, two-and-a-half minutes after the first seismic activity became detectable in James Bay—the quaking subsided. Early and I exchanged furtive glances, as though we worried talking would restart the tremors.

Just as I was about to speak, to say those audacious, conjuring words ("I think it's over!"), another deafening *crack* split the air. The ceiling gave…and came down.

Early screamed; I did too. The table buckled—and split in a *V*-shape between us.

No, please. Not like this.

Wood, metal, plaster, concrete rained down.

I'd later learn that this building, like many others in the city, was not at all prepared to deal with an earthquake of this magnitude, despite its being right on the coast. Had the owners retrofitted the building's foundation with slab, updated its 100-year-old metal, or reinforced exterior suspension lining—implemented *any* number of precautions against this easily-foreseeable disaster—the ceiling might have held. The substructure might not have caved. The table might have...

"Early?" I asked, coughing, wiping plaster dust from my face and eyes.

Silence for several seconds, then: "Hi."

Relief washed over me. I checked myself: muddy, dusty, but unbroken. Enough of the table had held to create a protective bivouac. I pulled myself—and Sufjan, still in shock—out from beneath the heap of building materials.

The ruined ceiling sloped down from the apartment above; shelves, bookcases, an annihilated dining room set all sat in a heap atop ours. The balcony doors were shattered, glass belched all over the floor.

"Oh god," I said.

"We need to get Mom," said Early, still beneath the wreckage.

"What?" I knelt and began moving rubble. The air stank of dirt and whiskey. Early's half of the table had taken more of a beating than mine.

"Mom. Need to pick her up."

"Early," I said, as I worked. "Your mother's dead."

I managed to heave aside a clump of concrete, revealing Early's face. It was all I could do not to vomit.

Blood streamed from his forehead, from his eyes. His right eyeball protruded grotesquely from the socket, red and distended. A piece of concrete and bloody rebar, matted with some of his hair, lay at his knees.

"Pick up Mom," he said, staring everywhere and nowhere. "She'll be off work soon."

I wrestled Sufjan into his cat carrier and raced outside. Standing at the cracked sidewalk, legs shaking, I called for help—for anyone. Dozens of my neighbors, too—some bloodied, in shock—stood in awe of the violent metamorphosis our neighborhood had undergone. Men, children, elderly women all screamed for help. A cacophony of sorrow and desperation, my voice at its heart. The air smelled of smoke and spilled gasoline. An emergency siren howled in the distance.

Sufjan cried in his carrier beside me. I wondered why I wasn't crying too.

Buildings nearby got it even worse than ours. A two-story walk-up had collapsed into its parking lot. A high-rise a block away had split down the middle: half of it remained upright, the other half sloped to the earth like a mountainside after an avalanche.

Jagged cracks of asphalt jutted up from the road, upturning cars and streetlights. Winds were picking up, whistling. Briny air speckled my face.

I walked to the end of the block to get an angle on the ocean-front. Waves shattered against the breakwater. The tsunami—the

earthquake's true devastation—hadn't struck in earnest yet, but it was beginning. White-capped waves leapt into the sky.

Stunned and useless, I watched an elderly man help a much younger guy try to push his vehicle out of a sinkhole. *Just how old is the average person on this block?* I shuddered to think of the people unable to reach safety.

It took nearly two hours to get help. Two EMTs, obviously exhausted, entered the apartment building with a stretcher. I couldn't bear to follow them, unable to face whatever damage two hours—those two precious post-traumatic hours—had done to Early. They exited minutes later with him beneath a sheet. He was still alive, they assured me. The sheet was for protection, they said. Their shaken, bloodless faces told me all I needed to know about his condition.

While one EMT loaded Early onto the ambulance, I heard the other one speaking to me from somewhere distant, dreamy. He apologized, but I was not allowed to join them. The hospitals were a zoo. "There's an emergency shelter nearby," he said, pointing. "Away from danger."

I stared at the ruined building. "Can I go back in? My—my medication."

"It's not safe. What meds?"

"Paxil."

"Find a pharmacy," he said, already climbing into the ambulance.

I moved my deadened legs in the direction he'd indicated, walking mechanically for god knows how long. A splash brought me back to reality. After several blocks, the water had risen so high that I was wading in about six inches. Down the shoreline, the sea was higher now—much higher. Huge waves easily overcame the seawall.

The current ran something up against my ankle. Something moving. Something alive. Tentacled. An octopus?

No—it had more than eight arms. It was about eight inches across, body like a gallbladder, the flesh blueish and orange with spots of white. Its legs looked like the flowers of a sea anemone. *Is it trying to wrap around my leg?* The sight of it writhing against my soaking sneaker made my stomach churn.

I kicked whatever-the-fuck-it-was into the current and—hopefully—back out to sea.

The emergency shelter was a hastily repurposed high school gym. Dozens of green army cots had been set up along the walls. I'd taken one in a corner, Sufjan's carrier stuffed beneath. The first night, he and the other refugee animals kept everyone up whining, mewling, barking. Not that most of us could sleep anyway, with the whooping winds and waves of the tsunami outside. We'd been assured that this gym was "perfectly safe," as if that made anyone feel better. Eventually, we—along with our pets—settled into a malignant, exhausted acceptance.

Whenever I tried to fall asleep, I saw Early's face, his eye bulging at me accusingly. It was everything I could do to keep it from my mind. Revulsion, pity, anger nettled at me. But I still hadn't cried.

The morning after the quake, the storm outside began to die down. I was surprised how quickly a facsimile of domesticity manifested in the gym, particularly for the elderly. Victoria, British Columbia, skews older than most of Canada, due to its temperate climate; James Bay—an expensive and picturesque neighborhood at Vancouver Island's southern tip—doubly so. An octogenarian couple across from me had pushed two cots together to create a "queen-size." Tables had been propped all along one wall and covered with coffee machines, teapots, sodas, revolting McDonald's orange drink, and sacks of donated food. Someone had set up a flatscreen, theoretically, to keep up with the news but, practically, dominated by children swapping between *Peppa Pig* and *Cocomelon* and *Larva Island*.

All I'd managed to escape the apartment with was Sufjan and my phone. My clothing—jean shorts, Converse, and a University of Toronto hoodie—was a dirty, soggy, mouldering mess.

I hadn't left my cot since waking. My phone screen was furiously red with dozens of unread messages and missed calls. I'd done my tertiary responsibilities—*I'm fine, Mom*—and tagged myself *Safe in The "Big One"* on Facebook, but couldn't bring myself to do anything more—to think, to care. My body and mind seemed drugged.

Early's father, Ron, included me in a family WhatsApp chat to inform us that Early hadn't died but was declared critical on arrival to the hospital. Hospitals still weren't allowing visitors, but Ron was receiving updates from the doctor. Extended family members kept DMing me with thoughts, prayers, condolences.

When Ron gave us the news I felt nothing. Not indifferent, exactly. Just numb.

I kept thinking back to the night Early and I had first met at some grimy two-story punk bar on College Street in Toronto. "Name's Earl, but you can call me Early," he said, extending an oblong hand, his face plastered with a goofy smile. "Only guy you'll ever meet with a nickname longer than his real one."

That memory used to make me smile. But now his eyes weren't funny, joyful; they were bloated and blood-red, sagging hideously out of his skull.

The question for his family now was whether to leave Early on life-support. Ron wanted my input, too. "Be honest," he said.

What *did* I want?

I thought about switching places with Early, if the beam had fallen on my half of the table, not his. Would I want them to pull the plug?

The answer, a resounding *yes*, came instantly. I didn't want to die (did I?) but the idea that, just like that, it could be over? Not suicide, but something better, cleaner, more noble? An easy out. All your worries, pain, frustrations—gone in an unshameful instant.

The thought was comforting. Bright. Welcoming.

The truth was, the truth I now supposed I was taking to my grave—or at least to Early's—was that the relationship hadn't been going well. Nothing special, the usual millennial stagnance: the same three takeout spots, the same bi-weekly bottles of wine, the once-cute, now-tired running jokes. Minimal shared interests outside of the odd Netflix show, fewer shared friends. Rudimentary, infrequent sex. Probably should have ended already, but we'd been together so long, our lives so intertwined—and I such a comfort-seeking fucking coward—that I couldn't bring myself to pull the trigger.

This situation…solved all that. A horrible, nightmarish, scorched-earth solution, sure. But a solution nonetheless.

Yeah. Not sure Ron would've appreciated my honesty.

I rose and made my way to the coffee tables. The gym smelled of wet clothing and animals, the air full of the oblivious laughter of children. It was past noon and the coffee station had been ravaged. I poured myself a cupful of tar-like liquid anyway. The sugar packets had been devoured, so I was forced, shuddering, to use stevia.

On my way back to my cot, I noticed some cruel grown-ups had turned the TV to a news station. I joined the small crowd. Onscreen, shots of the ruined inner harbor. The Empress Hotel, the centerpiece of Victoria's postcard heart, with a huge fissure from its chateauesque steeples to its perfectly manicured lawn. The beloved tearoom in shambles. Across the street, the Parliament buildings and Royal BC Museum in heaps of crumbling and mangled brick. A yellow taxi had made a new home in the front window of The Blue Fox restaurant.

A frazzled news anchor reminded viewers that this quake—the dreaded "Big One," 9.4 on the Richter scale—had been inevitable, had been predicted by every seismologist, geologist, volcanologist, tectologist, and astrologist on the west coast. The ticker at the bottom of the news screen read: *The Worst Prepared City in North America?*

Sensing discomfort, someone switched to another channel. A scientist in coveralls and galoshes walked up a rocky beach. The newscast cut variously between pools of fish and wet wildlife.

"While it might be too early to ask anyone to look on the bright side," said the scientist, with the jovial professionalism of one accustomed to explaining complex science to idiots, "one silver-lining is that this affords us eggheads a chance to observe species we might not have had a chance to otherwise."

Cut to: the scientist holding a strangely wormy, tentacled creature in his hands. A creature I recognized.

"This little guy is a previously unknown genus of echinoderm, or sea cucumber. He and his buddies have been spotted all along the coast. *Pelagothuria Galatix*, we're calling him; or 'P.G.' for short. You can see by his coloration that he's not your average coastal life. Very likely, he lives much deeper in the ocean, but the collision of the plates forced him up to shallow waters."

He held the P.G. close to the camera so viewers could become intimate with its bluish-orange flesh and wriggling tentacles. My breath caught in my throat at the sight of the hateful little creature. Something about its abject wriggling made my head spin nauseously.

I returned to lie down on my cot.

I found the dead woman early the next morning, her body hanging from a pipe in the communal gym shower. She looked about forty, her face long and drained of life, purpled tongue lolling out of her mouth. Her eyes were a fine, bright blue, and didn't look dead at all.

I'd awoken before six, tossing and turning on the uncomfortable cot before giving up and deciding on a shower. She must have done it in the middle of the night. I stared at her for several minutes before going to get help.

A couple of NEVs—Neighborhood Emergency Volunteers— rushed to blockade the women's changeroom. EMTs arrived shortly after that. Despite their efforts to be inconspicuous, everyone was awake and buzzing by seven. Her name went around: Deborah Delaney, forty-eight. Her husband and two children had been killed in the quake. She'd been the lone survivor of her family.

"Survivor's guilt," said the elderly woman across from me. I joined her as she chain-smoked furiously outside of the gym. "Suicide rates always rise after natural disasters, but the death toll doesn't include those who can't grin-and-bear afterwards."

I nodded and shared a cigarette with her, thinking that maybe calling it *survivor's* guilt was a misnomer. They hadn't survived, after all.

I followed Mitchell, my newly acquired teammate, into a crumbling, Michigan Street home, feeling along in the dark. The house had been thoroughly ravaged, with rifts and splits running along its walls like an epileptic spider's webs. My stomach lurched with every step, each floorboard either too soft or too creaky. We'd been assured that these houses were safe to enter.

You signed up for this shit, I reminded myself, nearly tripping over a warped plywood floorboard.

Lacking anything better to do, I'd gone down to the NEV center— an awkwardly-hijacked Liberal Party campaign office—to volunteer.

Anything to distract me from my lack of tears, my lack of feeling, my inability to mourn my boyfriend's rapidly oncoming death. I felt more guilt at my own apathy than real sadness. But I told myself the tears would come, that it was simply impossible to mourn a person who hadn't died yet. I assured myself the pain was on its way.

"One thing no one's talking about," said Mitchell, "is the housing market, man. This is going to *fuck* real estate in this city."

"Uh-huh."

Mitchell was a tall, hefty boy of about twenty-five. He had a bushy beard and sure liked to talk. He and I had been assigned to help the "red-tag" crew, city engineers who were going through areas hit hardest by the quake and assessing whether the buildings needed to be torn down. Our job was to examine each home to make sure nothing valuable—or living—had been missed.

Mitchell ran his flashlight along the drooping ceiling; layers of drywall sloughed away like sunburnt skin. He turned to me, grinning. "Pretty sure you could still rent this place for two grand!"

"Heh."

"I'm telling you though," said Mitchell, "if you thought housing in Vic was bad before, just wait." He examined the living room and bedrooms, while I turned into the kitchen. His pedantry became a little quieter but still echoed effectively through the one-story home. "I see some optimistic twerps on Twitter thinking that this is going to cause a crash—L-O-L. Nope, scarcity principles."

I rolled my eyes. I hadn't loved the idea of being paired with a random dude when the NEV organizer put us together, but Mitchell quickly turned out to be more of a nuisance than a creep. He seemed to think talking constantly about real estate and investments and decentralized how's-its was distracting from our grim environs. It felt more like being saddled with someone else's anxious internal monologue.

I opened the fridge and helped myself to a leftover Diet Coke. It was warm and the fridge emanated a mildewy stench, but I welcomed the kick of caffeine. I eyed the cupboards, wondering what else the homeowners wouldn't miss, when Mitchell's scream tore through the air.

I put down the soda and moved back to the foyer. His scream had come from the bedroom hallway. "Mitchell?"

"I'm okay!"

I turned a corner and saw him up against the wall, shining his flashlight into one of the bedrooms, covering his mouth with his other hand. I took several steps forward before he noticed me.

"No, Emily," he said. "Don't go in there."

"What?"

"Don't look."

Even in the dim lighting, I could read the fear in his eyes, but my curiosity took hold. I swept past him, ignoring his protests, and looked into the bedroom—a kid's room with a small bed, *Pokémon* and Jack Harlow posters on the walls. It didn't take long to see what had freaked out Mitchell.

A man's body lay crumpled against the wall. He had something thick and gelatinous wrapped around his head. His arms lay out on either side of him, undersides deeply slashed from wrist to elbow. Dried blood seeped into the carpet like scarlet angel's wings.

I choked back nausea and knelt before the body, illuminating it with my flashlight. His dead skin was an unholy white. I ran the light up his shirt, neck, and head.

The thick tentacles of a sea creature wrapped securely around his face, its polyp-esque flesh a horrifically familiar dark blue-and-orange. The man had likely been dead for awhile—skin slip had begun around his neck and limbs—but the P.G. showed no signs of loosening its death grip.

Up close, I could make out the creature's steady, rhythmic breathing.

"What we're hearing from experts, sources close to the situation, is that certain varieties of sea life *may* have had adverse effects upon some of the, um, coastal life," said the egg-shaped man on the screen. "It is being referred to as an 'UESE'—an *unfortuitous ecosystem event.*"

That, I thought, *is a 100% made-up term.*

We watched the screen from the back of the NEV center surrounded by dozens of other volunteers. It was the morning after Mitchell and I had stumbled on the dead man. NEVs around the province were asked to attend this "digital informational session." We gathered around a big computer screen beneath a red poster featuring a smiling Liberal candidate, his arms crossed above the slogan: *Expect Better!*

The biologist onscreen went on about posterities and precautions, insisting that we always stay in pairs and never go out at night. Though this meeting had been set up with an educational guise, Mitchell and I were not the only NEVs to have found a dead body under similar circumstances. Up and down the west coast, reports poured in of dead bodies, their heads tightly swaddled by these odd, colorful sea creatures.

Deaths after an ecological disaster aren't exactly unheard of; what stood out was that, to a corpse, none appeared to have died in the earthquake or ensuing tsunami. None had been killed directly by the sea creatures, either. None had been asphyxiated or poisoned, so far as the experts could tell. The methods were various—slashed wrists, drowning, gunshots—but the motive was uniform: suicide. Outside of this, there weren't any discernible patterns. Cause of death appeared to be the quickest way out the victim could find.

The room erupted in chattering when, onscreen, the egg-shaped biologist's face was replaced by a computer-generated P.G.

"Fucking *facehuggers*," muttered Mitchell. "Fucking *xenomorphs* incoming, man."

The bluish flesh of the creature flipped around, its digitally rendered limbs wombling about at a couple frames per second.

"It is likely P.G. inject their victims with a toxin, something that exits the system rapidly or is, so far, undetectable. I can't overemphasize caution. It's very likely that these victims are in extreme discomfort after, err, attachment occurs."

He cleared his throat. "Our working theory is that this toxin—whatever it is—causes extreme pain. *Overwhelming* pain. Likely, this sharp influx of pain causes victims to search for ways to rapidly commit acts of self-harm."

"You can just say *suicide*, dude," I whispered under my breath.

"What was that?" asked Mitchell.

"Nothing."

Wet night wind whipped my face. It wasn't raining exactly, but cold vestiges of the tsunami continued to haunt the air. It was nearly midnight. I stood outside the emergency shelter, drinking a shitty Tim Horton's coffee. I held a frantic Sufjan at the end of a long leash. He'd predictably begun to go stir crazy stuck in his carrier, so the old smoking woman had lent me a dog leash and adjustable collar.

"It's fun!" she'd said. "Cats actually *love* going for walks!"

Sufjan had spent the first five minutes outside catatonically terrified, feet bolted to the ground like he were about to take a charge from a sumo wrestler. Now he was just rolling stupidly in a puddle.

Yeah, lady. Fun.

Figuring that he was going to need a cleaning anyway, I sat on a curb and let it happen, staring at my phone. *Seething* at my phone might be more accurate. Mitchell might've been annoying, but he was right about one thing. Every apartment in this already absurdly expensive city had leapt about 25%. Charity and benevolence in the wake of catastrophe were, evidently, only virtues up until the opportunity to cash-in. *Sorry you had your life violently deracinated, bro, but The Market has spoken.*

I wanted to throw my phone against the gym wall, *smiled* at the thought of it breaking into pieces. Just as I was about to drag Sufjan inside, my phone rang—an 800 number.

"Hello?"

Silence.

"Who is this?" I asked.

A sob, then Ron's voice: "He's…he's gone."

"Oh god."

"I'm sorry."

"I'm sorry, too."

We sat there on the line, crying—or maybe it would be more accurate to say that I sat in silence, Sufjan yanking on the leash, while

Ron cried and periodically blubbed, "Oh Earl." Still the numbness ruled me, like my entire body had been dunked in an anesthetic bath. *What the fuck is wrong with me?* I'd had more of an emotional reaction to rent prices.

After a few minutes, I realized Sufjan wasn't moving. I looked up to see the leash lying slack on the wet cement.

"He's gone," I said.

"I know, I know," Ron sobbed.

"No, I—sorry. I have to go."

"It's okay, take your—"

I dropped my phone and bolted upright, stepping onto the soppy grass, shaking a mangled baggie of cat treats.

"Soof!"

A meow—over by the school's dumpsters. The air around them burned my nostrils with an acrid stench. Sufjan cried out again. I turned into a labyrinthine area connecting the main body of the school to several outbuildings and portable classrooms. Sufjan's mewls carried over the air—directionless echoes bouncing around the blackness.

A memory reared up: the time I'd left the patio door open on my way to work and Sufjan had escaped. For nearly three days, we canvassed the neighborhood, postered, made tearful Facebook posts. Early'd been so angry and scared that he'd barely been able to look at me (until Sufjan had been mercifully picked up by the SPCA).

"Maybe you just don't care enough," I heard him say. *"Maybe you don't care enough about our cat."*

"Sufjan?" I called out.

I skulked down an alley alongside a tall building. The meowing had ceased, the only noise the echoing squelches of my wet Converse. I kicked myself for not dressing more warmly. I turned a corner and stopped when I saw movement in the dark.

"Soof?"

I stepped forward, heart thudding. The shape's motions were oddly smooth, like blood pumping through a vein of darkness. I stopped moving; it did, too.

Not Sufjan.

It was too dark to make out details, but I didn't need them. I knew what it would be. It turned its attention to me, wriggling those stubby tentacles as if it were trying to feel the shadows.

Then it illuminated.

The P.G.'s limbs became bioluminescent, sapphire blue. Parts of its flesh pulsed with vivid tangerine spots. It rose on two tentacles, prone on its haunches. Its many limbs pointed vaguely at me, floating and hovering in the air with smooth, underwater movements. The tips of its tentacles lit up periodically with quick flashes of white incandescence.

I thought, dully: *They didn't cover this in the digital informational session.*

For several moments, the creature and I stared each other down. I called out to Sufjan again but received no replies.

I took a step back, muttering, "Stupid fucking sea cucumb—"

It launched. Before I'd even planted my back foot, the P.G. had cleared the gap between us and collided with my head. I tried to scream, but its appendages were already wrapping around me. I fought, but it was incredibly strong. Its tentacles—sickly moist, impossible to grasp firmly—pulled me into a hellish hug.

I tried futilely to tear the creature off. After several seconds, my vision was completely black. I expected to choke, but no—my

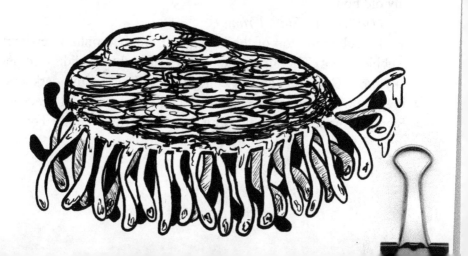

breathing was steady and clear, as though oxygen pulsated through the creature's molecules.

No, not oxygen. What I breathed was thicker, wetter—vapor? *It's breathing back,* I realized, panicked. I felt the noxious haze fill my lungs, my entire body. It *exhaled* into me.

This is it.

I fell to my knees on the wet pavement, bracing myself. What had the biologist said? That there would be pain, extreme pain.

I felt…something.

Pain? No no no.

Not pain—something…wonderful.

Joy.

I stood, filled with softness, sweet euphoria. I was lighter than I'd ever been—lighter than I'd ever thought possible. I wanted to run, to jump, to soar.

What had they been talking about, *pain?*

They had no idea. This creature was not a predator, but a friend. It didn't want to hurt me, to hurt anyone. It was a gift. An enlightening.

Blissful symbiosis.

A light appeared in the darkness, a white jewel nestled in vantablack. It called out wordlessly. Called me towards it. I moved. My legs—my old legs—stepped forward, rushing towards the beckoning light.

(Hadn't I been looking for something? Someone?)

I hit a wall. My arms reached out, gripped metal. A ladder? I climbed, one rung after another, felt watery wind against the flesh of my old body.

(This is—no. Stop. Wrong.)

I reached the top of the ladder and climbed onto a new surface. Rubble. Roof. The air up here was colder, but it didn't bother me anymore. Cold was an old concern. The light in the darkness was bigger now, brighter. Welcoming. I felt its warmth. I reached out. Stepped forward. My old feet hit a metal barrier. I climbed over.

(Stop.)
The light spoke no words but all the same said: *"Finally, Emily."*
(Don't.)
"You are home."
Then I sobbed with impossible ecstasy and stepped off the ledge, into the light.

HOWLS BUREAU OF INVESTIGATION

HBI

H.B.I.

SPECIAL AGENT *Joseph Andre Thomas*

Joseph Andre Thomas is a writer and literature teacher living in Vancouver, British Columbia. He is a graduate of the University of Toronto's MA in Creative Writing program. A recipient of the Avie Bennett Emerging Writer scholarship and the Canada Master's scholarship, Joseph's writing has appeared in *The Puritan's Town Crier* and *Untethered* magazine. He was a contributor to and a co-editor of the anthologies *Howls From Hell*, longlisted for a Bram Stoker Award ('Superior Achievement in an Anthology'), and the forthcoming *Collage Macabre: An Exhibition of Art Horror*; he has work forthcoming in the debut anthology from Black Cat Books.

🐦 @bunttriple

MEMO: *Evidentiary imagery provided by P.L. McMillan.*
Agent headshot provided by Leah Gharbaharan.

HEAVY RAIN
by TJ Price

I'm standing in the doorway where you last stood before you got up on a chair, slipped the belt around your throat like a necktie, and kicked the chair out from under you.

I imagine for the hundredth time how you expired, gasping like a fish in the air. Shitting yourself. Pissing yourself. Twisting like a windchime in a gale.

Two months have passed, and I still cannot entirely scrub the stains from the floor.

Our life was golden. Well, maybe a little tarnished around the edges. We still clasped one another in the evening hours. We still smiled when we talked, held our sides when we laughed, when we shared our inside jokes.

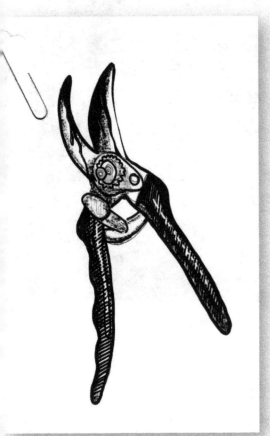

But you didn't like to have sex, and I did. I found other men. You didn't like to do much with your body. You started moving away from me whenever I touched you, like I repulsed you, or maybe you knew what I was doing.

So you hit fast-forward on your life, you wanted to see the credits roll. You wanted the fade to black, the stippling darkness, the sudden blast of white on the projector screen as the movie ended.

You hated yourself more than I could love you.

Since you took my heart and then fled to a place where I could never get it back, I took the pruning shears from the shed in our apartment building's little backyard, and I snipped off your left index finger.

Everyone thought it was something *you* did, before you killed yourself. Something bizarre, a kind of inexplicable symbol.

Where did it go? they all asked. The men in uniform scoured the garbage, the apartment. They asked me, when they thought they could slip it into conversation between the "I'm sorry" and the "for your loss."

I told them that's how I found you: minus one finger. When they found the pruning shears in the shed, still stained ruddy with your blood, they assumed you did it to yourself.

"What pain he must have been in," your best friend from work whispered to me at the funeral. It was meant to be some kind of sympathy, but it came off like a headline ripped from the tabloids.

Other than work, you preferred to keep to yourself. You liked a small crew: the smallest was you and me and the dog. Even the dog's gone now, too. Couldn't stand to look at her anymore. A nice family took her in.

She's romping on a farm somewhere, I'm sure.

I read about how to preserve your finger online. It's in a Mason jar, screwed tightly shut, full of what the Internet calls "strong water," which is water with a lot of grain alcohol in it. The finger does not float. It leans against the side of the glass, pointing towards Heaven. It is crooked slightly, too, as if it is saying "come hither."

I keep your finger next to our bed, on your nightstand, so I can see it any time I want. When I can't sleep, I focus on the whorls of your fingerprint, or the flaking keratin of your nail. You never had much in the way of nails, being an inveterate chewer.

And I can't stop sighing, or crying. I keep typing out texts to my friend, even when she's at work, and then deleting the text before I send it. These are invariably a combination of

Help me or *Today is a bad day* or *I can't stop crying* or *I saw his ghost today.*

The last one is a lie. I've never seen your ghost, but I've tried to convince myself that I have.

When the rain starts, I am thinking about how the weather has been so strange lately. Thunderstorms, big enough that the knick-knacks on the shelves jostle one another in fear. The temperature is chilly in the morning, but brutally humid by midday. The world can't take any more moisture: it is an over-filled sponge, leaking out around the edges.

To make things worse, last night the air conditioner gave a big rattletrap sigh and quit on me. I've thrown open all the windows to their fullest, gaping out on the world like yawn-stuck mouths. The heat of the day has stealthily crept in, too, its cloying humidity as predatory as kudzu vines. When an errant breeze kicks up, I stop and close my eyes for a moment, relishing the ephemeral coolness as long as I can.

Splat.

I open my eyes. Something has hit the floor, rolled under the cabinets in the kitchen, and left a translucent, jellied stain, along with a bright-red smear.

The most logical solution is the obvious one. I stick my head out the window, casting about this way and that, trying to find the culprit. Someone's playing jokes, tossed something in through the window.

It's either that, or something has fallen from the sky.

I turtle my head back inside and hunt for the invader, getting down on my hands and knees and following the red smear it's left behind. I press my face onto the cool linoleum to see what it is.

To this day, I still wonder which of us saw each other first.

The intruding object looks like a peeled, squashed grape, with a milky film like a mold saddling the middle of it. It's peculiarly white, from what I can see. I pull back from the dark recess, my bile rising, before I look again to confirm what I have seen.

It's an eyeball. I almost expect it to blink, as if it's as stupefied to see me as I am to see it.

Outside: a low grumble of thunder, like a sentinel guard dog issuing a warning, and the sound of wet, descending from the clouds.

I reach under the cabinet and draw the eyeball out. It's slimy against my fingers, trailing a bit of its ocular nerve, like a little braided tail. The iris, though cloudy, is strikingly familiar.

In fact, you had eyes that were just this color. Deep blue, but green too, like the ocean before a thunderstorm.

A car alarm goes off somewhere nearby, wailing like a disturbed infant, piercing and shrill. Someone screams, and for a moment, the two sounds intertwine in a ghastly weave before the screaming stops, as abruptly as someone pulling the plug on a sound effects tape.

I set the eyeball down on the counter and turn to look outside again, concerned.

The rain continues. It thuds against the roof, and I think: *hail?* But then the noise shifts, unutterably. It sounds like when you used to pound at the steaks with your fists to tenderize them. *Wham. Wham. Wham.*

Something flashes by the window, something bulky and large, like a wrapped package from the butcher's. I think: *who is throwing meat off of the roof?* It's big enough to be a leg of lamb, or an unbroken set of ribs.

A moment passes, and another object whizzes by outside. I hesitantly creep towards the window.

There, caught by the railing of the fire escape and dangling like a bizarre ornament, is a severed leg. It's cut off crudely somewhere above the knee, with a great chunk of thigh still attached, and, judging by the amount of hair on the calf and shin, it's a man's leg. The skin has a ruddy glow to it, as if recently amputated.

As I stare at it, completely mesmerized by the sight, I notice another strangeness: the street below is littered with body parts, as though God has grown angry with his dolls and dismembered them all over the neighborhood. There are arms up to the shoulder; hands, splayed out like fallen leaves; a foot here; a torso there. Scattered around are clumps of nameless flesh and gristle, strips of muscle and fascia, gleaming like wet seashells in the dim afternoon.

I do what anyone would do. I do what *you* would do. I twist around and look up.

The clouds are gray and black, like ink droplets in curdled milk. The wind is ghastly and hot, like the humid breath of an abattoir.

I recoil in disgust, back inside the apartment, and not a moment too soon.

That insistent, arrhythmic pounding on the roof becomes louder, even thunderous, and for a moment I mistake it for applause.

But it is not applause. It is the sound of things collapsing; the sound of ruin.

I wonder where you are before I remember you're dead, and then the deluge begins.

It lasts for approximately ten minutes before the body parts stop raining from the sky, but it takes much, much longer than that to get over the shock of what's happened. When the kitchen window shatters from a dismembered arm, fingers grasping at me as if it is alive, I admit it—I turn and flee, out into the hallway, down the two flights of stairs to the front lobby, to look out at the world through the small window in the door.

Someone running is struck down by a chunk of tissue that seems half-formed, glistening in the light. They are knocked to the side, their head splitting against the corner of a building in a red splatter. Cars careen to the sides of the road, barking up stoops and crashing into the front of the buildings opposite. Alarms wail, barely audible over the sounds of the fleshy rain. *Thud, thud, thwap.* Glass shatters. Horns blare.

As the alien downpour finally ceases, I cautiously open the front door. A severed hand falls from the awning and *splats* to the concrete right in front of me. One of its fingernails is oozing blood into the crescent of its cuticle, as if recently chewed.

Everywhere, there is ruin and wreckage: blood-stained people lifting themselves up from prone positions on the sidewalks, wrestling with limbs and other fleshly encumbrances. Some come out from recessed entrances, fearful eyes trained on the gloomy sky above.

The power lines sag from their poles, fizzing and sparking, some of the wires bent down to the street, and everywhere there is a dense *stillness*, a shared quiet that reverberates from panicked eye to panicked eye. No one is quite sure what to do. Who to call.

From the distance: a siren, getting closer. I tense up, unexpectedly reminded of the night I found you hanging in our doorway. After I took the shears to your hand.

It was only fair.

But then I called the police, and I remember hearing that same lonely siren uncurling from the seethe and buzz of the city, homing in on me, and, I suppose, you, as your lumpen body swayed from side to side.

Someone is crying. Someone else is screaming. It could be me. It feels like a bomb has gone off, or some hideous artifact of war has landed in the middle of the street, with all the assorted, blood-spattered bits of bodies lying about. Manna from heaven for cannibals, I think to myself.

Where has this rain of flesh come from? Surely not heaven. Surely not the clouds. Even now, they are shifting, disassembling, letting the fury of the summer sun beat down on the scene below. The storm, such as it was, did nothing to dispel the sticky humidity, and a scent of iron weighs down the air. On the wrought-iron fence, a foot is pierced through the middle, like stigmata.

A woman is crouched over someone else, just down the sidewalk. The would-be rescuer is open-mouthed, staring at me, shouting something in Spanish. In one hand, she holds a detached arm at the elbow, waving it at me as if trying to get my attention. The fingers at the end of the hand wiggle—all except for one.

The hand is missing a finger.

An index finger.

I go to the woman, walking towards her in a daze. She is yelling at me, gesturing to the crumpled, unmoving figure on the asphalt even as she hurries down the street away from us, leaving the severed arm behind. I think about yelling after her, but I swallow it instead. What good can I do for this poor sap, struck down by a flailing arm from the sky? I kneel down anyway, to touch their pulse.

I stand up. This person isn't breathing, and dark blood flows from a dent in the side of their skull. This person isn't alive.

The arm's presence is disquieting enough, but for it to seem somehow familiar, as well? Vertigo shifts my world from one side to the other as I pick it up, gingerly, by its elbow. It's heavier than I thought it would be.

The sirens are multiplying, as if a swarm is about to descend all at once. I back away from the corpse and feel something squish unpleasantly beneath the sole of my sneaker. I lift my foot to see jellied strings connecting it to the sidewalk: another eyeball. Swift remorse jolts through me, immediately followed by revulsion, as though I've stepped on a cat's tail.

I run back into the apartment building and slam the door behind me. My heart is thudding. I'm covered in a sheen of sweat.

And I'm still holding the severed arm.

Your arm.

Standing there in the stuffy dimness, I can barely breathe. I shift the arm around me, grappling with it like an unwieldy rifle. I press its still-warm palm to my own. I interlace what fingers it has left with mine, until we are holding hands, you and I.

It almost feels holy, in this sweaty cloister of an apartment foyer, leaning against the wall.

The stump, right where its index finger should have been (right where the shears lopped it off) twitches, and I scream, hurling the arm away from me.

It lands on the carpet with an awkward thud. For long moments, I dare it to move, to come to life and start crawling towards me, dragging itself along the floor by its bloody fingertips.

It does no such thing. It doesn't move at all.

In fact, it looks lonely.

Your finger is crooked even further now, I swear it. Perhaps it's the slow degradation of the flesh in the strong water; the muscle inside your finger is contracting slowly, or something. I'm sure there's some kind of explanation for it, but I can't come up with one.

It's been approximately thirty minutes since the police have arrived on the scene, and nobody knows what to do with all the fallen flesh, with all the carnage that's been wrought. The whole neighborhood's been cordoned off.

No one knows what's happened. Reports are trickling in on my phone. They're analyzing the flight paths of airplanes that might've traveled overhead, that might've loosed some cargo, or something. They're looking for anomalous weather conditions that might've disturbed a cemetery somewhere, and brought the limbs to fall upon us like some kind of Biblical plague.

Night's about to fall, and I have no power in the apartment. No lights. The entire neighborhood is without power, and there's a stuffed quiet, as if sosmeone has taxidermied the whole block.

Nobody knows which department is in charge of what. I've seen trucks roll through marked DEPT OF SANITATION, and I've seen men in HAZMAT suits, and the police have been going door to door. They even rang my doorbell, but I didn't answer. Pretended I wasn't home.

In the dark, I sit here fingering your suicide note. The one that's creased and folded around the edges, from where I keep it in my wallet. The one that's stained with my tears. The one that begins *Dear Noah. I'm sorry.*

I'm so angry that I crumple the note up in my fist, then smooth it out again, like I have a hundred times before, and try to read it further, even when I know it now by heart.

> *I hope you understand, someday.*
> *This is the only way I know how to escape.*
> *I long to be free of my body.*
> *But I will miss yours.*

> *Love, always—*

> *Adam.*

Lightning sighs voicelessly across the sky. I strip off my t-shirt, which is stained with your blood, and lunge at the jar in which your finger is kept. The water sloshes uneasily as I grip the top and unscrew. It takes some doing—I'd screwed it on tightly—but finally it pops free. There's a sharp, acrid odor that rises, and your finger is there too, pointing at me.

As if it knows what I'm going to do.

Hours pass, and they still haven't cleaned up the street. Men in uniforms and hard hats stand outside, bickering with one another. One man points to another man, who points to another man. Most of them stand around smoking cigarettes, gawking at the ruin. Body parts still festoon the scene, some of them incongruously positioned in trees, or hanging from fire escapes. Another arm, the same as the first, is laying on the sidewalk, and it's this that I crouch by.

I've wrapped your finger in paper towels, patted it dry of the strong water. It's got such a strange, gummy texture to it, and it's so cold when I pull it out of its little shroud.

When I place it on the stump of the arm's missing finger, I feel a jolt. A spark.

And when I blink, there's your arm, made whole again, up to the shoulder.

At once, I understand everything.

I turn my eyes up to the sky in a sort of supplication. I wonder: will there be more of you, like this? Can I find all of your disparate parts? Can I somehow undo what you've done, through puzzling you back together?

There: an ear, nestled in the leaves of the neighbor's holly bush.

There: a finger. So many superfluous parts. Are they all you? I only need nine more fingers to make ten. Ten toes. Two feet. Two hands.

Teeth. So many teeth, littered around like tiny pebbles. I count them out as I collect them from the ground. From a neighbor's bird-bath, where they lay like innocents in the shallow puddle.

I go about gathering you up, piece by piece. On the second trip back to the apartment, I bring a backpack. Your backpack, the same one you wore when we climbed Catamount, that Adirondack mountain. I put my hood up and wear sunglasses, though the sun is long since set. The sky is a haze of purplish blue, smeary with the aurora of streetlights. I do not stop when questioned. I run, stooping only to snare a gobbet of muscle that I need to restructure your cheek.

It's like sculpture, I discover. Each piece fuses marvelously back into place.

The power has still not come back on. I work feverishly in the dark, while the hot, stinking wind blows in through the shattered windows.

I am possessed of the wildest, strangest hope.

Finally, I have all of you, your entire corpus, laid on the floor in front of me, right down to the ligature scars on your neck where the belt snapped your spine. You are complete, but without breath. Without life.

I prise open one of your eyelids with my index finger and thumb, and I breathe your name into the air. Lightning answers, illuminating

the room in stark white for a half-second, and I swear I see your pupil dilate beneath the thin white clouds of death, departing.

I swear I see your lips tremble, start to move. Start to say my name.

"No…" Your voice is a harsh whisper, scratching against your throat. Your face starts to contort, your mouth opening in a wide howl, and I clamp my hand over it, to muffle your scream.

"It's all right," I reassure you. "You're home now. And I'll never let you go again."

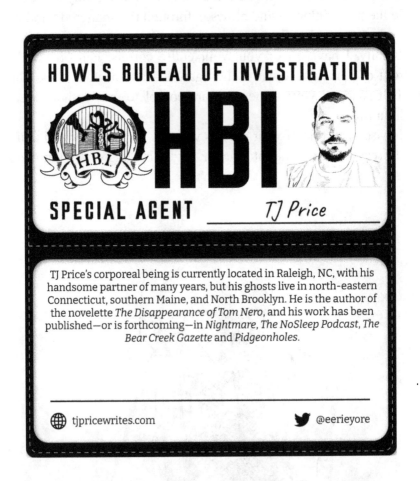

HOWLS BUREAU OF INVESTIGATION

HBI

SPECIAL AGENT — TJ Price

TJ Price's corporeal being is currently located in Raleigh, NC, with his handsome partner of many years, but his ghosts live in north-eastern Connecticut, southern Maine, and North Brooklyn. He is the author of the novelette *The Disappearance of Tom Nero*, and his work has been published—or is forthcoming—in *Nightmare*, *The NoSleep Podcast*, *The Bear Creek Gazette* and *Pidgeonholes*.

tjpricewrites.com   @eerieyore

MEMO: Evidentiary imagery provided by Christi Nogle. Agent headshot provided by Solomon Forse.

A WAR IN HELL
by Mike Adamson

Nobody says Peter Ferris didn't have the guts to dream. When you live in Hell, dreaming of escape is all the life there is.

By strange roads does a university professor in the antiquities come to wield an automatic weapon, leading the desperate and the damned. When I settled with my good lady to teach the roots of culture in the British Isles I was a passionate academic, a family man; but fate has its own ideas, and none were left untouched when the world changed. Now I stared into a pit that seemed to fall away to hell, and my heart raced, for all it held could be our salvation.

"Swing it around!" I yelled over the wind, the radio channel breaking up in my ears as I clung to the safety lines. The pit, yawning in the storm-blasted wasteland of Baldurgan, outside Dublin, was a gaping black maw, surrounded by spoil heaps where the big drilling rig had chewed into dense soil.

Skies of brown cloud and bits of flame, sizzling hail, winds that drive grit to strip flesh—oh, this is purgatory, but we have the slim pleasure of knowing we didn't actually make it ourselves. Hell was waiting all along, the malice that dwells hidden and forgotten in the deepest places of the Earth.

No one really knew where the *Things* came from, or quite what they were; but their appearance, on the heels of "The Rock" was too great a coincidence. They either came on the rock, which seemed unlikely, or our sweet Earth had always harboured the hounds of perdition, and the rock merely set them loose. In the early days we were unable to credit them, much less their incorporeal nature, and scoffed when holy men and sages told us they were eaters of souls. But we came to believe, through hard years of relentless battle.

We fought times without number as population dwindled, but now we fought with a purpose, because I had found the way to end their dominion over life.

Below, work lights flashed in the gloom, tension on the chains telling me the load was in motion. "Grab a hold!" I sent a thumbs-up to the crane driver, and we began to recover line.

But evil knows when it's under threat, and defends itself. You get a gut feeling, and the wise come to trust it. As the load inched back toward the wan and angry daylight, I turned in a crouch, weapon in my hands, and peered through my grit-fogged faceplate. I could almost taste their foulness in the back of my throat.

Speed is their greatest weapon; all they need do is take you in their jaws to consume your very soul. In the moment before they attack, I always seem to shift into quick-time, my mind processing information faster than I could have ever imagined before.

I felt the precognitive rush—and, in a heartbeat, we engaged the enemy.

They came out of the storm like shadows of only slightly greater substance, swirls of dust that somehow coalesced into shapes of nightmare, bounding like great beasts—some wolf-like, others akin to bears or hyenas, yet all the size of an ox, and as bent on insensate killing as the first moment they clawed free of Hades. I roared a warning, and the machine pistol in my hands barked, a clean line of fire to the heart of a hulking shape that dissipated in flurries of black vapour. On they came, over and over; only a solid hit would stop them—anything less and they flowed together, and attacked again.

Shoot, aim, shoot, load, shoot—the rhythm had become automatic. A dozen guns fired as one but the shadow-beasts seemed without limit today. First one gun-hand went, then a second. That scream, that terrible scream, as the soul is ripped free of mortal anchoring, was like torment upon an exposed nerve, for we knew that fate awaited us all. Bodies lay where they fell, but all that those people ever were was flown, not to some better place, not to reincarnation, but *consumed*, merely fuel for a bestial life-force.

I covered the right side of the crane, protecting the driver, my son Jimmy on the left. He was seventeen and had learned to be a soldier. None were born to this, but we wanted to live. So we stood our ground, fed the guns, and sent the horrors back to the nothingness from which they came—and counted each scream as our numbers lessened.

The platform was almost at the surface when the crane cab was dealt a terrible blow, the plastic windows crushed in on the driver. I raked the belly of the thing hulking above me, then stepped up on the long track to wrench the door open and drag the driver free, bleeding from a great head wound where the transparency had clubbed him. I could only lay him to the track, squeeze aboard as I forced the transparency back from the controls—and was faced with a terrible reality. It took two levers to operate the crane: I had to put my gun down.

Trust your people, my gut said—so I put the Uzi on the dash and throttled the big electric motors, to start recovering cable again. *Not far now, please, God, if you're still there!* "Deep team, be advised, attack in progress, come up firing!"

A Thing stooped by the open cutting, snarled into the blackness, and was raked through by a burst square in the face. It flowed apart and vanished, and I heard fire slackening all around. My boys and girls must have got on top of this fight—and we were almost out clean with the prize!

But as I let myself relax for a moment, the crane driver, stretched on the track below me, babbled a warning, trying to claw upright. I saw a monolithic apparition, like a bear crossed with a dinosaur, drawing together for the strike. The platform and its load broke surface beyond—I couldn't take my hands from the controls, the load was vulnerable, the team crouched about it firing in all directions. I could only shout a warning for anyone to my right to *get that one!*

Too late—the strike, the shriek, and the craneman's body collapsed as the abomination fed with loathsome pleasure. Sickness shot through me as I divided my attention, slewed the crane to set the platform down wide of the pit, then released the controls and snatched for my weapon. Confusion—the blasting wind from the glowering sky, the scream, the guttural utterances of the beast. I flinched from the horror, the whole witnessed in that fragmented way, like flicking through still pictures...

But before I could level my Uzi, the beast was raked through and dissipated before my eyes. The assault was over, and we survivors, panting with the shock of battle, stood alone under a sky more Venus than Earth.

I turned to the load: a metal-bound stone chest, decorated with carved spirals from Celtic antiquity. I managed less a smile than a grimace, to raise my gloved fist to the boiling heavens for a moment.

"Let's get it on the truck," I shouted over the wind. "I want to be back across the sea the first moment the weather permits."

But as my team jumped to their tasks, I felt a coldness in my right arm, and rubbed it abstractly. Then my stomach turned, as I feared—not reasoned, just feared—that in that final clinch, some part of the Thing had brushed against me. My heart raced behind my ribs, for while I knew it was not an automatic death-sentence, once touched one was never quite *right*. The chill of the grave, it would never leave me. In fact, some said, it called the Things like bait... and they abhorred a kill left unfinished.

"Cursed be those who yet breathe, in this Year of our Purgatory, 2079, for from Heaven did come the avenging blow, which smote open the innermost folds of Hell, and poured forth upon the ruined Earth all the evils of the ultimate Pit. Thus have our sins found us out. Yet God remaineth merciful, for in creating this intermediate moment before the enfolding damnation of the Inferno, He offers us the chance to expurgate our failings and transcend our basest natures. Thus we may yet win through to the foot of God's throne..."

The preacher was droning on again, where the alleys crossed under ancient corrugated iron sheeting, rusted through, dripping a constant reminder of the fury up above. It roofed the space between rows of survival shacks, squalid shanties dug into the earth and piled high with soil, gravel, anything to protect against the elements. It kept out the tormenting wind, but rats and mud were the most common companions.

The preacher seemed old, beard straggling on his chest, his Bible so tattered and worn it was held together with C-clamps on the spine. He had been raving this stuff so long it no longer mattered if anyone listened, only that it fomented in his soul and came out between his rotten teeth.

How the world had changed in the seven years since the coming of the rock: an asteroid fragment that got by the Spaceguard defences, and that alone made it seem preordained to many. It shouldn't have been a planet-killer, but every planet has a weak spot, and this one found ours. An oceanic fault line split like imperfect marble under the careless blow of a sculptor's chisel, ruptured the crust and the seas poured their vastness into the raw interior; and, like Krakatoa, the resulting steam explosion was far more destructive than the initial shock.

Nuclear winter was a foregone conclusion, ironically, for at a stroke the world became too cold, and modern high sea levels fell away as water was locked up once more in ice. But the endless darkness beneath clouds of dust and ash brought agriculture to an end, forests perished for want of sunlight, and the life of sea and land, already pressed to the brink by the anthropocene, faded quickly.

It was what the asteroid unleashed from the hellish depths beneath us, however, that sealed the fate of the planet Earth. That which came for *us*.

I just got in on the crawler from Sheffield, having rounded up some gun-hands for pay, making it back to the underground redoubt above Hathersage, in what was once the high fells of Derbyshire. Here in the Peak District, part of the mountainous spine of Britain, life barely clung on, hiding from the furious winds, growing food underground, condensing water from vapour…And hoping—praying—that the Things didn't come, at least not today.

My research took me to Ireland, across a night-black sea that raged four days out of five, and the ferries braved it a few days in a month. But my expedition was successful, if at a cost. Ten went with me, six returned, and my son had lost faith in me at that choice I was forced to make. One more kick to the bruised belly of a man; but he would understand, one day, if this crazy scheme worked.

I had called ahead from the crawler terminal. I passed by the preacher and my hand rode my gun-butt to keep shadowy figures in the archways of hooches and hovels, and when I knocked at a stout metal door I hunched against the chill and damp until I heard the security slit drawn back, and looked into eyes I knew. A rattle of locks and bolts, and the door was opened to me. It closed, was rebarred, and I looked into my wife's haunted features, into the bottomless pits of my daughter Meg's dark eyes, where she sat with a weapon to guard the way—but I could smile for them.

"It's done," I murmured, unwinding a filthy scarf from my lower face. "I got the gun-hands. We have the incantation." They came to their feet, hardly daring hope. "Believe," I assured them in a growl. "The last piece of the puzzle is in place."

"Tell me, Peter," Danielle whispered, her expression grave but hopeful, framed by a straggle of dark hair. We sat together at a table of rough plank, an LED lamp between us. She had found the makings of a stew. I had no doubt the meat was rat—what else was there, besides one's neighbour?

My hand trembled, the spoon dripping, so I set it down. "It was hiding, all these years, in the *Yellow Book of Lecan*. Not in the text, which is well known, much of the *Ulster Cycle* and other ancient compositions, but in the manuscript itself—the hand-written volume of 1318 in the collection of Trinity College, Dublin. We were able to find it under the ruins, its protective case was undamaged. We subjected it to a wider range of tests than ever before."

Danielle placed a hand over mine. "Was it…complete?"

"We were lucky, only two pages carried the hidden information, and both were present. With the hotcore generator, we were able to fire up the old quantum resonance scanner at St James's Hospital, and we knew at once there was more than met the eye. We got a reading of a mineral impregnation in the vellum. Nothing visible, just microparticles deep in the material."

"An unknown *palimpsest?*" Her smile was alive with a thrill of discovery such as I had not seen in years, so far had her academic fire been driven down.

I nodded, managing a little stew. "Typically, when a manuscript was reworked, it was an old pagan text being wiped away to allow a Christian substitution. A lost treatise by Archimedes turned up when a medieval manuscript was carefully imaged. But this is different."

She brushed my stubbled cheek with a hard hand. "A pagan text under a pagan text?"

"Precisely. It must have been written years in advance, letting the mineral inks soak in deeply, before the surface pigment was completely cleaned away. Yet the scribes knew exactly what they were doing. The key to finding the invisible text was the overlying writing itself." I managed a smile. "The map to finding the Cauldron of Plenty was on one page in which the cauldron is described, the invocation to *use* it, behind another."

She closed her eyes and seemed to give thanks in some silent prayer. "We may never undo what has become of the Earth, but the Earth is not the only reality."

I drew out my phone, called up files and flicked them to a terminal on a side table. They opened automatically, images of the ancient writing fluorescing in parts of the spectrum never seen by living eyes. "How was the information meant to be recovered? Probably chemically, like applying a reagent to make traditional invisible ink momentarily legible. But we could resolve the microscopic pigment granules themselves and map them, giving us a conventional image."

Danielle crossed to the terminal and slid on her carefully guarded spectacles, to squint, enlarge the image and catch her breath. "It's Middle Gaelic."

"I was able to read it at once."

"The cauldron?"

"Was in a safe place. Under St Brighid's Well, at Baldurgan. We had to tunnel twenty metres below the old deep water level. It was sealed with resin in an iron-bound stone chest." My voice faded and she glanced back with a frown, reading in my expression, my hesitation, how hard it had been. I nodded, exhausted. "That's when the Things came." She returned and took my hand. "We lost four men. We slaughtered them by the bushel, but they kept coming." I couldn't ever get past seeing a man's soul torn out. My whisper could barely be heard, and I knew Danielle had seen her fill too. Every survivor had. "Jimmy…He won't be forgiving me for a long time. I had to make a choice, Dannie. I chose to get the artefact to the surface. It cost a life I might have saved, but at cost of leaving the team that brought it up in an exposed position." My hands were shaking again and she squeezed them gently.

"He's young. He still has to realise that life cannot always be about absolutes." She knew I would speak of it when I needed to, and instead nodded to the terminal. "Are we ready to do this?"

"As we'll ever be. Come first light, the Things will know what a *real* fight means." I rubbed my arm under the table, wondering if I should mention it. Was I jeopardising the project, this close to completion? But I could not make the words come.

The seven years since the coming of the rock had been a journey of the damned for the survivors of planet Earth.

Everyone lost someone, and all bore the marks of hardship. We fought for every last scrap, and only the strong survived. I paid my gun-hands in clean water and full bellies, and they were happy because they fought the same fight with or without my employment. They had joined the project team at the bunker, and I would have my family there by dawn.

The Ferris clan had been nobody special before the rock fell. I was just a teacher of ancient history, but I knew what to do. They called me mad, yet I was the only one offering an answer. Technology had failed us, science was out of ideas when faced with the Things, and religion had nothing new to offer. But in folklore I saw parallels, the beasts of which our ancestors spoke, if not these then equivalents—the world was teeming with monsters, if one believed legend, and maybe, just maybe, people had encountered these creatures before. If so, the Things had stamped themselves upon our racial psyche so indelibly we still feared the unknown, the dweller in the dark, listened with the soul's ears for predators, and told stories which circled endlessly a forgotten archetype. The dragon, the chimera, the gorgon, hell-hound and lich, vampire and shape-shifter…

Why not raise one legend to another?

Perhaps few remained who could see in our scourge an echo of all that had gone before, but *I* could, and I dared imagine.

In the legends of these islands, Ireland was settled from across the sea, from the cities of four island kingdoms, each of which brought with them a sacred treasure—the Stone of Destiny, the Spear of the Sun, the Sword of the Moon and the Cauldron of Plenty. Though considered expressly mythological, a tangible tradition existed. A contender for the stone is well-known, a simple block of rough-cut sandstone brought into Scotland by the first kings of the Scoti, seized by Edward I in 1296, and long held at Westminster. Much doubt remained, some felt the real stone lay in the Hill of Tara. But if one can exist, why not the rest?

I came upon obscure ancient references to their resting places, and though the sword and spear would have been potent weapons against the Things, none today could wield them. Only the cauldron could bring us what we needed. Legend described it as a portal to the Otherworld: whether the next life, in which the ancient Gaels believed so fiercely, or some parallel reality, the tales were unclear, yet most explicit in the properties to be expected. The cauldron gave its bearer an unending supply of all that life could demand, whether inexhaustible food and drink, or indeed the power of regeneration. When the cauldron was carried to the field of battle, the slain would be dumped unceremoniously into its mystery, and return, reborn as mindless killing machines, grim servitors to fight on relentlessly, and *that* was all we need know.

An hour from first light, the cold, dank, underground streets lit with a few solar-powered LEDs, Danielle, Meg and I sealed our home for the last time. I had called the bunker, and a dozen gun-hands waited at our door to guard us on the last journey. We crept through the gloom, weapons in hand, each praying for whatever providence might gift us. The Things could come without warning, and though we had long observed that they manifested in open spaces, not tight enclosures, one could never be too careful.

The settlement stretched hundreds of metres in every direction, a stinking warren in which the dregs of humanity clawed for survival. Doom had already laid its clammy hand upon far too many, and for many who yet drew breath, there would be no tomorrow. But some might see the sunrise, if they had the courage to embrace the *other*.

We passed the corner on which the old preacher had stood yesterday, and I wondered how he would fare if presented with a choice—let the Things eat his soul, or acknowledge another religion? Perhaps he would die with a prayer upon his lips, and I would not fault him for remaining true to his creed.

The bunker was part of an old factory, basement levels holding storage racks and tanks. Here we manufactured ammunition and fuel, and the community owed us more than they knew. All above was scorched brick, wiped nigh-clean, like so much of the old world, but perhaps that mattered little now.

We passed through steel doors under the eyes of cameras and guards, and I found the project team clustered about their charge. The Cauldron of Plenty was a typical cooking pot on three stubby legs, the sort Iron Age metalworkers churned out by the thousand, but it was the size of an old-time whale-ship's vats, a bulbous body beneath which fires burned to render blubber to oil. It stood on a wide platform, atop a scissor-lift, beneath metal doors we would haul open, and, all about, the chamber was decorated in the sigils and signs of a lost faith.

I looked around the faces I knew, those who had accompanied me on the desperate quest into Ireland, those who had guarded our citadel for years, compatriots in this insane venture, and the many who had joined us to chase the faintest flicker of hope. They needed a speech, and the words came easily, though I struggled to ignore the cold in my arm that reminded me, come what may, we could do no more—win or lose, today was our last stand.

"You've walked this way for years, my friends, now I'll ask you to walk the last mile. The sun's coming up, soon we'll open that trapdoor, go up into the light, and we'll fight—as we've learned to. But, gods willing, we'll not do it alone today. Are you with me?" A cheer made the air shake, as guns were raised in gloved fists. "Then let's make a stand like they used to, the sort the bards sang of for a thousand years—for that's our heritage, and our glory, if we let it be." I made a circling motion of the hand. "Crank up the generators! Everyone to their places! Let's get this done!"

I caught Jimmy's eye, where he stood with the combat team, and saw, if not forgiveness, then understanding. He would fight with a will. Danielle and Meg hugged me, then pulled back with the troopers as I was passed a tablet displaying the transliterated incantations. Here was the hidden substance, locked away since the Middle Ages, words that called forth a fury the world had not seen since time immemorial, and I had the audacity to read them. But with one's back to the cosmic wall, why not risk all?

The gun-hands headed for the stairs, to unbarricade steel doors and stand by. The Things would come—but this time we *wanted* them to. Generators thrummed in their pits, the lights went down, and I began to read. I stood with the cauldron, one hand on its chill rim, and my voice echoed out with words unheard in an age. Part of me expected nothing at all, that to throw such defiance at fate was presumption at best—but were the Things not real?

Ah, but the force of life bound up with the ancient rites was itself timeless, a vigour quite independent of the mundane, and I felt the iron vibrate softly, growing warm under my touch. With a wolfish grin, I gave the signal, and brawny arms hauled to open the trapdoor above, great metal leaves parting as wheels squealed on overhead trackways. A slash of stormy orange dayglow came in on us as my voice boomed out the oratory that took the cauldron from inert iron to a veritable gateway between the worlds. And, it seemed to me, the spirits of the vessel chuckled, drew great breaths of air and flexed muscles unused since Rome had walked these lands.

The scissor-lift's hydraulics gave voice, and the platform rose through the aperture, the angry, glowering sky expanding to fill my world, and in moments I stood exposed in the gritty wind, my arm spasming with cold-shock. I roared out the final phrases of Middle Gaelic to complete the invocation, then slung the tablet, hefted my Uzi, and crouched by the thrumming metal—waiting, waiting…

Among the tumbled remains of the factory, the gun-hands emerged and took cover behind brick and stone, to scan the sky with infrared glasses. *They* would come—they always came, especially when a *touched one* remained to be claimed. For long moments I waited, my back to the warm metal, then a coalescing cloud of dark vapour descended, and we opened fire as one.

Thirty machine guns barked dragon-tongues of cordite flame as battle was joined, the cloud-creatures slashed apart as they formed, and I almost felt the spirits smile with glee. The Gaelic pantheon was bloodthirsty, and to be presented a resolute foe was an invitation to the slaughter in which they revelled.

A shimmering column of red light rose from the cauldron's depths, pierced clouds that gave back in roiling circlets of vapour, and the Things flinched, checking in their assault. The distorted shadows of bear, wolf and tiger paused, sniffed the cosmic winds, and a roar to shake the bedrock of the world rose from countless throats—but it was not directed at *us*.

They came from the red light: shambling humanoid forms clawed out of the cauldron, tumbled over the rim and rose like misshapen gargoyles.

I backed away, ran for the cover of a ruined wall, and panted over a dry throat as I saw them come: rank after rank of spectral figures, each clad in the remnants of ancient armour, clutching spear and shield, axe or mace, and the first among them formed ranks and strode forth as more, ever more, appeared from the ruddy gleams.

The Things held back as if spell-bound, and I feared they would turn-tail, that there would be no decisive clash. I stepped into the open, to wave my chilled arm at the vaporous, boiling outlines. "Come on! Don't leave the job half-done!" I offered my limb, knowing Danielle would realise what it meant, but the bait was enough.

A wolverine-like titan bounded for me and I drew a clean line of fire, but in the same moment a spectral spear pinioned the beast and it

went down ten metres short. A terrible silence held sway as each side stared down the other, then the Things broke into full, baying advance. The undead warriors from a lost epoch exploded into the charge, as ever more poured from the cauldron like a foul flood.

The ground shook to the pounding tread of a multitude, and all became a fury unseen since the world was young. On all sides the Things closed with their ancient foes, and vanished in gusts of vapour moment by moment, for the risen warriors were bereft of souls—there was nothing for the Things to devour, save the most tainted dregs that might yet cling to reconstituted flesh. The undead were flung like leaves before the sledgehammer blows of paw and fang, yet rose with the inevitability of some force of nature, to stab and slash with tireless thews, and a cold, unreasoning rage born of thralldom to gods and kings whose realm lay beyond that glowing doorway.

The wind shrieked above us, thunder drummed as lightning rent the sky, and the snarl of machine pistols was lost in the building tempest. All about, the sterile, ruined earth was churned by the inhuman armies, and the clamour of battle rose to a crescendo, a mad panoply of tearing and ripping, slashing and hacking, of risen sundered limb from limb, yet also the steady dissolution of the beasts, one flurry at a time. They came on from the aether in numbers we had never imagined, as if being drawn from every corner of the world to counter the endless army of the dead, and under that horrific sky I knew then we had the battle we needed. Here and now—drain them white, send them down into whatever hell awaited them, and the world would be blessedly free.

But all things come at a price, one I had already agreed to pay. Someone must rebalance the scales for the temerity of opening the portal, and somehow, I knew, one last beast would come for me. I was strangely calm as I changed magazines and slammed home the first round, feeling the Otherworld yawning wide for my soul, my arm numb almost beyond use. All thought of loyalties, of wider purpose, paled as I raced out of cover to avoid the slashing paws of a monolithic apparition, a hulking creature like a reptilian gorilla. It bounded over the ruins and took a line of tracer to its midst, yet kept coming, bowled the undead warriors aside like tenpins, and its fetid breath promised ultimate corruption.

I heard Danielle scream my name through the tempest, and my regret was that I could not share whatever paradise I hoped to buy for them.

I backed up against the cauldron, among the scrambling, clawing armies from beyond, and shouldered my weapon for the last time. I emptied the magazine in barking defiance, spent cases jingling around my boots.

Then the beast crumpled before me and I was bowled up and over—into the cauldron.

Only the greatest heroes could descend to the Otherworld. It was to confront the gods, to pass not through the gates of death, yet reach the Summerlands. Those cast dead into its mystic cavern returned as we had seen them, but what of one neither dead nor untainted?

When I regained consciousness, the sounds of battle were distant. A pale light shone far above, and I reached for it, wondering if it were the Moon. Then I blinked and found Danielle at my side, and Meg and Jimmy, and many another from the project, and the town beyond. She shushed me, a finger at my lips, and drew me up, to gesture to the moving columns about us.

In a line that snaked into shadowed depths and distance in this strange world, the undead came on in rank and file, their blank orbs unblinking, jaws slack, and striding with the spasmodic action of imperfect reanimation. They trooped toward the final climb, ever upward into that circle of light, and would do so until their dread task was accomplished. Yet from that pale eye also descended a second line, figures in ones and twos, making their way into the warm depths where, it seemed to the more sensitive among us, new worlds of opportunity awaited. As I watched, the preacher went by, bemused by all he saw. He no longer carried his battered Bible.

Without a word, I enfolded my family in my arms and we joined the line wandering into the gloom of this new and special world, seeking the light, and all that our ancestors had known, glad to turn away from the ruined world behind. And abruptly, I felt all would be well.

My arm was warm.

HOWLS BUREAU OF INVESTIGATION

HBI

H.B.I.

SPECIAL AGENT *Mike Adamson*

Mike Adamson holds a Doctoral degree from Flinders University of South Australia. After early aspirations in art and writing, Mike secured qualifications in both marine biology and archaeology. Mike has been a university educator since 2006, has worked in the replication of convincing ancient fossils, is a passionate photographer, master-level hobbyist, and journalist for international magazines. Short fiction sales include to *Metastellar, Strand Magazine, Little Blue Marble, Abyss and Apex, Daily Science Fiction, Compelling Science Fiction* and *Nature Futures*. Mike has placed on over two hundred occasions to date, totaling over a million words.

mike-adamson.blogspot.com

MEMO: Evidentiary imagery and agent headshot provided by Maia Weir.

FLESHIES
By Thea Maeve

Even in the air conditioning, Raven was sweating, making it difficult to finish her winged eyeliner. When she thought she nailed it, a small bead of sweat smeared a wing, denying the smooth lines she longed for. By the time Serena arrived, she feared her foundation would already be gone. The humidity had been so intense and constant, it was suffocating. She yearned to ditch the Louisiana swamp for a cooler climate. Somewhere without Confederate flags and people who would vandalize her car and weather that made her makeup run.

One day, she thought as she inspected her eyeliner in the mirror. Not perfect, but decent enough.

"Serena's coming over," Raven said, loud enough for her mom to hear her from the kitchen.

"Okay, sweetie." She was already preparing food for everybody.

"Can I talk to you real quick?" her dad asked from the hallway.

"Sure." Raven came out of the bathroom to find him leaning against the wall. He was a towering man with a gentle soul. His eyes turned downward as he spoke.

"I heard Mrs. Garnier is leading the protest today. She knows about you and her daughter, and it pains me to repeat what she said."

"Don't tell me," Raven said.

"I just want you to know. That old bitch scares me, and her husband is a headcase. With her drumming up all that transphobic nonsense at Bible study, I wouldn't be surprised if it was one of them that tagged your car."

"I'll be sure to lay a curse on her then. I'll fuck her up."

Raven and her dad laughed.

"I'm sure you would," her dad said. "I just want you to stay safe. I know you love Serena, and me and your mom are here for you."

Her dad came in for a hug. Raven never had a doubt her parents would support her, so when she came out, it felt casual. Her love for her parents was unparalleled, and in soft moments like this, it made her cry. But it was euphoric to cry in her daddy's arms, where the entire world would melt away and she, for a moment, was immortal.

A knock sounded at the back door.

"I love you," Raven said.

"I love you too, hun."

"Now I gotta run to the bathroom and check my eyeliner because of you."

Her dad laughed heartily.

"Let me see." He held her head up and looked into her blue eyes. "Looks perfect." His smile warmed her heart.

"Thanks, Dad."

"Go get her," he said.

Raven had an extra bounce in her step, as if she was dancing to the kitchen in a ballet. Her black skirt spun around the corner, with her deep purple hair swaying in the air like Van Gogh's *Starry Night*.

Lamb kabobs with tzatziki sauce sat on the counter in the kitchen waiting to be eaten. And Serena stood at the door, beautiful with a thin long-sleeved white shirt and high-waisted denim shorts.

"Serena!"

Serena hugged her like the world was going to end. Her citrus perfume seemed to be laid on a little thicker than usual, but Raven liked the smell.

"How are you, love?" Raven asked.

"Good, now I'm with you."

"I'm happy you're here. Did your parents try dragging you to the protest?"

Serena hugged a little tighter, as if the question itself hurt.

"Yeah. And they didn't like that I wouldn't go." She laughed. "They said I'm grounded for a week. Then left me completely alone as if I couldn't just walk out."

"Idiots." Raven rubbed her back. "You okay?"

Serena gave Raven a kiss on the cheek, waited a moment, and then kissed her on the lips. Raven loved moments like these, when the world faded away and nothing mattered but her and Serena. Oftentimes, she was stressed about school and the town and her own body and her future, but when she was with Serena, she could finally live in the moment.

"We have lamb kabobs if you want some. I know it's one of your favorites, Serena," Raven's mom said. Serena would come in through the backdoor to avoid rumors from the neighbors, and Raven's mom always made some food for her. When she found out Serena loved Greek food, she was excited to cook more dishes. Tzatziki sauce was the drug her mom was addicted to.

"God, I would love some. You're amazing, Mrs. Williams." Serena took a lamb kabob and dipped it into the sauce, and with that, the meal was christened. Everybody could dig in. All talking ceased as they enjoyed the juicy meat.

"I got you a gift," Raven said after her food had settled.

"Wait. Me?" Serena asked.

"Yes. You," Raven said. "Who else?"

"I don't know. Your mom, maybe?"

"Oh she doesn't need to get me a gift," her mom said. "Her happiness is enough of a gift for me."

Raven rolled her eyes. "Why am I the only one in this family who isn't so corny?"

"I'm not corny," her dad said. "I'm just peachy."

"Oh my God. We're going to my room. I can't handle this anymore."

Her parents laughed, and so did Serena. Raven grabbed Serena's hand and started for her room.

"Thanks for the lamb," Serena called as she was pulled out of the kitchen.

The walls of Raven's room were midnight purple, and canvases hung on the wall from their time painting together. Raven's favorite was a sunset over a lake that Serena painted with red and blue hues.

"I love your parents," Serena said.

"I know. I love them too. I just can't handle the dad jokes at a certain point."

They embraced, and Raven forgot about everything in the kitchen, and even the anti-Raven protest at the school. All that existed anymore was Serena's hazel eyes, like wandering through a forest filled with trees and ferns and faeries. They kissed deeper and more passionately than before. Serena traced her hands down Raven's back to her thighs. Then she pulled back, and giggled.

"So, you got me a gift." Serena smiled slyly.

"Um, yeah. Yeah. I did." Raven struggled to gain her bearings.

"You're blushing," Serena said.

"Don't say that!" Raven covered her face. "It'll make me blush more."

"Oh, I know."

"Such a tease." Raven grabbed a small rectangular gift off her bed. It was wrapped in leftover birthday wrapping paper even though Serena's birthday was five months away.

"Happy Birthday to me," Serena said.

Raven laughed. "Girl, just shut up and open it."

Serena tore the wrapper and revealed a beautiful gold and black tarot card deck inside. Her jaw dropped. The gold shimmered like it was real, highlighted by white lines in the fine details of the artwork.

"It's so pretty," she said.

"I knew you'd love it."

"Thanks. I don't know what to say." She shuffled through the cards, looking at the different art.

"I love you," Raven said. They'd started saying that to each other a few weeks ago, and it still gave an electric jolt through her heart to say it.

"I love you, too," Serena jumped into Raven's arms and kissed her again.

They fell into bed and made out until they were sweaty and out of breath. Then they cuddled, Serena's head on Raven's chest, listening to her pounding heartbeat steady itself.

Raven scanned Serena's body. Fresh bruises sprinkled her arm. She long suspected Serena's dad beat her, but felt it was up to Serena to say something. Raven's stomach twisted, and she wanted to cry, but she held it in for Serena's sake.

A knock sounded at the door.

"Girls." Mrs. Williams cracked it open. She spoke in a low voice. "The protest's coming to the house. They're almost here."

"What?" Raven said, her temples pounding.

"Stay in your room, lock the windows, close the curtains, and keep out of sight," her mom said. "We'll take care of this." She shut the door firmly.

"Okay." Raven brushed Serena's brown hair, "Fuck. I can't wait for college," she said. "Get away from these cunts."

"Did you get an acceptance letter yet?" Serena had already received acceptance letters to NYU and PSU.

"Not yet. Denied by NYU though." Raven said. "What if I don't get into any of them?"

Serena thought for a moment. "We'll just apply to more."

"Yeah…" Raven sat next to Serena and hugged her. "It just feels, sometimes, like I have no future. Like I can't have a future. I have to move away from here. But what if this shit happens everywhere? What if I keep moving until there's nowhere left to go?"

"If that's the case," Serena said. "I'll be there with you every step."

The sounds of the protest started faint, like a blurred buzz coming from a PA system. The sounds were rhythmic like the drums of an old rock song, then more distinct. "Protect Our Girls!" a megaphone blurted, followed by "God Hates Pervs!" from the crowd.

Eyes closed and faces flushed, Raven and Serena kissed each other, like it would be the last time. As if the stars and the planets passed between their lips. Goddesses enshrined in eternity. The water-color, oil, and acrylic paintings all blended together around them. If they could get through this tonight, perhaps, together, they could get through forever.

Something clinked against the window, and Serena detached from the kiss in shock.

"What the fuck?" Raven asked.

Raven discretely pulled the curtain aside. The protest filled the street. A few signs read "NO to boys in girls restrooms" and "Save Our Children." Most signs said DEU 23:1, the Bible verse somebody tagged on Raven's car earlier that week. In the front was Serena's mom, Mrs. Garnier, with a megaphone, and next to her was Mr. Garnier. He wore camo and held a rifle pointed up. Several other men were strapped as well. Raven wondered what depraved minds would cosplay as the army because there was one trans girl at school.

Mrs. Garnier stepped forward. "This house is a place of devil worship and witchcraft!"

She's coming out hot, Raven thought.

"They have wrought upon our town degeneracy, perversion, and homosexuality! In Sodom and Gomorrah, God took no mercy on the souls of people like this! We are here to send you a message, James and Pamela Williams: Get your house in order. Your son is a pervert! He wears dresses, long hair, and exposes himself to girls in the bathroom. We will not tolerate this anymore, lest God bring His wrath upon the town!"

"For fuck's sake," Raven muttered. "Does she think she's the Pope or something?"

Serena stayed on Raven's bed, hugging her knees into her chest. "I'm sorry for her," she said.

"You don't need to be sorry," Raven said. "It's not your fault."

Something smacked the window again, and again. As Raven faced Serena, the glass shattered and a large rock thudded across the floor. Raven collapsed onto her hands and knees, forearm searing in pain. A glass shard stuck out of it, glimmering in the light.

Serena dove down to help. "You're bleeding."

"I know. Fuck." They scrambled into the corner of the room, and Raven worked on removing the shard. She feared it would gush blood like a geyser when she pulled it out, but the blood oozed slowly down her arm.

Raven's parents appeared in the doorway. "What happened?" her dad asked.

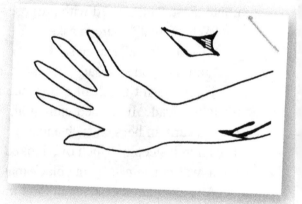

"The fuckers threw a rock through the window, and she got glass in her arm," Serena said.

"Jim, you need to say something to them. I'll get the first aid kit. I can't believe they came here."

"Hey!" Mr. Williams ran to the window. "This is private property, so you need to get off my land."

"OK, Groomer," Serena's mom retorted over the megaphone. The crowd laughed and another rock flew through the window.

"I'm calling the police," Mr. Williams said.

"I'm not coming to help you," Sheriff Frank Descartes said. The crowd laughed again.

In the distance, a looming darkness was fast moving and heading their way. It swirled like a school of fish, tumbling on top of itself, veering back and forth before adjusting toward the protest, always toward the protest, as if it could smell them.

Serena's hand squeezed hers. She had been crying, and Raven wanted to wipe those tears away, tell her everything would be okay, even though they both knew it would never be okay. Or, at least, their version of okay would be different than everyone else's.

An okay that would be perfectly adapted to sitting inside a burning building and remaining calm, always able to find each other, and survive.

Mrs. Williams poured antiseptic on Raven's wound. It stung like hell, making Raven cry out. Then she wrapped a bandage around her arm, working quickly, like a medic trying to get a soldier out of the line of fire.

"Does it feel better?" her mom asked.

"Do you see that?" Raven pointed out the window into the distance.

"See what?" Her mom looked up. The fog was closer now, and within the town limits. She now doubted it was a cloud. It was intentional. Fast. And moved with purpose.

"What's that?" Serena asked.

"It's not good," Raven said.

"Jim. Do you see that?" her mom asked.

There wasn't much of a distance now. It was around the block, ready to invade. It seemed unnatural. Not so much of a fog, but more like a swarm of bees on such a massive scale they could destroy a city. The church steeple, which overlooked Raven as the tallest building in town, was consumed by the black mass.

And then another scream. And another. Another. And they were becoming more rapid. The protestors outside finally turned to see the swarm absorbing their town. It was almost upon them. They froze for a second, before rising in a new uproar more chaotic than the protest before. Signs were tossed aside and families corralled their children to scatter in different directions.

"Everybody get inside," the sheriff shouted, barely audible among the commotion. Then he sprinted down the street, but his legs were unable to keep up. He skidded forward on the pavement, and the cloud neared his flailing body.

Raven couldn't help but smirk at his predicament. He was getting what he deserved. They all were.

Before one family reached their home, the swarm peppered their bodies in a million places, and they shrieked before being devoured completely into the darkness. It then crashed through the crowd like a tidal wave, their bodies drowning in its power. Deafening shrieks sucked all the oxygen from the air.

The sheriff scrambled back to his feet, but it was too late. His body was absorbed into the black void, his screams quickly choked out into a high pitched squeal. And then he was silent. They were all silent soon after their bodies were taken.

The Garniers dashed through the front lawn, and Mr. Garnier smashed the rest of the glass on the broken window. Raven wondered what made him feel welcome to come here, or perhaps in desperation, he didn't care. Mr. Garnier tumbled inside where his rifle skidded across the floor, and Raven thought for a moment that it might fire.

"Dad," Serena said. He took no notice of her. Instead, he reached his arm out to grab her mother.

"Jump up, Joan," he said. Her footing slipped and her head slammed into the brick beneath the window.

"Mom!" Serena jumped to her feet to help Mrs. Garnier.

"Serena. What are you doing here?" her mom asked. "I told you to stop hanging out with that tranny pervert!"

"I just wanna help you," Serena said, looking at the swarm crossing onto the front lawn. "There's no time."

Raven grabbed Mrs. Garnier's arm to pull her over the window.

"Get off me, you vile beast," she said, wrestling her arm out of Raven's grip. Mr. Garnier elbowed Raven in the face, causing her nose to go numb.

Serena extended her arm again.

"Mommy, please," Serena sobbed. "Let me help you." Raven never heard her beg like that, brought to the end of her wits by her own mother. Why couldn't the woman love her daughter? Love who her daughter was? Who her daughter loved?

Mrs. Garnier latched onto both Mr. Garnier and Serena. She cried out as her skin scraped against the cut glass on the window frame, causing her to back up.

Then she screamed. Bugs swarmed her. Sluglike, several inches long, slimy, jet-black. Wings beating fast like a dragonfly's. They squirmed into her hair. Latching to her skull.

Her eyes opened wide and the bugs bit deep into them, replacing them with black tails. They swarmed into her open mouth, filling it entirely until she gagged. Mrs. Garnier lurched forward and hurled. The vomit sprayed across the ground, a messy green filled with living wormlike creatures, flopping around like flies without wings.

"Hel—" she cut off again as more filled her mouth, and they coated her skin until she was a shadow of who she used to be. Then the shape collapsed to the dirt, and stopped moving, except for the bugs, wriggling with the joy of a newfound meal.

There was no time to think. No time for Serena to process losing her mom to a monstrous swarm. No time for Mr. Garnier to mourn the loss of his wife. They all ran for the door. The swarm cascaded in through the window like ocean waters pouring into a sinking ship.

"Get a towel," Mr. Williams shouted, and Mrs. Williams ran to the linen closet.

Bugs flew in beneath the door, first one or two, and then a small swarm. They latched onto Mr. Garnier's leg, and he stomped hard. Mrs. Williams skidded back and plugged the base of the door with a towel. Mr. Garnier tore them off his ankle and crushed them with his fist.

"Leeches." Mr. Garnier looked at them; his eyes were glazed over, and Raven wondered if he could see at all.

"Leeches don't fly," Mr. Williams said.

"These are blood sucking leeches if I've ever seen one," Mr. Garnier shook his head in disbelief. "How could this happen?"

"Raven." Serena's voice was soft and timid, her mouth quivered. It was as if she searched for words, but couldn't find them on her tongue. Raven hugged her, and they stood in the hallway together, too shocked to cry. She pulled Serena's head to her chest, like she had before all this happened and wondered if it could comfort Serena. Mrs. Garnier may have been the queen bitch of the town, but she was Serena's mom nonetheless.

It was quiet in the house, which made the noises outside even louder: the battering of their walls, new screams echoing. The town was sucked dry by a million tiny bites. It was a rough way to go, but at least it seemed quick. The only comfort to be had in the face of such tragedy.

They all sat for a long while in silence until the battering of the house went away. It was gone, as swift as a tornado storming through a town, leaving devastation in its wake, and disappearing forever. A freak weather event. Nothing more, and nothing less—the world taking its course.

Mr. Williams checked the peephole in the front door, then opened it. The crisp, refreshing air with a faint iron hint circulated into the home. The world was so full of color that it would be easy to mistake it for any other hot summer afternoon.

Corpses lay up and down the street. Their skin, peppered red, shrunk onto muscles and bones, as if vacuum-sealed. Leeches had sucked them dry.

Mr. Garnier rushed outside. "Joan," he cried out. "Joan, Joan, Joan, Joan." With each muttering of her name, he fell into sobs, crying over her body.

Raven was glad they were out of her sight; she pulled Serena in tighter. Serena didn't cry, or make any sounds, she only listened to Raven's heartbeat.

Mrs. Williams joined Raven's dad at the door and together they stepped outside to observe silently as Mr. Garnier descended into grief. Others throughout the town joined him as the silence officially broke. Cries bellowed into the air as if they were in Hell, begging for release from eternal torment.

Dean Garnier came storming back into the house and he slammed a Bible at Raven's feet. *No doubt a protest prop of Mrs. Garnier's,* Raven thought.

"Serena, get away from that boy."

Despite the massive protest in front of her house, despite them trying to pry her from Serena, despite…everything, Raven was still stunned to hear those words in this instant, after all those people died outside to an unexplainable phenomenon, including his own wife, Serena's mother. Raven snarled at him.

"It's your fault," he said.

"Dean," Mr. Williams said.

"*You.* You brought this upon us."

"What the fuck are you talking about?" Raven stepped forward.

"We harbored you here, degenerate filth, and God has punished us for this. He sent a plague to wipe us out. You're a Sodomite taking advantage of our hospitality."

Raven laughed. "Your 'hospitality'? Oh, I was really feeling the love from y'all."

"Dean, this has nothing to do with her." Mr. Williams put his arm on Mr. Garnier's shoulder, but the man wrestled out of his grip and turned to face him.

"It has everything to do with him. Don't you see?" Dean patted his shoulder, searching for something. He stomped past Raven and into the bedroom.

"Dean," Raven's father followed him. "You're not thinking right."

"Get out of my way."

"Not until you put that down. We need to talk this out."

"Honey, what's going on?" Mrs. Williams asked. She slowly crept closer, a renewed fear to her step.

Raven knew though. He had the gun and he wanted to kill her because he was batshit. She pulled Serena in close and hugged her. Serena rested her head on Raven's shoulder. It seemed to be all she could do at the moment. Holding Raven. The rest of her was lost somewhere deep inside her own head, hiding from the world.

"Now, Dean—"

His sentence was cut off by a loud blast. Blood splattered out of his back and speckled the wall behind him before his own body slid to the floor.

Raven's heart dropped and she nearly lost her balance beneath Serena's weight. It woke Serena from her trance and she looked into Raven's eyes. The hazel took a lighter hue than before.

"Jim!" Before Raven's mom reached her husband, Dean emerged from the room and smacked her in the head with the butt of his rifle. She collapsed hard to the ground.

Mr. Garnier aimed the rifle at her head and pulled the trigger. The back of her skull shattered across the floor like broken glass.

Raven didn't want to take her eyes off Serena and see the bodies of her parents. She couldn't remember them like that. Her knees weakened, but Serena kept her standing. Two of the three people Raven loved lay between her and Dean Garnier, and she couldn't allow Serena to join them.

But Serena had a will of her own. She stood in front of Raven and faced her father.

"Dad," Serena said.

"Don't make me shoot you too." His rifle was aimed at her chest.

"You've got to stop. Mom just died, and now…me?"

"I don't wanna kill you but I will if I have to."

"Raven has nothing to do with this."

"He killed your mother. He killed everyone. He summoned Satan and God needed to wipe us all out because of his sick perversions."

Dean Garnier stepped forward, and Raven was prepared to outrun his gun and flee with Serena to anywhere at all. Anywhere but this cursed town.

"No," Serena said. "It was a freak weather event. She didn't summon Satan."

"Flying leeches? It's impossible. It had to be God. He punished us. We…He…It's the fault of that boy you're with!"

"Please," Serena was crying now.

"My daughter will not take the side of groomer perverts."

Raven wrestled Serena into the living room just before Mr. Garnier fired his shot. It shattered a living room window, and outside the leech swarm appeared to be returning. They now had a way into the house.

Go home. Raven thought, unsure if she was asking Mr. Garnier to leave them alone, or calling for the leeches to scare him off on their way back to the swamp.

Serena dragged Raven into the pantry and they huddled together beneath the shelves. Raven prayed for the leeches to return, to fill the house top to bottom—outside the pantry. Already preparing, she removed her shirt. Pressing it at the base of the door, she sealed off the crack at the bottom.

Boots crunched against the floorboards.

He was in the kitchen, sniffing out his prey.

The handle to the pantry turned, but Serena grabbed the knob, holding it shut.

He let go.

The two girls took a breath of relief.

It was silent.

Raven stared at Serena's hand still on the door, losing herself in its ashen skin, goosebumps, hair raised, with a death grip on the doorknob. Would this be their grave? It certainly wouldn't be the worst to die side by side with your lover, surrounded by food, sacrificed to aid their bodies in their trip to the afterlife. It was a hero's burial. She just noticed her own arm was wrapped around Serena's waist, bonding them forever. She wondered if dying together made it easier to find each other in whatever comes after. Perhaps they would spawn at the same spot, or maybe their spirits would directly rise from their bodies, and they could hold hands entering the pearly gates of heaven, hell, or Valheim. Wherever they would be, they would be together.

That's all that mattered now.

A loud blast shook Raven from her trance. A bullet splintered through the wooden door, smacking Raven in the shoulder. She collapsed backward, with her head ringing from the impact. Serena pulled her in and cradled Raven in her lap.

The house trembled as the leeches stampeded in through the living room. The kitchen filled with their scratching against the walls. Another loud blast and another. No bullets came through the pantry. He was shooting at the leeches.

Then he laughed. His laughter boomed so loud, Raven heard it over the ringing in her ears. It maniacally bounced through different octaves and speeds unlike anything Raven had heard before. Then he became muffled and his body thudded against the ground and he was silent. Dead.

Raven wondered what would drive a man to laugh in a moment like this. But she didn't have time to think.

A leech was squeezing through the bullet hole, barely fitting. Its mouth opened, exposing a circle of sharp miniature teeth. Raven smooshed the leech, smearing blood against the wood. Another leech came through the hole and bit into her hand. In all the chaos, Raven

was amazed the bite was rather painless, like a finger pressing into the center of her palm. She pressed harder against the hole, the leech sucking her blood, and the door battered against its frame with leeches hammering the other side. The closet echoed the pounding, and exacerbated to a crescendo which rattled their brains.

"Please leave. Please leave. Please leave," Raven muttered.

Serena pressed herself against Raven, tears streaking her face, falling onto Raven's bloody shoulder. The pantry was the entire world now, and it was closing in. The cans of soup clattered upon the shelves. A box of spaghetti dropped next to Raven. She wondered if the walls would crumble. Raven leaned her head on Serena's and they both cried. They fought to be together, protected each other, and finally, it was the end. They had no words for the moment, just each other's touch and presence and love. Combined, they were a supernova preparing for destruction, shining brightest in the dark abyss.

The noises stopped. It was as quick as the snap of a finger, a tornado passed fully through leaving in its wake devastation and peace.

Raven lifted her hand off the hole. The leech was gone, leaving a round wound behind, which had a little bit of blood trickling out. She looked at Serena, their eyes wide with shock. Somehow, they survived.

Within the blood and their embrace, neither of them wanted to move. Perhaps, if they sat for long enough, Raven's parents would come greet them with another meal they might all enjoy together. Leaving the pantry would only acknowledge the devastation to their town, their families, and their lives. But the gun wound was very real, and the pain snuck up on Raven until it overwhelmed her. She clenched tighter to Serena as she started to cry.

"It hurts," Raven said.

Serena looked down at her, the words stirring her from a trance state. "We need to get you to the hospital."

"Okay." Raven wasn't sure what she said okay to: a trip to the hospital for her wounds, or leaving the pantry at all.

Serena lifted Raven to her feet, and Raven bit her tongue as her shoulder seared in pain.

"Here. Let me help you." Serena lifted Raven's arm around her shoulder, keeping her upright as they re-entered the world.

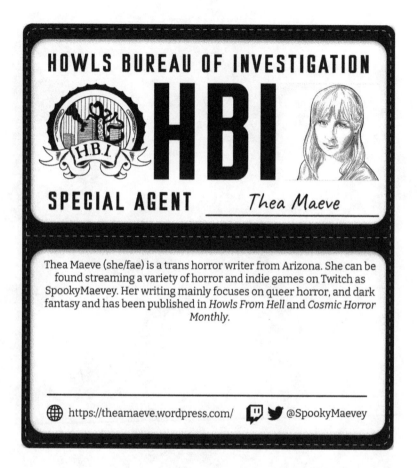

HOWLS BUREAU OF INVESTIGATION

HBI

SPECIAL AGENT — *Thea Maeve*

Thea Maeve (she/fae) is a trans horror writer from Arizona. She can be found streaming a variety of horror and indie games on Twitch as SpookyMaevey. Her writing mainly focuses on queer horror, and dark fantasy and has been published in *Howls From Hell* and *Cosmic Horror Monthly*.

https://theamaeve.wordpress.com/ @SpookyMaevey

MEMO: Evidentiary imagery provided by Christi Nogle. Agent headshot provided by Maia Weir.

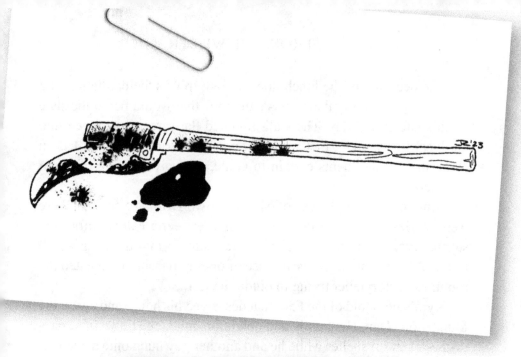

A TORNADO OR SOMETHING LIKE IT
by C.B. Jones

A toddler ripped from the arms of her mother…

Atmospheric winds so strong they tore the hide right off a herd of cattle, skinning them alive…

And a family of five killed in the place they were told to shelter all along—the cellar, where the tornado created such a vacuum their lungs were sucked right out of their mouths…

Kyra recalled these anecdotes and more on her drive home, the drive that was taking her toward a horizon full of dark clouds congregating into a massive wall. It was like the whole world was being covered by the domed lid of a silver serving platter, the edge about to meet the earth. There was a green tint to the air, the landscape now a photograph developed all wrong.

Earlier, during lunch, her coworkers had gathered around the dingy, windowless break room and regaled each other with tales of their own tornadic experiences. This is where she heard about the cows, the family in the cellar. Everyone knew the story about the mother, from a legendary tornado that had struck over a decade ago.

The occasion of the lunchtime story swap was the prediction of a PDS—a "particularly dangerous situation" that would befall the state on this late spring day. The wall-mounted flat screen was tuned into the local news, and a meteorologist waved his arms and prattled on about the developments certain to come, a carnival barker of doom and gloom.

Amongst the employees of Miller-Brown Drilling Services, there were stories of close calls and near misses, eerie calms before the storms, twisters seen from afar, a truck thrown into a tree. Like all roundtable bullshit sessions, a sense of one-upmanship permeated the room, each storyteller trying to outdo the last.

Kyra's boss told of the F5er that destroyed his house and swept the foundation clean. His family and neighbors hunkered down in a state-of-the-art storm shelter while he and another guy hung onto a chain as the cellar door rattled in its frame, the monstrous storm threatening to break in with its almighty strength.

Not to be outdone by the boss, Colt Harris, the Venture Pipeline Supply sales rep, told the story about the cattle. He said it was a thing that definitely had happened down in Texas. Had heard about it on the news.

"What about you, Kyra?" her boss asked. Kyra had been content to just sit back and quietly listen, but her boss was always trying to get her to come out of her shell. "Any 'nader run-ins?"

Kyra didn't have much to offer. In her twenty-seven years of living in tornado alley, she had been fortunate. She had never seen a tornado, even from afar. The most inclement weather she had ever experienced was a thunderstorm with strong winds and golf ball-sized hail; a few large branches scattered around the yard, the hood of her ancient Camry now with the texture of dimpled cellulite.

But she was recently acquainted with other types of storms. Maybe she could tell the break room about the tornado that had wrecked her life in the past month. The collision of circumstances that left a trail of broken pieces a mile wide: a cheating boyfriend, a layoff, and a cat gone missing. The turmoil of it all sent her fleeing for shelter. She had moved back in with her mom, whose boyfriend had connections for an office job at a drilling company down in the rural town of Suttonville.

Yeah, you might say I know a thing or two about being hit by a tornado, Kyra thought. *Or something like it.*

Instead, she simply said, "Not really. Been lucky, I guess."

Folks seeped out of the breakroom, and soon it was just Colt and Kyra. On the TV, the meteorologist pointed to a weather map. There was a line of splotchy yellow-and-red blobs stretching the length of the state.

"It's gonna be a bad day," said Colt, pointing at the screen.

"You can tell from all that?" Kyra asked, looking at the paint splatters of the Doppler radar projected on screen.

"Not the weather map. The tie. He's wearing the red one. That's how you can tell. When he's wearing that bad boy, shit's gonna get real."

"Maybe they'll let us go home early," Kyra said, picking at her leftover pad thai. A nervous feeling boiled in her guts, evaporating her appetite.

"Hope he does. I've done canceled all my calls after three. Don't you got a ways to drive home? If you want, you could come over 'til it passes. I've got beer and lawn chairs. Can show you how we handle tornadoes out in the country."

Kyra smiled, could only say, "Maybe," to this offer. Sure, it sounded kind of fun, and his affable personality usually put her at ease. But such overtures always made her anxious, always caught her off guard. She'd talked to this guy, like three times, maybe? If that. It made her nervous just thinking about it

"I'll text you my number in case you get in a bind. What's yours?" Colt said.

On the surface, he wasn't really her type. A little too much of a redneck vibe going on. She had grown up in a town not far from here, where guys like this were a dime a dozen. They had never really done much for her.

What could it hurt, though? He had a teddy bear-like quality to him, burly and thick-forearmed, a straight-tooth grin that cut through a lush, red-brown beard. Might be easier to get to know him through texts. For her, it was always easier to communicate that way, especially in the beginning. She gave him her number.

HOWLS FROM THE WRECKAGE

But now she was driving north, the wind was picking up, and fat raindrops pelted her windshield. She was beginning to regret not taking Colt up on his offer. She thought of calling him.

Perhaps it wasn't too late to turn back around?

But no, the town where she worked was miles behind her and the storm itself seemed to be wrapping around her current position. Nothing to do now but persevere.

Some morbid part of her wondered if this might be the day she would actually witness a tornado, live and in real time. From a safe distance of course. Hadn't she heard that the max land speed a tornado could travel was something like forty-five miles per hour? She could easily outrun that in her car.

Kyra scanned through her radio presets, each one preempted with storm coverage from local news stations.

Nate Hopper (Stay Alive with Channel 5!) was frantic, as he was apt to be. While he rambled on at high speed, Kyra tried to gather relevant facts and details. With a storm system so large, the coverage was jumping all over the place. Suburbs north of the city. Towns and rural communities she had never heard of. The goddamn panhandle.

"Let's go now to just south of Suttonville," Nate said over the airwaves. "This system is picking up energy down here, folks. You're gonna want to keep an eye on it. We've already got reports of hurricane strength winds rolling in. Power outages and damage to some buildings. Cam, you're there on the ground. Tell me what you see."

Kyra topped the hill overlooking Suttonville, craned her neck to look back. A huge portion of the town was covered in a massive shroud of conglomerated clouds, yet another section was completely untouched. The delineation was striking.

"Nate, we've got a pretty massive wall cloud down here, and I'm starting to see some significant rotation. Still seeing quite a bit of vehicles out and about on the roads, too."

Kyra changed stations and got a different meteorologist, this one covering a bedroom community north of the metro. She'd have to flip back to panicky Nate Hopper, the anxiety in his voice giving rise to even more anxiety within her chest.

178

"Folks if you're out there, if you're thinking about stepping out to drive anywhere, you need to let this thing pass. This system could drop at any minute," Nate said.

What Kyra was driving toward was bad, but what was behind her was worse.

The rain turned torrential. A constant din of raindrops pummeled the windshield while her wipers made futile swipes against the onslaught of water.

A cop car rolled by with its lights flashing.

She thought of pulling over, letting the storm pass. But that seemed like a worse option. For one, a stationary car was the worst place to be. The tornado could throw a vehicle with ease. She'd be a sitting duck.

She had always been told if it came down to it, you could lie facedown in a ditch and the tornado would move over you. It wasn't smart enough to go down into ravines or depressions. That's how basements and cellars worked.

Nothing about that seemed appealing. Besides, the ditches were filled with rainwater, miniature rivers of Coke float-colored water rushing past.

The winds picked up. A white plastic bag flew past the road like a seagull. A small branch followed. Thin trees bent over, their tops trying to touch the ground. Her phone buzzed, and she saw there were several missed calls and texts. All from her mom.

Are you headed home??

A loose cow tromped down the road.

Be careful.

She passed a white sedan in a ditch, hazard lights blinking. No driver.

Looks bad.

179

The racket of the raindrops intensified and she realized she was being peppered with pea-sized hail.

Call soon.

Kyra's phone drifted in and out of service. She couldn't get a call out.

"Wait a sec, wait a sec. Let's go over to Greer, up by Highway 76. This is…this is something else, folks. A completely unprecedented situation. We knew today was gonna be a major day, but this is different. Zoom in over here. By my radar, we've got rotation. This is gonna get ugly. If you are in this area you *need* to get underground."

Greer and Highway 76. That was the section she drove through every day on her commute home. The wall clouds were closing in.

There was a good road coming up though. She could cut the storms off. Go around them. It was a sensible option. She'd only have to drive through more pummeling rain and heavy thunderstorms.

Her phone buzzed. A momentary signal. She looked down. A text from Colt. A photograph from his point of view: pair of boots propped up on a wire spool, can of Michelob Ultra posed just so in the frame, mountainous thunderheads towering in the background.

That could've been her sitting beside him. Safe and sound. No other obligation except work acquaintances.

Goddammit, why hadn't she just waited before going home?

Kyra made the next right. She was going to drive around this motherfucker.

"Tornado on the ground! Tornado on the ground!" screamed the broadcast. "Suttonville, this thing is headed your way."

"Where?" Kyra said through clenched teeth.

She pushed hard on the gas. Passed a farmhouse, a grain silo, a barn. A small church. That did it. Next place she saw, she was going to bang on a cellar door and beg for shelter.

I love you. Please be careful

Please call and let me know you're ok.

The car accelerated through the driving rain. Standing water on the road. A loss of control, a sudden rush of feeling like she was floating. The world through her windshield turned and spun. The car ignored the tugging of the steering wheel and it all happened so fast.

Head jarred and teeth rattled, the car came to rest in a ditch. She screamed in fear and frustration and pressed on the gas. Yanked every which way on the steering wheel. Pounded the horn, a desperate call for help to no one.

And suddenly: an eerie calm. A decrease in rain. Silence on the radio.

From the speakers, a heart-stopping sound blared out, the sound of an alarm clock mated with a dial-up modem. This was followed by a sound like a dial tone. A robotic voice began to speak.

"The National Weather Service has issued a tornado warning for the following counties…"

Kyra stepped out of the car, ankles sloshing in water. Behind her, the reason for the alarm. It didn't even look like it was moving. Just

a vast, static pillar stretching toward the heavens. Awe-inducing in its size, she couldn't help but stand motionless before it. Transformer pops flashed electric blue at the base of the gargantuan, churning mass.

Fuck this.

She ran down the road in the opposite direction. In the distance and off to her right in the middle of a small clearing stood a house. It was dilapidated and abandoned with a roof half-caved in. Chunks of siding were missing, and animal burrows formed underneath the crawl space. A pair of eyes peered at her from that space. A black cat with its head ducked low.

The house wouldn't be much for shelter, but what if a cellar existed here, before?

Down a short gravel turnoff and across a cattle guard, she got a closer look.

Jackpot.

A concrete pad jutted from the dirt with a rusty metal vent pipe sticking out. She could see a metal door.

The menacing blackness of the tornado was closer now, blotting out everything behind it, filling that entire side of the world. Its roar was the sound of a freight train full of the faint howls of forgotten ghosts.

With exertion, the cellar door creaked open.

Like opening a crypt. Fitting.

Your final resting place.

Shut up.

The smell of damp earth and mildew filled her nostrils. The air inside was warmer than expected, and it wrapped itself around her in a comforting embrace. One part sauna, the other part stale fridge.

But there was something altogether unexpected.

She had expected to need to use her cell phone for illumination, but inside, the cellar wasn't dark. She could easily make out all the details visible within the front entrance.

A row of ancient farming implements. Smudged mason jars. An old can of paint. The edges of an aluminum utility shelf on which a lit candle sat and flickered, casting dancing shadows about the room.

Somebody was already here.

"Hello?" she called out.

And on the walls she saw the grinning faces. The empty eye sockets. Serpentine tails dangled from matted gray fur. A string of dead possums in various states of decay, hung up like paper lanterns.

Kyra wanted to turn and run. This was wrong. *Very* wrong.

The candle's faint glow left the rear of the cellar spared of light. Only pitch blackness back there. How deep did it go?

What about the stuff on the cement cellar floor? The overturned extinguished candles. The scrawled arcane symbols (was that a pentagram?). The oily stain.

Still, the tornado came, a landlocked maelstrom devouring everything in its path. There was no other option. Kyra descended the cellar steps.

She sat on the bottom step, pulled the cellar door shut with the attached chain. The freight train noise of the tornado was dampened by the closed door, and Kyra's heavy breath and thundering heart filled her ears.

Not much longer, she thought. *This will be one to tell around the break room.*

Kyra's breathing slowed and she gripped her phone. Still no signal. She thought of turning on its flashlight and illuminating the dark, damp corners of the room, but just couldn't. Ignorance was bliss.

With her breathing slowed and her heart no longer pounding in her ears, Kyra could hear something within the room.

A steady heavy breathing.

Sonorous wheezes.

Rhythmic, wet crackling.

Faint grunts from the blackness.

Something *was* here.

Something ritualistic. Something summoned.

A shuddering cry caught in Kyra's throat and her bladder spasmed while she huddled down on the bottom step. She tried not to whimper too loudly, covered her mouth with her hand.

By her ankles, the rusty chain slithered past. The door was being sucked open. Kyra grabbed the chain with all her might, wrapped it around her hand and leaned forward with her back to the door. The steel door clattered in its frame while the storm outside jerked again and again, the forceful winds hungry to come in.

As if Kyra could ever outpower a tornado. The best thing would be to get to the very back of the cellar, but there was no way in hell she'd go back into the dark with that thing. So, she clung to the chain with all her might, felt it squeeze her fingers with bone-cracking force.

The breathing of the thing was louder now. She could just imagine the shape of it in the dark back there. Standing. Waiting.

Kyra prayed for the first time since she was a child, begging to whomever was pulling the strings on this goddamn chaotic world to please show her some mercy.

But whatever was listening only mocked her with a voice like her own.

"Please. Please. Help. Help me."

The awful tornado sucked the words right out of Kyra's mouth and spit them back at her, pounded at the door with frantic purpose.

The freight train sound had morphed into the roar of a jet engine and the storm now tugged at the door with a new frenzy. More debris pummeled the outside. Barometric pressure shifting, the air in the cellar turned weightless and the light of the candle snuffed out, and Kyra's screams joined the cacophony and the storm screamed back.

"Stop! Stop! Stop!" Kyra sobbed, both to the storm and the creature inside.

And suddenly, it did.

The chaos and noise was followed by that same eerie silence that had preceded it.

The thing in the back of the cellar howled. A creature of some sorts. Perhaps a rabid possum leftover from whatever sick ritual that had occurred here the night before.

Perhaps something worse.

Kyra felt in the dark for the shaft of one of the farm tools. There had been several with rusty blades and the fingers of her good hand felt the rough splintered wood of a handle.

"Who's there?" she called, her voice a shaky rasp.

She swung the tool blindly in an arc parallel to the ground, striking only the aluminum shelving against the wall. Taking a few steps forward, she raised the tool above her head and brought it down. It struck something soft and then clattery, and the wailing noise grew louder and higher pitched until it was familiar to Kyra's pressure-dulled ears and somehow everything clicked and suddenly she knew what it was.

With the tornado now passed, she burst through the cellar door and into the now-bright daylight, running and running and never looking back.

Before

"It ain't much, but it'll help you get back on your feet," Bill said, watching Alice survey the empty mobile home.

She opened cabinets, looked in the fridge, traced a finger along windowsills. Baby Eli crawled along the freshly laid carpet and cooed. She turned to her Uncle Bill, the overall-clad teddy bear of a man, and smiled. "It's perfect." She couldn't keep the tears from coming.

"Now don't start, you'll get me going," he said, wiping the corner of his eye and clearing his throat. "What else was I gonna do with it? Never got no rent from that damn ol' Jim Felty. Shoulda known better. He left this behind and while the inside was in piss-poor shape, I had to recoup my costs somehow."

Alice hoisted Eli up on her hip. "Well you've done a good job. It's like new."

"And I know that being a woman out here in the sticks all by yourself might be a bit scary, but back here in the trees, nobody'll even know you're there. Can't even see it from the road. They see that abandoned house and think that's all there is. Might not hurt to get a dog or something. I know you're a cat person."

"We'll see. Smoky's pretty protective."

"Oh, one thing you might worry about, with storm season coming up and this being a single-wide and all. There's a storm cellar up by that old house. It ain't much and I caught some kids messing around in there last Halloween, but if worse comes to worse you can go down there and ride out the storm."

Riding out the storm. Alice felt like that's what she'd been doing the past year. An abusive and absent ex and a difficult pregnancy and no child support and no job and doing it all on her own. It certainly felt like her life had already been hit by a tornado. Or something like it.

Alice had resisted going into the cellar as long as she could. After a bout with croup and many restless nights, Eli was finally resting comfortably in his car seat. No need to go down in that dank place just yet. All she would have to do is grab him by the handle of the seat, and make the short jaunt to the cellar. With her other hand, she would carry Smoky, who was already tucked away in his cat carrier, tensed up and hissing. She'd look like a traveler with too many carry-ons trying to make her flight in time.

Weeks prior, Alice had done a cursory check of the cellar. It wasn't actually that bad. No snakes. Only a few spiders and cave crickets. There were already candles inside. Some kids had used it for a makeshift horror movie set or something: a chalk drawing of an inaccurate pentagram on the floor and strung-up rubber roadkill. After the initial shock, she'd had to laugh. Seemed like something she and her friends would've done back in high school. She remembered a time when they had staged true crime scenes, taking pictures of them with Polaroids.

Uncle Bill had called earlier that day, telling her to "be sure and watch the weather." He was out on a fishing trip in Colorado, asked her to swing by and check the cows when it was all over.

On the news, they had warned how today was something called a "particularly dangerous situation." Now, the weatherman on the radio had gotten more frantic, his warnings more dire. A tornado had formed down south in Suttonville and headed to her location in about twelve minutes.

Alice sighed. Time to go.

Outside, the atmosphere was striking. A greenish darkness settling down over it all. Carrying her precious cargo was more difficult than expected. Her shoulders and arms grew heavy and trembled.

Halfway to the cellar, disaster struck. The latch of the pet-carrier gave way, the top opening like a clamshell.

Smoky tumbled out onto the grass, paused for the briefest of instants, as if considering Alice's pleas to "Stay!" After weighing his options, he darted away, a black blur. Back toward the trailer.

This was fine. She still had time. Leaving the door open, Alice carried Eli down into the cellar and set him at the foot of the stairs. She lit a candle and set it on an aluminum shelf. Aside from the edgy wannabe Satanic stuff, the place looked cozy.

She managed to get a text out to Uncle Bill:

In cellar with Eli. Getting Smoky.

Alice hoisted Eli's car seat and carried it to the back of the room. There was a concrete ledge back there that served as a bench. The perfect place to set a baby carrier. He'd be safe and sound while she went to go get that damned cat. Propping the cellar door open a crack with a brick, she set off.

If she didn't find him in five minutes, she'd just have to come back.

Smoky would probably be fine regardless.

Somehow animals always knew what to do.

HOWLS BUREAU OF INVESTIGATION

HBI

SPECIAL AGENT   *C.B. Jones*

C.B. Jones is an author from somewhere in the middle of America. His work has appeared on *The NoSleep Podcast*, *Cosmic Horror Monthly*, and the medieval horror anthology *Howls From the Dark Ages*. His debut novel, *The Rules of the Road* was released in 2021. He has never seen a tornado.

🌐 www.therulesoftheroad.net   🐦 @writersjones

MEMO: Evidentiary imagery provided by Joe Radkins. Agent headshot provided by Leah Gharbaharan.

A THING OF HABIT
by Cassandra Khaw

He had been waiting for the world to break. *Hers*, specifically. He knew it was coming, the telemetries of social media such that he could see how the floor beneath her was shifting, the seismic implications of her multiplying calamities. Momentum was a thing that grew like water, or love. If only she'd been cognizant of that. He would have saved her from her car crash of a life.

Wanted to still.

Because unlike her, he believed in fidelity to his promises.

Less so, fidelity to his wife. What a tedious thing she was, rinsed-out by the years, charmless: dishwater congealed into a person. Had he been a bad man, he'd have abandoned her. But he wasn't. He had promised her Da he would shelter her, keep her safe, fed, plump and content. For all that he disdained the woman, she did yield him two sons, and they were as bright as she was dull. An heir wasn't nothing. Two could even be construed as something. And he would honour that, if not his wife herself, on account of the fact he prided himself a decent man, a good man.

He found her—his wife never looked in on him when he was in his office, giving him copious time to search—hospital with ease, like he'd done this a thousand times prior, tracing her movements like the curve of her knuckles. He'd cautioned her too: to be careful with the photos she put online, to strip them of billboards and shop fronts, anything the enterprising could use to augur a location. He'd *told* her. Yet there she was, trussed-up in bandages like a sacrificial hog, providing clear direction to where she lay invalid.

He ran his hand over his wispy thatching of blonde—it seemed luminous now in his dotage, an angel's halo of flyaway strands, nearly white in the wrong light—hair, and thought hard about what he would wear: if a suit would be more apt, if he should come in houndstooth, or perhaps, he would arrive in tweed with a drift of cigar smoke clinging to his hems. Appearances mattered, after all.

It'd been years since the two of them spoke, longer since they'd met and though he had seen so very many photos of her, every one of them possessed a staged quality he disdained, a glossiness he knew was absent in her daily life. In person, she was messier, more a puppy than a woman, in need of a leash and a hand at her collar: holding her, guiding her, bettering her.

He stood then, pushing away from his cluttered desk, possessed by a sudden itching urgency. Though it seemed unlikely she would be discharged from the hospital any time soon, tragedy was magnetic. Others would come. Old lovers, new flings. What friends she might have accreted. He couldn't imagine there being too many of the last, given the rot of her. But still, who knew? And either way, he would not risk it. Easier to go now before she was buried in visitors, easier this way to ensure she wouldn't be distracted.

The night nurse raised her head as a man approached her counter, the sound of his footsteps as steady and decorous as a sleeping heart. He was, as men went, unremarkable. Tall, but not notably such. Narrow at the shoulders but broad at the hip, with long arms and a soft chin that sagged into a wattled throat. Nonetheless, there was something professorial to him, in his stance and his expression; something sweet about the bouquet of wildflowers he clutched in one gloved hand.

"Name?"

"Sebastian Samuel."

The alliteration pleased the nurse, as did the man's voice and its docile accent. "Who are you here to see?"

The way he said the patient's name pricked at her. He spoke it with a lover's intonation and, looking the man over again, the nurse decided he was much too old for the patient. Unease crawled through her. Yes, there was something wrong here.

"What's your relation to her?"

The man smiled. Seconds ago, she would have called it a pleasant smile, a kindly one: warm and practised. Now, she saw it as a dollar-store veneer, picked up cheap by a man with even poorer intentions.

"We're friends."

She nodded, assessing him with greater care. The leather coat he wore was ill-fitting, billowy enough to hide any manner of sins. "Friends? How'd you meet?"

He cocked his head.

"We were in university together, she and I," The man gave an embarrassed laugh. "She was in her first year, and I was exploring the possibility of restarting my life. I know it's usually the other way around: the older man serving as the mentor, but she was the one who led me along this new life—"

His words were white noise. She watched his face instead, studied his mouth, his eyes and she was twenty-five again, listening to an old boyfriend tell a different story about why her cheekbone had a comb of bruises. How tender he'd been and how tender this man was as they invented their improvements on the truth. How sure their voices. How still their eyes, like the moment after a crash, when the body is still bargaining to stay more than meat.

The nurse readied herself to alert security, only to be interrupted by a bloom of pain behind her right eye, spreading as she forced herself to speak.

"You're not on my—"

Her tongue, heavy, refused the rest of the sentence. She felt his hand on the knob of her wrist. "It's alright. She knows me."

The agony spread until her vision went oily with migraine auras. Still, the nurse tried to rally, tried to find words, convinced even in her suffering that this was not a responsibility she could shirk, not unless she wanted blood on her hands.

"It's alright," he said again. "You can let me through."

Let him through, came another voice in parallel, like a cool hand on a fevered brow: a woman's voice, soft and almost motherly. The man the nurse would have fought until he choked the life from her. But this second voice, with its soporific calm, she could only drown in.

"He's going to hurt her," the nurse whispered hoarsely, a statement that knitted the man's brows together before he shook his head, patting her hand with more vigour.

"That's what she tells people," he said in a pained tone. "I don't understand why, honestly. I have never hurt her, and I promise I won't begin now."

In reply, the nurse did nothing but whimper and sank her head down onto the tangle of her arms, where she moaned heartbrokenly to herself. The man waited until it became clear she was too preoccupied for further conversation before he departed, whistling softly, the wildflowers set down beside the nurse as if in condolence.

She was not where he thought she would be, which did not surprise him somehow although he was naggingly certain it should have. Her bed was empty save for a jumble of blankets. The bedside dresser held none of her valuables, and while the adjacent machines were still on, they were wiped clean of any records of her vitals.

It was a taunt, he decided. Her being recalcitrant again. Rebelling for the pleasure of being infuriating, an overgrown child arguing at the prospect of a bedtime. Had he been a different man, less kind, he might have lost his temper. But he had made a long study of her uneven

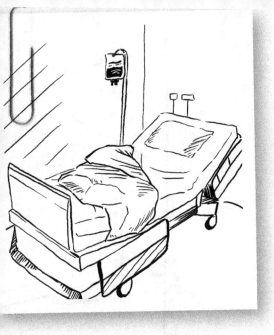

temperament. No doubt this was her needing someone else to vilify, someone to paint as adversary so she could justify the events leading to the accident.

And honestly, better he be victimised in such a fashion than have her illusions broken. He understood his role in her life even if she was oblivious to her own responsibilities towards him. He was older, after all. The mature one. If he didn't lead by example, by stately grace, how was she to model her behaviour on him?

He breathed in the antiseptic air, the sharpness of it and—

Blood.

He could smell blood.

Upon registering the scent, he realised he could see it, too, a mottling of red along the linoleum, thickening at the doorway into a spray and then a trail wending into the corridor outside. It was red still, warm where he ran his fingers through the slickness. Recent.

Fear squeezed his heart. What had happened? He followed the blood to the hallway and there, the walls were soaked through. How had he not seen it then? Why hadn't anyone else taken notice?

A part of him wondered if he should alert the hospital staff, but the lateness of the hour and the eccentric nature of his arrival made him decide otherwise. Authorities would only complicate things, and if she was hurt, he would not be delayed by bureaucracy. If she was in need, he would not be slowed. He would go to her, as he'd promised he would. Loyal to the last of her days.

So, down he went through the hospital, plunging between hallways. The blood led him through a maze of stairs, past rooms heaped with sleeping patients and nurses in their respirators. No one stopped him, no one commented on how he barreled through the corridors, perhaps sympathetic to the urgency in his pace and the panic in his expression. Lower still he went, the windows wicking to concrete walls, and there was a smell now of clean dirt and cold water, and his footsteps rang as if on steel. The light dwindled to a spluttering glow, shed by a row of naked bulbs.

Here, sang a voice in his head as he arrived at another corridor, wheezing from his exertions, his breath pluming through the air. At the end of the passageway stood a single door, slightly ajar. Light knifed out from the gap, a pale blue like an old woman's eye.

Here, said the voice again.

Here, it repeated, with increasing eagerness, matching each of his forward steps, cajoling him onwards, quickening as he did. Until meaning dissolved into droning compulsion, and he couldn't separate the sound from the hiss of his breath, or the roar of his heart. The door singed his fingertips as he closed them over the metal, so cold it was, but he barely noticed, mesmerised by what he saw within.

It was her.

After all these years, they were in the same room again. He had pictured a better venue for their reunion: a low-lit bar paved in dark wood, a table in a Parisian cafe, a place under a shawl of gold stars. Instead, they had this morgue, with its halogen lights and its steel lockers, the air smelling of freon. She sat in what he came to realise was a pentagram of a kind, filigreed on every side with symbols he did not recognize.

"Are you going to apologise?" she said, both arms gloved in red.

"For what?"

She cocked her head. "The accident."

"Why would I apologise for the accident? I had nothing to do with it." An itch began under his scalp.

"You had everything to do with it," she said, her eyes and hair both as dark as he recalled: a moonless black against the golden skin. The hospital gown made her seem so small, and he wanted nothing more than to blanket her in his arms, protect her against that chill. "You don't remember?"

He shook his head. The itch spread down his neck, the nape and his shoulders pebbling. "I don't know what you're talking about."

"You made sure I was in the right place at the wrong time," she said, uncrossing her thin legs. "Well, that's being too generous, I think. What you did wasn't really an act of precision. You made sure everyone there would die—just in case there was a small tiny chance I'd escape that mess of steel and bodies."

"I would die for you," he said with more fervence he thought he could master, shocking himself. He'd been convinced the years had withered any capacity for passion, but here he was, struck by an adolescent zeal, full of fire again. "I promised you that, didn't I? I would do anything for you."

"You killed so many people. Do you even know how many?"

"I missed you so much."

"I don't even know who you *are*. We shared one class."

"For a *year*."

"You know," she said as though he had never spoken, and he hadn't flayed his heart open for her, laid his vulnerabilities down for her like an oblation, a tribute. "While there is power in death, there is just as much power in its proximity. Those hours when you're struggling to survive, when no one's sure if you'll pull through. If you know how, you can use it to call Death, to offer it someone else."

She traced a circle through the air with a finger, and he felt under his skull the hum of a bone-saw. It went right under the bone, drilling through the meninges. He wanted badly to undo the top of his head so he could scratch, run nails along tissue, dig into brain matter. Anything to stop the itching.

"And when it saw I had you to offer, it said yes so quickly, I basically cannonballed back into life."

"What?"

"You can make a ghost of anything," she said, her features seeming to flatten. "Especially when they're halfway there already."

"I wish you would stop talking in riddles," he chuckled hazily. "I have the beginnings of such a headache, and it would be nice to have a little quiet."

"It's about to get worse, I'm afraid."

She said what he was sure was his name, except it was also a crack of bone, a *pop* of something coming loose, and he reached up to pat his skull, was relieved to find that his skull had indeed uncorked enough that he could pry it open like a lid. He reached inside (what was he doing?), was comforted by the heat wafting up into his palm (stop) and the oily warmth of his own brain (this wasn't right). The itch had tunnelled down, deep down, into the wadded-up folds. He scooped at the lobe with his nails, was rewarded then by a burst of clarity. *How many times has he been here before?*

"You wouldn't let me go. I won't let you go either."

He drew a breath, ready to argue, but his hand found a branch of gristle, and he was pulling before he knew what he's doing, tugging, until his vision became an oil-spill of images, whiting out at the rim, and he saw his desk again, cluttered and threaded with spiderwebs, and—

HOWLS BUREAU OF INVESTIGATION

HBI

SPECIAL AGENT · *Cassandra Khaw*

Cassandra Khaw (they/them) is an award-winning game writer and former scriptwriter at Ubisoft Montreal. Khaw's work can be found in places like *The Magazine of Fantasy & Science Fiction, Lightspeed,* and *Tor.com*. Khaw's first original novella, *Hammers on Bone*, was a British Fantasy Award and Locus Award finalist, and their recent novella *Nothing But Blackened Teeth* was a *USA Today* bestseller, Bram Stoker Award nominee, and Indie Next Pick.

casskhaw.carrd.co · @casskhaw

MEMO: Evidentiary imagery provided by Leah Gharbaharan. Agent headshot provided by Molly Halstead.

* BLOOD SPLATTER ANALYSIS
BD-1149R

UNZIPPED
by Bridget D. Brave

Mia woke to pitch black nothing.

She couldn't feel her arms.

I've broken my back.

Panic set in.

Calm down, dumbass. Take two seconds and evaluate the situation. Feel that god-awful pain in your left leg? Mia's breathing slowed. Her leg *did* feel like it was full of broken glass. *You broke your knee, dipwad. If you were paralyzed, you wouldn't be able to feel that shit.* Mia grimaced and tried to stretch her shoulders forward to determine how badly her arms were hurt. She received only painful prickles of pins and needles shooting from her biceps to her wrists. They were numb, but still there.

Her head felt woozy, throbbing pain dully announcing itself at the base of her skull. She winced and gingerly turned her head from one side to the other in an attempt to orient herself.

She'd been at the South Zipper pass, the widest of the three narrow necks that led into Giant's Room Cavern. Mia remembered an unexpected depression in the stone tunnel where her foot slipped and... something happened.

Her strongest memory was of the low rumble as she'd reached the passage entrance, loud as thunder or a car crash. Then there was a hazy recollection of the rocky earth beneath her undulating, then cracking her jaw against the lip of the opening. Mia could still taste the tang of blood in her mouth.

Shit. She'd hit her head. She must have knocked out her headlamp. There was—something she was supposed to do if that happened. *Don't panic. Stop. Stop right now. You have a system for this, think about what you learned.* She paused and tried to take a deep breath, the words of her Project Challenge mentor echoing in her head.

When the fear takes hold, deep in the dark, close your eyes. Focus on where you are. What can you hear, before you open your eyes? Find yourself in your moment. Breathe, Mia. Breathe.

Another raspy breath and she moved her head forward, analyzing her surroundings as best she could. There wasn't any light coming from beneath her, but she could tell something was wrong. First, the sound was all mixed up, echoing in a way that didn't make sense. Second, the water that was dripping was hitting her chin first, sliding up her cheek, and into her hair.

Mia tried to brush the wet tangles away from her face and again felt the resistance of her unwieldy and numb arms.

Something thudded dully against the side of her face, eliciting a short scream. It felt like cloth. *There was someone in the dark with her.*

The panic overtook Mia, constricting her chest further as she sucked in noisy breaths. The thing hit her again, and she felt an accompanying twinge of pain in her wrist.

1...2...3...breathe. Mia closed her eyes and pictured her happy spot, the place she was supposed to go to when she felt panic in a caving situation. For her it was a television studio, the local news anchor telling a tale of her accomplishments before they cut to footage of Mia at a rock-climbing wall, the voiceover explaining all she had overcome. How her grades slipped after the death of her sister. How she had fallen into trouble first with other students, then with school officials and finally the law. How the Project had saved her from a disastrous pending charge for felony assault and put her on a path of recovery, a path of strength. How the skills she had learned had helped her save her life more than once.

You are safe. You mapped this out. This is just another obstacle to your true self. You need to get your bearings and go back the way you came.

The panic subsided, and Mia took stock of her situation. She was lying on her belly in a tight passage, most likely the bottleneck entrance to the Giant's Room Cavern, as it was the most narrow. The quake must have caused some shifting, making it even more narrow than usual.

There was a tight constriction at her waist, with solid rock beneath her rib cage. While she was slim enough to fit through any of the three entrances, she had hoped to use the largest for this, her graduation from the Challenger program. For the past nine months she had worked with Challenger counselors, peer role models, and her assigned mentor to set an attainable goal and help overcome the fear that led to what her high school had referred to as "behavioral outbursts that are disruptive to the academic environment."

"Had enough of Chelsea Martin's bullshit and punched Chelsea right in her stupid face" was a more accurate representation. Chelsea had pushed and pushed, calling Mia names, mocking the drawings she doodled in her notebook, leaving crude insults on notes, culminating in Chelsea locking her in a janitor's closet during fourth period. Mia was there for hours before the custodial staff discovered and freed her in full view of a group of senior boys, Mia already a snotty mess from her panicked crying. A response was inevitable. Unfortunately, Mia's response had broken Chelsea's nose, and then the real nightmare began. Mia spent two nights in a juvenile detention facility awaiting her first hearing before her lack of criminal record and history of decent grades allowed her a diversion program.

Challenger was created by the state of Missouri to help "troubled teens find a more appropriate outlet for their frustrations," according to the pamphlet Mia reviewed with her mother and appointed public defender. She would discover the root of her anger, set a realistic goal, and achieve that goal in order to receive a non-felony charge and the ability to return to school. Therapy uncovered a laundry list of fears for her to choose from. Accomplishing this caving expedition, overcoming her claustrophobia, her fear of being alone, her fear of the dark…this solo push through the dark cavern would signal her emergence from the program and a return to her normal life. She'd worked too hard to fail now.

You're the one who wanted this, now get your ass up and out of here.

She attempted to brace her feet, finding her boots scraping ineffectually against the rock on either side of them. Pain shot through her left leg and she pitched forward. Her upper body flopped in response, the static sting shooting through her extended arms. The menacing cloth presence again crashed into the side of her head.

It's your arm. It's your own goddamn arm. You're upside down.

She was hanging in a narrow crevice, with blood dangerously pooling in her head and arms. Mia screamed but the sound came out wheezy, and not nearly as loud as she had hoped. That's when she heard the voice above. *No, not above, you idiot. Below.*

"Is someone up there?"

The voice was male and sounded young.

"Yes," she said, disturbed by how hoarse and weak her own voice sounded. "Help me."

"Are ya stuck?" He had that thick accent that morphed from southern-fried to almost Cajun. The boy was a local.

"Yes." She paused, struggling for breath. "There must have been a cave-in."

"T'weren't no cave in, lady," he called back cheerfully. "That was the Madrid, chugging back up."

"Madrid," she repeated.

"Funny thing, they call it the New Madrid, but I don't think I'n never heard anyone mention the Old Madrid. And the New Madrid, well that's old as anything. Maybe they should change the name."

"Help me," she wheezed.

"Oh shoot. Here'n I go again, yappin' where there's work to be done." A yellow beam of light shot past her, then swept back across the crack in the rock and into her eyes, blinding Mia. "Wowee. You did go an' get yourself proper stuck."

The light turned from her, leaving behind purple and blue stripes of afterglow dancing across her vision. There was a scratching sound, like something scuttling across loose gravel, and then the light returned. She squinted, unable to make out the boy holding the lamp.

"Canya move yer hands? Reach out?"

Mia managed to wiggle her arms by shaking her shoulders from side to side. The prickling sensations as feeling returned to her limbs made her cry out.

"Yeah," he said sympathetically. "They probably went to sleep after hanging like that for so long. Circulations all messed up." He pronounced "circulation" like "cerck-yoo-lah-chun." It made her feel a little giddy, like she might laugh.

That inclination passed the moment he started to pull on her hands.

It felt as if he were going to yank the arms out of their sockets as her lower body prevented her from budging. "Stop! Fucking stop!" The burst of adrenaline brought her back to full alert.

"Sorry, sorry," the voice said again. "I'nt mean nothing by it. No reason to get a-cursin'. Just tryna see if I could pull you out. Hoo." He whistled low. "You are a young thing, ain'cha? Skin like buttered cream. You ain't a miner, tell ya that. Despite yer mouth." More loose gravel noises as he moved. "How did you find yerself stuck down here?"

"I'm caving." She took several gasping breaths. "I'm in Project Challenge. The others are waiting at the entrance. They'll be looking for me."

"I don't rightly know'n what that is, m'afraid. But that's not here nor there, gotta get yous out. Maybe if'n I had some rope." The voice sounded further as if he were moving away from where she hung.

"Don't you dare leave me!" she gasped in desperation.

"Ain't goin' far," he called back. "You just stay put, y'hear?" Then he let out a peal of laughter. "Stay up, I says. Like you'n go anywhere, anyhow." Another echo of laughter, further away this time.

Mia startled back to consciousness, unsure how much time had passed. There was no sound in the cavern below save for the steady *drip drip drip* of water. She was freezing, her clothes still soaked and heavy. Mia attempted to flex the muscles of her stomach, wriggling her hips as much as she could. She stayed stuck in the same position.

With difficulty, she tried to bend her arms at the elbow and felt both wrists sear in pain in response. She relaxed and let her arms hang free again, screaming against gritted teeth as the flesh on the back of her hands scratched across the rough stone.

She half-dozed and dreamed of her bed at her parents' home, the sound of nightbirds filtering in through the windows. Only in this version of her bed, someone kept tucking the covers around her tighter and tighter, constricting her chest and making it near impossible to get enough oxygen. She awoke with a start that sent a fresh electric shock of pain through her limbs.

Someone set down something heavy below. "You'n still with us?"

"Yes," she croaked. "Did you call the police?"

"The police?" he said incredulously. "Even if'n had a phone to call them with, there t'aint nobody to call. No jury's diction, they tell us. Here."

There was a sour tang to the water he poured into her mouth, but she was grateful all the same.

"Call a park ranger, please," she asked. "Tell them my name is Mia Anderson and I need help."

"You'n said you was part of a project? You got any others stuck up there too?" The voice was almost teasing.

"No," she said. "No, I'm alone. That's the point."

"Not much'a project, if you ask ol' Rufus. Making young pretty things crawl through the dirt on their own."

She laughed despite her situation. "No," she said weakly. "It's something I had to do."

"Projects up there puttin' guns to people's heads, shovin' 'em inta caves?"

"It's my community rehabilitation."

"Dunna know anything about that." Rufus chuckled. "I ain't even got much of any kind of commune-ity."

"You aren't missing out on much," Mia said quietly. After all, her "community" was the whole reason she was down here, courtesy of Challenger: a daycamp-meets-prison that paired her with the mentor who'd put her down here alone: Bethany Chambers.

Bethany had been the outdoorsy type and thought that helping Mia conquer her fears would lead to "inner strength and a new outlook on life." This had mostly involved grueling workouts, exhaustive map-reading, and endless irritating "life mantras" from her mentor. This caving trip, a green level she could "easily" do by herself in less than an hour, was the final culmination of months of training. Bethany stood with two of the camp counselors, waiting for Mia to re-emerge transformed. This was supposed to be the moment she could prove that she wasn't worthless, that she was capable of great things.

Mia had pictured a dramatic moment of reveal, like they did on the makeover shows. Her father couldn't help but forgive her for every-thing she put the family through, not once he saw Mia smiling and sunkissed, her new strong muscles rippling in her upper arms. This was supposed to end with networks asking her for interviews where she would sit in a bright room on a velvet chair and a nodding sympa-thetic woman would ask questions about overcoming her weaknesses and finding a new passion that was good for her mind and her body.

That was what was keeping her going; that was what brought her here. *That* was how this was supposed to end.

Mia began to sob.

"We'll get you sorted proper," he said in a soothing tone. "You'nt gonna die like this."

"Die? You think I'm going to fucking die?" she gasped, another wave of panic hitting her.

"Don't worry none. Rufus knows these caves like the back of his hand, he does. I'nna get you free."

Scrabbling sounds again and then the rough caress of leathery skin against her hand.

"Rufus?" she groaned. "Your name is Rufus?"

"Far'n I can tell," he said jovially. "Not many 'round to call me one thing or another no more."

"Rufus, you're going to help me."

"I'mna do my darndest."

Mia's mouth pursed shut, the tears making her whole face feel wobbly. Something rough wrapped around her left wrist, then her right. It stung, but in a vague, far-off feeling way. That numbness wasn't a great sign, she knew. She felt the tears threaten again as she allowed herself to wallow.

The interview's velvet chairs and cheery lighting were replaced by a taller stool, with a dramatic black background. *A story of survival against all odds.* The sympathetic journalist with perfect silver hair nodded solemnly as she explained how the plucky teen nearly gave up hope until this nice man found her and saved her life. Then they would introduce Rufus, shy and nervous in the big city, receiving a reward as he smiled at her from across the studio—

The fantasy exploded in a sheet of white-hot pain as he began to tug. Ropes. He'd put ropes around her wrists.

There was the sensation of the soft skin of her inner palm tearing. *Bracelets of Fortune* popped into her head, a half-remembered tarot book she and a friend had discovered in her older sister's steamer trunk, the illustrated guide to palmistry in the appendix of illustrations. The thought was almost giddy, despite the bile threatening at the back of her throat. *He's tearing off my skin.*

"Rufus!" she shrieked, feeling the pull go slack. "You have to stop. It's hurting me too much."

There was only silence below, but the ropes remained loose.

"Can you go to get someone? Please?"

"There'n nobody to get. I keep sayin'."

"Please," she sobbed. Her chin quivering.

He didn't answer, but she thought she heard the slip of gravel again.

"Rufus?" she called out.

There was no response.

Positive and Negative are more than resistant forces—they are a mentality! Wake up each morning and decide if you're going to adopt a mentality to win, or a mentality to quit. Commit to that decision.

Mia once again tried to swing her arms to get the blood moving when she heard the sound of someone far below her feet. *Above, stupid.* Right. Above. She sucked in as much air as she could and managed to groan something that might have been an attempt at "hello" or "help" but came out more like "heeeeeeeeeeeeeeeurh."

Still, it was enough. "The fuck was that?" and then scrabbling. "Is there someone back there?"

Mia could only cough in response.

"Holy shit." It was a woman. "Are you—can you hear me?"

"Help...me," Mia called weakly.

"Okay, okay. Shit. Shit shit shit." Loose gravel sliding. "I can see your feet. Hang on, let me see if I can…. *Shit.*"

A beam of light passed by, showing the dirty sleeves of her jacket. "Are you stuck?"

Mia grunted.

"Okay, okay. I'm going to need you to stay calm. I can see where you're wedged, but I don't think I'm strong enough to pull you out by myself. My husband is behind me. I'm going to double back a bit."

"Rufus. Find Rufus," Mia gasped.

"Rufus?" the woman called. "Is he in there with you? Is he also stuck?"

"No," she breathed. "No."

"Okay, sweetie. Just stay calm. Shallow breathing. Try to stay awake. I'll be back."

Mia drifted in and out of her haze until she heard the voice return.

"Holy *shit.*" A man's voice. "And she's alive?"

Mia managed to make a "mmmmmrgh" sound as she regained consciousness.

"We're going to get you out." It was the first woman again. "We just have to figure out…"

"Do you see how her fucking leg is twisted in there? If we pull on her leg, we might break it off."

Mia felt a wave of nausea hit. "Don't. Don't take my leg."

"Oh, oh honey. We're not going to take your leg. We're gonna get you out, okay?" the woman said.

"Fuck. She sounds like she's just a kid. What is she *doing* in this part of the caves? I don't have a fucking signal down here."

"Neither do I, but we can't just leave her."

The words faded and all went dark for Mia once again. She dreamed of the interview stage. Bethany, her perfectly coiffed mentor was there, arms wide open in greeting. Only when Mia looked down, she saw blood. Bright arterial crimson blood, shiny and slick soaking her jeans, ragged and torn flesh hanging at the end of stumps where her hands had once been. She jarred awake again and let out a yelp.

"There she is. Can you tell me your name?" The woman's voice now.

"Mia," she said back hoarsely.

"Okay, Mia. I'm Diane, and I have Brian here with me. Is Rufus your boyfriend?"

"No," Mia responded roughly. "He wasn't with me. He was trying to help me."

"You came down here alone? Do you know where he went?"

"He lives somewhere near here. He found some sort of exit out of the Giant's Room."

"Giant's Room...?" Diane's voice trailed off. "Mia, you took a wrong turn awhile back. You're not anywhere near the Giant's Room Cavern. Is that where you were trying to go?"

"Yes."

There was a moment of tense whispering before she heard Diane again. "Honey, you're a lucky girl. I don't know how, but you must have missed the signs and took the wrong direction at the main fork. You're in a section they call The Devil's Throat. It's a tight squeeze down and just keeps going. No one's ever attempted it fully."

"Rufus is down there!" she wheezed. "He said there's a way out. I can hear birds and crickets."

"Mia." Diane's voice was full of sympathy. "It's miles straight down. There's no one there. I think you might be confused after hitting your head."

Mia sobbed in response.

"It's going to be alright. How old are you, Mia?"

"I'm sixteen." The tears threatened, and her chin quivered.

"How long have you been here, do you know?"

"No. I fell during the quake and I think I slipped into this spot."

From further down the passage, Mia heard the man's voice say, "Quake? Did she say quake?"

"Look, we have no idea how long she's been down here. She's probably a little confused, definitely dehydrated." Diane huffed in exasperation. "Who the fuck lets a kid come down here alone? Okay. Okay. Mia, I'm going to get you out of here. Just stay with me, okay? I have to crawl back out so we can get some things ready."

Mia drifted again. It was silent when she opened her eyes, limply trying to stretch out her arms and will the feeling back into them. Her fingers were now completely numb.

Somewhere, in the darkness below her, a scratching sound followed by a harsh whisper. "You still there, girlie?"

Mia made a muffled "mmmhmmm," her mouth dry, tongue unwieldy.

"I got'n an idear during my walk here. You know how we get stones out of the wells?"

Mia grunted noncommittally.

"With a bucket and rope! Anyhoo, no point'n wastin' time. I gots everythin' we need, 'cept that bucket, but you wouldn't fit in it nohow. The crank's rusty, but it'll do the job just'n the same. Just gotta be strong for me, Mia. You know'n how to be strong?"

Mia sobbed. "What are you going to do?"

There was the sound of a metal pulley spinning and the ropes again tightened around her wrists, searing feeling back into her limbs with a ferocity that sent bright flashes across her eyes. She screamed with a fury she had no longer thought she was capable of as she felt the flesh start to separate with the sickening stretchy-wet sound of tearing.

Bracelets of Fortune popped into her head again, imagining those deep wrinkles below the fleshy plump of her palm splitting to reveal the unnatural white and purplish-green gore of the meat below.

Above her, another scrambling noise and then Diane's voice.

"Mia? Mia, what's happening?"

"Get me out!" Mia shrieked in panic. "Get me out, get me out, he's pulling my hands off."

She heard Brian and another man join the shouting above her feet. It sounded like a heated debate punctuated by her shrieks. At last Diane screamed, "Just fucking do something, listen to her!"

Someone grabbed at Mia's thighs, clawing at her pants and trying to drag her upward, increasing the pressure on her wrists as she felt the skin begin to rend.

A beam of light from one of their flashlights swept past her. There was a moment when they had nearly managed to pull her up before she slid back down into the crevice. One of them grasped her reinforced cargo pocket on the side of her leg and gave a heavy pull.

She felt their hands on her waist, dragging her back by the band of her pants, her lower back scraping against stone as they tried to work her free. The ropes around her wrist slackened.

She heard Rufus muttering under his breath as he drew closer, reaching up into the cracked cave ceiling. There was a strange coldness to his exhalation, one that smelled of low tide and something danker, darker, older. Then a whispery sensation much too near her face that reminded her of the vacation her whole family took to the North Carolina shore when she was very, very young.

It sounded almost like the crabs that would gather on the rocks below their beach house, scratching and slipping along the wet surface, their chitinous bodies rasping and scraping as their tiny pointed feet tried to find purchase on the damp stone.

Someone wedged the flashlight into the crevice, and she finally got a look at her hands in its beam.

Deep maroon grooves encircled her wrists, the flesh above gray and dead. That should have been the worst thing she'd ever seen, would ever see again.

It wasn't.

Bethany crept into her mind, like a harsh whisper too close to her ear. *Think about what you desire from this journey. What will you emerge from your trials with? What will you leave behind? Who are you going to be when you finally learn to stand? Where will you be?*

Mia's eyes widened, watching as the grooves opened, splitting the flesh and leaving behind stringy tendrils of connective tissue. Her fingers wrinkling and deflating as that thing pulled at her.

Whatever Rufus was, he didn't have human hands. He had *claws*. Elongated fingers that featured one too many knuckles; black and gnarled, their long, needlelike nails yellowed with filth.

The monstrous fingers skittered higher, feeling emboldened now that they no longer had the darkness to hide in.

The thickened talons sank into the open wounds at her wrists and began to peel back the skin as her rescuers reached in around her ribcage. With a soft, moist *squick*, the flesh of her hands slipped off, neatly and whole.

Mia shrieked until her lungs ran dry, inhaling with a guttural groan before she began to shriek again. The last image she saw as she was dragged upward were those blackened, unearthly fingers withdrawing into the earth, clutching their new prize.

She laid on her back, numb to all the noise and commotion, only hearing snippets of the exclamations of her rescuers when they first saw the breaks in her leg, the deep lacerations on her thighs, and finally her skinned hands. They wrapped her in towels. They reassured her.

Rescue services were on the way. Such a lucky girl. The Devil's Throat! No one had attempted that since the last man who died in the 40s. A few more feet and she would have slipped right into that tunnel. No one would have ever found her. The legend is that there's no bottom to it, just keeps going down and down into the earth. Had a brother once, tossed a coin in. Never heard it land. Lucky, lucky girl. You're going to have some stories to tell, girl. They just need you to stay awake, Mia. They need you to try to stay with us, Mia. Can you try to sip this water, Mia? Can you hear us, Mia?

All Mia could hear were the quiet sounds emanating from the great crack in the earth beside her, where a voice cooed soft as a sigh as it slipped onto its gnarled and knotted fingers a soft new pair of kidskin gloves.

MEMO: Evidentiary imagery and agent headshot provided by Joe Radkins.

THE LAST SERMON OF BROTHER GRIME
by Timaeus Bloom

MAY 21ST - 4:17 PM

Who am I writing this for anyway? No one reads it. Well, that's not exactly true. Occasionally, I'll get a couple of stars to show that someone "liked" it. Very rarely any comments though. I dunno. The topic of this blog has changed so many times—so many templates have been used, art posted. At first it was gonna be a space to review Korean horror films, then maybe a place for moody poetry. On and on. Hunting knives (nope), candid photos of people sleeping (tacky), Linux programming (snooze). You don't care. And I don't either. So I'll just "eh, whatever" this page.

Anyone out there like barbecue? How about crazy people? I've got a two-for-one special for ya.

For those of you who don't know me (all of you), I'm a bigger guy. My dad calls me "stocky," my mom says "lovable." Me? I'm not one for labels—I just know what I like. And your boy likes barbecue.

I thought about making this one of those "foodie" blogs, where I talk about whatever I'm eating and give local places ratings, but I've never been especially good at that. When friends or whoever ask me what I gave the newest comic book flick from 1-10, I just say it was "good." I figured if I was judging food, I wouldn't have to think too hard. If something tastes like shit it's all on the tongue. Leave my brain out of the equation—it's never good for much anyhow, always getting in the way. Ask my ex.

Last week, I found myself in front of a couple piping-hot pulled pork sandwiches, a greasy pile of crispy steak fries, and a styrofoam cup of the sweetest iced tea I'd ever tasted. I fancied myself a food critic. Hell, Guy Fieri does it.

Puck's Barbecue is the worst kind of artificial. I was tilting back in an old wicker chair that still smelled like it was just from the factory. Long, fabricated orange marks ran down the table legs to emulate rust. The floors had the kind of dried stains and faded warehouse tiling I'm sure some stylist was paid way too much to reproduce.

Every order came with "All the peanuts you can crack!" The gimmick was that since the floor looked shitty any way (not real shitty, fake shitty) it was okay to just toss them on the floor. A troupe of table bussers in faded overalls, all with the same right cotton strap unclipped and flapping across their backs, were all too happy to swoosh by with those big industrial floor brushes and sweep those pesky peanut shells away. It was fun! It was rustic! It was quaint!

It was…fake.

As I torpedoed a steak fry from the command ship that was the remaining chunk of my last pulled pork sandwich into a plasmid shield of Heinz Ketchup, the screeching sound of wooden chairs being shoved aside kicked my head to attention. Then came the familiar sound of mumbling that often followed confusion.

A short man in a dingy, white button down and an equally swampy-looking pair of white slacks bustled into the center of the restaurant. A light blue checkered tie, faded and wrinkled to hell, swayed around his neck instead of under the collar. Resting precariously at the top of his head, on a knotted and misshapen puff of an afro, sat a short-brimmed straw hat with a floral design—one of those hats a retiree might wear in a gated community.

"Heed me," he said dramatically, taking long pauses between the "heed" and "me."

"What is to come ain't because of me. You done this one to yourselves, pops."

That "pops" came out dry and matter-of-fact. Uncomfortable parents held their children close.

The young, freckled college student who had led me to my small corner table half an hour earlier moved quickly to interrupt this bizarre oration.

"Brother Grime's got time for you, my man. But he ain't got all the time. A reckoning's coming. Where ya wanna be when it comes? The Grotesque has got something fer ya."

I watched him slide a long, spindly arm, ashy as a chalkboard, across one of the iron tables that held a family's leftovers boxed and ready. Grease and pudding, sauce and mashed potatoes splattered nastily to the floor, with a fair slosh of it attacking the server's pristine, egg-white sneakers.

"The hell, dude?" he said, mortified.

"Hell, it ain't," the ratty tramp said, cleaning a line of dark, runny black Get Back sauce from his left arm. I'd heard worse monologues.

"It's here. Right 'chere. The trash and slop, the filth you leave is shouting loud and it can hear it—"

But he couldn't finish. In the middle of his condemnation, a woman in a black polo shirt and two overalled teens were on him. They weren't gentle. Each took hold of his gyrating body as tightly as they could, and they pushed him forward and toward the plastic, neon EXIT sign. His tight smirk seemed to say that, for now, enough had been said.

Weird, right? I know. I didn't stay too long after that. I thought it was kind of cool, honestly. It was sort of odd how, as soon as the nut was removed from the restaurant, everything eerily reverted. Once the yeeted leftovers were cleared and the table bussed, the indignant "What on Earths" were pretty much capped by a stark return to normal.

You'd think—maybe—that as a thirty-something black dude that went to an inner-city college, gentrification would be familiar to me.

I meant it when I said Puck's Barbecue felt fake. It was in that newly renovated part of downtown that was attracting all the business. Old shotgun houses and brick buildings with community-driven murals had been felled, giving way to a brewery, concert hall (Foster the People, here next Thursday), a little shop that sold over thirty flavors of cookie dough, and Puck's.

I figure the weird guy in white was just someone who'd been de-housed. Most people (at least not the family outing kind with the yappy dogs) don't like to see their own mess displayed in front of them, I guess. It's uncomfortable.

Anyway, I liked the food. I give it 4 out of 5 on belly feel or whatever.

MAY 22ND - 1:34 PM

I see the hashtags worked. That's pretty awesome. 11 likes.

I also see Taco Bell has brought back Mexican Pizza. I haven't had that since I was in high school. It was good. Would it be on-brand to do a review of that?

Just a little update on last week's post. I recalled something about that homeless guy, "Brother Grime"—is it rude to assume he's homeless? He had that look about him. You know what look I'm talking about. It's more than just dirty clothes or worn skin—even more than that smell of old meat or just staleness. As his little short-brimmed bahama hat bounced every which way on his Soul Train puffball, I couldn't help but look into those eyes. They reminded me of my Grandfather's: sharp, ruby-red veins spidering throughout the sockets like the roots of a tree. A stubborn tree that knew what the world was and wouldn't be deterred—definitely not by any overalled zillennials serving up banana pudding cups while "Life is a Highway" played out of tin-covered speakers.

With all the talk of the weird stuff at Puck's, I almost forgot to mention the icing on the cake. When I went outside, I was annoyed, yet unsurprised, to see the cops had been called. Hillside's Finest. The polo'd manager was complaining with the best of them.

"This is the last time. We can't have that kind of thing happening around here. It scares the guests. And the smell. It's just—this is a restaurant. What if—"

She turned to stare at me as my large feet tapped across the restaurant's porch. Yes, it had a front porch. And rocking chairs. Even a little gift shop on the way out where you can buy those wooden train whistles and sticks of sugar cane. Was that wood creaking manufactured too?

"My apologies, sir," she said to me. "He's been an eyesore ever since we opened up a few weeks ago."

An eyesore. Not pretty enough for the jugband aesthetic? Seemed to be just the fit to me.

I shrugged robotically. "Dinner and a show."

MAY 23RD - 5:28 PM

Today was one of those annoying Saturdays when I'm asked to come into work: inventory day. Driving home, I was that annoying mix of tired and hungry. I didn't really want to go anywhere except home, I guess. By the time I was wheeling back into my neighborhood, I was adamant that rummaging through the pantry would suffice. I'd have something at home to hold me over until I was recharged enough to pop back out.

Before I realized, I was taking a left turn I wouldn't normally take. I made my way up the tight two-way street until I saw the quaint image of an overalled white man with blue eyes, a tangled beard, and a corncob pipe nestled between gapped teeth. Popping out of his mouth was an egg-shaped speech bubble like out of an old comic book. He was welcoming everyone to partake in the "Best barbecue this side of the Mason Dixon." Right here, he added, at "Puck's."

His bulbous head turned around to stare at me. But now he had the face of Grime, staring down at me from ten feet above. He licked his lips as black slime seeped down his jaw like drool. He took the pipe out of his mouth, and pointed it straight at me.

I shut my eyes with such intensity that pain seared my temples. Just a lack of sleep, yeh?

I opened them. All hopes of an exhausted brain playing tricks dashed by old-timey dialogue:

"You're hungry, boy! I knows it. Yes I does!"

He "spoke" in those same speech bubbles.

"Why dontcha park them pretty wheels of yours and have a plate?"

From nowhere, like an old Looney Tunes skit, he pulled out a plate piled high with what looked like intestines lathered in ketchup and charred tongues with a sweet coating. A cartoony silver scent trailed from the sign and into the vents of my car. I held my breath. I felt the upchuck of vomit.

"Whatcha on 'bout?" He sounded playful. "Too good fer a city boy? Just a lil' old bite fer the road, Young Blood."

He reached a liver-spotted hand into the food and grabbed the largest tongue; orange glaze dripped from it. It wiggled like a freshly caught trout gasping for air.

"Open er up now...that body an' the blood they hand out on Sunday ain't got nothin on this 'chere..," he said, reaching a long arm outside of the sign and sending globs of the glaze dripping into the street as he reached toward my car.

I shuddered to attention as a car horn blared behind me. I was holding up traffic.

When I turned back to look at the sign, it was the old white man again unchanged, except now one of his eyes was the same dull brown of the lunatic from yesterday. The other was winking at me, as if it shared a secret only the two of us were privy to. The faint remains of that terrible scent clung to my nostrils.

May 24th - 8:13 PM

I went out for a walk today. Like millions of fat people before me, I've got a long history of losing and gaining. Lost as much as sixty pounds once and felt good about myself. Really liked it when people would do double takes, or joke that they could see my neck now (my friends are kind of dicks).

So, when I got off work today, I decided to go for a walk. Call it a moment of clarity. Not in any particular direction, but just to meander around the neighborhood.

Maybe you'll not be surprised that my feet dragged me toward Puck's.

Puck's, with its chimneys and wide-open doors. You could smell the gristle from blocks away, hear the old honky tonk crooners from stereos singing about lost loves and starry nights. But tonight, as I made my way down the remodeled pavement, past bike racks in the shape of old trains and college kids with their small shirts dotted with stitchings of anchors or bananas, something seemed a bit off about the newly polished neighborhood.

Everything was a bit too quiet. There wasn't much in the way of real talking or laughter. It took but a few more short steps for everything to become clear.

As I made my way toward the end of the freshly paved cobblestone road, I saw a congregation of people filling out the side alley that connected the restaurant to the street. There was an eerie quiet to this crowd, who looked onward toward the center stage. I noticed among them my next door neighbors, Mrs. Gutierrez and her husband, confused and not as enthralled as the others.

There he was. Grime, wild and unkempt, looking like a modern-day sharecropper in the ratty shirt of an office worker and that same dangling, wrinkled tie around his cracked neck.

"Now what y'all missin,' chillen, is the source. That TV is a liar, and so are them folks talkin' about cleaning up our neighborhood..."

The crowd was transfixed, staring up at this Southern-fried Homer, spilling parables by street lamp. All of them looked worn and shut away. These were the old inhabitants, and likely no small number of them had been displaced. Their gathering was a direct attack against the city council's "Yesterday's Hillside Renewed!!" agenda.

"What was so wrong about our lil' communitee? They say it was filthy? Messy? Served us just fine, didn't it? Served us good. We lived how we wanted. Ain't that right? I said AIN'T THAT RIGHT?"

A deep and monotone "THAT'S RIGHT" emitted from the crowd, like it was one breathing, pulsing creation. These blank faces lacked emotion and were as flat as their seemingly automated responses. They yelled at his beck and call like an audience caught by the aura of a televangelist. All that was missing was a self-righteous "BE HEALED."

The accuracy of that comparison cannot be understated. He proselytized and damned better than any of the Southern baptists my grandma dragged me to as a kid.

"Now I'ma tella ya somethin'," he preached on, reaching out an arm dramatically and scooping air, commanding his flock to come forward as he lowered his voice with cutting severity: "There's something out there that can return it back—get us how we were. They say we filth? Trash? Sheeeit. What's wrong with that? Better to be coated in our own shit than washed in their fake clean. Dirt be real, and Grime be real."

He turned around and leaned over into the dumpster. Letting out a few grunts, he pulled out a big clear plastic bag with a thick knot atop it. This "Grime" tossed the bulk onto the pavement with a hard, squishy thud.

"Whatcha got here now?" he asked aloud to no one.

Bringing his dingy and yellowed nails forward, he slashed into the plastic bag, ripping it with ease. Dipping both hands in, he pulled out a browned and warmed slab of raw meat.

"You see this here, chile?" I swear those eyes rested on me.

His hands dripped with the ooze of the rotten meat. He then took in a full, pleasurable whiff as if intoxicated by a perfectly primed ribeye. It was almost sexual.

The world around me and the priest began to twist and transform. We were no longer in Puck's alley. The walls had the white and pink lines of butchered flesh, and the cobblestoned street was warm and pink, lifting us up and down like a salivating tongue. Above us: a black, oily tapestry. It slowly waved like the minor tide of some accursed sea.

"They don't understand," Grime said. "But you do, dontcha, Young Blood?"

"Where are we?" I asked.

"Home, Big Man," he responded as he moved toward me, still holding the molded meat. "That Grotesque is comin'. And we gone need ya."

"For…what?"

"Everythang, Young Blood. Everythang."

He let that chunk of meat drop to the ground with a nasty splat that tempoed the squishing of our squirming floor like a distorted metronome and cupped my face in his hands.

I didn't pull away.

He spread the residue on my face like paint. It hardened into putty as he covered me with his hellish facemask. His knotted fingers worked over my skin. He took weird care, telling me to close my eyes before he covered them in the mud or to take a deep breath before he waxed over my mouth and nostrils.

Upon completion, Grime took a few steps back and placed his hands lazily on his hips, admiring his work.

Letting out a few high-pitched giggles, he said, "Lookin' prom ready, Young Blood! Take a lookie yerself."

"Look where?"

"Behind ya."

I turned around. Behind me was the small crowd of people I'd seen transfixed before him at the dumpster. They all stood motionless and unchanged, except for their faces. There were no eyes, just mouths and rows of teeth. Each mouth seemed to grin at me, as if smirking from a dirty joke I hadn't heard, as lines of black fluid dribbled down their chin.

"Where…are…eyes?" was all I could manage to say.

Grime spun me around to face him. His hands on my broad shoulders steadied me. "You ain't never needed eyes to see."

I screamed myself awake.

MAY 26TH - 12:11 AM

I think I'm ready to give up this blog. No, not yet another instance of changing topics. I don't think I want to blog any more. You see, I ran into the Brother again. No, that's not true. I went looking for him.

MAY 27TH - 2:30 PM

Another post. But that's okay. You want to read this. I'm sure of it.

I'd actually dealt with him before—not him, exactly, but his work. I live a few streets over from Puck's Barbecue, about a block. It's a typical apartment: three floors, shitty air circulation, managers that never seem to be around unless you're a second late paying rent. Thin walls, too. Sometimes the sounds of my neighbors going at it are so loud, so close, you'd think they'd ask for my consent. It's not the worst, though. When I told the oblivious couple who owned the place I'd always wanted a view, they gave me the second floor.

Anyways, when I was returning home last summer from whatever the fuck I was doing, I'd see ratty sheets of paper on the doors of my floor. Some days they were scattered pieces of notebook paper, strips of newspaper, burger wrappers—any sort of trash. They were stickied to the door with gum, tape, whatever. Gibberish was often sprawled haphazardly across the sheet.

One day I read, "Ur Junk is Its Treasure," on another "Wayste Not Want Not." Because my apartment was near the end of the floor, I walked past all of them. The thinly carpeted floor with its dull orange sconces lit up each door as if bringing attention to each decree.

The most memorable one was the door opposite mine. Mauve lipstick shouted across a dingy paper towel, the brown ones you'd find in a gas station restroom: "IT COMETH IN SLUGS."

I thought it was some kind of college club or "Go Green" movement. Younger kids who knew that to spread a message you needed to do something more than clip flyers under a windshield wiper (doesn't that just bring more trash?) Using garbage to get the word out—the kind of calculated irony that might lead a disinterested someone to offer a halfhearted "interesting" before littering the hall with a balled up scrap of tissue paper. Turns out, at least according to Darrel (older white dude with a seemingly infinite supply of cargo shorts and gray shirts), it was some old man with a fro, a weird look, and a straw hat.

Darrel had stopped by out of the blue.

"Hakeem," he'd said, questioningly. "You've lived here this long and don't have a peephole?"

Before I could reply I heard the buzzing sound of a spinning drill tunneling into my front door. His thought was that, with strangers like Grime around, a renter needed to know who was knocking at their door before opening it up.

You know, I never understood how he got into the apartments in the first place. The front door has electronic locks that require an oblong plastic stub to activate. Somehow, I knew a locked door couldn't stop him. Did a locked door stop rodents or bugs? Rodents, like refuse, always find a way to be just where we don't want them.

MAY 27TH - 7:36PM

We were together now, teacher and student.

He looked as bizarre tonight as he did every other day. He was doing that thing people of a certain age do, when they chew constantly as if smacking on the sweetest gum in the world. The fro was still misshapen, and that brimmed hat was still hanging on for dear life.

He looked up at me.

"This ain't right, Young Blood. This. Ain't. Right."

Every experience handed down to me as a kid about dealing with strangers had left as Grime's folksy ick seeped into my mind. There was a weird charm to him that left Puck's and the establishment coming off as the real villain, and him as some sort of putrid Pied Piper, leading children away from the real contamination: artificiality.

Looking into those lined, wooden eyes, as brown as tree trunks and as knowing as the earth, I didn't feel fear. Not compassion, either. I was looking at my grandpa again. Not someone I was especially close to, but a man I knew who'd spent every day of his life just getting by; be it selling drugs, opening up a two-bit carwash, or being told once again by some stern-voiced boss, dripping with fake sympathy, that he just wasn't the kind of guy his crew was looking for.

Was it respect I felt? Unsure. But it was…something.

"What isn't right?" I asked.

He kicked around inside of the steel box that had become his makeshift throne, stepping over laundry detergent bottles and smashing through soda cans.

"Where's the trash? This won't do. They won't like this, Young Blood. Not one bit."

The old nasty dumpster had been cleaned, and was now being used for recycling. Likely done to halt the weird preacher's incomprehensible exercises.

"Who won't like this?" Curiosity was not just killing my cat, it was torturing it.

"The Grotesque, son." He held up his arms. The bony limbs flailed like spaghetti noodles. "They sing with fleas, wade in bile, and caress in excrement. They come knockin', Young Blood, I'ma answer."

Leaving one hand raised, he pulled down his pale slacks. His legs, like rotten pieces of bark, shimmied as he danced and sang aloud with no semblance of being in tune. I could make out that he was crooning the chorus of Al Green's "Love and Happiness," using it as the driving hymn in which to devote himself to his coming master.

"I soil for thee," he cried, eyes looking at the low ceiling of the garage. A black tear slid down his wrinkled face. Then came the dripping of water.

I stepped back, not even toying with the notion of his yellow spray splashing me.

But it wasn't yellow, was it? What came out of him was slow, thick like molasses. A dark liquid that flowed like syrup. It was viscous, plopping hard and twisting around him on the floor. And then the gelatinous substance separated, forming into nasty black little leeches that slithered around his legs like gnats on a succulent vine. The sucking sound of his benefactors increased as they continued to entwine around him. Sucking. Turning. Sucking. Turning.

"'Bout that time, Young Blood. 'Bout th—"

But his words were cut off as the slugs spread from legs, to torso, to mouth. They devoured him in a twisted coating of their own design. New armor donned for the battle he foretold.

Backing away in disgust, I shoved the lid of the dumpster closed.

MAY 29TH - 9:00 AM

Today is the last day I write something, because tomorrow I won't have fingers. I won't need them. Grime said so.

"Them digits, sonny son son, are for thinkin' work. Turnin' knobs, and pushin' buttons. Don't need em. We gone take your hands tomorrow, give you hands like these…"

He grasped my palm. The wrinkles and bent fingers that once made up his urchin's excuse for hands had smoothed, polished. His hands had de-aged—become smooth and pretty. A few remaining leeches clung to him, licking and draining him of who he once was.

A sticky sinew spread between the gaps of my fingers. Once each space was coated and webbed like a toad's, it hardened.

I looked down at my new flippers, something out of a B-grade monster movie. I could still wiggle my fingers but it was hard.

"See this? That all you need. Those are scoops. Will help you stick—help you shovel food. And they perfect for prayer. What you need fingers for? Just stick and pray."

He stepped out of what remained of the green bin. He gave me a slap on the back. It was strong. The slap of a young man's renewed strength.

"You hungry, Young Blood? There's gonna be a shindig at Puck's around…"

He scanned bare flesh, miming the checking of a watch.

"Tooth-hurty."

He walked away, leaving a trail of sludge and dying leeches.

There was that hymn again: "Love and Happiness."

Returning to my room and locking the door, I kept hearing the plopping of those slugs hitting the cardboard boxes. Droppings and droppings.

It was actually easy to fall asleep. I'd been carb-loading. Dunno why. Been a depressing year. I've just found myself…munching. Not even especially hungry. When I'm worried, frustrated, scared, happy—I eat. Last night it was two packs of ramen. Cheap stuff, good stuff. Even cracked an egg in the pot. I was out by eleven.

When I woke up, it was all over.

I left my eerily normal apartment, and strolled for the upteenth time through my neighborhood, or what was my neighborhood: a cacophony of sounds and distortion devoured my senses. The priest's presence filled the street. Long tendrils of viscera, oozing and gyrating, snaked along the roads and sidewalks, lamp posts, and neighboring buildings, stretching under the doors and sewage drains in search of life.

The door knob of each small building pulsed, the handles replaced as if visited by late-night carpenters. They were spongy and brown, a dark brown pupil in the center of each. The eyes on every knob followed me, curious to know where I might go next.

As if aware that I refused to turn them, to step into their thresholds that were now entrances to the whims of the Grotesque, they slammed open.

Despite all the nightmarish changes, I could identify Puck's. It remained the same, a tribute to what was. I walked over the throbbing veins of the world that now was. And the restaurant began to breathe.

"Come in, Hakeem. You'll let the cool out...."

Mrs. Gutierrez stared up at me, long silver hair plastered to her skin in wet knots. Where her eyes had been sat the wagging tail of a slug in each moist socket. Punching into her torso was a long, black vine. Her chest was flayed open as if something had chewed itself out.

"Where is Mr. Gutierrez?" I asked.

"He chose not to serve," she answered matter-of-factly. The vine raised her limp body forward, gesturing toward a flight of stairs and raising her forward and upward.

I followed up a simple wooden staircase to the restaurant's second floor. It was fairly plain with more tables, a few old gas station signs to keep the down-home flair, an empty stage for performances, and a line of windows. I stared through them, and the world had changed yet again, as if it was slowly growing into a new suit.

What I saw was filth, everywhere. Wrangled...corpses? Of all twisted fashions, dirty and toad-like, leaping across lily pads made out of the stretched skin of the uninitiated. Somewhere out there, one of these converts was bouncing on Mr. Gutierrez.

Where there had just been streets, flowed the same chunky, gurgling fluid Brother Grime had used to sanctify the recycling bin.

The clouds, too, seemed to be made of that same flowing nasty black. There was no sun. But a sphere hung all the same. The distorted face of a toad, puddied with a woman hung expressionless and unmoving. Her mouth was open in a snarl, black sludge flooding out of it and slopping into the flowing streets like a hellish waterfall. It looked like a sick child's view of Venice—save the gondolas.

The Grotesque? I thought to myself.

And further outside, each building inhaled, breathing in unison with the doorknobs. Each building kept its familiar structure, but now they were fleshy. Raw pieces of enormous meat that had once been stripmalls, gyms, or fast food joints dotted the dreary landscape. They were all medium rare, some of them dark meat, others light. I saw ribs, steaks, ham hocks, all weeping blood with each inhalation. Had Grime been kicked out of an Olive Garden instead of Puck's, what would his visions have conjured then?

I turned abruptly as I heard the vine rustle. Mrs. Gutierrez sighed and twisted toward me to look out the window.

"My, my," she said in annoyance as if today was any other day: "Looks like rain."

HOWLS BUREAU OF INVESTIGATION

HBI

H.B.I.

SPECIAL AGENT *Timaeus Bloom*

Timaeus Bloom fancies himself a makeshift magus, Eldritch underling, and shadowy specter that began writing way too late. He now types away in the most inopportune moments playing catch up. Timaeus is proud to represent Black authors in speculative fiction.

🐦 @of_ichor

MEMO: Evidentiary imagery and agent headshot provided by Leah Gharbaharan.

AGAINST THE FLATS
by Jennifer L. Collins

The amorphous forms could have been Ziploc baggies, upside down and puckered with air…but they weren't. Lined with flashes of pink and purple venom, the colony of Portuguese men o'war flooded the surface of the tide between the shore and the useless boat.

Kyle floated face-down in their midst, the water around him darkened by the muck which had been slurped from his body by the tide.

Miguel stared at his lifeless twin from what counted for a beach, a numb weight spreading through his gut and into his deadened limbs. He could feel himself wilting in the heat of the sulfurous flats, melting, and thought absurdly of the old "This is your brain on drugs" ad that focused on popping fried eggs. That's how he felt now, and smelled, what with the stink of the territory they'd just wandered through.

A flock of pelicans flew overhead, fleeing out to sea rather than remaining behind to tolerate the bellowing of gators in the distance.

Or the dead body and the jellies in the tidewater.

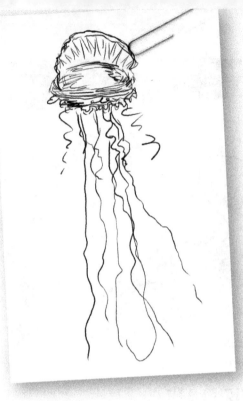

Bile rose from Miguel's gut, fed by the murmurs of his friends and the glare of sunlight on Kyle's corpse.

Just short of where water lapped the surface of the mud, Ruthie stood holding her arms tight against her chest. "Where the hell did all these jellyfish come from?"

"They're not jellyfish." Richard's fingers trailed dried crumbs of muck through his beard. "They're siphonophores. Colonial organisms with a bunch of single biologics acting as one."

"Doesn't really matter, does it?" Miguel reached for Ruthie's shoulder, clutching it once before he collapsed down to his knees beside her—his eyes remaining on his twin drifting in the tide. What counted for ground in the flats rose by a few inches, squelching around his feet and ass as if to greet him. "Whatever the fuck they are, they killed my brother."

Kyle's body bobbed some ten feet away from them, his banana-spotted trunks a yellow beacon of bad faith in the middle of the creatures' inflated sails. Tentacles wrapped around his legs like neon bracelets, and his pale limbs had gone bright pink with stings. Twenty feet beyond him, the boat they'd rented rocked in the water, mocking them.

"I don't understand why he would have gone in the water with them here." Sierra picked some caked mud from her arms, staring forward. "He should have waited. Or come back for us."

Miguel up-ended a bottle of water over his hands, fighting down a blanket of anger at the filth coating his skin and filling even the crevices beneath his nails. Like his friends, he'd become caked with the stuff in traipsing through the flats at their backs, wandering around in search of pictures of gators or snakes just to pass away the Florida day and say they'd done it. His legs ached from the effort of pushing through the knee-high mud all morning, but his brain had gone numb. Richard scowled at him pointedly, judging the waste of water, but Miguel couldn't bring himself to care at the moment.

His twin was dead. Stupidly, senselessly dead.

The weight of Kyle's body circled around his heart and pinched his throat. Ruthie murmured something unintelligible, but an old friend's comfort was nothing in the face of a lost twin.

Lost for no reason other than that they'd wanted to play in mud like toddlers and see some mangroves and an alligator in the wild.

"What are we going to do?" Ruthie leaned forward and looked down into the water. "Do we have to, uh, swim around to get to the other side of the boat? Pull Kyle in after we get back to it?"

"Don't even think it, babe." Sierra pointed to the edges of the boat, where men o'war spread beyond each side of it. "These things have tentacles that are like twenty feet long. Even if there aren't any on the other side of the boat, their tentacles are there."

"More like a hundred feet."

Ruthie's eyes narrowed on Richard. "Huh?"

"Their tentacles can be like a hundred feet long, is what I said. That's why none of us are stepping foot in this water right now. And it's why our buddy hasn't floated away." Richard choked on the words, and then spoke softer. "He's anchored to them."

"So, what about *Kyle*?" Miguel looked up and around at his small group of friends. "We let him drift off with those things? Besides, this doesn't make any sense. They're not supposed to be deadly."

"Not in small doses, no, but that much venom all at once? How many stings do you think he got walking ten feet into this water?" Sierra leaned over as far as she could, staring down into the lapping tide.

When she turned away from the deadly scene, she headed over to their twenty-pack of water bottles, now mostly depleted, and began pulling bottles from the plastic. "Richard, help me out here."

Miguel shifted to observe, ill with the sight of his brother drifting among the men o'war and their tentacles. He scooted back in the mud, ignoring the inches-deep sludge rising around him. "What the hell are you doing?"

"We can wrap this plastic around my legs and cover up my skin, and I can get out to the boat." Sierra pulled up another bottle and propped it in the wet ground. "I'll keep my feet under the mud to avoid getting stung."

Richard froze with one hand in the plastic, and then jolted up and pushed her back from the water bottles, eyes going wider than the men o'war's sails. "You're off your fucking feed if you think I'm letting you go out there. You do see our friend's body floating face-down, yeah? Right friggin' there?"

Sierra licked her lips, taking a few seconds too long to meet her boyfriend's eyes. "Richard, we've been back on the beach for a half hour. He hasn't moved, and neither have the men o'war. What do you propose?"

Struggling to his feet, Miguel tried to ignore the suck of the ground wanting to hold onto him as he angled away from his brother. "Not a suicide mission."

Sierra pushed some sweaty bangs away from her face. "That's what the plastic's for," she argued, gesturing down to the shorty wetsuit she wore. "And if Ruthie's still got her knife, I'll cut off my sleeves for extra protection. I'll be fine."

Ruthie finally turned back to the group, pulling her pocket knife from her shorts and holding it out to Sierra, who yanked down the top of her wetsuit so that it hung around her waist. After adjusting her bikini top, she began sawing at the sleeves.

"This is absurd," Richard said. "How do you even know the wetsuit'll keep the stingers off you?"

Sierra shrugged, still focused on her task. "It's worked before when I've been snorkeling and encountered jellyfish. On men o'war's tentacles, too. And it's not like I'm crossing a channel. I won't have to go in past my waist, the water's so shallow. The wetsuit goes down to my knees already. We'll use these sleeves to cover my calves and up to my knees, and I'll keep my feet under the mud and glide forward like I would if we were worried about stingrays. The plastic'll tie everything up and add protection. When I get to the boat, I'll use one of the fishing poles to pull in Kyle and call for help."

"Or just drive down the beach and we can meet you," Ruthie offered.

"Not gonna happen." Sierra finished one sleeve and began sawing off the other. "No telling how far these tentacles stretch or which direction this colony came from. I don't trust the water to be clear for you guys."

Miguel looked past Sierra to the flats behind her. They'd trekked maybe a half-mile in, but he couldn't remember how wide this flat was before it reached open sea on the other side. One mile? Two or three? More? "Maybe we should just cross the flat. The other side faces the mainland, so there should be more boat traffic. We can signal for help from there."

"You're the one who didn't want to leave your brother and the boat," Ruthie pointed out.

"Yeah, but I don't want us all dead, either."

Behind them, Richard muttered. "I can't believe we left our cells on the boat. Fucking Kyle, man."

Sierra slid past Richard to face Miguel, resting one hand on his arm. "This is gonna be fine, okay? I don't want to leave Kyle alone to cross the flats any more than you do. Plus?" Her eyes darted in the direction of his gaze, across the glaring horizon. "We don't know how deep this flat gets or how long it would take us to cross. The sun's gonna set in a few hours. We don't need to be caught ass-deep in mud with a bunch of gators and snakes when it's full dark out."

"Not to mention how much the sun's taken out of us," Ruthie said quietly. She held out one burned arm by example. "I've been using lotion all day, but I'm burnt. Even if y'all aren't tired yet, you'd be exhausted before we made it to the other side."

Miguel swallowed down protest. His legs felt like lead, and they'd eaten the little bit of food they'd brought along.

"This'll work, y'all." Sierra pulled up the now sleeveless top of her wetsuit and zipped it shut once more. The detached sleeves reached above her knees and landed tight against her skin, a few inches above where the suit's hem ended, covering her skin all the way down to her ankles. "Help me out, Richard?"

Together, they tore strips of plastic from the edge of the water-bottle packaging and tied it tight below her knees and above them, holding the torn sleeves to the lower portion of her suit. With the lower portions of the sleeves tied tight to her ankles, they wrapped the remaining plastic around her thighs and waist to offer more protection against the tentacles.

And then she turned around to the group, all of whom stood near the water without letting it touch them.

"I don't like this," Richard muttered. "Maybe I should go. I know more about these things anyway."

Sierra came up close and tipped her head back in search of a kiss, waiting silently until he relented and brushed his lips across hers. "It's gotta be me," she pointed out. "I'm the only one wearing a wetsuit, and y'all's boardshorts and t-shirts wouldn't do a thing to protect you. *Plus*, none of y'all would fit into this suit even if you wanted to trade places with me."

Miguel licked his lips, looking for an argument and finding none.

She wrapped her arms around Richard, leaving a long line of muck caked along his chest, and rested her head against his t-shirt for a minute. "I'll be fine."

Her voice didn't tremble. Didn't even sound doubtful. But the glance she shot at the ocean of Portuguese men o'war in front of her suggested something less than confidence.

Even in the glare of the sun, Miguel's limbs went suddenly cold. Weighted with Sierra's plan and the distance to the boat.

"You'd better be fine." Richard brought her in tighter against his chest, his grip digging into her suit as he held on. "We gotta celebrate your twenty-first next month."

She pulled away with a laugh, though it didn't sound real over the lapping of the water. "Margaritas, baby. Lots."

Miguel held his breath as she stepped within an inch of the water, letting her feet sink into the squelching mud without fighting the pull of it.

She slid one foot forward, then another, and kept going in a stilted stingray shuffle. Soon, she was knee-deep in the water, Portuguese men o'war floating on every side of her. She glanced over her shoulder, her eyes finding Richard's where he stood a few feet from Miguel, tight-lipped.

"I'm fine, see?" Without waiting for a reply, she turned back around and slid further into the sea of tentacles and sails covering the blue water of the Gulf. This close to the Keys, the water was the tropical turquoise of desert isles seen in movies. It was only slightly darkened by the silt being stirred up with her passing and the flat behind them, but the purple-pink edges of the creatures surrounding her made it more surreal than anything.

"Ouch, damnit!"

"What?" Richard demanded. "Is it through your suit?"

Sierra shook her head violently, a sob breaking out of her throat, but she didn't turn back to them. She held her arms up in the air, jiggling them wildly as if to shake off cramps. "No, no, no! I'm…I'm fine. Just…" Whatever she might have said bled into a whimper as she froze where she stood, and Miguel thought he could see a tremble starting in her arms and shoulders as her head shook.

"What?" Richard called.

"The plastic's slipping!" Her forward progress had stopped, and she swayed where she stood, waist-deep among the men o'war's sails and mere feet from Kyle's bobbing body among them. "The mud must've…fuck, fuck, fuck…I can't feel my left leg," she sobbed out, "and the tentacles…I think they're wrapped around my knee!"

"Shit." Richard started to take a step forward, just stopping himself from putting his bare foot into the sail of one of the creatures. "Keep going, Sierra! You're closer to the boat than us!"

"I know." Her voice broke in a wail of pain, but she didn't seem capable of moving, and then Miguel saw what she was about to do before the others did.

"Don't, Sierra! Don't!" His scream seemed to vibrate off the siphonophores, and a few dipped below the surface, sensing a threat.

But her hand was already edging along the surface of the water, as if building up the courage to dive.

"No!" Richard screamed. "Sierra, no!"

"I just…have to…get them from around my knee…and then I can—"

Her words broke off in a scream as she dipped her hand down, angling in the water and reaching down until the water gaped at her elbow, sails all around her, and then she jolted upward.

Blue tentacles hung from her arm like alien entrails, and the siren of her wail broke the air in two.

She swung her arm upward, trying to dislodge the attackers, and turned with the motion. A tentacle flung upward and caught her across the cheek. It smacked her eye, and the whole left side of her face went instantly red as she screamed.

Ruthie gripped Richard. He shouted Sierra's name, shifting them both closer to the water.

"Miguel, help me!" Ruthie yelled, jolting him into action.

Richard fought against the two of them as Sierra wailed, frozen in the water, and then, suddenly, she went silent. Richard used the distraction to slap himself free of Ruthie. Miguel just kept her from falling into the waiting tide while their friend splashed forward, screaming Sierra's name in between curses and pushing forward through the creatures' venomed tentacles.

Miguel turned away and pulled Ruthie to face the flats with him, Richard's cries turning into curses and whimpers behind him.

When he chanced a glance over his shoulder, Richard had reached Sierra and pulled her into his arms. Her limbs and face were a blazing cranberry color except for where tentacles tangled blue upon her skin, and she hung limp against him. Richard himself was hyperventilating, stings multiplying against his arms and face and legs as he cursed and moaned in pain.

Yanking Ruthie's face hard against his chest, Miguel shut out the torture behind him, though Ruthie sobbed and tears began streaking through the sweat and mud on his own face. His friends weren't making any progress toward the boat, and he didn't have to look to know it.

When Miguel turned around again, Sierra and Richard's forms were tangled together in a heap, partially submerged. They were within arm's reach of the boat. And nearby, his brother's body dipped peacefully in the tide, Kyle's once-pale skin reddened with sunburn and venom.

"I don't understand how they could all be dead."

Miguel didn't bother answering. He only gripped Ruthie's hand tighter and trudged another step forward, pushing his leaden legs through the muck of the flat. They had to keep going. They had to cross the flat and get to the side facing the mainland, where they could signal for help, and they had to do it before their bodies gave out. Ideally before the sun gave out, too. Action was more important than conversation right now.

Plus, there was no point repeating what he'd already said, and what Richard had told them when they'd first found Kyle. One sting was one thing. Five stings was one thing. Hundreds of stings, with tentacles wrapped around legs and arms and torsos, and thousands upon thousands of nematocysts—venom-filled, every one of them—when in open water and with more of the poison sinking in every moment, arresting organ function and blood flow…that was something else.

Still, Richard's mini-lecture echoed in his ears, even as the deadened brown of the flat mocked everything they'd known that morning. Everything they'd thought prepared them for this godfor-saken place.

We were stupid to come here. Stupid to think we were smart enough to be here alone. And now they're dead. Maybe we are, too.

Kyle and Richard had never had a chance. Sierra had, maybe… until the mud had melted away with the water, and her makeshift armor slipped along with it.

Ruthie knew all that. She just couldn't accept it, and Miguel's throat was dried up and aching from the attempt at making her.

He forced his left leg another step forward. He and Ruthie were both caked up to their waists now, having stepped in murkier patches along the way. Senses dulled to the swampy rotten-eggs smell, bodies numb with weakness. They'd reached a point where there was no sight of the ocean in any direction.

No matter where he turned, he saw mud.

Occasional mangroves and branches and dead logs broke the surface of the muck, and he was certain that if he'd slowed down and observed carefully enough, he might have picked out snakes and any number of other creatures who called the flats home, but he only really noticed the sparks of color that crossed his sight as birds. Otherwise, his focus remained on the horizon.

"I'm so burnt," Ruthie muttered. She stumbled beside him, and he gripped her hand and pulled her along. "Why did we come here?"

His sight went reddish for a moment, blurring, but he didn't stop.

If they got sunstroke here, they were dead.

"I need to stop, Miguel. Can we take a break?"

He almost didn't answer, but she tugged at his hand, her mud-gloved fingers slipping from his before she gripped his wrist again and pressed for an answer. "If I stop, I'm not going to be able to make myself get started again."

She barked what might have been a hoarse laugh. "Then don't. But I'm going to sit on this log. Just give me a minute."

All he had to offer was a short nod. Eyes on the distance ahead, he let her hand go.

He had to keep walking. No matter what.

One, two, one, two, one, two, one, two...

His right leg was one. His left, two. He counted, and counted some more. His brain had gone heavy and dead with sun and grief and disbelief hours ago, but he could count.

His leg caught on a branch, and he stumbled forward, cool mud splattering up against his forehead as he fell to his knees. Somewhere behind him, Ruthie called his name as he caught himself, his forearms and biceps swallowed up by the flats. The stuff caked all of him now except some small bits of hair and face.

He bit back curses and squelched oozing dirt in his fists before he pushed himself, stumbling, back up to a standing position. Carefully, he took stock of what was ahead of him, marking it as the horizon opposite their boat and their dead friends, and then he let himself turn back to find the one companion left to him.

Ruthie was maybe ten yards back, lifting herself off a half-submerged log. She waved at him, hefting the small knapsack of remaining water bottles back onto her shoulder. He should have taken it from her even if it had been her turn to carry it.

"I didn't mean to get this far ahead of you." The call came out as a whisper—he was too weak to yell.

She trudged a few yards from the log and stopped, looking up to where he waited for her and seeming to focus. She waved, and he waved back. She smiled, and he smiled back.

And then, as if in slow motion, she wavered where she stood, and collapsed sideways into the flats.

"Ruthie." The word stumbled from his lips slower than her body had crumpled, and then he moved. Each step took breaths upon breaths of sulfurous air, the flats burning his lungs in mockery of his efforts. Near thigh-deep in mud, there was no way to move fast. High-stepping only slowed him. At first, he could see Ruthie's shoulder and half of her head. Not her lips or nose, though. Then, he saw only some hair.

Then, nothing.

No skin or fabric or face or lips to breathe with. No bubbles. No indent in the ground to signal where she'd fallen and lay submerged.

When he got to where she must be, he dropped to his knees and scraped his arms and hands beneath the surface, pushing sludge around. He didn't scream her name or call for her. His throat had gone closed with sobs much, much earlier.

She's gotta be here.

When one of his knees ran up against a fully submerged branch, he fell sideways and went lips-deep in the mud. He came up sputtering, spitting out brown muck that landed in clumps and then blended with the surface, no sign of disturbance.

Swinging his body to the right again, he kneed his way forward, and then he moved forward again and to the left.

And again. And again. And again.

When he found her, when his knee struck body and his hands landed against what was either leg or arm—*Ruthie's* lower leg or upper arm—too much time had passed since she'd gone under, and he knew it, but he dragged her up anyway.

It was her leg, and her sneaker flung sludge into his face when he hefted it above the surface. He dropped it to wipe oozing ground from his eyes before reaching back down and finding her shoulders.

Her head was encased in mud. No holes for eyes or lips or mouth. She might have been a dummy dropped by a plane, lifeless and plastic and empty of soul.

And he knew it.

Staring at what had been his best friend, he swiped at her skin and tried to find a pulse, but felt only cold sludge against her throat. Pushing fingers into her mouth, he dug out more of the suffocating ground, and then a scream finally erupted out of his throat against the weight of her corpse, slackening the air around them where he knelt.

He closed his eyes, counting. When he opened them, she was still there, and he closed them again and kept counting.

By the time he'd convinced himself he was living in a dream, and was able to open his eyes to see it, the mud had dried on his cheeks and on her features. There was no wetness or give to it anymore.

I'll take her with me. And when I wake up, she's going to laugh at me and then get mad at me for seeing her like this, even in a dream.

He pushed himself to his feet, and looked off to the horizon to center himself on the destination. There, between those two groups of mangroves. Five fingers left of where the sun was setting. That was where he was going.

Caked in mud, Ruthie was heavy.

Miguel's legs had been leaden for hours, but his arms took the strain and numbed within a few yards of where he'd found her. His back to the sinking sun, he kept pulling her along the surface of the flats. Her lower body trailing through the mud, leaving a wake that eased shut behind them.

When it went near dark, he stepped backward and landed waist-deep.

The mud was getting deeper.

He froze in place, Ruthie growing heavier in his grip with every passing second. If he needed a break, it had to be now.

"Just do it," he muttered, barely aware of what he was thinking or doing. "Or it'll be too late."

He turned and lowered his friend back beneath the surface, resting her just ahead of him, where he'd only been thigh-deep instead of waist-deep.

Stretching his arms out across the muck, he willed the cramps to leave his body. Then, gently—ever so gently—he sat down on Ruthie's body so that he could rest while keeping his head above the mud, and do so without losing track of her.

"I'm not leaving you behind, Ruthie. We'll get help, and then we'll come back for the others."

He rested his head back slightly, wondering if the surface of the flat would hold him. It didn't quite, but he let the back of his skull lay there as he turned his face to the night. Jolting, he just caught himself from falling asleep and sat straight again.

"Gotta stay awake. Gotta stay awake, Ruthie."

He crossed his arms, squeezing ooze from between arms and chest, and willed himself to sit still and tense. He'd just close his eyes for a minute. Two, maybe.

The night stilled around him, he breathed deep. The mud remained wet and soft, and he could feel Ruthie's Fitbit against his thigh, through the muck, telling him she was still there. When he shifted, the surrounding flat moved with him, and so did her body, and he could pretend she was still alive. Supporting him. Just waiting for him to pick her up.

"The stars are pretty," he muttered to her. "Kyle would like this."

He closed his eyes again, resting. Promising himself he'd stand up again any minute, and pick her up and keep going.

When the scales hit the back of his neck, he didn't recognize them as more than a breeze at first. But when they kept running across his skin, he opened his eyes.

The snake drifted along the surface of the muck, its body sinking only a centimeter or so into the surface as it moved, but it seemed to be recognizing him as a break in its territory. A branch-like thing for resting above the muck of the flats it was used to.

The snake's muscles flexed along the back and front of Miguel's neck, and he tried not to breathe.

In the moonlight, he saw the pattern of its scales, and he recognized it from the pictures they'd reviewed before setting out that morning.

An eastern diamondback rattler.

Because of course it was.

The snake's muscles flexed against his neck, and it circled him, slithering unconcerned along the surface of the mud and finding purchase around his neck and jaw, appreciative of the solid surface it had stumbled across between branches and mangroves.

This flat must connect to land at low tide. Maybe I don't have to signal a boat after all.

The thought was an easy one. Sun and the flats had stolen his ability to panic.

The snake wrapped itself loosely around his head. His mouth was parted, breathing overtop of one length of its back. There'd yet been no sound of a rattle, so the thing wasn't panicked. That was good.

He stayed there and still, centering himself on Ruthie's Fitbit cutting into his thigh and his heartbeat, felt in his throat and against his crossed arms.

He could outwait a fucking snake.

A breeze rose up, and the snake shifted against him.

For a moment, he thought about what would happen if he opened his mouth and bit the thing. Like the sudden aborted thought to leap from a high ledge when one crossed it, the urge was there and then gone, suicidal and then deadened.

He swallowed the urge down, and he kept breathing.

The snake shifted, caking off some of the mud against his neck. Tickling him. He willed himself frozen, holding in a curse. Still no rattle.

But when the sneeze came, the sneeze came.

Two lances of pain stabbed his skull above his right ear, and he jolted upward out of the muck as his hands and arms moved to dislodge the thing. In another moment, two hammer-blows of stinging pain struck just above his left eye, and though his arms found the snake's body and swept it sideways, the next bite, the third bite, took him in the left wrist, catching and holding before the snake's needle-like fangs released him with a tear of skin and disappeared into the night.

His throat closed, his sight already gone.

When he sank down beneath the mud, the wet sludge casing over him eased the sting where the snake's fangs had pierced him above the eye, some form of moist relief hitting his brain with the venom.

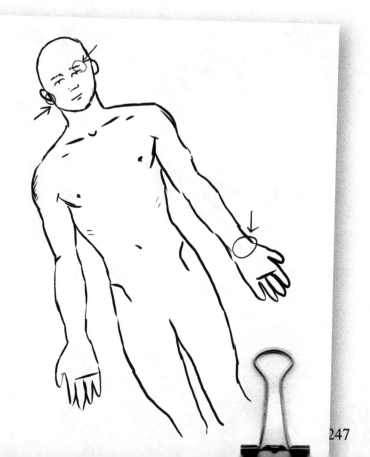

His body settled across Ruthie's, easy and slow. Oozing ground squelched between them. His throat wouldn't work, but he felt the flats easing into his ears, deeper and deeper, filling him like wet concrete. Slipping and drifting and squeezing into his nose, and then through his lips and down into his throat. Easing in, wet and opportunistic.

Landing fully and settling over Ruthie's body, the movements were easy and slow, settled and heavy. His body bloated with the mud atop the venom of the snake, cradled against the flats' rough ground.

Filled, swallowed, and dead where even the night couldn't reach him.

Against the Flats by Jennifer L. Collins

HOWLS BUREAU OF INVESTIGATION

HBI

SPECIAL AGENT   *Jennifer L. Collins*

Jennifer has a river dolphin tattooed on her foot and a large corn snake tattooed on her back. She suspects that, had she known they existed, she might have grown up to be an environmental terrorist—she's both thankful and a little horrified that that never happened. Jennifer has work upcoming in *Cosmic Horror Monthly*, and her first poetry collection, *Oil Slick Dreams*, was published in 2016. Meanwhile, her first novel is under submission to publishers. She lives in southwest Florida with her husband and their five rescues—three needy cats and two large pups with endless energy.

🐦 @wytwavedarling

MEMO: *Evidentiary imagery provided by P.L. McMillan.*
Agent headshot provided by Maia Weir.

HOPE IS A SAD SONG
by Gully Novaro

Screams bring me back to life, and with life comes pain.

The pain of being under a building's worth of debris. The pain of broken bones and bleeding wounds, of dust in my eyes and inside my lungs, stinging like bees.

Adding on to the familiar pain of failure. Of being too depressed to do my best, incapacitated by grief and guilt after my wife's suicide. Of being the single dad who doesn't know how to talk to his daughter. Of being the negligent cheapskate who doesn't change the water heater that leaks gas every now and then.

Now I can add bringing the building down to the list.

"Dad!"

Michelle's high pitched voice breaks my trance. Her sobs and whimpers echo through the darkness, joining the white noise of setting

251

rubble, rushing water, and rat squeals—their presence wasn't just a rumor after all.

I move, and my wounds come alive, sending signals of agony to my brain. The fallen concrete has crushed my left arm; it feels as if my bones have been replaced with broken glass, biting into my flesh. There's also something cold and metallic impaled into my abdomen and keeping me in place.

"Daddy, help me!"

I can't remember when Miche last called me daddy. One year ago? Three?

I open my mouth to reply, but dust and the claustrophobic taste of stagnated air rebel in my lungs, turning the answer into a coughing fit.

"Daddy, is that you?"

"I'm here, baby!" I manage to rasp. "Are you okay?"

"I'm scared!"

"Are you hurt?"

"No, I don't think so. But I'm stuck, Dad, I can't get out of the tub."

She had been taking a bath when it happened, and that may have saved her life.

On the other hand, if she hadn't taken a bath, the heater wouldn't have…No, I shouldn't think like this. It isn't her fault. It's mine.

That damned water heater. I should have gotten rid of it when it became a hazard, when it first started malfunctioning. I couldn't fix it myself, and I couldn't afford to replace it either. I should have at least turned it off.

But I didn't dare disappoint my daughter again. Being poor, working all day, barely seeing her at all. Being the reason why her mother…Asking Miche to live without hot water—all because I was too much of a loser to afford a new heater—was more than I was willing to put her through.

I felt as long as we were careful, we could still use the damned thing. And for over six months that held true.

Today it finally blew up, and it brought the building down on top of us.

"Stay still, baby! We're going to be okay!" I say. "You are okay, I'm okay, someone's going to get us out. We are going to be okay."

Okay has become my mantra, willing it to be true through repetition.

I can hear Miche humming to calm herself, as she does whenever she's nervous. I've never paid attention to the song before, but I recognize it now, and it pierces my soul. The song Pam used to sing to her every night, before she died.

I start to sing along. "Hush, little baby, don't say a word."

Miche quiets down, and I hurt for her, I hurt for her mother, I hurt for us. Then she sings back to me.

"Mama's gonna buy you a mockingbird."

Sirens wail in the background, tears well up in my eyes. Our voices fall in sync.

"And if that mockingbird won't sing!"

Every inhalation brings searing pain to my side—a reminder of the iron bar going through me—as I sing along. But the dust has settled, and the air—even though it smells of sewage and rust—is a relief.

The sound of water is now reduced to a constant dripping, the rubble has settled. The rats are still squeaking. Are they louder? Closer? Will they join our song?

"Papa's gonna buy you a diamond ring," I sing, ignoring the rats. Miche sings "Mama" instead.

Someone will rescue us soon. The firefighters should already be on scene. Every time something like this happens, someone survives. The news calls them a miracle.

Today, we shall be that miracle.

I smile, despite the pain. Hope is a ridiculous thing, and yet so hard to resist. I wonder if it's some kind of chemical reaction, a bodily response against despair. Or maybe it's idiocy. I let myself hope anyway.

"And if that diamond ring turns brass."

As we sing, I take inventory of my injuries, now that I know Miche is fine. My left arm is probably gone—I don't even try to move it. The pain is a sleeping bear, and I dare not wake it up. My legs are stuck between the rubble, but I can wiggle my toes and tense the muscles. Probably bruised but otherwise unharmed. And my right arm is free. I touch my stomach; it's caked with blood, but the wound is not as dangerous as it seemed—the iron bar has only gone through fat and muscle, about two inches deep.

"Mama's gonna buy you a looking glass."

A choir of squeals join our song, the volume rising as they approach. The crescendo in an ode to fear. Something walks over my legs as their chorus reaches its climax, and I scream. I kick out, hitting nothing, and I wake the sleeping bear. I scream in pain, as both my stomach and arm send spirals of torment to my brain.

"Dad!"

I hear Michelle in the background. And the squeaks move toward her.

"Dad, something's in the bathtub!"

Fuck.

"Kick it out!"

"I can't see, I can't find it!"

"It's more scared of you than you are of it!" I tell her, hoping it's true.

"There's more! They're walking over—" Then she howls.

Needle teeth start biting at my foot, it hurts even through the shoe. I can't help but imagine the pain Miche must be in, without any clothes to protect her. I kick, hitting nothing this time, but the symphony of suffering on my left side plays again.

My wails join Miche's, and the sirens outside—a very different tune than the one we sang moments ago. Help is coming, but I doubt they will make it in time. We need to survive a little longer. I need to protect her until they get here.

I bite my tongue and try to rip off the meat, fat and skin that keep me immobilized. Miche's screams get louder. I move my body, but the iron bar is stuck. My flesh is a sinewy steak hanging from the metal fang that tried to bite it off. Blinding fireworks show up before my eyes. As the pain comes alive, I feel the rush of blood flowing through the expanding wound. I'm nauseous and lightheaded, and I want to lie down. But I'm not giving up on Miche. I'm not failing her again.

One.

Two.

Three.

I twist my body with all my strength. My abdomen breaks free of the iron bar, and I scream as my side gushes blood. At least I can move now, a little bit. I get my legs from under the rubble; the rat hasn't let go of my foot yet.

I grab its fat body with my hand and smash its head against the ground. And I do it again. And again. Even after it stops moving, even after all I'm holding is a beanie baby of gore, I keep smashing the dead thing against the floor.

"Help me, Daddy!"

Her voice reminds me of what I'm supposed to be doing.

"I'm coming, baby! Fight them off! I'm coming!"

My left hand is still a chewed-up mess under a concrete jaw. I try to pull my arm free, as every nerve in my body begs me to stop. I can't. Miche keeps screaming, and that hurts more than everything else. I tug—skin, muscle and sinew stretch, no longer restricted by bone. It snaps clean. I taste blood as I bite my tongue to hold off the pain, and I keep pulling.

Tears run down my face, blood seeps down my chin, and I pause. I put my hand on the ground for support, and I'm met with a sharp, cold bite. Glass…and a frame. The only framed picture in our house is the one with Pam and Miche at the beach, their last picture together.

Miche keeps it on her nightstand, so it being here, in our living room, must be a sign. A final beacon of hope.

Miche's shouting is incoherent now.

I haven't tried my best since Pam killed herself, but I will now. Ignoring the pain, I grab a piece of broken glass, hold it like a knife. It digs into my fingers, down to the bone, but I won't let go. I pull my left arm as far as I can and cut the skin and muscle with ease, but the sinew won't cede. I pull as tight as I can, but all I manage to do with the piece of glass is strum it, like a guitar string. B sharp.

"Papa's gonna buy you a mockingbird," I scream, hoping she hears me.

My hand drops the glass shard, defeated and useless. But I must go on.

It's only sinew.

Only sinew.

I shut my eyes, put my mouth to my shredded arm, and bite. It *has* to give. I gnaw at it with my front teeth, see if I can puncture it with my canines, and slowly wear it down. A small piece of flesh gets inside my mouth; the taste of blood and raw muscle makes me gag. I don't waste time trying to spit it out, I force it down my throat and get back to biting.

The sinew snaps and I fall to the ground, landing on my head. I glimpse light above me, hear voices, then everything fades to black.

Incessant beeping brings me back to life. I open my eyes to a bright white light, and the framed picture of Pam and Miche. A nurse gasps and rushes over. Seconds later, the room is full of people.

A miracle, they call me.

I ask for Miche.

They tell me I'm the only survivor.

They say her death was instant, but I know better.

I'm alive, and with life comes pain.

HOWLS BUREAU OF INVESTIGATION

HBI

SPECIAL AGENT — *Gully Novaro*

Gully Novaro is a Non-Binary writer from Buenos Aires, Argentina, with love for all things out of this world. Their work aims to explore feelings of dread, solitude and wonder, and has been featured in *Wyrms: An Anthology of Dragon Drabbles*, *Well, This is Tense*, and the *Dystopian Drabble Showcase, Vol. 2*, among others.

MEMO: Evidentiary imagery provided by Leah Gharbaharan.
Agent headshot provided by Christi Nogle.

SYSTEMIC INFECTION
by Michelle Tang

"Rot starts from within," Nina explains to me. "You've got to clean it out, all of it, or things will never get better." Sweat beads her brow as she tugs out long swaths of gauze from deep inside the wound.

I flinch as Simone's whimpers turn into prayers. Into screams. Clumps of purulent discharge cling to the long strips of ribbon gauze, tied end-to-end, staining them brown and green and yellow and a bright, bright red, like a magician's never-ending handkerchief.

I have to raise my voice to be heard. "Should we…can we give her some more pain medication?"

"This is all the doctor ordered for her. Six tablets. It's enough to kill a horse. But Simone likes to be dramatic, don't you?" Nina curls her upper lip at the patient's tears. "Hold still! Be grateful your mother talked the doctors into admitting you—you think they have money for morphine at the public hospitals?"

"It hurts." Simone weeps as she writhes, fingers digging into her pillow, struggling to stay still. She's only a few years older than myself, not even thirty, but she looks like a small child as she cries.

259

Nina's eyes gleam. "It has to be clean, or it won't heal. I have to be thorough."

"Tumahimik ka! Some of us are trying to sleep!" one of the women in the ward room shouts. Many of the nurses refer to these three patients as manananggal, but I try not to think of them so cruelly—they are not vampires, or if they are, they only drain energy. Still, they look the part, with starched white sheets always drawn up to their waist, as if they don't exist below their torsos. As if, like manananggal, they fly away to search for victims, leaving their legs behind.

"We're almost done." I rub Simone's shoulder, casting about for anything that might help, and finding only empty words. "Take deep breaths. Almost there, Simone."

Nina shoves clean ribbon gauze into the crater where Simone's thigh muscle should be. I stare at the tissue, covered with yellow slough, beading scarlet. I stare at the grey of bone.

We finish the dressing change, Nina packing the gauze so tightly that it peeks through the dehisced wound like stuffing from a ripped chair. As we clean up the plastic detritus of the procedure, Simone lies still, shivering and pale, staring at the wall as though she could see through it, as if a pain-free refuge glimmers on the other side.

My eye catches on small pale circles in Nina's scrub pocket as she bends forward. I freeze, Simone's whimpers still ringing in my ears.

"Hey, you going to cry?" Nina straightens up and pulls me aside, toward the middle of the ward. "Look, I feel bad for her too. But you can't show kindness in this job. If your heart is too soft, the patients will take pieces of it until there's nothing left. You'll see."

I think of my siblings and how we've struggled this year. At how much weight my youngest brother, Georgie, has gained since we could afford food again. At how Marielle smiled for the first time in months when I brought home chocolate. I wonder what my mother would do in this situation, when so much is at stake, or what my father would want a nurse to do if I was suffering the way Simone does. I miss my parents so much I have to fight back tears. Georgie and Marielle's little brown faces flash into my mind again.

I say nothing about the six morphine pills I've seen in Nina's pockets, pills that should have been given to Simone before the dressing change.

Simone is an ashen thing the next day, burning hot and shrunken like wood from a waning fire. A stench emanates from her wound, as if her body decays without giving her the courtesy of first letting her die. The three manananggal in the room complain loudly, shouting insults at the younger patient.

"Stop it." I stand in the middle of the room, turning to face each of the women. "Can't you see she's suffering?"

"We're all suffering here. And she makes it worse, with her screaming yesterday and now her smell." One of them wrinkles her nose.

"Send her to another room. Another floor. Anywhere but where we paid good money to recuperate." Another fans away from her face as if that will waft away the stink.

Eleanor, the one I like least of all, spits on the floor. "Move her to the dumpster, where she belongs."

These three have been here for weeks, recovering from their cancer surgeries. They bonded over bullying other patients. They bully the nurses as well, expecting us to abandon our care of others to fluff pillows or clean up bodily fluids for their amusement. I'm certain they can each afford private rooms, but they would be rendered powerless there, deprived of a captive audience.

"There's something wrong with Simone," I tell the charge nurse. "I think the infection's worse."

"Matter of time." The charge nurse heaves a sigh and glances at the telephone. "She's Dr. Chiu's pet patient. Said she's more VIP than anyone this hospital has ever had. I don't want to be around when the doc finds out she's going sour."

"Maybe we can start antibiotics...shouldn't we at least ask?" I wring my hands together. "In other hospitals I've trained at, they would take wound and blood cultures. Start fluids."

"They can do it next shift." The charge nurse flips another page of his magazine. "I'm not paid enough to deal with Dr. Chiu's temper."

The shift passes slowly. I rush through my work, checking in on Simone between each task. The young woman hasn't made a sound, but a tear trickles from her clenched eyes to the sweat-soaked pillow. Her small frame is shivering despite layers of blankets, despite the Manila heat.

"Simone?" I whisper, crouching by the bed, somehow afraid another nurse will catch me. "What's wrong?"

It doesn't seem like she'll answer, at first. I straighten up, stretch my sore back, and then Simone cracks open dry lips. "It hurts so much. Can you please call my mom to come see me? I'd like to say goodbye. In case..."

Systemic Infection by Michelle Tang

What might I say to my own parents if I could see them? What might have given me some comfort this past year? "I will. I'll call right now." And yet there's a resistance to my body, unseen but powerful, like a riptide pulling me away from shore. Some of the nurses won't want me to get involved. Some will say I'm asking for trouble. But who am I to turn away someone asking for their parent, when I so badly yearn for mine?

During the chaos of shift change, when we are giving report to one another and the doctors are preparing to round, Simone's mother slips in. She is tall for a Filipina, her hair long and wild, tan skin unlined. She strides through the hospital halls like the chief of surgery himself, but no one bats an eye. The woman nods to me, as if she knows my face just from hearing my voice.

I point with my eyes and lips towards Simone's ward room, in case she's never been.

Too late, I think of the three manananggal and what cruelties they might exact on a worried mother, what words might slip like scalpels into a grieving heart.

The stench seeps into the hallway, warm and fetid.

Dr. Chiu wrinkles his nose. "What's that smell?"

The odor is unbearable, so powerful it feels like a living thing, and yet it is death that rides the air and fills our lungs. The charge nurse I spoke to feigns confusion. "I thought I smelled something earlier, but it's suddenly much worse. Someone must have skipped a dressing change."

Even though my day is over, I follow the odor to Simone's room with Dr. Chiu and the other nurses, as if it beckons us. It fills me with growing dread and each step is harder to take. As if it's last year again, and I'm reaching toward a phone ringing in the middle of the night. As if it's doom that taints the air instead of a poor woman's infected wound.

Every patient in the ward room is asleep. At least, I hope they're just asleep. They lie on their sides, curled like fetuses, unmoving and silent. Even Simone, whose ribbon dressings lie in a putrid tangle on the floor by her mother's long skirts.

Her mother is so incandescent with fury, I cannot bear to look at her. She's an archangel descended from heaven with a flaming sword. She's Lucifer himself, too glorious to behold.

"You promised me you would take care of her. Like she was your own, you said." The woman's low voice throbs with emotion. With power.

Dr. Chiu, a man who has brought nurses and other doctors to tears with his arrogant rudeness, falls to his knees in supplication. No one even gasps. We are frozen, as helpless as the patients, who I only now observe are staring at us with pleading, wide eyes.

"I have. I promise you. I've taken out the cancer, the margins are clear. We can deal with the infection. You'll have Simone back home soon." Sweat is a circlet around his bald head, a ruined king genuflecting to his usurper.

Simone's mother bends to speak to Simone, whose eyes flick over towards Nina. The strange woman straightens up again and glares at the soiled dressing she's pulled out of her daughter and thrown on the floor, before she points at Nina. "That one is never to touch my daughter again. I expect every nurse to count out my daughter's pills in front of her before the dressing changes. And no one is to remove what they find in her wound."

The look on her face, the burn of her dark gaze, sears into my mind. It burns, as if I stare directly into a solar eclipse. Dr. Chiu clambers to his feet, back bent like Atlas carrying the sky, and brings Simone's mother to the hallway for privacy.

Nina swoops towards me, but her anger is a candle compared to the inferno I have just witnessed. "Had to run tattling to mommy, didn't you? You're going to regret it."

"I didn't say anything." But she is gone, leaving my words to hang in the air. I swallow them back, push back other, harsher words that are scrambling out of my throat. I need this job, and I won't survive without the other nurses' support.

Another nurse, Julia, pats my shoulder before she leaves. "Some of us forget patients are still people, with their own thoughts and voices. Even if they're afraid to share those with us."

Dr. Chiu returns without Simone's mother. He is pale and snappy, a shadow of the man he once was. Simone is to be moved into a private room. Blood is to be taken, antibiotics to be started, and I am to redress the infected leg, leaving whatever the powerful woman has left in the wound untouched.

It feels like a punishment. My shift has already ended.

I count out morphine from the paper cup before Simone swallows them. Six tablets, Thirty milligrams of relief. While we wait for the drugs to take effect, I help the ancient service assistant, Ferdinand, move Simone's things. The manananggal are silent for once, sitting up in bed half-covered once more, their eyes predatory. I pity the next victim assigned to this room.

When it comes time to replace Simone's dressing, no one will help me. Even Julia averts her gaze when I ask at the nursing station. Nina has been here for decades, her influence quite strong, and she has advised the other nurses that I am not to be assisted.

Dr. Chiu placed new wound care orders in Simone's chart before he left. The instructions are…peculiar. Gentle irrigation with saline, no suction, light packing. It feels like mere ritual instead of the vigorous efforts we were making before. Simone has left her room dark, the streetlights outside the window providing scant illumination.

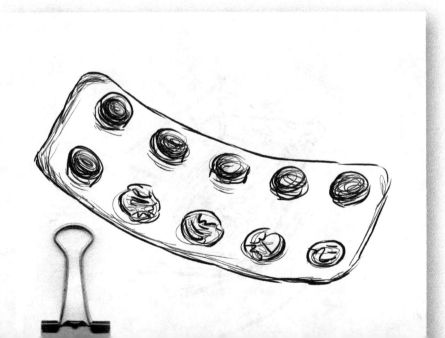

I don't want to wake her. For the first time, she seems comfortable, relaxed. I set out my supplies and lean over the wound, squinting in the dim light.

Deep in her thigh, against the yellow slough of Simone's wound bed, something moves.

Perhaps she hears my gasp, because she gives me a sleepy smile. "Don't be afraid. My mom did this for me."

My hand trembles as I reach for the light switch. I do not want to see, but I must finish this last task so I can go home. I fix my siblings firmly in my mind. They need me to be brave.

The gaping hole in Simone's leg teems with insects. Maggots, hundreds of them. They squirm and roll, their pale, worm-like bodies glistening in the light like shattered teeth. They are the size of rice, but fatter and more yellow. And they are…they are feeding.

It is for Henry, the man of the house now that my father is gone, that I hold in my screams. For my sister, Betty, that I gently rinse the wound with saline, careful not to disturb the bugs. For Marielle, I dare to dry the area before filling it with sterile gauze. Georgie…little Georgie is the reason I wait until I have finished, until I've cleaned my supplies and run to the change room, before I allow myself to vomit.

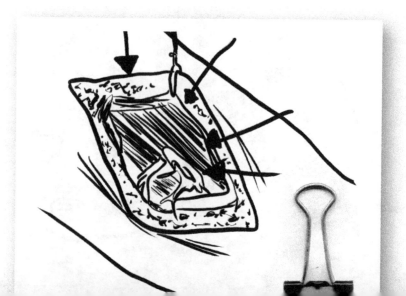

Systemic Infection by Michelle Tang

Instead of resting or eating that night, I clean our small house, throwing away old food we can ill afford to waste and scouring the kitchen until my hands are raw and red. I can't get those bugs out of my mind, can't bear to think of them festering, multiplying in our cabinets and fridge. When I finally sleep, I dream I'm on a sinking boat, and the undulating sea is made of shredded, pale flesh, while a low, throbbing voice invites me to dive into the deep.

I wake up at dawn to ready the children for school, and then I sleep again, dreamless and restless, until my siblings return home once more. It's time for my night shift. Some sense of foreboding takes hold of me before I leave, a sense of gathering storm clouds, and I kiss each of them goodbye as if it's my last chance.

The moon rises full and bright in the Manila sky. Some nurses say that full moons make patients more anxious and nights more strange. I've always been mesmerized by its cold, clear light. Tonight it feels like a bad omen, a peephole through which a malevolent god can watch humans suffer.

Nina shushes the others as I enter the nursing station. The tactics of a schoolgirl. Despite my best efforts, the whispers and baleful eyes eat away at me, and my grief waxes as full as the moon shining above our wing. I look at my patient assignment and school my expression, sure the others are waiting for my reaction. Among three other patients that require the most care, I have been assigned all three manananggal. It will be a long night.

The foul smell is gone when I pass Simone's room, and I take the time to smile at her. The antibiotics, or maybe the maggots, have helped. The thought lightens my step, despite the dread at my heavy patient load. A prisoner on death row loses nothing by skipping to the gallows.

I am washing Eleanor when she knocks over my basin of soapy water a third time. I am soaked, my shoes a sloshing mess.

"Oops," she says. "Going to call Simone's mother again, since you don't have one?"

I don't know how she found out about my parents. My colleagues must have told her. Her words—and the betrayal of confidence—strip something vital from me. Whatever was holding me upright and functional disappears with her unearned malice. I try to rationalize: Eleanor feels helpless and she wants to reclaim a sense of power; she is afraid, and uses this to feel brave; I am lucky to have my health. My thoughts aren't enough to contain the pain, which has not faded over the year, but metastasized like a tumor. Suddenly the razor edge I've balanced on all year sharpens—shears me in two. There is no end to my troubles: my job will not improve; I must raise my siblings alone, hiding my stress and grief. My parents will never return.

I burst into tears.

The ward room is silent, each patient a spectator watching me sob. I can't stop, and I can't move. My legs give way until I drop to my knees, gloved hands hiding my face. I am ashamed, but I can no more stop my tears than I can change human nature. I hate this unit, how it teems with abuse and corruption, cruelty passed from doctor to nurse to patient like an infection. I hate how it holds us hostage, makes us witness the abuse unless we choose to leave or join in. I hate how it chang—

Screams ring out. Agonized, terrible screams.

"Mama!" Simone shrieks. "Mama, help me!"

My own troubles forgotten, I run to her room to join the mass of nurses watching from the doorway. It smells like blood and the sea in the hallway.

Nina's eyes are frenzied, her face shiny with sweat. She is sitting atop Simone, ignoring the woman beating at her back with weakening fists. "There are bugs inside her!" she bellows at us, her gloved hands digging, digging. "Unclean filth!"

"They're maggots, Nina." The charge nurse holds both of his hands out, his voice calm and soothing. But his face is strained, his eyes so wide I can see white all around his iris. "They're eating the dead flesh away. Dr. Chiu told us not to touch them. Nina, please. You're hurting Simone."

The canister of coarse table salt from the break room falls from the bed onto the floor. Only then do I realize what Nina is doing. Streaks of red and crystals of white are caked on Nina's gloves, splattered on her scrubs. She is scrubbing the bleeding flesh with rough salt. Nina rakes her fingers through Simone's wound, strewing a handful of dead maggots in our direction. Simone's hands patter weakly against Nina.

We are frozen in horror, all of us, until ancient Ferdinand pushes through. "You're killing the girl," he snarls, and pours an open bottle of saline into the wound to flush out the salt.

Blood and dead maggots float out of the hole in Simone's thigh. It is larger than it was yesterday. Nina's hands have torn the tissue and skin in her zeal to clean the flesh. People drag Nina off Simone, and the salt has been rinsed away, but Simone doesn't stop convulsing.

At first, I think it's pain. And then I see her lips are blue and bloodless, her movements faltering, her breaths rattling.

The code lasts for an hour before Dr. Chiu calls it. Simone is dead. He runs his hands through what's left of his hair, shaking and furious. "You don't know what you've done," he repeats. "You've cursed us all."

I shudder as I remember Simone's mother. I do not envy the doctor tonight.

"I tried to save her," Nina pants. She glares at us all, daring us to say otherwise. "You were all witnesses. I tried to save her."

The silence has its own stench: of complicity, of shame.

We cover the body with a clean sheet, and Ferdinand mops up puddles of half-dead maggots, striped with blood, encrusted with salt, like bloated sea creatures from the deep. The air in the unit is filled with nervous anticipation. Even the patients are quiet.

Simone's mother does not come right away. I sit with her daughter's body during my breaks and when I chart, so she is not alone. It is uncomfortable, yes, the feeling of a silence waiting to be broken by a cleared throat or a new topic. But my companionship is all I have left to give her. It is not nearly enough.

Nina is subdued as she works. All of us are. It is a night of shivering anticipation, of trembling dread. Something is coming. I feel it in my bones.

She arrives when the clock strikes two a.m. The Witching Hour, as my parents called it.

I gather my charts when she enters. Dr. Chiu, the coward, has long since gone home.

The brilliant burn of the woman has faded, banked into embers by grief. She is dressed all in black, her hair split into two braids. Her eyes are wet like fresh tar. "My daughter. My only child, what have they done to you?" She gasps as she draws the sheet back, keens as she traces her fingers over the jagged rip in Simone's cold thigh. I don't dare look to see if she notices the nail marks scraped through the wound. "I failed you, mga anak. I failed you."

I hurry out before I hear her last words to her daughter. I have enough things to haunt me at night.

She is inside close to an hour, before she reappears in the doorway. Her face is drawn and flat, like she has died alongside her daughter. She beckons to me. "Simone tells me you have been kind to her. I thank you for that." I ignore the way she uses the present tense. Sometimes that happens, before they've accepted their loved one is gone.

"I want to show you something," Simone's mother returns to her daughter's corpse.

I take a few steps inside before I stop. The air is strange, heavy and humid with energy. It makes my skin crawl.

She turns to the covered figure on the bed and whistles as if calling for attention. "Now, my darling." Her voice is low and throbs with power.

The sheet covering Simone's body flattens against the mattress. As if her body has collapsed, or turned to dust in an instant. Hundreds of insects skitter from the bed, flying and crawling and twisting, and only my fear that I'll swallow one keeps me from gasping.

They leave the room and invade the unit, like a plague of locusts. The nurses begin to scream, and then the patients' voices join in, a late night choir of the damned.

Some insects return to Simone's mother. They carry string between their mandibles. No, not string—hair. She crouches, long black skirts sweeping the floor like the train of a wedding gown. She ties these strands of hair to various insects, to cockroaches and burrowing wasps and centipedes. Then she sends them forth again, captains of her armies, and where they go, more creatures follow.

Simone's mother grips my shoulder as she leaves. It reminds me of comforting Simone while Nina changed her dressing. "You are no stranger to loss. If I see your parents, I will ask them to send you a sign that they're still with you. As a gesture of my thanks."

Then she is gone, and Simone's bed is empty, and the room is heavy—drowning—with magic.

Insects swarm the unit, crawling into scrubs and into nostrils, eating at flesh. I tie a wet towel over half my face and venture out.

The three Manananggal are covered with crawling things, as are the rest of my patients. The women shriek as insects burrow into their skin, choke on many-legged creatures crawling down their throats, swat futilely at bugs feeding on the thin rivulets of blood that seep from new wounds. Their abdomens swell, grotesquely, impossibly fast. They are nine months pregnant in the space of seconds, and then their clean white hospital gowns become speckled with red. Blood blooms like flowers, oozes like honey, and I can see, from the undulations beneath their flesh, that the three vampires are being devoured from within. Eleanor grows until her skin splits open like a too-tight dress, and a stew of writhing insects spill out of her. The largest one, the cockroach, has a strand of Eleanor's brown hair tied in a neat bow around its thorax.

I try to pull one of the women out of bed, to escape. Her forearm wriggles strangely beneath my palms, and I cannot bear to hold on.

Ferdinand calls my name, and I follow him out to the nursing station. There is one other nurse, kind Julia, who is untouched by the insects, but the rest of my colleagues are already half-devoured, yellow fat bubbling through split skin. Still, they struggle to escape the swarms, screaming in pain as they whip themselves with wet towels, while they flail with lit torches they've made of rolled patient charts.

One frantic nurse sets another colleague on fire. Nina's purple scrubs are the only way I recognize her. Even her eyes are being eaten, fat grey maggots feasting on what's left of her corneas. They fall through the holes they make in her sclera like tiny round popcorn covered in vaseline. She turns in my direction, shrieking. Half of her tongue is gone.

An alarm blares, deafening me and drowning out the sound of insects. Ferdinand grabs for me. "It's the fire alarm. We have to go."

Smoke billows into the unit, from the makeshift torches igniting paper charts and cotton scrubs. I want to evacuate the patients, but there are none to save. I wait with the survivors from my unit out on the sidewalk while the firemen arrive. Their hoses will not work—only worms spill out while the fire devours what's left of the old wing.

It doesn't take long for the surgical ward to burn down to cinders. The smell—of roasting lechon—makes my stomach rumble, and I retch at the realization that it's not the smell of pork I'm salivating over. We wait with the crowd until the fire dies, until smoke fades like spirits, until ashes float in the air like escaping insects. I take care to keep my distance from those, just in case.

The rest of the hospital, newly built with firewalls, remains untouched.

When there is nothing left of my workplace and my coworkers but char, I walk home to my siblings. Sweat trickles down my back like dozens of tiny legs, and I can't stop shivering.

And then I see two butterflies. They dance together in the coming dawn, fluttering near me. They alight, just for a moment, on my shoulder, before they fly toward the rising sun. I think of Simone's mother, of my parents, and despite the night I have just experienced, I feel comforted. There are forces beyond my understanding in this world, clearing out rot, and perhaps…watching over me.

So many of those patients and staff were innocent, their only crime not speaking up. And yet, in the end, healing has to be all-encompassing. People can't change if corruption has already taken root.

Rot starts from within. You've got to clean it out, all of it, or things will never get better.

Systemic Infection by Michelle Tang

HOWLS BUREAU OF INVESTIGATION

HBI

H.B.I

SPECIAL AGENT   *Michelle Tang*

Michelle Tang writes speculative fiction from Canada, where she immigrated as a toddler. Her short stories have been published by Cemetery Gates, Escape Pod, and Flame Tree Press, among others. When she's not writing, Michelle works as an oncology nurse and lurks on social media.

MEMO: Evidentiary imagery provided by P.L. McMillan.
Agent headshot provided by Cassie Daley.

FOREVER HOME
By Chelsea Pumpkins

My phone blares, ratcheting me awake. The emergency text tells me I have mere minutes to evacuate. Protocols flip through my mind like a rolodex, but come up empty for "tsunami." Shit.

Documents, photos, T shots, hard drive, heirlooms—what could I save in minutes?

What can't I live without?

Pekoe.

I call to him as I rummage through a pile of crumpled clothes. "Pekoooooe." My sleepy voice cracks on the high-pitched syllable.

I yank on jeans, sports bra, hoodie. I slide my feet into sneakers, and unplug my phone.

"Pekoe, kitty-boy, c'mere." I clear my throat, trying to keep the edge of panic from my tone. He'll be able to tell.

The warning wails again. I look at my screen.

MOVE TO HIGH GROUND
IMMEDIATELY

I drop to my knees and look under the bed—nothing.

"Koe-koe puff." I try every stupid nickname I'd invented over the years. "Peeky-pie."

I run to the bathroom, to the sink where he sometimes sleeps on hot nights.

Empty.

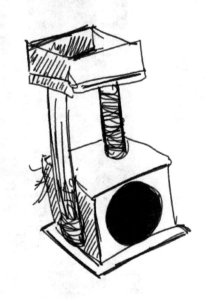

I riffle through the towel closet, in case he senses the danger and is already hiding. My pleading coos grow too shrill, so I cluck my tongue for Pekoe until my mouth goes dry.

A scared, strained mew calls back to me from downstairs.

I rush down to find him. As my feet hit the landing, I hear the booming rage of water crashing down the street. The firework shatter of windows, the groaning of metal, the snapping of centuries-old tree trunks.

It's here.

My limbs are electric with panic, fingers and toes buzzing with static. I'm screaming for him now and listening for his little voice over the roar of the approaching ocean waters. Thuds pound against the house, and the walls creak against the pressure.

I dash to Pekoe's cabinet for treats, desperate for anything that'll draw him to me.

My sneakers slosh in the kitchen. Water sprays from the edges of the back door and the spurting stream climbs up the door jamb inch by inch. We're out of time.

Pekoe's crying, the throaty sound of alarm in his voice. I picture his dilated pupils and ears pinned back, frozen in fear. He needs me.

I need him.

We promised to protect each other. From day one, when he scrambled into my arms at the animal shelter—his big kitten ears filled with mites, and his eyes goopy with infection. The two of us strays, once abandoned, now bonded. He knew we could heal each other.

A wall of floodwater bursts through the door and knocks me off my feet. Briny sewage chokes me and tosses me in its angry current. I grasp for something sturdy to hold onto, to get my feet under me, but the deluge has unanchored everything in arm's reach.

The undertow drags me through the door, out of the house, and I fight for air on my front lawn. My feet touch the ground and I waste no time propelling myself up with all my strength. I burst through the surface, my arms flailing for any type of life raft.

My neighbor's plastic chaise lounge rushes towards me, bobbing in the mad waves. It collides with my face, smashes my nose. I taste blood. I lock my arms around the chair and throw my leg over its side. It's enough to keep me above the churning water.

The current pulls me further from the house. I row with the one arm I can afford to use, but it's futile.

"Pekoe!"

I spot him in the bay window—a bead of orange among the gray fury of the tsunami. His lips and whiskers pull back in a constant cry for help. His tail whips behind him as he paces. He shakes a front paw, and then a back one. The flood is at the windowsill.

"Pekoe, run. Upstairs! Go to bed—bedtime!" I'm yelling nonsense, anything to try to get him out of there.

The ocean claws at me, trying to capsize me and swallow me whole. It's hungry for my body, my breath. Wrenching, choking, dragging.

It can't have me.

I paddle with my right arm, pulling water back with all the power in my upper body, and kick ferociously with my left leg. Waves rock my chaise liferaft and pummel me with debris. I dodge tires and trash barrels and tree limbs while trying to maintain purchase.

Pekoe still pleads for me in the window, the water now clutching his ankles.

My throat is raw and ragged from screaming back to him.

Against my effort, the current pulls me further out, beyond my yard and into the street.

I can't leave him behind.

I abandon the chaise with a lungful of air and dive into the brackish rapids. They suck me down, turn me over, and tumble me among the wreckage.

The waters won't relent. I've used up all my oxygen, and my body fights against instinct to gasp for more. My clothes are heavy chains, conspiring with the sea to hold me under. There's no telling which way is up, which way is home.

I open my eyes and watch everything rush around me. A stroller appears from the murky current and before I can move out of the way, it slams into my ribs. I'm betrayed by my nervous system with a sharp inhale. The sea assaults my nose and mouth, and my chest heaves as it struggles to clear the water in search of air.

I plunge my arms through the water and pray I'm swimming up.

Within an instant, a whack at the back of my skull turns everything black.

A child's tantrum wakes me from a nightmare, and I instinctively reach behind my bent knees for Pekoe's curled sleeping body. The empty space knocks the wind out of me. Night after night. It was easier in the hospital with the constant drip of painkillers flowing through my blood. It was easier to be numb.

Attempting to escape the crying, I turn over in my bunk and wince as my bruised ribs throb. The threadbare FEMA-issued blanket clings to my sweat-dampened skin.

I can't tell what time it is in this windowless arena. I listen for the clatter of aluminum trays and coffee canisters that indicate breakfast is soon, but it's quiet beyond the noises of sleep and fear.

I think about mornings with Pekoe. How he'd stir from his slumber with my alarm clock and headbutt my face as I tried to snooze for an extra nine minutes.

A distant memory now, and a desperate hope.

The shelter begins to stir, and I slink to the showers during the breakfast rush. I claim the furthest stall to avoid questioning glances and wash quickly with tiny hotel bottles of cheap soap and conditioner.

My overgrown hair drips down my back as I wait in line for burnt coffee and cold scrambled eggs. I pull the dispenser for scalding liquid, and the smell transports me to my kitchen, where Pekoe would sit on the barstool and chat with me while I'd prepare double shots of espresso. I got an earful every day while he impatiently awaited his breakfast.

The reunification desk opens at eleven and I sit on my bunk with shaking knees until then, hoping today will be the lucky one.

"Have you found any cats? Mine is orange with a white stripe—"

They cut me off there and wave me away.

I hold up my hand-drawn sketch of Pekoe, in blue ink—the best I could muster.

"No pets," they say, and I can see they're tired of repeating themselves day after day.

No pets.

Dismissed like a child's plaything, as if disposable, replaceable. Pekoe isn't just my *pet*, nor am I his keeper. They don't understand.

To win an animal's favor is easy. All it takes is a little food, a little patience. But to earn an animal's devotion—to forge a language and intuition of each other's deepest needs, to bind your spirits together in a strand that withstands time and space—that's another thing entirely.

Rejected, I return to my bunk, lay on my back, and stare at the ceiling as lights flicker and birds flit among the trusses. I close my eyes and try to quell the pulsing ache behind my eyes, unsure if it's grief or hormone withdrawals. Doesn't matter. It's probably both.

After lunch, lines queue at the phone booths where people call families, banks, insurance, and utility companies. I wait my turn to hear the authorities tell me my house is still condemned and unsafe for re-entry. With every day denied, my chest grows tighter. How many days can Pekoe survive on his own? Will he revert to his days in the feral colony, where he had to scavenge, fight, and hide to stay alive?

I wander aimlessly for hours until the next meal. I stop by the donated clothes table, searching for baggy tops and anything resembling a binder. I meander outside to get some sun and hope it's not time for Millie to be out walking Bindi, her therapy dog.

When I first got here, Bindi was my shining light. Millie would let me sneak a scratch behind Bindi's ears, and Bindi would lick my hands in thanks. They're the only two who'd look at me instead of through me, perhaps because they're here alone too.

But after a week or so, the sight of Bindi soured. She became a reminder of the void in my bed every night. Why was Bindi more deserving of rescue than Pekoe? Pekoe may not have a labeled vest, but he is just as much a necessity to me.

He's my will to live, my purpose for being. He's my every smile and every good day. He plucks my worries from their festering vines and keeps them in a faraway place where they can't hurt me. When I'm lost to the darkness that boils deep within me, my kitty boy guides me out.

The way he curls up on my chest and purrs until my tears dry.

The patter of his paws across the floor as he runs to greet me after a long day of work.

The silky spots behind his ears that I stroke until I fall back asleep.

He is as essential to me as air and water, and in every day that passes here without him I'm withering away.

A volunteer church van drops me off at the end of my driveway. In the five weeks since a neighbor fished my limp body from the rising tide, my home has fallen into a state of dereliction and decay. An orange FEMA "X" marks the siding—disaster hieroglyphics I can't decipher. Don't want to decipher.

The lawn is dotted with lagoons of rotten water where fat, black flies tap-dance atop my bloated collection of books. Unopened medical bills, soggy throw pillows, my favorite coffee cup...Pekoe's scratching post. My life has been disemboweled and my vitals are scattered outside for everyone to see. My grandmother's rocking chair lies splintered and graying as the centerpiece of destruction.

The south-facing wall of my bungalow is torn away completely, my living room like a dollhouse—one whose furnishings have corroded.

Five weeks. *Weeks.*

He could survive if he found his way out, found some food.

I'm rigid with fear, but propelled by hope as I walk through the cavernous entrance to my ruined home. Our forever home.

The smell hits me first, in the back of the throat—sulfuric, marshy, and the pungency of excrement. The odor is so strong, the room tilts beneath me. Unsteady on my feet, I reach for my bookcase for balance, but it's no longer standing. In its place, rows of stains mark the levels of standing water on the wall, the first one high above my head.

I stumble against the wall and the force of my shoulder leaves an indent in the sodden plaster. The scent of mildew is pasted onto me with smudges of gray streaking down my arm. I rub the marks to erase them, but they darken beneath my touch.

Dishes clatter around the corner in the kitchen sink. *Pekoe?* Flashbacks of scolding Pekoe for licking my dirty plates send my heart fluttering. I jog into the room.

Two red, beady eyes peer over the sink edge at me. A white rat stands guard while two ragged black ones scour the sink for food.

"Get!" I bang my fist against the water-logged countertop from across the room. It barely makes a sound. "Go on, get out of here!"

They scurry out of the sink, down the cabinets, and through a collapsed hole in the floor.

The floor sags around the hole, and from where I stand I see chewed wires and fallen pipes—the broken bones of my house. They dangle over standing water, which glistens like an oil slick. Noxious fumes drift up and singe my sinuses. My vision blurs.

Toxicity dwells here now.

I cover my face with the bottom of my t-shirt, turn around, and continue my search.

The pulse in my ears slows, and every step weighs heavier. I want to run, but a trudge is all I can muster. My heart yearns against impeding forces, and an unclearable fog descends upon my mind.

"Peeee-kooooe." The call slips from my mouth like a syrup, my lips swollen and sticky around his name. My voice sounds far away—a ripple. An afterthought.

I trail my fingertips through the slimy film that coats the walls, leaving a snail's trail under the tiny portrait gallery of those who gifted me their love. The floodwaters have transmuted my grandmother's porcelain smile into a scowl, and her antiqued eyes follow me as I drift by.

I reach the bottom of the stairs and wonder if I'm dreaming.

A sunbeam gleams through the window on the landing, and Pekoe sleeps on his side in its warming center—his favorite place to nap. Dust motes glint around him in an ethereal aura. They twinkle in my eyes as I float up the stairs to meet him.

I kneel on the landing behind him, in benediction.

His shiny orange coat has dulled to rust, his once fluffy undercoat filthy and matted. I comb my sluggish fingers through his faded stripes and fur falls from its roots in clumps.

I turn his tiny stiff body over to find a sticky, black gash in his abdomen. My chest fills with lead. There's no room left in me for breath.

"No," I whisper. "No, no no."

The edges of his wound are ragged and scabbed over. *The rats.* Flies pick at the remains of Pekoe's entrails. I stick my swelling fingers into the putrid void and pinch one of them between my thumb and forefinger.

The fly struggles in my grip. I pluck its wings from its thorax and watch it twitch helplessly in my palm. I drop it, and its raisin-like body bounces once on the molding carpet before coming to rest.

My shallow breath rattles in my lungs, up my windpipe. I bark out a wet cough into the crook of my arm, and it comes away splotched with muck. Confused, I wipe my mouth and a ropy strand of mud stretches between my fingers like a web. I turn my hand over and see that my nail beds have turned bruise-purple, and the bloodless color slithers down towards my wrists.

I cradle Pekoe's head and turn his face to mine. His shimmering green eyes have faded to milky gray. They don't meet mine anymore.

He stares unfocused and unblinking at the space above me. Fuzzy black mold creeps down his cheeks from the rims of his eyes.

"I'm sorry," I tell him. "I didn't mean to leave you."

His faded pink nose wriggles. I hold my breath and lean in closer. A pair of maggots crawls from Pekoe's nostril. He's filled with life, but not his own.

I wipe them away and pepper my precious boy's face with kisses until it's damp with my tears. I press my lips to his cold little nose and squeeze my burning eyes shut.

Instead of my body warming his, his corpse turns my lips cold. The chill spreads into my mouth. My tongue swells, first against my teeth then past them, protruding from my icy lips.

I pull Pekoe to my heaving chest and gulp for air as I rock him.

Pekoe's abdomen expands against my clutching arms. *A breath?*

He feels heavier. He balloons out, farther than his diaphragm and ribcage would contain.

Not a breath.

I turn him over again, and we're face to face.

Murky runoff drips from Pekoe's ears, then from the corners of his molded eyes.

Brackish water streams out of my nose and pours off my chin. My eyes sting with salt, as they did the day of the tsunami.

Pekoe's lips flare and water squirts from his mouth, too.

I open my mouth to scream—it's all that's left in me. Cold water surges from all the openings in my body. From his too. His waves crash onto me, and mine onto him, until we're both engulfed.

We're a pair now, drowning together.

Together.

For Argo

HOWLS BUREAU OF INVESTIGATION

HBI

SPECIAL AGENT — *Chelsea Pumpkins*

Chelsea Pumpkins is a writer from Massachusetts who stays curious about all things macabre. When she's not reading, writing, or watching something spooky, you may find her hiking in the White Mountains with her husband and sweet pitbull, Moose. You can read her stories in various horror anthologies and in *Shortwave Magazine*. She is the editor of *AHH! That's What I Call Horror: An Anthology of '90s Horror*, and a co-host of The Cutthroat Queens podcast.

www.chelseapumpkins.com   @ChelseaPumpkins

MEMO: Evidentiary imagery provided by Christi Nogle. Agent headshot provided by Maia Weir.

THE CHILDREN OF THE EVENT
by Carson Winter

The first person to see the wave was a fisherman. Like most of his kind, he was strong, fond of water, and a heavy drinker; he wore rubber boots and a yellow coat slicked with salmon guts. It's important to stress that there was nothing heroic about this fisherman. He was a normal man. He had friends and family. One bar server remembered that he used to show off on Friday nights, after the day's catch, impressing local women with his trick shots.[1] There was nothing that made him more special than all the other men and women who died early that morning, but because he reached for a radio, we know that his name was Jaycee Washington.

To this day, his body remains undiscovered. But it's his voice, his gasping SOS, that became the soundbyte that defined a catastrophe:

"Hello? Hello? This is, uh, Jaycee."

"Jaycee, this is the coast guard. What's going on? Over."

---

1   Anonymous interview.

"Something's in the water. Something's...[*inaudible*]"[2]

The water crashes against the deck and Jaycee is presumably thrown overboard. That alone is enough for a tragedy. A man is dead, lungs filling with icy salt water. But as we know, fate is not so kind. Because after *Carbon Angela* goes down, the water stills. Then, after an hour, it breaks.

It's hard to talk about what happened next, because it's absurdity incarnate. Karin Delle of the Northwest Linguistic Institute posits that's why we collectively decided to call the creature the Event.

The name stuck. The being, or whatever it was, crawled out of the ocean. Scaly, with black skin and red markings. A crown of curved horns. A maw of dripping fangs. A large distended stomach. Observers calculated it as standing roughly seven hundred feet on its hind legs, and half that on all fours. Its tail was as long as its body and then some. It came to the coast first, scuttling ships and killing men like Jaycee Washington, before climbing onto shore. Most people heard the Event before they saw it. Its deep resonating roar rumbled through the earth, announcing its arrival.

Just as its weight crushed through the docks, sending shards of splintered wood careening through the air, two Coast Guardsmen made the decision to sound the alarm, eleven full minutes after Washington fired off his warning.[3]

The broadcast was hastily put together. Press releases were rushed; news anchors and radio personalities were interrupted mid-sentence with breaking news.

Brian Seneca of WDFQ said, "It was like nothing I'd seen before. We'd done emergency announcements before, of course we did. We're

---

2   For myself and others, this was history. I remember repeating, "Something's in the water, something's in the water," while watching the news, doing the dishes. These words became a part of us.

3   In the aftermath, this prompted a public debate. Some commentators praised the Guard for their reaction time. Others dismissed it as too little, too late.

the news. But this carried with it a certain gravity. I could tell it was serious when the information hit us and the producers just looked at each other in disbelief. One of them, Randy, came up to me, dead serious, and said, 'Read the prompter. It's not a joke.' And that was that. I did it. Soon after, we were evacuated."[4]

The Event destroyed fifteen blocks of newly renovated waterfront property, burying restaurant-goers and the workers that served them in crumbling rubble. It continued its march of destruction for two hours, tearing through commercial and residential neighborhoods alike. Thousands perished during the Event's initial landfall. Whether by accident or design, however, is an entirely different matter.

---

4   Seneca went on to mention that the evacuation itself was a surreal affair. "We were hustled out of the building, into a news helicopter, and flown 15 miles up north. We were terrified. The helicopter could only fit so many personnel. They took us first, 'the talent.' I never felt so guilty in my life. When we were safe, I watched it fly away. I didn't realize it was never going to come back."

One woman, one of several dozen to live in the city center and survive its destruction, said, "...[I]t wasn't doing much but walking, really. I was shaking. I'm still shaking thinking about it. We were all huddled up under a fallen support beam. I could still see out to the street though. Its claws were yellowish, as big as me, if not bigger. And I couldn't see much, all I had was a triangle between two slabs of drywall, but I could tell that it was bending over, like it was about to do something. Which terrified me, you know? Because until that moment, I didn't realize that it had thoughts. It was *doing* something. I didn't like that, I didn't like that at all."

What the Event was doing in that moment, is an example of dramatic irony on a cosmic scale. The woman, who wished to remain anonymous, was a partial witness to a paradigm shift.[5] Many of us, this author included, did not know what the monster was doing in the city. We evacuated early, or lived in the suburbs and quietly quaked, glued to the news. Those who lived in the city had front-row seats to what the rest of us could only imagine.

Helicopter footage showed us what happened in those two fateful hours. The Event crashed through buildings, first knocking them gently with its snout; then, when the tenants in waiting fled, it flattened them completely. This routine was repeated many times. But when the people ran into the streets—and there were a good many—the great beast unhinged its jaw and leaned over them. It becomes obvious, through the footage, that the Event was *sucking* people whole into its maw. Hundreds of them.

There is one short clip of footage from a supermarket, where the camera is so shaky you can barely see anything but white walls and glass doors. What you can hear, briefly, is one man screaming, "Jesus Christ! It's eating them!"

Street after street, this continued.

For observers, the horror seemed to last an eternity—and for many of us, the image of the great behemoth, crushing our structures, and vacuuming up our friends and family, would come to define that

---

5   Many of those interviewed for this piece wished to remain anonymous, for reasons that will be obvious later.

morning. We sat together in our homes or evacuation sites, hugging each other close. We knew that our lives, or rather, our reality, had changed forever.

At noon, sitting in my one-bedroom apartment, twenty-five minutes east of the city, I heard one of my neighbors in the hallway screaming, "It's gone! It's gone! The monster left!"

I, and others like myself, wiped the sweat from our brows and gave into our own nervous energy. We left our apartments and walked outside, watching the plumes of smoke rise up into the sky.

An hour later, someone's teenage daughter pointed at her phone: "Look at this," she said. "Look at this." Soon, a group of adults gathered around her, to see the video. So many people crowded around her that others were left to ask, "What's it called? What are we looking at?" and then they too pulled it up on their phones.

We were all watching the same helicopter footage. There it was, the Event, stretched out in the remnants of our city, its posture reminiscent of a cat voiding a hairball. Its back arched, jaws parallel to the earth. It retched. We all watched the video hundreds of times, over and over again.

The Event hacked and hacked and then, a mass of twisted limbs came from out of its stomach. We couldn't make it out clearly from the footage until it zoomed in.[6] At the end of the video, you can see a large hill of wet humans squirming, separating from each other. The video cuts, a short time jump, and we're left with a lingering shot. The monster is gone, the Event is over, and on top of the rubble, an army of glowing survivors survey their surroundings.[7]

---

6   An entire article could be written just on how we, humans as a collective, experience trauma on a mass scale through second-hand reporting. Many of us, myself included, never saw the Event, nor felt its presence until hours after it had left. And yet, we still have in us a deep throbbing sense of despair, of loss and terror.

7   This went on to become an iconic image. The videographer who captured it refuses to be named and has donated the image to the public domain.

It was obvious that the people had changed in some way. We'd seen them on the news, listened to them talk. They described being in the monster's stomach as something akin to a womb, although they said it smelled of rot and sulfur. By all accounts it was dark, hot, and humid. They floated in a pool of thick saliva and stomach acids, gasping for air. Of the 376 that were swallowed, every one of them claimed that a warm calmness washed over them. When they came out (or were born, as some commenters put it), they glowed a peculiar green. In news segments, I watched them curiously as they struggled to articulate their feelings, as if they were newborn fawns taking their first steps with the English language.

The bias arrived immediately.[8] One man, a first responder who attended to the newly born, said, "I had an immediate reaction to them. I couldn't put my finger on it, but something wasn't right. They were normal, they looked like us, I thought. But, something inside me felt repelled by them."

This man, who wished to remain anonymous, captures the popular sentiment against the Children of the Event (who would go on to colloquially be called the Children). Although by all accounts they presented themselves as earnest, eager to help, and curiously humanitarian, their alien gestalt was almost universally off-putting.

The Children reintegrated as best they could. They went back to their families, hugged their loved ones (even when those loved ones cringed at their touch), and the rest of society began discussing the Event with a feverish intensity.

The first matter, of course, was where did the monster come from? The answer was: we did not know. This ambiguity created an ugly back and forth as officials theorized loudly on television. The Event was from the ocean, it was a lost creation from prehistory. Or, it was a product of our invention—a byproduct of environmental waste. Religious officials held an uncomfortable notion that it was the biblical Leviathan. Fringe metaphysicians maintained that it was a God, a spiritual reckoning given shape and form to punish us.

---

8   I myself admit to this, although I'm not proud of it. The first time I saw one on
     television, I recoiled.

We never received a definite answer. So, naturally, the question "Where did it come from?" became "Where did it go?"

That, too, proved to be unanswerable.[9] Observably, the Event came from the ocean and returned to it. Nations gathered to sweep the depths, but the Event was never found. It was as if it came to life, then dissolved into unlife. And all it left of itself was tragedy. And, of course, the Children.

My first interaction with one of the Children was at a volunteer event.[10] We gathered to begin the rebuilding process. There was also the hope of rescuing survivors, despite the utter devastation surrounding us.

We were brought together by the destruction of the city and we were determined to do something about it. That's all anyone could say at their television, for a while. "Somebody has gotta do something!"

---

9   Ambiguity tolerance is a part of a country's cultural makeup and reveals how a culture deals with uncertainty. Ambiguity theorists such as Rosha Hundvirst believe that, while the United States typically is identified as being an ambiguity-tolerant country, the Event challenged this cultural norm in some way, and since then, neuroticism has become more acute and pervasive. This represents one of the few great cultural shifts we've seen happen in real time.

10   I did this, in a way, to challenge my own biases.

Collectively, we came to the agreement that this is what somebody ought to do—show up and sift through the wreckage.

It became apparent very early on that there were Children among us. The eerie glow that emanated from them unsettled me deeply. I tried my best not to show my discomfort, because we were there to do a job. We were there to do something.

I was tasked by one of the Children, who was wearing an orange vest and a hard hat, to go with another of his glowing fellows, a man named Carlos.

Carlos was kind and friendly, often giving me advice on how to traverse difficult terrain. He smiled at me gently, helped me when he could.[11]

"Over there," he said. "There's more over there."

Carlos led me to the hollowed-out foundation of an apartment building that he seemed to know intimately, or rather, innately. We dug through rubble. I didn't talk much, because I didn't have anything to say, and also I was afraid of maybe saying the wrong thing. As if I would open my mouth too long and I'd have no choice but to ask about what it was like inside of the Event.

Carlos, it seemed, knew the question on my mind. But when he would look up at me, a smile spread thinly on his lips, a twinkle in his emerald eyes, it was like he was daring me to ask, to say something. That day, Carlos found twelve corpses amongst the rubble. I found none. When we reported to the organizer though, Carlos made sure to say *we* found them—a fine gesture, to be sure.

Everyone said it would take years to rebuild the city. We had all started to buckle down, ready for the long haul, while living in fear of the Event returning. It never did, thankfully. But some of us felt like it should.

---

11 On the day of, it was impossible to read this as anything but pointed condescension.

In actuality, most of the destruction was cleared in weeks thanks to the hard labor of a group of efficient community-minded teams. It came as no surprise to us that they were made entirely of the Children. At bars and at restaurants, in conspiratorial whispers, we told ourselves that it was okay. *Of course they're taking the initiative, no one knows the Event better than them.* But even that thought left a cold clump of icy dread sitting in our stomachs.

I made an appointment with Marshall Wallace, the Senior Director of ReBuild—a non-profit organization dedicated to funding the re-development of the city. Wallace was a barrel-chested man who seemed ill-suited for his button-up shirt and slacks. He looked like the sort that found more joy in the solitude of nature, or as a calloused-hand in the trades. Wallace confirmed as much shortly after we met. When he shook my hand, I tried not to recoil, lest his glow penetrate me.

He pointed out a group of construction workers. "I used to do what they're doing," he said. "But not anymore."[12]

We sat under a tent, a sort of makeshift lunch space. Wallace was gracious and intelligent and looked me in the eyes.

"How do you feel about what people call you?" I asked.

Wallace sighed. "It's just a name, I guess. I don't think about it much. Except in the dark."

"Because of the glow?"

"Right."

"Have they figured out why that happens?"

Wallace shook his head. "Your guess is as good as mine, bud."[13]

"Some people have said that the Children have changed in some way. Do you agree with that?"

"I don't know shit about that, bud. I think we all changed. That's what happens when something like this happens, right? Being in the

---

12 While upward mobility is often a theme in whispered tales of the Children, it's important to note it's not always so. Most of the Children haven't reported a significant change in salary.

13 Currently, we have no credible scientific discovery regarding the Children's glow.

belly of the beast, so to speak, it gives you perspective. I'd say we're just like you, doing our best in a difficult time."

It was because of men and women like Wallace that the rebuilding began at all. While some of us held vigils and made talking points of the catastrophe, the Children acted. And not to be outdone, we followed.

There was pushback, of course. There was a sense that in the wake of the catastrophe, we were moving too fast. That we were not grieving adequately. This grief was for change. Because things *were* changing.

I first noticed the "Seawatchers" gathered in a long line along the boardwalk. I was on my way to interview a woman who worked in the rebuilding effort. They leaned over the railing, carefully eyeing the soft curvature of the horizon. Some of them locked arms; some of them wept. It was as if they were both mourning and pleading, all at the same time. These Seawatchers were urged internally by a sense of melancholy longing to be swallowed by the Event, to rest in its stomach acids, suspended in bile with their new brothers and sisters.

They could be seen from blocks away, many of them wearing glow stick arrangements to emanate a chemical shade of emerald—a weak substitute for the Children's natural glow. But, like the Children, they were resented and reviled. "It's disgusting," said one anonymous source. "Foul. Just look at them, the way they—I don't know—grovel."

I approached the Seawatchers with curious empathy. I too watched the same footage they had; I too felt a deep emotional reaction. We all did. Every one of us lived under the weight of the Event. The Seawatchers though, transubstantiated an invisible slice of the zeitgeist into something concrete—a movement.

They stood there in shifts, at every time of the day. Even in the dark hours of the night, they glowed—albeit artificially. They held each other and looked out to the sea and wished for one more chance to be something special.

It's funny how even in times of disaster those pesky human needs still roil under the surface. Death screams and rubble can only suppress our desires to be loved and recognized; however, they cannot annihilate them. Standing in the cool breeze, smelling the ocean, I felt what they felt, for a time—that everything we loved was gone, and soon everything would march forward, with or without us.

The Seawatchers, all in all, were a harmless sect. They watched the sea with pensive despair but did little more than loiter. The Children commented on them only when pushed. When it came time to renovate the waterfront and undo the damage from the Event, the Children paused construction. They created a plan to respect the mourning of the Seawatchers and worked with their representatives to find a work around. The Seawatcher representatives could not hide their glee at shaking hands with the Children. Some wondered if this was the plan all along, to force their attention.

The Seawatchers continued on, as the new waterfront was built under a new architectural vision. They stood in their false glow, totally unaware that a new event was upon them.

I did not consider myself a Seawatcher, but I did spend time with them. They were the only ones who were willing to wear their hearts so plainly on their sleeves. It was exhilarating, in a nihilistic way. The desire to wish the Event back to shore, after so much devastation, was akin to an intrusive thought. It was driving into traffic, jumping off a bridge, playing Russian roulette—pure catharsis.

It was on a cold day in November when tensions reached a fever pitch. At first it was a minor bit of counter protesting. Four people, sans glow, holding picketing signs across the street. One read, "Green Unclean," while another urged Seawatchers to "Run toward the light." They laughed and jeered and did little more than tease. But then, slowly, more joined.

It wasn't until that day in November, six months after the Event, that I felt a more acute friction.

There was no name for the protesters. We just called them people. They were not the Children, they were not Seawatchers. They were just people, like myself. Ostensibly, they had no loyalty or connection to each other, besides the fact that they did not glow and did not want to glow. They came from all walks of life, and many of them brought weapons.

The tide was higher than usual that morning which caused some new chatter. The Seawatchers were prone to assigning value to randomness. They talked amongst themselves. "It's here," they said. "There's something in the water."[14]

For some reason, they were more elated than usual. The week before, a whale carcass washed ashore, and there was only a murmur of excitement. But on that fateful day, the crowd erupted. Speaking to one expert on crowd dynamics, Dr. Linda Wolk, this explosion in activity could've been building for a long time, and it was likely *because* it had been building, and nothing else. "When people get together in groups, especially for a cause, they want to see results. Eventually, through either fact or fiction, they'll find them."

As the tide rolled in, large waves foaming and frothing in collapsing crescents, the Seawatchers cheered. They jumped up and down, screaming. "Yes, thank you! Yes! It's coming! Take us!"

I watched it come in, bemused, but also energized. I bounced with them too, throwing my body against them, back and forth, screaming nonsense.

Later, I was told that the people—the regular, plain people—were pacing, agitated. I didn't see them at all, I couldn't. I was with the Seawatchers, bellowing my lungs out in the glow of filtered light.

Somewhere down the waterfront, a bullet found its target. We did not hear the gunshot. They found the body and then slowly hushed those around them, craning their necks like meerkats as the next rifle kicked and sent another Seawatcher sprawling to the ground, blood rushing from their neck.

Silence overtook us in a wave, spreading whisper to whisper, until it reached myself and beyond. I did not know what had happened; I only knew to be quiet. Many of us, for a moment, thought that the Event had returned, so we turned back toward the ocean to look for a great shape rising from the water.

---

14   This was a rallying cry of sorts for the Seawatchers.

As another volley of shots arrived, another handful of Seawatchers fell to the ground, dead. Pandemonium struck soon after.

The Seawatchers, once docile and melancholy, turned toward the protesters in rage. The protesters, in turn, ground their teeth and reloaded. They didn't wait to fire, they kept killing until the rush of the crowd overtook them, until their bodies were trampled under the false glow of angry boots.

I ran, dodging people and bullets, ducking behind outhouses and construction equipment. The city's pressure cooker of rage exploded all around me, and I ran into a dig site, through the skeletal beginnings of a building I could not recognize. I went up a flight of iron stairs that looped about like the curves in a roller coaster.

At the top, I collapsed, hot breath steaming into my palms. I stared down at the wreckage below me, the violence that overtook the streets.

People were being pounded into paste. It was a squirming mass of wriggling bodies, tearing each other apart. Those who ran stomped away in splashes of blood.

Police cars and ambulances arrived soon after. Men and women exited the vehicles with riot gear and an emerald aura. They used minimal force, I realized. As I watched from my perch, I saw the crowd disperse, the violence mute itself. Once enraged murderers were taken calmly into the backseats of police cars. Green EMTs mended wounds for both people and Seawatchers.

I watched this for hours, a sickness growing inside me.

By the time I left my hiding spot, the streets were clean and quiet.

There was no great violence after, no more events—capital or lowercase. Time marched forward and so did we, as best we could, with the knowledge that our home was not our own. The new world will belong to the Children and their children.

And yes, there were births. The Children reproduced, but only with each other. They bear illuminated children that don't cry much and hit milestones early; they're a friendly, insightful bunch. Now, in the city, I can't help but think the only people I see anymore glow

a vivid emerald. They're eating sandwiches, talking about the news, pushing their brood in new baby carriages. Sometimes, they open the door for me and smile as if they're holding bile in their cheeks.

There is no more blood in the streets though. There is no more rubble. They don't live with the memories of before and after.

The city is different. The towers are taller, thinner—like needle points reaching to sew a seam in the sky. They have no windows. Some of them are short and squat, round and metallic. Others curve and loop, serpentine, around the older buildings, threatening to constrict them with their new construction.[15]

But now that the Event is long gone, unable to be located the world over, and the city is rebuilt, it seems that that just isn't enough. The old buildings that survived are now being demolished. Glowing men set the charges and stare solemnly as they crumble. The city is almost done, I hear, but that's a funny thing to think about. The word "done." When is a city done?[16]

---

15 We didn't think about how strange these were when they were built. We accepted them. We didn't even consider that the world that we were building, under the direction of the Children, was a new one.

16 We'll know when they tell us.

HOWLS BUREAU OF INVESTIGATION

HBI

SPECIAL AGENT   *Carson Winter*

Carson Winter is an author, punker, and raw nerve. He's a minimalist weirdo, a conversational absurdist, and a vehemently bleak-minded writer making his home in the Pacific Northwest. You can find his short fiction within the pages of *Vastarien*, *Apex*, and *The No Sleep Podcast*. His novella, *Soft Targets*, is out now from Tenebrous Press. In addition, he's the co-host of the horror writing craft podcast Dead Languages. If that's not enough and you want more Carson Winter roiling in your stomach and mind, find him in the spaces below. But please, be careful.

carsonwinter.com   @CarsonWinter3

MEMO: *Evidentiary imagery provided by P.L. McMillan.*
Agent headshot provided by Joe Radkins.

DETRITUS
by Lindsey Ragsdale

News travels like lightning among our small crew of forty, out here in the middle of the Pacific. Footsteps pound across the metal decking of the *Panamax Garnet*. I'd been in the galley when Michelle burst in, red-faced and out of breath: *There's someone in the water.*

All eight of us pour out of the small room and ascend four decks up the narrow staircase, bursting through the hatch into bright sunlight, and run down the upper deck to the trash nets at the stern. More crew members join our exodus, boiling up from various doorways and hatches like ants escaping an anthill, until nearly thirty of us crowd by the upper deck railing, peering down at the lower deck.

Captain Connors and Amanda, the ship's doctor, crouch near a still, pale form laid out by the deck crane. They're mostly blocking our view, and I can't make out any details—just a pair of legs, bare-footed, lying still. Mario and Jin, who've been on winch duty, stand off to the side. Their mouths are set in grim lines. Jin's wringing his cap in his hands.

Jodie. Please, don't let it be Jodie. I step back and scan the gathering crowd, mouth dry. But Jodie's running towards me, the relief in her brown eyes no doubt mirroring mine. I grab her hand and pull her close.

"Do you know what happened?" I ask.

"No," she responds. "I ran up here when I heard about a body. Do you know who it is?"

I shake my head. Below us, Mario and Jin unfold a tarp, spreading it over the person on the deck. *The body,* I remind myself and shudder. A sudden sea breeze catches the tarp and flips it up, revealing the person's face. I gasp and recoil.

There are plastic shards sticking out where the eyes used to be.

Memories of my dead father's face bubble forth before I can tamp them down. I squeeze my own eyes shut and clench my jaw. Whisper my calming mantra over and over, trying to calm the screaming that's building in my brain, rising like a torrent. *You're safe. You're loved. You're safe. You're loved.* Over and over until the pounding in my ears dies down and I'm able to unclench my white-knuckled fists, red grooves left where my nails dug into my palms. His face has haunted my dreams ever since I found him dead, and now in my mind I've replaced those loving eyes with stabbing shards. One more memory now tainted by violence, just like all the rest.

Arms encircle my shoulders, slowly, tentatively, and Jodie murmurs against my back. "Is this okay?"

She knows. She's the only person I care about who knows about that day when I came home after school and found my father lifeless on the couch. And she alone can give me the comfort I need right now. I give a small nod and lean back, letting her scent and presence envelop me like a womb. Jodie is my safe space.

Urgent whispers rise from the crowd around us. *What's going on? Oh my God, is that a body? Who is it? When are they going to tell us?* The questions build like a wave, mirroring my growing unease. Jodie guides me away from the knot of volunteers who've gathered by the upper-deck railing. Voices fade until all I hear is our breathing, the creaking of the ship, and the endless lapping of trash against the bulkhead far below.

"Thank you," I mumble, opening my eyes. Jodie's a head taller than me, which means we fit together perfectly when holding each other close.

She smiles. "Of course. Let's go below deck. How about we find you a comfortable chair and some water?"

All I can do is nod, and she leads me by the hand back to the open hatch leading below, beckoning me with its promise of a safe, enclosed space. Away from the open sky and sea, the fretting and questions from the crowd, and the never-ending tides of garbage.

"Can I tell you what happened?" Jodie asks, breaking the rhythm of shoveling and sorting. We're decked out in rubber boots and gardening gloves, hair tied back, sweating in the sun as we sort through the mountains of trash on the lower deck, separating biodegradable trash from plastic, smaller pieces from larger ones. This makes the garbage much easier to process back on land.

The onboard winch whines behind us as it brings up another net from the sea's surface, full to the brim with plastic detritus. Cups and wrappers and straws, broken toys, pieces of boats, shoes, and God knows what else all tangled with kelp and by-catch. I wave to Michelle, who's operating the crane today, and she releases the net when it's a foot off the deck. Seawater and debris spills across our work area, the sudden brine and rotten-fish stench making us gag, and Jodie and I wait for it to disperse before raking through the mess.

I take a deep breath. "I think so." I'd spent the rest of yesterday hiding in my bunk, avoiding all conversation and gossip about the dead body. Jodie must've cautioned the others, because at breakfast I got sympathetic glances and small talk about the weather and work, nothing else. I felt both grateful for their kindness and ashamed of my weakness.

"It was Harvey," Jodie says. "Did you know him well?"

"A little," I say. Harvey was one of the old-timers, and this was his fifth season at sea cleaning up the Pacific Garbage Patch. Our friend circles didn't overlap, so I didn't know him well, but he was friendly enough. I'd only served one clean-up shift with him over the past two months. "Did they find out if he fell overboard?" I continue, dragging my hand across my forehead to wipe away sweat. "Any of the cameras catch anything?"

"No," says Jodie. "I guess they're still investigating. They want to give Harvey's family all the information they can when we dock in two weeks." We rake garbage in silence for a few minutes, and she sighs. "You've heard the rumors, right? About the state of his body?"

"Jesus, Jodie, I saw his face." I lean on my rake, feeling faint.

She pauses before continuing. "I'm telling you this now, so you don't get caught off guard hearing it from someone else. So, Harvey was all cut up, and...*filled* with trash. Like someone had taken a knife—"

"Jodie," I interrupt in a steely tone, "Really. That's enough."

Jodie is silent. I love her more than anything, but sometimes she doesn't filter out gory details. "Just trying to do you a favor, okay? It's a small crew. Better you hear it from me now, than later."

"I appreciate what you're trying to do, but I'm good. Really."

We shovel and rake in silence until Jodie speaks again. "I'm going to take five, you?"

"Sure," I say, standing straight and rolling my shoulders to loosen them up. Jodie sets her shovel to the side and heads past me to the water station. I catch her shoulder as she walks past me, and she stops.

"Jodie," I say, in a gentle tone. "Thank you for helping me yesterday when I almost had a panic attack."

She looks straight ahead. "Rachel. I'm telling you this because I love you." She pauses her raking, and I know what she's going to say. It's an old conversation we have time and time again. "You really should talk to a professional. What you went through, as a child, is super fucked up. Finding your dad overdosed when you were twelve?" Jodie turns to face me. "I don't blame you for freaking out the way you did yesterday. But talking to a counselor could help you process the guilt I know gets all kicked up when you remember your dad."

"You're the help I need," I say in a rush. "I'm fine when we're together. Really."

Detritus by Lindsey Ragsdale

"But what if I can't be there?" Jodie says. "How will you deal with it on your own?"

I shake my head. "That's not going to happen. We love each other." I kiss her, and she embraces me, tucking my head under her chin. "You're the best thing that's ever happened to me. The only person who understands me and my issues. Why should I tell a stranger? How are they supposed to help?"

Jodie sighs. I can feel her breath tickle the hair at the top of my head. "Okay, Rachel," she says, defeated. For now. She kisses my forehead and walks past me, stripping off her gloves. "I'll be back in a second."

I walk to the portside railing. The deep blue sea we read about as children is not what I see. The sky is blue as could be, but the ocean is dotted with trash in every color, a veritable kaleidoscope of debris bobbing gently with the waves. The Great Pacific Garbage Patch has tripled in size over the past forty years, and *Panamax Garnet*'s mission is to clean up as much as we can each six-month season, while the weather is fair.

The trash is endless in variety and quantity. If I strain, I can hear the dull thuds of the larger chunks hitting the hull below. Faded orange buoys, flat pieces of watercraft, old teal nylon fishing nets. Punctured tires, blue rubber barrels, wet mildewing rope coiled around the lot. Plastic tubs, food containers, cloudy water bottles. And this is just what I can see with my naked eye. Microplastics lurk in the empty spaces, from old trash broken down by waves, wind, and sunlight, into pieces so small they are only detectable by microscope.

Panamax Garnet uses a system of nets and hooks to filter what garbage it can out of the ocean, five times a day. We make

our winding way through the thickest part of the gyre, scooping and sorting what we can get our nets and hands on. The trash we sort and collect in old shipping containers onboard, offloading them when we resupply at port.

This is Jodie and my first two-month tour, and I hoped it wouldn't be the last. The work is messy and physically taxing, but my fellow volunteers are a welcoming bunch, the food isn't bad, and I feel a deep satisfaction at making an actual difference in the world. That, or the hard labor, or a combination of both, help me sleep soundly every night, keeping the ghosts in my mind at bay. Plus, Jodie and I are working and living together almost 24/7. She's crazy about the environment, and it's thanks to her we found this opportunity.

But now, with Harvey's death, for the first time in six weeks I yearn to feel dry land beneath my feet. I turn away from the railing and the endless roiling of garbage stretching all the way to the horizon.

Captain Conners addresses everyone later that afternoon on the upper deck. "Starting tonight, at 1900 hours," the Captain continues, "and at all meals, we will be calling roll. If you're not working, please stay below deck, for everyone's safety." His eyes are troubled as he scans the crowd. "We've increased our speed to dock earlier than scheduled. Any questions or concerns, please let me know."

"Is everyone in danger?" a voice calls out.

"How soon will we dock?" calls another.

The chorus grows, the crowd's anxiety churning to a crescendo. I tune the voices out as I stare down at the metal decking, gripping Jodie's hand as tightly as I can, and wait for it to be over.

There's little conversation over dinner. People pick at their food or cast nervous glances towards the hatch. No one lingers to play cards or board games after the meal, and Jodie and I head to our shared bunk. She's pale and scratching idly at her bicep, lost deep in thought. "Jodie, you okay?" I ask her. She nods, and I feel better. As long as she's okay, then I'm okay. "Let's call it an early night."

We prepare for bed without conversation. I'm reading a book as Jodie uses the bathroom. She's in there for a long time. I doze off before she emerges, and awaken in the dark with her lying by my side, muttering in her sleep. I stare up at the curved bulkhead, waiting for sleep to claim me once more, and I'm almost there when her voice rasps in my ear, and I jolt upward, heart racing.

"Did you see how he filled himself?" Jodie murmurs. She sounds almost drunk. "Did you see how he transformed?" Her voice is a low drone, completely unlike her normal speaking tone.

"Jodie!" I turn on the small light by my side of the bed. Jodie's eyelids are fluttering. I catch glimpses of white through the sliver visible between her lids. She tosses her head from side to side.

The sleeves of her pajamas ride up—I often tease Jodie for wearing full pajama sets, since she gets cold at night—and reveal what look like bracelets on her forearms. "What the fuck?" I stammer, and reach for her, but she pulls from my grasp.

"He's turned," Jodie says loudly, beginning to thrash. "He's turned with the tides."

I manage to grab a flailing arm, my heart pounding with worry, and pull Jodie's sleeve up. Her arm is covered in colorful bands. Strips of plastic. Tied so tightly that her arms are mottled red and purple and white where the circulation's been cut off.

I gasp and flash back to my father, lifeless on the couch, black tourniquet wrapped around his bicep as his pallid arm dangled off the side. Green eyes, full of shards, head tilted back, mouth open in a soundless scream.

Darkness swims into the corners of my vision, and my chest grows tight. I fumble for the words of my mantra—*you're safe, you're loved*—but they slip like spilt sand and are lost to me. Shaking begins as a tremble, escalating into full blown convulsions through my arms and legs. I squeeze myself into a ball, trying to regain control as the room spins around me and details are thrown into sharp relief; the edges of the nightstand, the red numerals winking from the digital clock, the rainbow bands striping Jodie's arms as she turns fitfully in her sleep, shouting nonsensical phrases which clang through our metal capsule of a room. Muttering fills the space, creeping in from the bulkheads and the dark corners, blending with Jodie's shouts, and I clamp my hands over my ears.

Pounding on our hatch echoes in the small space. "Hey!" a muffled voice yells. "What's going on?" Keys scrape in the lock—the crew, no doubt—and Amanda bursts in with her doctor's bag, followed by Michelle, who lives across the hall. Their eyes are wide and confused as they settle on Jodie, who's shown no awareness of her surroundings, only shouting and beating the backs of her bruised arms against the mattress. Amanda jumps into action, pulling a pair of scissors out of her bag.

"Rachel, hold Jodie's arm for me," she commands. I'm frozen, and Amanda turns to Michelle, repeating the request. Michelle grabs Jodie's left arm and the doctor deftly slices through the tight plastic bindings, which fall in scraps to the sheets.

Jodie gasps as her blood flow is restored, and the light comes back into her eyes. She winces.

"My arm!" she whimpers in her normal tone of voice. Amanda's seized her right arm and sliced through the bindings there, eliciting another sharp gasp from Jodie. "Hurts!"

I crawl over to Jodie's side and gather her in my arms, the spell broken. "I'm here," I mumble into her hair as she massages her forearms. "I'm here now." I blink away angry tears.

I failed the person I loved when she needed me most.

When Amanda asks me why Jodie had tied her arms so tightly, I have no words. "She must've done it in the bathroom before coming to bed," I say, tears choking my voice. "I fell asleep. I had no idea anything was wrong until she started yelling."

Amanda frowns. "I don't want to worry you, but I'd like to keep Jodie here for observation. It's normal for people to act strangely after a traumatic event, given everything that's been going on, and I'd rather she be right here if she needs medical attention."

I swallow the lump in my throat and fill in Amanda's unspoken words. *I'd rather Jodie be in the infirmary with the doctor, since you couldn't help her last night in your room.* "Do you think she'll be okay?"

"Honestly, I'm not sure," Amanda continues, taking notes on a clipboard. "People often talk in their sleep or have night terrors after witnessing traumatic events. But the meticulous tying of plastic bags around her arms…" She shakes her head. "It concerns me." She peers closely at me. "How are you doing?"

"Me?" I glance at the ground and swallow the lump in my throat. "Fine," I lie. "I just want to be here for Jodie if she needs me."

Amanda places a tentative hand on my shoulder. "I want you to know, Rachel, it's a completely normal response to freeze up like that when someone's in trouble." Her eyes are kind and pitying. "Please don't beat yourself up about it. I can see you're hurting."

I can't speak. Shame threatens to swallow me whole. Amanda gives me a pat as she stands up. "If you need to talk, let me know." She sees my tense shoulders, and her eyes soften. "I'll bring in a cot and blankets, if you'd rather stay with Jodie."

It's been three days since Jodie was admitted, and she sleeps most of the time. When she's awake, she's groggy and slow. I've gotten permission to skip work detail and remain by her side.

Feeling restless on my fourth day in the infirmary, I head to the galley for a snack. My footsteps in these narrow metal corridors echo louder than I expect, and I'm grateful for the bright lights flooding every corner, driving the shadows away. My nerves are almost settled by the time I duck through the galley hatch and come across Jin.

He's standing by the far wall, facing the far corner of the room. His shoulders are bunched and I can't see his hands as he rocks back and forth in place. Something rustles as I take two steps closer and a familiar briny smell fills my nostrils. Low murmurs, like hiss and static from a radio, are barely perceptible from an unknown source, but I don't dare take my eyes off Jin's back.

"Jin, are you okay?" I ask, taking a step forward. He turns to me, a glazed look in his eyes.

He's filthy, shirt and pants covered in rotting kelp from the garbage piles. Jin's cheeks bulge with what I realize are old plastic bags, browning translucent scraps trailing out over his jaw. He clutches broken disposable cutlery in his fists, and little drops of blood patter down onto the floor. Rustling comes from his mouth as he chews and chews. His dead gaze stares through me as I stand, rooted in place with confusion and disgust, until creeping terror wins out and I tear myself away. Jin mumbles something behind me, but I can't understand through the crinkling and rustling of what's in his mouth.

"Help!" I manage to choke out, stumbling back through the hatch into the hallway. To my relief, Captain Conners and Mario have just rounded the corner, and my shout interrupts their discussion. They sprint toward me and into the galley, and their voices escalate at what they find.

I huddle in the corridor, hands over my head, as the ship-wide alarm begins to sound, its shrill bleating following me down into an exhausted darkness.

Wherever Jodie is, that's the only place I feel safe. Amanda says we can stay in a private room in the infirmary until the *Garnet* docks. She brings us meals, monitors Jodie's vitals, and keeps us informed of what's going on outside, though I wish she wouldn't.

They found Michelle tangled up in the nets last night. Two more people are missing. The duty roster is falling apart. They've stopped all work. Nonessential crew is confined to quarters until we dock in three days.

Jodie continues to doze off and on, and I keep the door locked between Amanda's visits.

We're one day from shore when I wake up on my cot to find Jodie gone. Her bedsheets lie crumpled on the floor and the hatch stands open. I lunge to my feet, adrenaline surging, and bolt after her. How long has she been missing?

In the hallway, I make out a pair of bare feet sprinting up the perforated metal staircase, and I charge after them. Once I emerge onto the upper deck, everything's dark, stars dotting the velvety night overhead. All is silent but for the ship's creaking and the garbage rustling far below. I spot a white-clad figure running towards the stern, where the trash piles and filled shipping containers are stored, and take off after her.

Proper protocol would be to notify Captain Connors and the crew. Let them join the search; they know the *Panamax Garnet* better than anyone. But I can't fail Jodie again. I couldn't live with myself if I did. A selfish part of me, deep down, wants to save her, with my own two hands. Rescue her from whatever demons are plaguing her, just like she's caught me time and time again. I owe her that much.

Jodie's fled to the trash collection area at the far end of the deck. I make out a flash of leg as she darts into the labyrinth of shipping containers, hulking rectangular receptacles filled with the garbage we've captured from the sea, each as large as a tractor trailer. Most containers are closed and sealed, but a few half-filled ones are open to the sky, awaiting more detritus.

My hair whips around my face as the sea breeze picks up, and I shiver from cold and fear.

"Jodie!" I call over the scream of the wind. Bracing my arm against the lower deck railing, I creep one slow foot at a time forward towards the containers. Their straight sides loom up and around me as I stagger into the stacks. At least the metal sides provide some protection against the salt spray now coating my face and pajamas.

The faint stars far above my head barely illuminate the night. Nothing is as dark as a night on the open sea. The sounds of the trashy sea lapping at the ship's rusty flanks fade as the containers loom around me. I have the irrational feeling that I'll lose my way and be trapped in this maze forever. Several glances over my shoulder do nothing to reassure me.

The first three containers I pass are shut and barred. The fourth is open from the top. Metal ladders are set into the side of each container, and I climb up to get a better vantage point. I pull myself up, wet hands and feet slipping on the rungs.

In the container is a white figure below me, hip-deep in plastic.

"Jodie!" I shout.

She spins around, just as the deck is flooded with light. Amanda must've sounded the alarm when she noticed us gone. All the deck lights, upper and lower, have been turned on, throwing every dark corner into brilliance. In the sudden light, I see Jodie clearly, and recoil in horror.

Jodie's teeth are bared with an arm up to shield her eyes, blinded like a wild animal in the glow of oncoming headlights. Red streaks cover her arms and face and dot her pajamas, the crimson a sharp contrast to her sickly visage. She grips something orange in one hand and bits of bright green and yellow and blue dot her arms and face, sunken into the red slashes marring her flesh. Was she tying herself up in plastic strips again?

No. She has carved deep slashes into her arms and legs, and pushed filthy, briny garbage into her gaping wounds, coating herself inside and out with detritus from the shipping container. Lank seaweed tangles in her hair, and her gown is splattered and torn.

I have to save Jodie from herself.

"Jodie!" I shout. "We need to get you out of there!"

"No!" she screams, clutching the orange thing—I realize with a sick jolt that it is a box cutter—and wades through the plastic, burrowing away from the light, like an insect seeks its hive for safety. She sinks to her knees and dips her head beneath the flotsam, pushing garbage over her head with her bloody, mangled arms. Revulsion and nausea well inside me, followed by my constant companion of deep shame.

Jodie needs my help. I couldn't help my father. I can't even help myself. But I can help her. I can try.

I swing my legs over the side and sink into the trash. A pungent, oily stench worms its way into my nostrils, grimy, salty debris and long-rotten organic matter. I breathe through my mouth in shallow gasps. My feet tangle in various nets and wrappers as I wade through the garbage, pushing swaths of it out of my way. I grimace against the sharp pains in my feet and legs, caused by the jagged plastic edges all around me, but forge onward.

A sound grows that almost stops me in my tracks. Above the howling wind, above the ship's creaking, whispers rise around me. Muttering and fluttering, voices worming their way into my brain, chanting and pleading in a hypnotic tone:

Turn with us
Turn with the tides

Over and over, this sinister mantra pounds its way through my head, growing louder and louder from the trash stirring and settling around me. I am in the thick of it, and it's all I can do to push ahead, to save Jodie from the spell of whatever's possessed the pollution seeping through the sea.

Jodie's barely visible in her huddled nest, and I wrap my arms around her, heedless of the blood and slime and muck. She whimpers in my arms, still clutching the box cutter. "Be with me," she pants. "Be with us." Drops of blood roll down her fingers and forearm from where she's shoved pieces of a plastic straw under her fingernails. "Join me, please."

I pry the box cutter from her weak grip, slippery with blood and saltwater. "Jodie, I'm here," I whisper into her mangled ear. "I'll always be here for you." I hold her close.

"No!" she shrieks, lunging for the cutter. I wrestle against her surprising strength, cutting my finger in the process. We grapple, slipping in the trash all around us, which continues to whisper, growing restless, until I manage to cock my arm back and fling the box cutter with all my might away from us. It sinks into the mess and the muttering fades.

Jodie slumps against my side, eyes rolling back in her head. She's breathing shallowly, and she's bleeding all over us, but I hold her close and I repeat my words over and over into the shell of her ear. I will save her. I will do whatever it takes to keep her here. I lost my father, but I won't lose Jodie.

Over and over I whisper, even as the crew's shouts rise up across the deck.

You're safe.
You're loved.
You're safe.
You're loved.

HOWLS BUREAU OF INVESTIGATION

HBI

SPECIAL AGENT — *Lindsey Ragsdale*

Lindsey Ragsdale (she/her) is a writer from Chicago, Illinois. Her stories appear in the anthologies *Howls from Hell*, *Howls From The Dark Ages*, *Strange Weeds*, and *Nightmare Sky*. She loves reading, writing, cooking, and long walks by the lake.

@Leviathan15

MEMO: Evidentiary imagery provided by Maia Weir. Agent headshot provided by Solomon Forse.

STAFF AWARDS

 EMPLOYEE OF THE YEAR!

The HOWLS Bureau of Investigation proudly celebrates the work of

Christopher O'Halloran

 Christopher O'Halloran (he/him) is a milk-slinging, Canadian actor-turned-author with work published or forthcoming from *Kaleidotrope*, *The No Sleep Podcast*, *Cosmic Horror Monthly*, Hellbound Books, and others. His longer fiction can be found in anthologies *Howls from Hell* and *Bloodlines: Four Tales of Familial Fear*, with three novels just waiting to be put in the game, coach!

 COAuthor.ca   @Burgleinfernal

Christopher   has demonstrated excellence as   *Editor*

Employee headshot provided by Leah Gharbaharan.

EMPLOYEE OF THE MONTH!

The HOWLS Bureau of Investigation proudly celebrates the work of

Nick Cutter

Nick Cutter is the author of the critically acclaimed national bestseller *The Troop* (which is currently being developed for film with producer James Wan), as well as *The Deep* and *Little Heaven*. Nick Cutter is the pseudonym for Craig Davidson, whose much-lauded literary fiction includes *Rust and Bone*, *The Saturday Night Ghost Club*, and, most recently, the short story collection *Cascade*. His story "Medium Tough" was selected by author Jennifer Egan for *The Best American Short Stories 2014*. He lives in Toronto, Canada.

🌐 www.craigdavidson.net

Nick has demonstrated excellence as *Foreword Writer*

Employee headshot provided by Joe Radkins.

 EMPLOYEE OF THE MONTH!

The HOWLS Bureau of Investigation proudly celebrates the work of

Molly Halstead

M. Halstead is a graphic designer and book fanatic who spends her day fighting with Adobe products and evenings reading horror. When creating in her free time, she focuses on book and magazine design, horror writing, and traditional bookmaking and printmaking. She lives in North Carolina with her husband and two cats.

🌐 mhalstead.com

Molly has demonstrated excellence as *Formatter/Illustrator*

Employee headshot provided by Molly Halstead.

319

EMPLOYEE OF THE MONTH!

The HOWLS Bureau of Investigation proudly celebrates the work of

Joe Radkins

Joe Radkins spends his days illustrating, reading and watching horror. He is a co-host for a horror film review podcast: Partners in Fright. His story "Clement & Sons" and various art can be seen in *Howls from Hell* and *Howls from the Dark Ages: An Anthology of Medieval Horror*. He lives in Pennsylvania with his supportive wife and their two little padawans.

🌐 partnersinfright.podbean.com 📷 @thecinemaddiction

Joe has demonstrated excellence as *Illustrator*

Employee headshot provided by Maia Weir.

 # EMPLOYEE OF THE MONTH!

The HOWLS Bureau of Investigation proudly celebrates the work of

Leah Gharbaharan

Leah is a graphic designer and illustrator working in Cape Town, South Africa. Using both traditional and digital media, her illustrative work draws on the natural world and expresses her interest in disruption, ecology and patterns of change.

📷 @schism.art 🐦 @tigrrrly_

Leah has demonstrated excellence as *Illustrator*

Employee headshot provided by Solomon Forse.

EMPLOYEE OF THE MONTH!

The HOWLS Bureau of Investigation proudly celebrates the work of

Cassie Daley

 Cassie Daley is a writer and illustrator living in Northern California. Her first published short story, *Ready or Not*, debuted as a part of Fright Girl Summer in 2020. Her nonfiction writing has been published by Unnerving Magazine, and her short fiction has appeared in several horror anthologies. Her first YA horror novella, *Brutal Hearts*, was published in 2022. She is also the creator of *The Big Book of Horror Authors: A Coloring & Activity Book*, as well as an award-winning children's horror book, *Rosie Paints with Ghosts*.

🌐 https://ctrlaltcassie.com/   🐦 📷 @ctrlaltcassie

Cassie _____ has demonstrated excellence as *Illustrator*

Employee headshot provided by Maia Weir.

 # EMPLOYEE OF THE MONTH!

The HOWLS Bureau of Investigation proudly celebrates the work of

Christi Nogle

 Christi Nogle is the author of the Bram Stoker Award® nominated novel *Beulah* (Cemetery Gates Media, 2022) collection *The Best of Our Past, the Worst of Our Future* (Flame Tree Press, 2023). She is co-editor with Willow Dawn Becker of the Bram Stoker Award® nominated anthology *Mother: Tales of Love and Terror* (Weird Little Worlds, 2022).

🌐 http://christinogle.com   🐦 📷 @ChristiNogle

Christi has demonstrated excellence as *Illustrator*

Employee headshot provided by Christi Nogle.

EMPLOYEE OF THE MONTH!

The HOWLS Bureau of Investigation proudly celebrates the work of

Maia Weir

Maia's goal in every medium is to tell a compelling story. Whether the players are human, architectural, or shades of gray, she invites you to explore meticulously created dimensions of narrative. Educated and experienced in applied arts, she is passionate about animation, illustration, installation art, writing, jewelry design, and more. She works to uplift herself and other artists through the matrix of artistic expression.

Maia has demonstrated excellence as *Illustrator/Cover Artist*

Employee headshot provided by Maia Weir.

The annual awards banquet will also recognize three honorable mentions: Agents Solomon Forse, P.L. McMillan, and Michelle Tang. These agents have gone above and beyond as illustrators in addition to their work in the field.

ACKNOWLEDGMENTS

Another year, another intensive HOWL Society anthology workshop. The titles you see in this table of contents represent only a sliver of the stories produced over the course of the grueling, challenging, yet ultimately rewarding workshop process. In 2022, dozens of writers (ranging from unpublished to veterans) took part in the workshop: three critiques across three rounds, for a total of nine critiques each. Additionally, for the first time this year, HOWL Society added a mentor program in which protegées were paired with established writers to develop their stories one-on-one. The collection's editor, Christopher O'Halloran, then selected stories from a pool of those that made it through the workshop meat grinder. It's fair to say that most workshop participants went above and beyond the call of the official workshop parameters to help others produce the best possible version of their stories.

Though it is ultimately competitive to get into the anthology, the workshop process is anything but. For months, we shared disaster memes, pored over one another's stories, and proofread until our eyes hurt. Earthquake, blizzard, tsunami, drought, *kaiju*, raining gore, biblical apocalypse—you name it. If there was a creative way to destroy their characters' lives, someone brainstormed it. The quality of this anthology is thanks to the blood, sweat, and tears of everyone who took part in the workshop at all stages and levels, not just the names you see here. You will doubtless be seeing many of the stories that weren't selected for *Howls From the Wreckage* in print elsewhere soon.

Lastly—a very special thanks to Solomon Forse, one of HOWL Society's founders and beloved Thotfather, who took a step back from editing last year's excellent *Howls From the Dark Ages* (alongside P.L. McMillan) to oversee this year's workshop. He kept us writers on-schedule and ensured everyone received consistently high-quality feedback. Speaking for everyone who took part, your work is much appreciated.

Herding cats after a cyclone would be less challenging.

—Joseph Andre Thomas (bunttriple)

EDITOR'S NOTE

Haircuts, mom-jeans, and fanny-packs; out of all the nineties trends being dug up and revived like the living dead, I'm glad apathy isn't one of them.

These stories illustrate something crucial to fiction and crucial to life. That people need to care.

About their friends, their family, their communities. A beloved pet cat or the skin on their hands.

It was my honour and pleasure to assemble these fantastic stories about hope and despair. About triumph and complete devastation. Thank you to the production team at HOWL Society for giving me this opportunity and ensuring the success of this project. Solomon, Molly, Leah, Joe, Kris, Corey, Maia, and Christi—your contributions to art and marketing makes all the difference.

These HOWLS anthologies have an incredible track record of securing forewords from some of the biggest names in modern horror, and Nick Cutter stands among the greats. He has been one of my favourites for years, so thank you, Nick, for your kind introduction.

My appreciation goes out to every author who took the time to read an early copy of *Howls From the Wreckage* and provide your support. The horror community truly is a family, and that's never clearer than when our peers speak up for the scrappy folks.

This collection could not be released without extra attention from sensitivity readers. We want to shock and awe those who read this book; we do not want to do harm. Thank you to everyone who served in that role.

Thank you to every writer who submitted a story. The job of selecting which stories to include was simultaneously very easy and very hard. Very easy because I had such a huge selection of treasure to pick from, and very hard because I had such a huge selection of treasure to pick from.

Thank you to the mentors who helped provide new authors with one-on-one coaching.

Thank you Jenny, for your guidance and friendship.

Mat, Jennifer, and Chelsea, thank you for absolutely nailing the Kickstarter and promoting the hell out of this project while I was off watching my wife birth our second child.

Finally, thank you to the readers who took a chance on this book of chaos. It's been a labour of so much love from so many people. Having that love returned from your side of the page makes this all worth it.

—Christopher O'Halloran

THANK YOU TO OUR KICKSTARTER BACKERS

A
Adam "Chili" Stevens
Adam Eisenhut
Adam McInnes
Alan Lastufka
Alex Morales
Alexander Lyle
Alexandra Lee
Alice Austin
Amanda Holden
Amelia Campbell
Anastacia Russell
Andrew Beirne
Andrew Harris
Andrew Weldon
Andy
Anna Owens
Annice Brave
Anonymous
AnonyMouse
Art Morris
Ashely
Ashleigh Floyd
Ashleigh H.
Ashur Barre
Becca Futrell
bennett
Bess Turner
Bob Warlock
Bonster with the Goose Bone
Brian B.
Bridger Winter
Bridget Engman

Bruce Wehrle
Bryce
C. D. Kester
Caiden Keehl
Caleb "Kaiju" Stephens
Caleb J. Pecue
Carson Winter
Cassandra Byrne
Catherine F
Charles W. Anderson III
Chelsea Pumpkins
Chrissy O, NMD
Christi Nogle
Christine (Stine) Lea Fletcher
Christopher J Smith
The Cold Unfeeling Universe
Colleen Feeney
Connor Boyle
Cory the RADDAD Radkins
Cristian Kiper
Damarchus Tepes
Daniel
Daniel Hojnowski
Danny Jacobs
Darkhorserodeo
Dave Smith
David Swisher
David Wayne Wujek
David Worn
Denise Tuttle
Derek Devereaux Smith
Desiree Straut
Die!..ana

Doctor Mister
Dominic Surano
Dr. & Mr. Heidi & Paul Collins
DrasnianFrank
Drew Cox
Dylan Fowler
Ed McCutchan
Edward Abbott
Eileen Ryan
Eli H
Elijah Jones
Elise Ratchford
Elton Skelter
Emily Hughes
Emily Walter
Emmy Teague
Erich Hess
Erika M.
Ernie Ridley
Esraa Alhassan
Felix Graves
Finneus Earnhardt-McClain
Francesco Tehrani
Haley Strassburger
Hamed Soltani
Heidi Hansen
Henry Neilsen
Hollie F
Howard Blakeslee
A Howl From Sasha Brown's Butt
Hugh N
Ivan Smith
J Norville
J. Jason Lau
Jacob H Joseph
Jacob Rennick

Janelle Janson
Jason Cole
Jason Mortensen
Jeanette Mortensen
Jeff Bzdick
Jennie Donovan
Jennifer L. Collins
Jessica Enfante
Jessica mace-ball
Joe Radkins
Joey OConnor
John Corcoran
John Opalenik
Jonathan hixson
Jonathan Mendonca
Jonny Pickering
Joseph J Connell
Josh Buyarski
Josh McGinnis
Joshua Maestas
Josue"AKAMOUSECOP"Oyuela
Jude Deluca
Julia Morgan
Julie Sevens
Just James Horror Review Podcast
Justin Phelps
Kai Delmas
Kalyn Williams
Karl Andinach
Kay Popple
Kenneth Skaldebø
Kenneth T. Dodd
Kevin Granade
Kevin Lemke
kg
Kris Eversole

Kristin C

Kristina Meschi

L.T. Williams

LaShuna Garcia

Lauren Bolger

lentils09

Les Hernandez

Lesley Reed

Lindsey Ragsdale

Lor Gislason

Louie Rice Jr

Luisa O'Halloran

Lynne Walter

M.E. Bronstein

Mads

Martin Berger

Martina Almario

mathew wend

Matt Poisso

Matt Stepan

Matthew Maichen

Matthew Price

Mattie Davenport

Maureen Thomas

Melanie B.

Melissa Cox

Micathyel

Michael Clarkson

Michelle Hollands

Mike McQuillian

Mikhael Zereda Wijaya

MLtheimpossible

N/A

neal swanson

Neil Alhanti

Nicole Coster

Nikolaj

Patrick Barb

Paul & Laura Trinies

Payton Hamilton

Peter Morczinek

Peter Ong Cook

PunkARTchick *Ruthenia*

Quinn Fern

R. H. Newfield

Rain Carling

Rex Long

Richard O'Shea

Rick Howard

Rob Russell

Robert Claney

Roberto Inferno

Roth Schilling

Ryan

Ryan C

Ryan Marie Ketterer

Sadie Cocteau

Sal Cottrell

Sam Asher

Sara Kennedy

Sarah Duck-Mayr

sav

schism.art

Scott Miller PB3140

Sean Horkheimer

Sean Kelly Christensen

Shaun D. Burton

Sheena Perez

Shelby McElvaine

Stephanie Trinity Turner

Stephen Howard

Steve Pattee

steven duane allison junior
Steven Patchett
Susan Jessen
Susanne Stohr
Sydney Dunstan
Tanya Sutton
Teresa B. Ardrey
Thea Maeve
ThotFather
Tim Snider
Tomino
Weird Little Worlds Press
William Jones
Windi LaBounta
Wolfy
Zack Fissel
zen dog

ABOUT THE HORROR-OBSESSED WRITING AND LITERATURE SOCIETY

HOWL Society, located on Discord, is the most active horror book club on the web. With hundreds of members, the club offers readers the chance to join a supportive community where they can enjoy books alongside other horror-lovers while engaging in meaningful discussions and forming long-lasting friendships. Aside from serving as an organized platform for discussing books, HOWL Society is also home to a tight-knit group of horror writers. Additionally, members can participate in tangential conversations about horror films, horror games, and much more. Because the club aims to provide equal access to all readers and writers around the world, membership is 100% free.

THE BOOK CLUB

- No membership fees

- All club activity takes place on Discord

- Each month, club members vote on the horror titles that will be read in the following month

- The club reads one book per week, members obtaining copies of physical books, ebooks, or audiobooks according to their preferences

- Members are not expected to read every title

- Each book is separated into three sections and assigned to an individual channel

- Discussions for each section initiate on Mondays, Wednesdays, and Fridays

- During discussion, members use spoiler tags to ensure a safe discussion for those who choose to read at their own pace

THE WRITING COMMUNITY

- No membership fees

- All club activity takes place on Discord

- Mentors available for new writers

- Writing critiques continue year-round through an organized feedback system

- Each summer, club members vote on an anthology theme and take part in an online writing workshop with stories submitted for consideration in the annual HOWL Society Press anthology

Learn more at howlsociety.com.

CONTENT WARNINGS

"Don't Play in the Closet" by David Worn
Child Loss, Infertility

"(>executeRelease_)" by P.L. McMillan
Graphic Violence, Amputation

"Son of Yokozuro" by Caleb Stephens
Gore, Urban Destruction, Loss of Loved One

"Crickets" by Solomon Forse
Child Loss, School, Insects, Vomit

"You Shall Return" by L.P. Hernandez
Arson, Death

"The Richardson Family Reunion" by Ryan Marie Ketterer
Verbal Abuse, Alcohol Abuse, Gore, Poverty, Implied Child Abuse, Kidnapping

"Casualties of a Predictable Apocalypse" by Joseph Andre Thomas
Depression, Animal Attack

"Heavy Rain" by TJ Price
Suicide, Amputation

"A War in Hell" by Mike Adamson
Gun Use, Poverty, Graphic Violence

"Fleshies" by Thea Maeve
Hate speech, Transphobia, Graphic Violence

"A Tornado or Something Like It" by C.B. Jones
Suggested Violence toward Children, Natural Disaster

"A Thing of Habit" by Cassandra Khaw
 Gore, Hospitalization

"Unzipped" by Bridget D. Brave
 Claustrophobia, Gore

"The Last Sermon of Brother Grime" by Timaeus Bloom
 Gentrification, Insects, Rotting/Garbage

"Against the Flats" by Jennifer L. Collins
 Violent Death, Graphic Violence, Drowning

"Hope is a Sad Song" by Gully Novaro
 Claustrophobia, Animal Violence (Rats), Child Loss, Gore, Mental Health/Depression (implied), Suicide (implied)

"Systemic Infection" by Michelle Tang
 Medical Gore, Insects, Fire, Torture

"Forever Home" by Chelsea Pumpkins
 Animal Death, Insects, Person Experiencing Unhoused Conditions, Natural disaster (flood) with displacement

"The Children of the Event" by Carson Winter
 Gun Violence, Classism

"Detritus" by Lindsey Ragsdale
 Gore, Mentioned Drug Use, Body Horror, Self-harm

Printed in the USA
CPSIA information can be obtained
at www.ICGtesting.com
LVHW040010181023
761319LV00006B/673

9 781736 780077